GOD OF MERCY

GOD
OF
MERCY

A NOVEL

OKEZIE NWỌKA

ASTRA HOUSE | NEW YORK

tessy & joe—dad and mom[1]

For information about permission to reproduce selections from this book,
please contact permissions@astrahouse.com.

This is a work of fiction. Names, characters, places, and incidents are products of
the author's imagination or are used fictitiously. Any resemblance to actual
events, locales, or persons, living or dead, is entirely coincidental.

Astra House
A Division of Astra Publishing House
astrahouse.com

Printed in the United States of America

Publisher's Cataloging-in-Publication Data

Names: Nwoka, Okezie, author.
Title: God of mercy : a novel / Okezie Nwọka
Description: New York, NY: Astra House, 2021.
Identifiers: LCCN: 2021909549 | ISBN: 9781662600838 (hardcover) |
9781662600845 (ebook)
Subjects: LCSH Igbo (African people)—Fiction. | Igbo (African people)—Folklore. |
Igbo (African people)—Religion—Fiction. | Nigeria—Fiction. | Christianity and
culture—Nigeria—Fiction. | Magic—Fiction. | Magic realist fiction. |
BISAC FICTION / Fairy Tales, Folk Tales, Legends &;
Mythology | FICTION / Cultural Heritage | FICTION / Magical Realism
Classification: LCC PS3614 .W35 G63 2021 | DDC 813.6—dc23

FIRST EDITION

10 9 8 7 6 5 4 3 2 1

Design by Richard Oriolo
Map illustration by Alberto Castillo
The text is set in Arno Pro Regular.
The titles are set in Bureau Grotesque OneThree.

1. irrespectively

CONTENTS

CAST OF CHARACTERS

CHINEKE (also known as Chukwu or chi), Supreme Being
ANỊ, goddess of the earth
IGWE, god of the sky
ANYANWỤ, god of the sun
AMADIỌHA, god of lightning
IKENGA, god of industry
IDEMILI, god of the river Idemili

ỌFỌDILE (also known as Ekwueme), father of Ijeọma
NNENNA, mother of Ijeọma and first wife of Ọfọdile
IJEỌMA, first daughter of Ọfọdile and Nnenna
NNAMDỊ, son of Ọfọdile and Nnenna
CHELỤCHI, second daughter of Ọfọdile and Nnenna

NWAGỤ (also known as Nwakaibie), father of Jekwu
MGBOYE, second wife of Nwagụ and mother of Jekwu
CHINWE, daughter of Nwagụ and Mgboye
JEKWU, fifth child of Mgboye and Nwagụ

OLISA, brother of Ọfọdile and father of Ụzọdị
EZINNE, mother of Ụzọdị
ỤZỌDỊ, son of Ọfọdile and Ezinne

NWANKWQ, father of Ọfọdile

SOLOMTOCHUKWU (also known as Solomto), an ancestor of Ijeọma

NWABỤEZE, an Ichulu village man

MGBEKE, grandmother of Nwabụeze

IGBOKWE, dịbịa of Ichulu

ỤZỌKWESỊLỊ, eldest elder in Ichulu

NNABỤENYI, second oldest man in Ichulu

ADAỌRA, eldest woman in Ichulu

NGỌZI, an Ichulu village woman

OKOYE, an Ichulu village man

OBI IROATỤ, fifth descended king of Amalike

MADỤKA, aide to Obi Iroatụ

CHIKA, a woman from the Place of Osu

INNOCENT NWOSU, pastor of Precious Word Ministries

PHYLLIPA NWOSU, wife of Pastor Nwosu

SISTER GRACE, sister of Precious Word Ministries

JOHN, Pastor Nwosu's administrative assistant and nephew of
     Obi Iroatụ

IKEMBA, son of Pastor Nwosu

GOD OF MERCY

PROLOGUE

NOBODY IN ICHULU CARED FOR the erosion. Its tired old and its tired young were rebuilding the village indifferently. Its little ones were keeping weary smiles and discarding playtime, giving skinny dogs their place in the orange mud. Its surviving cassava leaves were drinking their share of light, with folded, wrinkled chaff corrupting the cassava's green. All in Ichulu, every person, every household, ignored the honored eagles soaring over them.

Igbokwe foretold the dangers this rainy season would bring, scurrying behind forest trees, booming his quivering cries. He pronounced them many weeks before the storm, several weeks before it came, and was not moved to read his cowrie shells the morning the message arrived. White paint adorning his old, small body bequeathed him with gifts like clairvoyance—as the gods themselves revealed a message in the skies once a cock had crowed its fourth crow. And when he emerged from his red-painted obi, with equanimity beside him, praying a small prayer and then trudging toward a goat-horn cup for water, his gaze met the clouds, clouds shaped in ominous ways—clouds shaped in symbols that he could not name, lurking within the sickly firmament of Igwe, the god of the sky. His eyes filled with panic. He opened the earth with the tip of his staff. Its bells were shaking with war on their lips. He could not wait for the town crier, his words were too urgent, he had to deliver it himself, every ear in Ichulu was to hear his solemn warning—

"It is coming! It is coming! Dangerous water is coming!"

The fear and confusion that followed traveled faster than the winds of harmattan. Nobody in Ichulu could say how water could harm. The town stretched along Idemili, a sacred river that gave the people a place to bathe, to drink, and to witness their faith in the god after whom the river was named—Idemili, the one for whom the river was. To touch the waters of the river was to touch the body of the divine. Irrigation channels ran from the riverbanks to the rippled farmlands: heaps of earth impregnated with the seeds of yam, groundnut, and other vegetation. The village did not thirst. The children did not drown. Idemili lived for Ichulu, and Ichulu satisfied him. It held past storms with ease given Igbokwe's divinations. If a storm's language became threatening, Igbokwe subdued Idemili with a sacrifice. Now, Igbokwe, consulter to the gods, warned that this long-sacred deity was to attack.

This wild pronouncement might have caused the village to ignore Igbokwe's cries echoing from within the forest. But the people of Ichulu knew Igbokwe's word to be good and believed him to be a matchless diviner. He possessed power known far past the ends of Idemili, which the white ones too had come to fear. On days filled with jeering and humor, the elders would remind the little ones of when the white ones lost their way, stumbling upon the village seeking to establish the laws of a foreign god—laws that would shatter the peace of Ichulu as well as the peace of the white ones and their village. They would say that the white ones first came with friendship woven into their smiles, promising to build schools for the children's reconnaissance and to build a church where the white ones spoke often of their god. Then, after four Eke market days, their friendship turned to enmity and their smiles converted to bullets. It was said that the power of Igbokwe's predecessor caused those inept schools to crumble, and caused the barren church to collapse. It was said that the power given to him by Ichulu's gods expelled the white ones from the village as they cried, "Their midget witch doctor has deranged me! Give me anything, anything to drink!"

"But what is *witch*, ehhhh?" the elders would say, chortling above the little ones. "Igbokwe—that shorter man you see—he is our dibia."

Ichulu remembered the wars fought by the town of Etuodi, and it remembered the negotiations initiated by the town of Umuka. It remembered, because neither the sword nor the tongue prevented either town from being toppled by the poison of a white god. "Where were the gods of Etuodi and Umuka," Ichulu's people would ask as they threw snaps of disdain, recounting how men were imprisoned for speaking to the ones called their ancestors; and how schoolchildren were mercilessly beaten for uttering the sounds they were taught to speak; and how the fate of Ani, the goddess of the earth, was sung of in dirge, as hidden voices seldom remained to pass on sacred memories.

Only the village of Ichulu remained as it was. It remained because of the divination of Igbokwe and his predecessors—divination that came through the one called their god. Chukwu was the life source of the line of dibias. While it was true that their homage to Ani, Ikenga, Amadioha, and the rest of the gods seldom wavered, they knew that the entire pantheon summed to nothing without the Supreme Being. Chukwu was the most of what any thing or one could be—the greatest among that which could be called great. Chukwu was called Chineke when Chukwu made creation; Chukwu was called chi when Chukwu became a friend; Chukwu was everywhere, unbound to any material thing. Ani had her earth; Anyanwu had his sun; Igwe had his sky; Idemili had his river. But Chukwu-Chineke-chi governed all creation. Even as the dibias worshipped Idemili, Chukwu was the one they had, the one who empowered them to guide and protect the village.

So when the present Igbokwe cried that dangerous water was coming, the people of Ichulu jounced in an unexpected fear. Men hurried to thatch the roofs of their compounds with the town's thickest palm leaves, nimbly weaving the leaves in the patterns of nests, and praying that Igwe, the god of the sky and the bearer of rain, would send them time. Women rushed to the market to sell a portion of their premature harvest, with a woman named Ngọzi already selling forty cups of groundnut, causing the others to wonder how a woman who could not conceive, how it was that she could quickly harvest and sell such an abundance of produce.

The animals, too, prepared themselves. The black nza birds flocked away from the town, dismantling their cushioned nests and migrating toward Ụmụka in the north. The vultures left the festering carcasses and sojourned northward as well, as the cows, cocks, goats, and rams allowed themselves to be sealed in barns by their owners and peacefully waited for the storm to come and pass. And the little ones, they felt no anxiety at Igbokwe's words, but grew eager in taking a thousand showers beneath the clouds—to feel the touch of raindrops—knocking, knocking—against their naked skin.

But on the day after Igbokwe's pronouncement, the elders of Ichulu gathered to discuss their plans to avert the storm. They knew they were required to offer something to Idemili, and they purchased a bull to appease the god of the river. Soon, they beheld four very young men pressing the animal down with taut bodies as Igbokwe opened the bull's neck with a blade, collecting its spilling blood with a metal bowl while praying over it and asking Idemili to protect the people of Ichulu. He reminded the deity that if he failed to send mercy to the village, the people would condemn him, and he would be chastised by the power of Chukwu—warning that the Supreme Being would send a new river, and the people of Ichulu would find a new god. He reasoned. He asked. He threatened. Still, when the elders looked to Igbokwe's face for signs that the sacrifice was taken, they wondrously found an empty gaze: abandonment and apathy.

Igbokwe was befuddled. He did not understand what could cause the storm, since he had placed four holy stones from the depths of Idemili in the four corners of Ichulu. The stones were feared throughout the village, as they had been among the stones living beneath Idemili, which kept the river clear and unpolluted. Nobody would dare move them, he believed, while thinking of the one he placed in the northwest corner, in the forest used for hunting; then thinking of the one he placed in the southwest, near Idemili, where compounds sat beside one another; then thinking of the third, placed by the iroko trees in the southeast, which separated Ichulu from Amalike; then the last one—the one he saw in his mind—lodged deep inside the northeast, fixed within the Evil Forest. He had blessed them each morning, and could not understand why they now failed, and dismissed the thoughts of accusing a faultless person, or an innocent town. And before Anyanwụ, the god of the sun, had departed from the day of sacrifice, Igbokwe knelt among his scattered cowrie shells cast within his obi, offering supplications to Chukwu, pleading to the Most Supreme that power be restored to those holy stones.

"Who? Who? Who would curse us this way?" implored the women selling food near sunrise.

"It could be those goats from the village of Etuọdị," one said as she adjusted her mat of greens.

"Sit down!" said another, while biting on her chewing stick. "Whose *gods* are greater than the gods of *Ichulu*? Or are you among the foolish—those *stupid* ones—who have forgotten the power of Idemili?"

"Then you have not heard of emissaries going to Amalike to remove the curse from Ọfọdile's child?"

Ngọzi, a childless woman, was pouring groundnut onto her light yellow cloth as she spoke good words to the others.

"Ijeọma? The mute? But for what?" said the woman with the chewing stick.

"Yes. Ijeọma," Ngọzi said, "It is a good word. My husband told me that after the sacrifice failed, Igbokwe spoke with the gods, and they told him that whoever cursed Ọfọdile's daughter also cursed the people of Ichulu with this evil water that is coming."

Ngọzi heard the women laughing, and saw them turn their heads from her—knowing that it was because she had not given birth to a living child.

But she continued pouring her groundnut, and disregarded their eschewals, leaving the market women to themselves.

OFODILE WAS SURPRISED TO SEE Igbokwe standing in his modest compound. He was thatching the roof of his red-clay obi when he saw the dibia below him, cloaked in a rappa of yellow and blue and holding his iron staff. Ofodile pulled at the ends of the raffia the moment Igbokwe's eyes fell on his, and felt his heart quivering at the sound of Igbokwe's bells.

"Welcome," said Ofodile.

"I see you preparing your house for the water," Igbokwe said.

"Yes . . . My family has been using time to prepare . . ."

"That is wise. That is very wise," said the dibia, while casting his eyes on a gliding falcon.

"Come inside," said Ofodile as he slid down from his raffia roof. "I know you did not leave your prayers with the gods . . . to inspect my thatching patterns."

"You are a keen man, Ofodile."

The two men entered the obi and sat upon its earthen floor, and Ofodile reached into a small bag made of goat hide, moving past his containers of snuff, searching for his chalk to begin drawing four lines on the floor, one for each day of the week. He reached into the bag again, after drawing the four lines, and removed a bright pink kola nut, one no larger than a river stone.

"Ijeoma! Ijeoma! Come here!" Ofodile said from inside his obi.

And before the moment passed, Ijeoma, Ofodile's nine-year-old daughter, appeared, wearing a green rappa that wrapped across her chest and reached the top of her ankles. Her hair was plaited tightly in very small loops with its blackness complementing her nighttime-colored eyes; her skin was dark; her nose was broad, curved at the nostrils like the petals of a flower; and her cheeks were high, resembling those of the one called her father, while her beaming smile indicated that she was ready to receive his instructions. I have heard you, she said within herself. Speak, my father, I have heard.

"Ijeọma! Go and get the ose ọjị from your mother. Have you heard me?"

Ijeọma nodded three times and ran to get the ose ọjị to halt any disappointment, then returned with a brown-nut cream plopped onto a metal dish. She placed it by Ọfọdile's outstretched legs, then left his obi once he lifted the dish with the kola nut, not seeing Ọfọdile present the dish to Ichulu's observant dịbịa.

"Igb . . . okwe—" Ọfọdile was ashamed to hear his voice delaying, and quickly turned from the dịbịa while coughing into his left shoulder. "Igbokwe . . . it is said that he who brings kola . . . brings life. That life, which Chukwu has placed . . . inside the loins of our fathers . . . and into the wombs, of our mothers, has not . . . forsaken us. It was here yesterday. It is here today. And it will be here . . . tomorrow—if tomorrow comes. Idemili, the god of this village . . . is a *powerful* god, he is an *enduring* god. He will protect . . . the life of his children. For what god, wants to go hungry? What god wants . . . his sacrifice to be ash and dust? No. Idemili will be, reasonable; he will be merciful. Let us pray, that the gods that we serve . . . continue to sustain us, our wives . . . and our children. Let us pray that our ancestors . . . will protect us, during this time of difficulty . . ."

"May the gods be quick in hearing your prayer," Igbokwe said. "May they answer it with the speed of Amadiọha's lightning."

Ọfọdile broke the kola nut into four pieces, one for each day of the week, and he placed them on the dish containing the ose ọjị, and then gave the dish to Igbokwe as he ate his own share, chewing deeply into the kola's gross bitter—the bitterness reminding him that all creation carries sorrow.

"Ọfọdile," Igbokwe said, "you know that my medicine has never failed Ichulu."

"Yes, yes . . . I-I-I know . . ." Ọfọdile said, reaching for his small goat bag.

"The Igbokwe before me, and the one before him—all of us from of old have been protecting this village from destruction, protecting it from floods and war. When the gods speak, I listen. When I speak to the gods, they hear. Now that this storm is coming, I have been asking them to show me, to teach me how to send it to another place. We have offered sacrifices. We have prayed prayers. None of them have been effective."

The dibia paused, and looked through the black of Ọfọdile's eyes.

"Ọfọdile, the gods have spoken. They have told me that this storm has been sent from our enemies. They have told me that the people who cursed us with it are the same people who cursed your daughter Ijeọma with muteness years ago, and they have decided to finally give me those people's name."

Ọfọdile glanced at the dibia, his face bright with anger as he raised his hands and pushed his mouth forward to speak.

"We would have fought," Igbokwe said. "The gods did not show us our enemies when Ijeọma had lost her voice, because they knew that we would have fought. And if we had fought, we would have lost."

"Give me their name!" Ọfọdile barked.

"It is the people of Amalike who have cursed your daughter and our village. I have tried to stop this curse with my divinations and I cannot. The gods have told me that the curse can only be broken by the medicine of Amalike's people."

"No! No! How can the people of Amalike still have the power of medicine! Did they not join the god of the white one!"

"Chukwu alone can answer such a question."

Ọfọdile stared helplessly at the corner farthest from him, watching ants gathering within it, pulling his bag forward to snatch his containers of snuff, thinking that, at the age of twenty-nine, enemies were fighting a war against him. And as he looked past the ants clustering within their tangled ball, he deeply resented the hopeful promise of his youth: that once he was a graceful dancer who could shift the muscles in his arms and legs and buttocks in ways that obeyed the pleasures of the drum, who could jump toward the heavens and flip backward over and again until he found the earth once more, who could tap his feet and clap his hands together more swiftly than a feather afloat—possessed by the spirits of dance. He was an extraordinary hunter and an attractive bachelor, and was told that he chased meat and beauties as if chasing nothing at all; and his age-mates gave him the name Ekwueme, because everything he said, he did; everything he wished for, he worked to obtain. And after rejecting the advances of several women from several lands, he chose to marry Nnenna, the one for whom his heart refused reticence, and together they gave birth to a child who lost the gift of speech.

Ọfọdile spoke hopefully then—speaking for healing to enter the one called his daughter; speaking for the ones called his gods to show his family mercy; speaking so that the village would hear his words and know that he would not be defeated. And as he spoke, he did: offering sacrifices until Nnenna said they could no longer afford to eat, consulting Igbokwe until the village complained that they too required consult, then wearing pride on behalf of the newborn child until that pride had waned and his child became to him regrettable, as he no longer did those things he had been doing for her. His desire to love Ijeọma had become quieter than the gossip he had overheard: that his daughter was abominable, and should have been sent to die in the Evil Forest like other abominable children.

He was angry at his self-declared defeat years before Igbokwe's visit, and his spirit had been broken years before he heard Amalike's name. And as a thread of raffia fell from his highly domed roof, landing gently on his legs, his mind revolved toward loathsome yesterdays and unmet promises, as he took a heavy snort from his now-empty container of snuff.

AMID THE SCURRY GENERATED by the pending storm, Igbokwe sent eight very young men to the town of Amalike, bearing the responsibility of informing its king that Ichulu wanted their curse to be broken. He gave them twigs to wear around their wrists so that they would be divinely protected, but tremors were curling beneath their throats as they walked atop the road toward Amalike. Eight very young men were keeping silent fears, and no one dared expose the truth dwelling within them; and Uzọdị, the one called Ọfọdile's kin, nervously swung his machete with his skinny right arm, scratching the orange surface of the earth.

"Who is the most beautiful girl in Ichulu?" Uzọdị said.

"It is Nnọnye," said Nwabụeze, "Have you not seen her breasts!"

"I have seen them, and they are ripe," said one of the other eight. "She has been licking too much ọgbọnọ soup!"

Laughter erupted among them, and it lingered for much longer than they knew it was supposed to linger, as they were not saying those things which dwelt within them—an act they were told was an act for women. Still, those things dwelling within them were screaming, screaming, calling it unfair to be sent because they were eight very young men. So they continued speaking aimlessly—protectively—of other things: things like the breasts of very young women.

And when the trees became sparse and the earth became a gray-colored brown, the eight knew that they had arrived at Amalike. They began asking a small child, whom they had seen running, to take them to the palace of Obi Iroatụ, the town's fifth descended king, and they were led by the child to the gates of a white-coated palace that bore the kind of stoutness of a towering hill; and the eight believed that its pillars were too audacious, reaching for the bowels of Igwe, the god of the sky, and laughing at the threshold of Amalike's birds. There was no honor, they said within themselves, there was no reason, building up what Chineke could whisper down, and with great discordance the eight of them approached the king's barred gates, quietly waiting for Amalike to speak.

"Weytin you want?" said the approaching gateman, wiping his oily nose with a shirt.

The eight of them looked about with confusion.

"Why does he not speak our language?" asked Nwabụeze.

"Because he does not come from where we come," Ụzọdị said.

"Ụzọdị, speak to him," said Nwabụeze. "Is it not the good word that you can speak like him?"

Ụzọdị recoiled, not wanting to speak a language that he had been instructed never to speak again, remembering the instruction of the one called his mother as he moved backward, away from the gateman.

"Go on, speak!" said one of the eight.

"If you can speak, *speak*, so that we can return to our home!" said another.

"Do not be like a woman!" Nwabụeze said.

"Close your mouth!" Ụzọdị said, quickly moving forward and looking below the gateman's eyes.

"We . . . c-come . . ." Ụzọdị began in English. "We . . . come . . . to see . . . king."

"Fro wee you don come?" the gateman said.

". . . Ichulu," Ụzọdị said.

"Wait hiyah make I go tell dee king."

The gateman turned and ran toward the palace with his slippers clapping against the cement as he went; and he quickly returned—unlocking the gate for the eight emissaries, then leading them into the palace—directing them through large doors and up carpeted stairs—and, finally, ushering them inside a glimmering room at the center of Obi Iroatụ's palace. And the eight of them saw twenty men of guns standing along the room's four walls, their heavy artillery borrowing light from the chandeliers protruding forth from the floral wallpaper, which bore the same design as the king's gold jewelry, which he wore as he sat atop his ivory throne—smiling at eight very young men.

"Young men, young men," said Obi Iroatụ in Igbo, "it is beautiful that you are here. But I cannot welcome you well without first breaking kola nut."

The king was given kola by one of the men of guns before praying over it. And after small portions had been divided, he watched the eight eat it slowly.

"Now, young men," said Obi Iroatụ, "why have you come?"

"Iroatụ," Ụzọdị began, "we are here to give you a message from the people of Ichulu. Someone from Amalike has cursed our village, and has also cursed the daughter of a man named Ọfọdile, the son of Nwankwọ. We want—"

"Wait," Obi Iroatụ said. "You boys have journeyed from the village of Ichulu to speak of what—a curse?"

"Yes," Ụzọdị said.

There was silence—and the king's terrible laughter broke it. He looked past the young men, searching for their collateral and for their weaponry.

Finding nothing except myths and machetes, he continued laughing wildly upon their faces.

"Is this the good word? You think this is like the ancient days, when we dealt with idle gods and foolish medicine. Eh? Do you think my town concerns itself with something as foolish as a curse?"

Ụzọdị considered the questions and heard in his memory faint echoes of the one called his father, reciting stories of old wars and battles. He knew that the strength of those ancient warriors meant Ichulu rarely lost or surrendered to any fight, since he could hear the voice of the one called his father humming the trance induced by the ikpirikpi ọgụ dance and telling him of the ways it strengthened the dancing warriors by summoning the spirit of Ikenga: "IKENGA, IKENGA, the god of our wars, would snatch their shoulders and spine, and their whole body would be like the sacred python . . . and the cantor would sing:"

Silence over slain enemies.
Silence over slain enemies.
Our children have been reborn!
May our kin never worry death.

"Goats! You people have betrayed your gods!" shouted Nwabụeze from the center of the room, ending Ụzọdị's thoughts.

"You have abandoned your gods and ancestors like wild animals!" Nwabụeze said, grasping the medicine tied around his wrist.

Six others began making exclamations in support of Nwabụeze: one crying that the obi was nothing more than the white one's shit, another calling him a fool, all of them, except Ụzọdị, who was quietly mouthing the words of the song being sung within him; he saw the king saying nothing, and looked upward to watch Obi Iroatụ stare at them with hateful eyes as though fire had consumed the blood running through his veins. He moved backward when the obi seized his staff and sped toward him; the obi was looking into his eyes—then swiftly moved across the bodies of the other seven.

"Do you know who I am? Eat shit! I said, do you know who I am? I will show you who I am. Bush animals. You think you can speak to me like I am one of your bastard fathers, grooming and licking the devil's anus. This is not Ichulu; my land will never be defiled by you animals! You! Go and get Maduka!"

One of the men of guns left the room and soon returned with Maduka, the obi's aide.

"Maduka, gather these animals and take them to that old obi outside. Men of guns, follow them."

They all obeyed: because they were all to obey. Twenty men of guns gathered eight very young men—pointing their guns to eight backs—leading them out of the palace to an old, crumbling obi—then pushing them against the obi's gray walls. And Maduka commenced what the king had wanted, collecting some ingredients from a box in the obi: alligator pepper, congealed blood from a bull, cassava root, and a selection of bitter herbs. He began mixing them inside a metal bowl, and told the obi that he would begin with a gentle nod of his head.

"Lie down!" Obi Iroatu said.

The eight very young men obeyed and quickly buried their faces in the earth, fearing the men of guns, knowing their machetes could not withstand their power as they began whispering prayers to the ancestors and to the gods—then screaming-screaming—believing that nothing could stop the obi standing above them—who was scratching their backs open with a seized machete.

"If this were in the days of our forefathers I would have killed you with this blade. You come into my town . . . and this one," he said, lifting the machete and pointing it to Uzodi, "If you ever fail to address me by my title of Obi, I will force your mother's clitoris into your mouth. Senseless bastard. I will teach you a lesson today. Maduka!"

Maduka stepped forward and began engraving a circle around the eight with a short branch from a tree. Then he put the branch beneath his arms and poured palm wine within the groove he had made, waiting for the white liquid to settle in the earth, lifting the metal bowl, the bowl which held the medicine thought necessary to enslave one to a god, dipping his finger into its blood and roots, and writing on their backs in spurious symbols as he recited incantations in an Igbo the eight found difficult to understand.

"I am finished," they heard him say.

"It is good, Madụka," said Obi Iroatụ. "Today, Ichulu will have eight osu to call its own."

The eight jumped.

"Did he say osu? Did he say osu?" Nwabụeze asked.

"Were you not minding your ears! I said you are now osu. Now, leave from here! Leave from my town, before I break your skulls."

The obi was laughing; he was laughing with his men of guns and with Madụka—all of them jeering and laughing as the boys began running, jeering at them, calling them osu, laughing as the men of guns shot bullets against eight backs—watching six very young men dropping to the earth, then choking on the pressing blood, rising to their lips, no longer shaking once their bodies stopped coughing and pleading and hoping—once their breaths, panting beneath the evening light, had drifted openly toward the moon.

Ụzọdị and Nwabụeze were not touched by the king's bullets, but bled from their backs by the machete's blade, having spun past the laughter of Obi Iroatụ and his men. They hurried down a narrow road leading out of Ama-like, and once they reached a distance far enough from the obi's palace, Nwabụeze fell to his knees as Ụzọdị stood quietly, Nwabụeze screaming and punching the earth with denial—weeping—failure—failure—from his family's expectations. They slowly returned to Ichulu with their insides charred by melancholy, youth's hope becoming a formless ash: future dying without a corpse to bury; and so could they; entertaining suicide; petitioning their deaths; tempted by the call of the river god's basin; one not looking at the other, not his eyes nor his shadow; not looking for any sign that what had happened had happened.

And the smaller boys wondered why they would not listen to the song they had composed for them, becoming silent the moment Ụzọdị's red gaze struck them, as many urged them to eat what was placed in their midst, with others wanting to know why; and they were told that the ones called their sons would never marry daughters of the soil, would never carry a chieftaincy title, that they were either an osu living or an osu dead. "Two are alive bearing that disgust within them," some people said. "Six are dead on a road in Amalike."

So the heavy water, and the dreadful erosion that followed it, became things the village named as vanity. Ichulu mourned the storm's destruction with apathetic eyes, and when it came, many saw the belly of the river pouring its contents over the village, then like a ruminant, swallowing them down again; they saw it beginning: Idemili flowing thinly through the irrigation channels, then filling each one, and spilling outward, growing wider and wider, sweeping through the village, seeing his muddy water rumbling through red-clay homes, unfurling its brown and white when it reached the surfaces of trees and stones, finding other things to push and eat, crashing and breaking the bodies of what Ichulu had grown and built, signaling no pause of any kind but bringing more water, more rumblings, and the shine of teeth from hungry alligators; then they saw the water suddenly rise—and felt their hearts trembling at the realization that high earth was not high enough, and surrendered themselves to the god who began taking them into the depths of his river.

Though as they were carried off, flowing along the waters of Idemili, those dying victims pitied the eight osu more than they pitied themselves, for they believed they would be forever known in Ichulu as freeborn. Their bodies were buried quickly: Ani had to be appeased; there were as many gunshots fired as there were mounds of earth; the collective grave; keeners wailed the names of entombed women; men boasted of the names of inhumed men, as the ancestors were invited—emerging from their holy anthills adorned in masquerade, dancing their dance, a dance of war and a dance of peace—speaking their good word through muffled groans, blessing the names of the fallen children, watching the village hear and not understand, hearing Ichulu curse the name of their enemies—tempted even to include the name of their greatest god—since Ichulu's anger found its root not in having their dead live among the ancestors, or their crops destroyed for the upcoming year—for their dead were still alive, and their barns were safe and full. They nearly cursed the name of Chukwu, of Chineke, and of each chi, for what they knew would be the fate of the very young men cursed by the obi of Amalike.

A few days after the storm, the male elders convened a village meeting to decide whether the six murdered emissaries would be buried, and if Uzodị and Nwabụeze would remain in Ichulu. Two hundred men came to the meeting, with their colored rappas, and their wooden stools, and their bare chests painted in uli. Many of them had their hair twisted in loose locks, or domed and plaited in styles which came forth through the hands of their brothers; some of them were bald; some of them were wearing bright feathers, plucked from many large eagles; and it was those two hundred men who decided together that Uzọkwesịlị, the eldest elder among them, would lead them in their village meeting.

"Ichulu, kwenu!" said Uzọkwesịlị.

"Yah!" chorused the men.

"Ichulu, kwenu!" Uzọkwesịlị said.

"Yah!" the men chorused.

"Ichulu, kwenu!"

"Yaaaaaaaaaaaaaaaaahhhh," the men sang.

"Children of my mother," Uzọkwesịlị said, "we all know what has brought us here today. Those animals from Amalike poisoned the bodies of eight of our sons, killing six. Six! All eight of them are now osu. They are now the slaves of gods. Children of my mother, it is not time to brood in anger. As our people say, let the morning take away evil; the one who asks for another person's death, let him go to sleep before the fowl. We must let the gods avenge on our behalf. Until then, we must remember the words of our fathers: 'No man enslaved to a god can live amongst the free.' The time has come for us to decide if we will bury those who became outcasts moments before their death . . . and if the two surviving will remain with us here in Ichulu."

Many of the men congregated were nodding in agreement.

"Ụzọkwesịlị's words are good!" said Okoye, a large, bearded man who sprang to his feet the moment the elder sat down. "We all know the tradition of this land. We *cannot* go to Amalike to bury the bodies of those six osu. It is an *abomination* to our goddess Anị. Let their bodies lie there for Amalike to bury. And the two osu that remain . . . they must be removed from this village *immediately*. If I told you why they cannot stay, I would be wasting my words. All of you know that the gods must be obeyed. Or have you forgotten what is sacred? Let us not waste time. We must do what our tradition tells us to do. If we do not, something worse than the flood our enemies have sent will find us."

Given the light tone of the murmurs spreading throughout the market square, Okoye knew that he had won the favor of the village men. Yet he returned to his stool uneasily, thinking that one man would be foolish and challenge him; he believed that man would distort the argument he had finished making, the same way he believed that man had distorted the heart of his lover eleven years ago. That man was standing.

"Men . . . of Ichulu . . ." Qfọdile began, with his red rappa wrapping plainly around his legs. "We must remember . . . the responsibility we have to our sons. We sent them . . . on our behalf . . . and we armed them with *machetes* . . . *machetes* that are like chewing sticks . . . compared to the mighty guns of Amalike. Our fathers told us . . . that we cannot live among osu . . . Still . . . our fathers would never allow their children to be discarded like waste. As our people say . . . 'When a corpse smells good, friends go home, but bad brothers come out.' We as fathers . . . must do, what we must to protect . . . and keep our children."

"Children of my mother, look at it!" said Okoye, standing again. "Qfọdile, are your motives truly pure? Is the son of your dead brother not among the osu? And what of your daughter? Was it not the failure of your loins that produced a child who cannot speak?"

A few men began to chuckle, and Qfọdile heard them.

"Men of Ichulu," Okoye continued, after caressing the length of his beard, "do not listen to this titleless man, who wears no eagle feather atop his head! We have already suffered the wrath of Idemili's flood for reasons unknown. Are you prepared to battle the other gods?"

"We understand, Okoye, but take your calm, take your calm," said many men. "Leave the father of the mute alone."

"Leave the father of *Ijeọma* alone," one said.

More men began speaking, and more commotion spread across the market square, and Ọfọdile remained silent to Okoye's insults. His lack of support among them made any response imprudent, and as he stared solemnly at the market square's earth, thinking of those things he would have said to Okoye, he also thought of those ways he would have struck Okoye's face, recalling that he had spoken because of a promise he had once made, a promise that Uzọdị's future would bring titles and chieftaincies—and that he had also spoken because of the men who birthed those killed as emissaries for Ichulu; those men, he knew, would blame him for the death of the ones called their sons, and would curse Ọfọdile's name, and shame him. They would tell Ichulu of the dishonorable man, Ọfọdile, and all in the village would shame him—the father of the mute—and he would lose more honor and would no longer have a place to stand within their glorious village.

"Please! Let me bury my dead son!" said one of those men.

The space was quiet except for the rattling of Okoye's stool.

"No, my brother," said Okoye, standing. "You cannot."

And as the meeting continued, most of the village men expressed their agreement with the bearded Okoye. They found no compelling word that would have them refute their tradition, and said among themselves, "Morality has been secured! We have pleased the gods! We have pleased them!" Some said the osu were lepers rejoicing in their own leprosy—an imprisoned people never—*never*—to be freed. Many argued that to protect the village, the anger of the gods was to be prioritized over the welfare of the young men. Those few who sympathized with Ọfọdile simply asked, "Where were the chis of those eight osu?" and accepted the retort that their personal gods were drunk, or sleeping.

And as Ọfọdile heard them say these things, he sat in the market square retrieving his containers of snuff, and watched the men permanently exiling two boys. The one called his kin had become an outcast, the one who would help him win titles was lost, and his breathing quickened when he told himself that he had failed Ụzọdị and had failed the promise he had given to the one called Ụzọdị's father—and that he had failed himself, that he had failed. He believed now, as he sat snorting through his containers of snuff, that life was vanity, complete vanity, hopeless from the curse residing behind Ijeọma's eyes.

PART I

A
GIRL
CAN
FLY

1.

THERE IS THE FINAL TRUTH; and Ijeọma knew it resided within her, tinier than a speck, when the blowing wind became like wings and her feet shook the branches of the leaning orange tree, knocking Ichulu's dust to the ground. It drew her upward, raising her like smoke from a burning fire, raising her to the nests of nza birds and the first scatterings of light from Anyanwụ, the divine sun. She rested there, suspended like fruit too precious to pluck or a thought too erratic to name. She rose to the sky, and nobody was there to see it.

The reasoning lay in her wind-blown wings. The pleasure lay there, too. And they joined with her spirit, to beat steadily, steadily, deep like the udu, deepening that which was lifted, that which her thoughts and body followed.

Her fingers stretched before curling inward toward her palms; her chest now rose upward, then fell to greet her heart—while the prickly dots, like a million rose thorns, flashed across her left cheek, then her lips, then her right earlobe; before passing into the air—returning to its abode—as she let out a sigh and magnified the wonder.

Tears were trembling in her eyes, and through them Ijeọma saw a single vision, printed past Igwe, the divine sky, with her lips moving: counting then recounting the faces of ancestors, and the faces of those unknown, celebrating their names, with promises guided by much hope. A promise of many prayers to those little ones, those whom she had not yet seen, those looking through her with truth and kindness, as she prayed and promised and felt more stilled than death itself, and in that stillness found the greatest of life—and in that life praised the Most Supreme for making any thing or one possible.

She closed her eyes. The sky closed, too: full clouds colliding within a moment. And Ijeọma found her feet touching the earth, and clutched her hands, now warm from the evening light; and she did not understand it all, not the faint vibrations in her bones, or the smell of sky-bound dust, or the rupture of what was thought to be known and understood as she heard Ọfọdile's footsteps, and ran through the compound to hide and find understanding in Nnenna's red-clay home.

"Ijeọma, where are you running?" Nnenna said, sitting airily by the house where food was stored. There was no response from the one called her daughter, and Nnenna turned her head, too tired to inquire after one child when another was latched to her breast suckling milk; she was nursing Chelụchi while resting in pleasant thoughts, while humming songs of peace, peace which would leave her body and enter that of the infant child to pursue and expel every kind of evil. And she stopped humming when she saw Ọfọdile mouthing words of shame, when she greeted the one called her husband, and he responded with offense in his glance—she knew that his efforts to save Ụzọdị had failed and she wanted to speak with him, to ease his frustrations, but his spirit felt cold when he passed her. So she stilled her lips, detached Chelụchi from her nipple, and dismissed those rising thoughts revealing her as the one telling Ezinne, the mother of Ụzọdị, that the one once called her son would not be returning to their home.

"Mama of mine, hunger is hungering me," said Nnamdị, the one called Nnenna's only son, while rubbing his belly with his right and left hands, looking at the one called his mother, who sighed a sigh, knowing she had little time to prepare a meal.

"My father, I have heard you," she said to the one called her son. "Go and get Ijeọma."

Nnamdị ran forward into Nnenna's red-clay home and returned with the one called his sister in his hands, pulling her toward a standing Nnenna, who was wrapping Chelụchi around her back.

"Ijeọma," Nnenna began, "go to the forest by the stream, and collect the firewood that I will use to make yam porridge . . . Have you heard me?"

Ijeọma nodded three times to Nnenna, with her eyes still and facing the earth, with her gaze focusing upon its dust as she nodded three times again, nodding yes to Nnenna, then quickly leaving for the firewood. She hurried along, thinking of what had happened above the orange tree, losing breaths to the awe of what she had seen, holding its joy, wanting to spread it across Ichulu and past the mighty banks of Idemili. The feeling she held: it was so piercingly simple she deemed it greater than any tickle or touch, greater than the little rocks pressing beneath her feet, as she thought of how to sign for it, and wondered whether it could be signed for at all.

And her thoughts of wonder continued, following her along the narrow path that led to the stream, but dropping like dust once she saw the one called her kin, walking to the Place of Osu. He cannot see me! she said within herself, trembling at the thought of being blamed for his exile, believing he had lost any pity for her. So she ran; she ran as quickly as she could, hurrying her legs through the bush, letting the PAT-PAT-PAT of her feet raise the tempo of her frame, feeling her heart leaping in her chest, touching the ground under her feet, *AH where is the ground where is the ground*—

"Chei! What am I seeing?" Ụzọdị whispered, his voice pointing Nwabụeze to the sky. They stood bewildered, mouths peeling open; they could not speak. And they saw her. Under the parting clouds and beneath the rays of Anyanwụ, they saw Ijeọma accept the sun's libations with her eyes—watched her reach toward the haze of Igwe and strike calm and ecstasy—witnessed her relish her welcome like a newborn dragonfly; watched her smile, watched the birds flap their wings in celebration of the wild image cast upon their eyes; heard the humble wind whistle and sing, then whistle and sing over and again.

"Who has given this girl the power to fly?" asked Nwabụeze as they gathered around Ijeọma's dappled shadow. She was levitating: her body was dangling above the ground, near the fruits of a slender palm tree. The question was not answered; and the two very young men looked on, transfixed; and the two very young men beneath the slender shadow soon grew to a crowd swelling with awe, as many people were now looking upon Ijeọma, and asking how her flying could be; knowing that their rising curiosity was not the result of unprecedented history, since the tradition of Ichulu was built upon those who had accomplished the extraordinary: some who had spoken the language of the sacred python and others who had spat flames from their mouths. There was one, even, whom the village would sing of, one who had flown from beyond the banks of Idemili to return to the village of Ichulu. His name was Solomtochukwu, but Ichulu called him Solomto for short, and he was an ancestor who had died many harvests ago; he was an ancestor both honored and remembered.

Suddenly—Ijeọma returned to the earth, descending as gently as a leaf. And once her feet touched the ground, her eyes lost their transfixion to the sun, and she saw the people around her, then signed to them, pointing to her eyes.

"Who has made it so that the mute can fly!" they said among themselves. "Is it that Solomto has returned?"

"We do not know," Nwabụeze said. "But what is she doing? Why is she showing us her eyes?"

"I do not know," said Ụzọdị. "I do not know. Ijeọma. . . ." He held her arm, then quickly releasing his hand since it was becoming warm. "Ijeọma, who has made it so that you can fly," he whispered, "And why are you showing us your eye?"

Ijeọma tried with much difficulty to answer, signing signs with her arms and hands and fingers, searching around herself, looking for translation as she held Ụzọdị's arms, then held the arms of those around them. *How can they know it*, she thought while signing signs, tapping her chest, *You do not understand, all of this, you are being told, understand my jumping, look at it, look, look.* Touching their faces, all of their faces, the girls and the men, all of those gathered, she touched their faces, holding them, wiping them, letting her fingers lift, surprise, and ease them, watching their faces almost surrender to the words she so desperately wanted to give, watching some lull as if in a dream. She moved again, signing signs over and again. Still, she could neither communicate what she saw in the sky nor the fact that she did not fully know the power behind her levitations.

"I will take her home and show her to her father," said Ụzọdị.

"That is wise," said Nwabụeze, "Let me follow you."

"That is beautiful," Ụzọdị said.

And the crowd dispersed with questions and with wonder: two ingredients for crafting accolade and gossip. And they had forgotten—through new concerns—that their outcasts were reentering the village, as their little ones were running and jumping with glee, singing the song of Solomto:

Solomto, Solomto has found his home.
Solomto, Solomto has given us a path.
Solomto flew above the ocean and through the air,
Solomto, Solomto will emerge from his grave.

2.

IT WAS ONLY AFTER THE shadows in Ichulu grew long and thin and the nza birds returned to their sequestered nests that Ụzọdị, Ijeọma, and Nwabụeze arrived at Ọfọdile's compound. Their journey there was silent. None of them had known what to speak, though Ụzọdị had recounted young memories of Ijeọma: the way she would mouth secrets into the ears of goats before their slaughter and would beg him to play at nighttime, running after him through the darkness of Ọfọdile's compound. And he watched her now: her high cheeks rising higher, a joyful smile, fascination lacing her nighttime-colored eyes. And he wondered at her thoughts, if they danced as burningly and as wildly as the excitement she was causing in the village, and if she had known that he was hoping for this excitement to release him from the name osu. Ijeọma's flying, he thought, could some-how break Amalike's curse; he knew Nwabụeze was thinking the same when Nwabụeze turned to him and raised his brow, grinning with mild recklessness. But Ụzọdị stared him into a deeper silence to prevent hopeless dreams from being spoken, to prevent Nwabụeze's verbosity from inciting another kind of death.

They arrived with Ijeọma when the evening had settled, and found Nnenna peeling the yams to be used for her porridge; they grew shameful when she dropped her knife and began staring at them in disbelief, because they knew she wanted them out of the compound on this day of their banishment.

"Our mother, we greet you," Ụzọdị said. "Is my father's brother in his obi?"

Nnenna remained silent, wishing that the very young man would not touch the one called her daughter—thinking of slicing Ụzọdị's hand, away from that of Ijeọma—then thinking of the consequences of speaking to an osu: sacrificial atonement, prolonged exile. But something overcame her, something like a tear, as she sighed a breath—Ụzọdị—he was a boy, a boy from the same lineage as her beloved, a boy who had sucked at the breasts of her dear in-law Ezinne, a boy upon whom misfortune had grinned. She could not remain silent at his words.

"Ụzọdị, he is not here," she said. "He is hunting. Why have you come? Ijeọma, where is the firewood?"

"There is no firewood," Ụzọdị gently replied. "There is something that happened on the path to the stream. The two of us . . . we saw Ijeọma flying."

"She was standing atop the air!" said Nwabụeze.

Nnenna remained silent, and her eyes began moving quickly—left then right, left then right—widening as if in search of something, seeing Nnamdị playing with sticks beneath the orange tree and Ijeọma holding onto Ụzọdị's hand while gazing at the purple clouds—as two very young men had told her that her eldest daughter, the one called her Ada, could fly.

"That is impossible!" Nnenna said. "I have known this child since she was inside of me, and she does not even jump! Now you are telling me she can fly? *You are lying lies—*"

"Ụzọdị, is what you are saying true?" said Ezinne as she moved closer to the four, looking warmly at Ụzọdị, the one called her son. She had overheard the conversation from her red-clay home, and now appeared in the middle of the compound, gazing at Ụzọdị affectionately, as her clean-shaven scalp played with the evening light.

"My mother, it is true," said Ụzọdị, looking down upon the earth. "Many people saw her fly, and the word is traveling quickly. We came so that you would know before the entire village. Will you tell Ọfọdile?"

"Yes. I will do so," said Ezinne.

"No, I will do it. If anybody will speak of *my daughter* to Ọfọdile, it will be me," Nnenna said.

They all understood. There was nothing more they could civilly say, so Ụzọdị and Nwabụeze left the compound. But Ụzọdị left the compound with unspoken thoughts, feeling unable to speak them in the presence of Nnenna and Ezinne, wanting to believe that if the one called his kin could be given the power to fly, he could be given the power to be free again—released from the curse of osu. And as he moved away from his former home, he wanted to return once more and pronounce it—but knew that he could not, believing that his freedom would never reappear, marking the difference between a wanted truth and the good word.

Ụzọdị continued walking, but his stomach fell at the fear of tomorrow, and the tomorrow that would follow to the end of his life. And his mouth released sounds as if a sparrow were dying within him, as he heaved and heaved until tears shot forth and screams shot forth and he shivered down to his knees, to the spinning earth, and to his friend Nwabụeze holding him in silence, weeping to the gods, naming every sorrow he could name: he did not want to live in the Place of Osu, he did not want to be estranged from his aspirations, too young to let his deepest hopes die: to become a chief, bear titles, and marry a freeborn woman; to restore honor to his family— they would no longer happen because he had done his duty as a messenger for his village. Ụzọdị knelt against the dark path praying to his chi, praying that his chi would untie the noose his enemies had fixed around his neck, praying that one day he would return home, praying that the nza birds that now flew above him would sing those prayers to Ichulu's gods and to Ichulu's people.

But the people did not hear the birds singing or praying. It was evening time, and the people were eating in their red-clay homes; and Nnenna, not having any firewood, went to a neighbor's compound to borrow some, then proceeded to cook yam for the compound of Ọfọdile. And when the water began boiling, she called Ijeọma to her side and began checking her plaited hair for loosened threads; and as she plucked at her strands by the light of the firewood, Nnenna leaned into a fragrance pouring forth from Ijeọma's hair: the sweet smell born anew after thundering and rain. A smile had settled across Nnenna's lips—Ijeọma, who Ichulu thought was powerless and weak, could fly. She could stand above any height, and look down upon the entire village, standing with an authority given by the gods. And she knew there would be few who would mock it, few who would call it strange, but those few were the kind of villagers Nnenna deemed more godless than anything else, the kind who did not truly see Idemili in the water, and Igwe in the sky, and Anyanwụ in his great sun. Ijeọma could fly, and Nnenna believed it was the gods who made it so.

"Ijeọma, is it true? Can you fly?"

Ijeọma nodded three times, smiling.

"How, Ijeọma? How is it possible?"

Ijeọma pointed at her right eye.

"I do not understand," Nnenna said with confusion. "Fly now. Show me, fly for your mother."

Ijeọma left Nnenna's side and jumped four times, slowly nodding her head twice, and seeing that, Nnenna began to lose her smile. But Nnenna lifted Ijeọma with an embrace, as if she had arms as broad and thick as wings, believing that nothing would ever worry her again, that the things she most relished—pottery and cocoyam, truthfulness and integrity—would always be at hand, across every season and within every moment. But a memory seized her—Ọfọdile. She knew the habits of the one called her husband, and believed his pursuit of honor gripped the throats of his thoughts and actions. It surged when Ijeọma was born, then died once they discovered that she could no longer speak.

Nnenna pulled Ijeọma to the earth and sat with her, enclosing her tightly, rubbing the back of her hands. She continued thinking of those days, many harvests ago, when Ijeọma would lie in her arms withdrawn, beaming mostly at the sight of the one called her father and refusing to be peaceful if he was not nearby. Even as an infant she looked like him, and Nnenna remembered each time Ọfọdile asked how his face could be in the face of this little child. "Idemili has taken it from his river water," Nnenna would say, and she recalled how brightly that would make Ọfọdile smile.

When Ijeọma learned to walk, Ọfọdile followed her steps, steering her from dangers that were not there. When she began to eat food, he scolded Nnenna for not checking the meals for small rocks and bones, an act Nnenna found romantic. It was then she knew that his love for Ijeọma was boundless like a wanderer looking upon the nighttime sky, and she believed that only a power vaster than the heavens of Igwe could quell Ọfọdile's love for Ijeọma.

But at the age of one, Ijeọma began to cry; and recalling it moved Nnenna to hold Ijeọma tighter, remembering again how Ọfọdile told her that he would go to Igbokwe's compound each morning, collect potent remedies, and offer prayers to powerful gods. But nothing brought relief to Ijeọma; not even a petition to Chukwu saved the crying child. And after the passing of three weeks, their newborn daughter could no longer make any sound.

Nnenna's heart now tightened at the memory of the village wanting to throw Ijeọma into the Evil Forest. Igbokwe intervened, pronouncing that her voice had not been taken by disease but stolen by an evil person, a person whom he did not then know. And once Igbokwe had made his declaration, Nnenna held the one called her child in her arms and watched Ọfọdile's esteem fall as quietly as a leaf falling from a palm tree, listening to them become the mother and father of the mute.

He will truly hate her now, Nnenna thought, while passing a finger through Ijeọma's hair. And she began offering soft prayers to her chi: that

Ọfọdile would soon love their daughter again, that Ọfọdile would never see Ijeọma fly; and her tongue became tense when she smelled the yam burning in the pot, just as Ọfọdile walked into the compound, carrying the corpse of a young antelope strung around his neck.

"Welcome," Nnenna said, hurrying to meet Ọfọdile after she removed the pot of yam from the firewood.

Ọfọdile said nothing in reply.

"Ọfọdile, I am cooking yam porridge for us to eat."

"That does not smell like yam porridge," Ọfọdile said.

"But I have also fed Chelụchi."

Ọfọdile remained silent.

"There is another thing that I must tell you," she said. "It concerns our daughter."

"What is it?" asked Ọfọdile. "Is Chelụchi ill?"

"No, Ọfọdile. Ijeọma can fly."

"What?"

Nnenna looked at Ọfọdile calmly, as if he should have already known the fact.

"Ụzọdị came earlier, and told me that he and many other people saw Ijeọma flying."

"I do not believe it. When the food is ready, send it to my obi."

Ọfọdile dropped the dead antelope at Nnenna's feet, then went into his red-clay home, rummaging through Nnenna's words. *It must be Amalike*, he thought. *They took her voice, now they are giving her the ways of wild animals.*

He moved through his obi, professing that it was not true—then knowing it was—and letting the words of his mind move him to action: Ekwueme. He decided that he would take Ijeọma to Igbokwe the next day, and stood with ease in the middle of his obi, finding great promise in his plans.

He heard two claps and saw Ijeọma carrying his food and a bowl of water at the mouth of his obi. He did not speak to her as she entered, but he looked at the way she placed the dish full of yams and the bowl of water in front of him, and the enthusiasm with which she waited for his instructions, and thought it all to be sickening, finding it regrettable, beckoning her to leave with the dismissive flutter of his hands. Then he washed his hands to eat his food and thought of those words he would tell Ichulu's dịbịa, hearing his own voice, imbued with much confidence, echoing throughout his mind.

3.

EARLY ON THE FOLLOWING DAY, before Anyanwụ called the sun to rise, everyone in the village had heard of Ijeọma's levitation. Ọfọdile had risen quickly, though, to chase the rumor out of the village before it reached the people's eyes, reasoning that while sound bred speculation, sight sealed truth; and the truth that his family was not an abomination was what he wanted Ichulu to know. He hurried into Nnenna's red-clay home and told her to prepare Ijeọma for her consultation, and once Ijeọma had emerged, he snatched her arm, nearly undoing her dark blue rappa, and hurried them along the path to Igbokwe's compound.

While walking atop the eroded earth, passing weary dogs and injured cassava leaves, Ọfọdile and Ijeọma crossed paths with Nwagụ, a member of Ọfọdile's age group. And Ọfọdile quickly remembered how the village had called him lucky and adored him in their childhood, especially the elders, who had given him the name Nwakaibie for being favored among their peers.

Whenever an animal was slaughtered and its entrails distributed, it was Nwagụ who would receive the largest share and would sometimes receive parts of the cooked meat. As he looked past Nwagụ's eyes, Ọfọdile recalled that Ichulu now said that Nwagụ's luck was kept alive because Mgboye, the one called his second wife, was expecting to give birth to their fifth child.

"How are you, Ọfọdile?" asked Nwagụ with a broad smile, his black-and-white chieftaincy fan fluttering in his right hand.

"It is well, Nwagụ . . . let us talk . . . another time, since I must go quickly."

"But you know that our elders say that one does not recognize a black goat at night. Morning is the time to greet one's brethren."

Ọfọdile quietly sucked his teeth. Trapped by the proverb, he allowed himself to stay with Nwagụ.

"Ọfọdile, I have heard that this daughter of yours"—he looked down at Ijeọma when he said *daughter*—"has been flying with the birds."

"You . . . have, heard it . . . but did you, see it . . . with your eyes?"

"You are right, my friend. My eyes have not seen it. But there is no problem. I am sure you have heard that Mgboye is expecting to have another child soon. I pray that it is a boy."

"May the gods hear your prayer," Ọfọdile said quickly.

"They will hear it. I know they will. And you, what of that son of yours, Nnamdị?"

Ijeọma listened to Ọfọdile respond, heard Nwagụ respond again, and looked at both men, seeking to resolve Ọfọdile's discomfort as she thought of things—quickly she thought of them: pouting, running—and then she crossed her legs, tightening her thighs and fists.

"Nwagụ," Ọfọdile said, "It seems as though . . . my child wants to urinate. Let us . . . talk again, in time."

"Let it be, then," said Nwagụ, "Fasten yourself to power."

"Fasten . . . yourself to power," Ọfọdile said.

And the two were turning, each moving away from the other, while Ijeọma ran behind a tall palm tree and pretended to urinate. She squatted to the earth with her blue rappa raised to her hips, counting to twenty to make her ploy believable. When she rejoined Ọfọdile on the path, hoping that he had not recognized her deceit, she signed to him that she was finished by brushing her hands together; and when she saw his brow unfurrowed and his high cheeks unmoved, she believed them to be signs of the full success of her plan, believing that Ọfọdile was quietly rejoicing at her craftiness.

Soon, she and the one called her father both stood on the earth of Igbokwe's compound and watched the dịbịa engage in his morning prayers. Only a white cloth covered Igbokwe's body, sitting softly below his waist as he raised and lowered his arms, straight toward Igwe's clouds, straight beyond Chukwu's lofty sea, to the rhythms of his murmuring lips, suddenly pointing at Ọfọdile and Ijeọma and honoring them both with a greeting.

"Ọfọdile and Ijeọma, welcome. I have been waiting for you."

"So you know why I am here," Ọfọdile said.

"I do," said Igbokwe. "It does not take the wisest of men to know that Ekwueme does not want his daughter flying."

"It is true," Ọfọdile said. "Please . . . tell me what is causing this to be?"

Igbokwe lifted himself while wrapping the white cloth around his waist, then walked toward Ijeọma to search her eyes for any evil. He blew air into them, which made them tear, and drank the droplets which fell forth. Then he took her arms and legs and examined them for foreign things, things like lumps or bruises. He found nothing, and moved to draw a circle along the earth by the tip of his iron staff.

"Ijeọma," the dịbịa said, "walk around this line."

She obeyed, and Igbokwe saw nothing unusual in her motions.

"Ọfọdile, I must speak to the gods. Your daughter must come into my obi so that I may speak to them properly."

"It is well, Igbokwe . . . let me go and check my traps . . . to see if I have caught anything . . . I do not want my meat to rot . . . my wife will not cook it, if it is rotten . . . I will return soon to see what you have learned."

Igbokwe commanded a pause between them, remaining silent as he looked through the black of Ọfọdile's eyes.

"A man who believes his chi is sleeping has already died," the dịbịa said.

Three nods was the response Ọfọdile gave, before he left the dibịa's compound and reached into his bag for his containers of snuff.

Ijeọma watched him go and wondered why he did not stay, wondering, too, why he seldom stayed—not when she was sick—not when she was scared—not when she wanted him present; leave, was what he always did. She wondered if it was for growing, or for weaning, or for another thing, wanting Ọfọdile—coming from Ọfọdile, without him, she believed she could not be. *Though he does not speak to me*, she thought, *and why, because if he could speak with me, the way he spoke with Nnamdị, if he could babble with me, the way he babbled with Chelụchi, if he heard of my flight through my speech, he would believe, he would know that my flight was something beautiful.* But Ijeọma could not speak, so he did not speak; and Ijeọma could now fly, and she wondered what Ọfọdile would think of it.

"Ijeọma, enter my obi," said Igbokwe, whispering as he spoke, watching Ijeọma enter timidly, then seeing her eyes moving across the many things in his obi: the decapitated heads of women and men, the benighted symbols on his obi's walls—written with his fingers and blood.

"Do not be afraid, my child. The gods only want me to understand why you are flying. Have you heard me? Do not be afraid."

Igbokwe saw her nod three times, and he nodded three times also. He turned to his wall to take a goat-horn cup and began drinking the water within it. Then he sat on the earth of his obi's floor and called out the names of Ichulu's gods.

"Amadịọha, Ikenga, Igwe, Anị, Ugwu, Idemili . . . Chukwu beyond the sky, Chukwu the all-powerful, Chukwu the all-knowing, the Supreme Being, the one who is everywhere and everywhere . . . Can you hear me? Can you hear your child speaking? I ask you because I do not know if yesterday you decided to discard your ears. You are my gods; if you discard your nose so as not to smell, who am I to question it . . . You have heard. I know it in my heart that you have all heard. Bring peace to this obi of mine. Hear the concerns of your child, and bring ease. I have come to gather the seeds of your wisdom . . . Did you not speak to me, in the morn of yesterday's sister, through the winds and skies? Did I not hear your words echoing through the soil of Anị? I ask that you speak again. You know what has happened to this child of Ichulu who sits before me. You know her, and have known her— even before she left the loins of Ọfọdile and entered the womb of Nnenna. Put what is known into my own mind, so that we, too, in this world may understand."

Ijeọma listened to the way in which Igbokwe prayed: the firm timbre in his voice, his unyielding honor for the gods, the simplicity of his spirit— which made truth feel true—feeling the prickly dots passing through her shoulders—moving her to trust Igbokwe's words and heart—then quickly— she saw Ụzọdị's eyes within her—He must not have anger for me; how can he have anger, if he escorted me to my father's compound and explained to my mother that I was flying; Ijeọma smiled at what disproved Ụzọdị's love to be unrequited, smiling with wide lips and teeth, asking Chukwu to strengthen him in the Place of Osu, to bring to him the vision she had seen in the sky, past the clouds of Igwe.

And as Igbokwe prayed, he lifted the horn containing his cowrie shells and began shaking it, then cast the shells atop his obi's ground. He read the patterns before him, deciphering every word the gods had spoken before picking up the shells again and putting them in the horn, throwing them, and casting them three times more. And when the message remained unchanged, his face rose bewilderingly.

Me! I must be loved! I must be loved!

How is this possible, Igbokwe said to himself. Chukwu, the greatest god of my people, is this true?

Ijeọma smiled with her lips and with her chi, a beam of light resting, now, on her forehead; she thought of Ụzọdị as her eyes looked toward the sun, past the roof of the obi, a tear now falling from her chin.

"It must be true! What the shells have told me is true!"

Igbokwe watched Ijeọma, and could not deny that joy had taken her as she sat peacefully in the air as though fear had hung itself from a tree; and so he laughed, he could not prevent himself from laughing, filling his obi with awestruck cackling; and though the message left him slightly disquieted, he could not find worry beneath Ijeọma's shadow.

And when he heard Ọfọdile's footsteps approaching him moments after Ijeọma returned to the ground, he left his obi quickly, not wearing any reassurance, not seeing Ọfọdile's face fall hopelessly.

"Ọfọdile . . . my child, my child."

"What has happened, Igbokwe? What is the problem?"

Igbokwe took time to gather his words—words he had thought would never be said together.

"Ọfọdile, I read my cowrie shells. I read them well. Chukwu, the greatest god of our people, is reclaiming power. Do you not see? The reason your daughter can be lifted to the sky is because Chukwu is recollecting power from Anị—and has been doing so for many months now. Your daughter, who many thought should have been thrown into the Evil Forest to avoid the judgment of Anị, is the vessel Chukwu is using to speak this message. Anị and Chukwu—the gods who once knew harmony—have disagreed through the body of your mute child. Do you not see it? When she flies, she moves upward . . . toward Chukwu and away from Anị. This was why Idemili and Igwe, the husband of Anị, conspired with our enemies to punish us with the evil water that came. Ichulu is the only village worshipping Chukwu as Chukwu wishes to be worshipped. Now the goddess and her friends are vexed at us and the Most Supreme because her power is no longer hers."

"How do we know that she truly flies? Only a few people claimed to have seen her."

"Ọfọdile, she was sitting above my head when you were snorting your snuff."

"Could it not . . . have been a spirit . . . you were seeing?"

"Are you calling your daughter a corpse?" Igbokwe asked.

"I have heard you . . . so how can we, stop her from flying again?"

Igbokwe widened his gaze. He could not understand why Ọfọdile would deny his words. This was not a mere possession or curse: the gods were at war.

"Ọfọdile, I do not control the gods. I am only their messenger. My medi-cine receives its power from them. I will inform them of what you have told me, but if you can pray to your chi, pray. Ask them to speak to the quarreling gods, and plead for a quick resolution."

"Igbokwe . . . I have heard your words . . ."

Ọfọdile beckoned for Ijeọma to come to him, and the two quickly left the dịbịa's compound.

4.

IJEỌMA WOKE TO NNENNA CHANGING into the rappa that Nnenna would wear for the morning. The cocks had not yet crowed, and the dew-covered compound was still dark; but Ijeọma stood from her sleeping mat and looked on inquiringly at the one called her mother, wondering where she was going, hope resting in her eyes.

"Ijeọma, I am going to Nwagụ's compound. They have said it is time for Mgboye to deliver her baby."

Ijeọma raised her brow, laughing within the silence of the morning, nearly forgetting that she had dreamt of her return to the sky, of black nza birds lifting her to a vision in the clouds. A child was being born, and the delight of it tickled her the way she tickled her infant sister, as though the day would never end; laughing more gleefully at the thought of playing with the coming child, she moved, pulling on Nnenna's arms: pleading.

"Ijeọma, you cannot come with me," Nnenna said. "You know this is only for those who have given birth."

Ijeoma's gaze fell at Nnenna's pronouncement, but she conjured the strength not to complain, understanding Nnenna's reasoning like every child in Ichulu understood it, knowing the village sacrificed much to protect its traditions. She raised her eyes and released Nnenna's arms, deciding, then, to consider other things: to return to bed, to wake at another time and clean the homes of the ones called her mother and father, to take a bath, and to sweep the leaf-filled compound; then she would pray to Chukwu—jump toward the Most Supreme and pray for Chukwu to make her fly again, and greet her vision in the sky, and thank the Supreme Being for giving her what she wanted, and thank Chukwu, thank the Most Supreme, for bringing me upward again, for giving me life to sweep the compound, and go to Idemili, and clean my mother's home, but take me up—and for that mama of mine, and Mgboye's baby, thank you, take me up again today, past Igwe—mama of mine, mama of mine; you will see me sweep the compound; and bathe at Idemili; and honor his water; greet Mgboye and her baby, greet them, and as Ijeoma signed to Nnenna, Nnenna said that she would do those things: that she would tell Mgboye and her newborn baby welcome.

Then Nnenna carried her belongings and met Ezinne at the center of the compound; she was wearing a purple rappa, while Ezinne wore the one for which she was well-known, a golden one that matched the light brown of her clean-shaven head. Together the two traveled to Nwagu's compound to bear witness to the birth of the one called Mgboye's fifth child. They passed the sleeping compounds as they went, and passed, too, the many sunken paths and fallen trees felled by Idemili's flood; and when they arrived, several women were already gathered at Mgboye's red-clay home. Adaora, the eldest among them, fed Mgboye warm udala to remedy her bleeding, while the others sang the promise that her pain would soon be forgotten as her screams echoed throughout the compound, alarming the goats and causing the calla lilies to shiver, and the women continued to encourage her with prayers, then good words, words like the crowning of her baby's head, and the appearance of the baby's umbilical cord; and with a powerful scream, she pushed its body through her own as he opened his mouth and joined in her crying.

"Chei! Let it not be so!" Nnenna shouted.

"I pray it is not so," Ezinne said.

All the women gathered, looked into the child's mouth, and screamed. The child had teeth—four on each row—and they knew that such a child was an abomination to the goddess of the earth and would soon be thrown into the Evil Forest. And they cried out for mercy and leniency, seeing that Adaọra would fulfill her duties, when her face remained stolid as she presented the child to Mgboye; and they cried out again, like the crackling of lightning, once Mgboye looked down to see what the others had seen, breaking into tears, weeping bitterly for the one called her son.

"I was going to call him Chukwujekwu! I was going to call him Jekwu! Aaaaaaaaaa-yeh-yeh-yeh! My chi! What have I done! What have I done!"

When Adaọra had finished cutting the umbilical cord and cleansing Nnenna's body, she took the infant out of Mgboye's arms and into Nwagụ's obi—then dodged a clay pot which Nwagụ had thrown furiously, nearly striking the elder. Not knowing where he was, nor what he had become, not knowing if any thing or one could be true—as life had not forged the beauty he thought it should make, possessed by fury, Nwagụ, the one who found luck through his chi, began lunging his fists through his obi's walls, craving to destroy it.

When the mourn had passed, Nnenna and Ezinne returned to Ọfọdile's compound and told him of the birth of Nwagụ's son. And he felt pity for the man, though he heard a song of glee resounding through his head; he dismissed it and thought of the child, knowing that before night had come the infant would be collected by Igbokwe, cry many cries, and then die of starvation inside the Evil Forest. He felt sympathy dwelling within himself, and honored the obligation of visiting a grieving man—waiting for Anyanwụ, the god of the sun, to stand in the middle of the sky before traveling to Nwagụ's compound. And once he arrived, he witnessed the man's sorrow, merciless and unrelenting, sorrow as wicked as an envious god, his broad smile no longer with him, his face loose and heavy like a sagging rappa. This cannot be Nwakaibie, Ọfọdile said within himself, this cannot be Ichulu's luckiest man. And he sat down with Nwagụ, and joined him in breaking kola.

"Nwagụ, I have heard," Ọfọdile said. "All of us in Ichulu have heard of your son, and it worries my worry. No man should ever know this kind of suffering."

"Thank you, Ọfọdile, but because of your daughter I am not yet defeated."

"Who is that . . . are you speaking of Chelụchi?"

"No, I am speaking of Ijeọma," Nwagụ said.

Ọfọdile's fingers immediately began trembling as he turned his face from Nwagụ's.

"Ọfọdile, I am speaking of your Ada."

"What . . . are you, saying?"

"I am saying that when Igbokwe came to my house to take the baby into the forest, he told me that it may not be permanent. He told me that Ijeọma's flying was caused by Chukwu taking power from Anị. He told me that if my son lasts in the Evil Forest for four days, it means that Chukwu was ending the conflict, and that sacrifices to appease Anị would not be necessary. If Jekwu survives this week, he will be allowed to return to my home."

"Is . . . your . . . word . . . good?

"Yes, my word is good. Had it not been for you, Ọfọdile, my child would not have any hope for life. All we can do now is pray that he lasts in the forest."

"I will tell . . . my household . . . to pray, for your child. I must go now . . . Tell your family, that I greet them."

"I will do so. Fasten yourself to power," said Nwagụ.

"Fasten yourself to power," Ọfọdile said as he left the obi, hurrying along the eroded path winding toward his modest compound; the words that Nwagụ spoke yielded a mighty wind, storming throughout his mind, tossing the present about like dust, making him oblivious to his feet atop the earth and the verdant landmarks guiding his return home; he was lost in it— walking as bewilderedly as a lonesome rat, wanting to cry out, but nobody was there with him on the sunken path, and nobody, he thought, would understand, or share his shame lest the windstorm bury them; there was nobody there to tell Ichulu that he had finally accepted that his firstborn daughter was an abomination.

"Nnenna, come here!" Ọfọdile said, once he had stepped into his quiet compound.

"What, what has happened?" asked Nnenna.

"Ichulu has fallen! Ichulu has fallen!"

"What do you mean?"

"Nwagụ has told me that Ijeọma has saved his newborn child."

"What?"

"Yes. He said that Igbokwe will keep the child in the Evil Forest for one week because Ijeọma is flying. If the child survives, the child will be returned to his family."

"That child will die! That little child will die of starvation!"

"Woman, is that what you heard! Do you not see that her flying is giving this village trouble? Our forefathers have always worshipped Ani; now your daughter's abnormality is challenging the goddess."

"Ọfọdile, Chukwu has done this to our daughter. She is a child with blessing."

"I see that you are becoming foolish! Go! Continue what you were doing. I have told you what I wanted to tell you."

"I will go. But if you call me foolish again, I will use the blade that I use to cook your food to cut off your tongue. And if you ever deny our daughter, calling her mine alone, that blade will cut off another thing."

Ijeọma saw the one called her mother moving away from Ọfọdile, having heard those words they spoke to each other, a river as long as Idemili moving down her face—not falling amid their words, but from one salient truth: in a fearful forest, a baby would painfully die. So she rushed toward the little space between Nnenna's home and the wall enclosing the compound, and although the thin patches of grass tickled her dusty feet, and the wind wiped the droplets from her face, the horror of the baby remained, grieving the footholds of her mind; Chukwu, where are you, she said within herself, wanting a levitation to ease her with its joys—wanting it to dip her into the Evil Forest to lift the child and fly toward refuge. But she did not control when she left the earth. Chukwu did. So she resigned her words to prayers, prostrating herself on the orange ground, ignoring the ants crawling along her legs, and ignoring the anticipated voice of the one called her mother, scolding her for dirtying her rappa.

That their belly would remain full, and that the mosquitoes would not bite them so much, were wishes for which Ijeọma prayed, and that the baby would sleep throughout their time in the Evil Forest and dream dreams of happiness, and for their teeth, their little teeth, that they will grow big and wide and make the most beautiful smile in Ichulu, and Mgboye and Nwagụ, what mother and father live as their child dies, and let them not curse your name in anger, Chukwu, let them not curse your name, give them hope, and the baby, too, are they sleeping in the forest, are they crying in the forest, what did that baby do, it was their teeth, but we have them, too, the baby had them early but there are some who do not have them at all, let me see them for myself, their smile, their evil smile, that baby can smile already?

Ijeọma laughed softly into her dusty rappa in realization of what the village failed to consider: the baby smiles; and this baby who had not breathed the air of the open world, or watched the lizards dance their silly, jerking dance, lay in an evil forest for smiling in the womb of the one called their mother. *How can they let them die*, she thought, wiping her face, then raising herself to a new thought of aiding the little one. She pressed her feet into the compound's earth, knowing the thought to be true: she was the one to save the smiling child from death.

DIARY ENTRY #931   DATE UNKNOWN

Chukwu where are you? I have been waiting for you to feed me in this prison cell. It was Igbokwe who told me of his dreams where yam fell from the sky in a barren place. The place had no harvest and no food. But there was yam coming from your hands. I know there is a reason for this dream. I know Igbokwe never dreams in vain. I know this; I know it must be true. So please feed me Chukwu. Please feed me because I am hungry. They've given me water but it is not enough. I need food. Human beings need food. And I have not cleaned at all. My waste is packed all around me. Can you not see it? Do you not smell it?

Chukwu please! Don't let these wicked people take my life. They are evil, worthy of nothing but your punishment. Don't let them triumph over me, but save me from them. Strike them down, all of them. They are starving me and I am hungry Chukwu. Please, I am hungry. I ask of you to feed me. Give me bread. I need bread Chukwu. Even if it is just a little. I will manage with it. I will survive with it. I know you will do it. The one that raised me to the sky will not deny me bread.

5.

THE BRANCHES OF QFODILE'S ORANGE tree hung low as their ripened fruit reached for the distant earth. The stout chickens in his compound looked upward at those embryonic suns, bobbing their heads and wondering if their beaks could penetrate those thick, golden skins. The feathered beasts did not wake the compound with their crows.

"We have lost time!"

Qfodile awoke to the smell of goat dung and ripening fruit, and to the fright of losing his consultation with Igbokwe. He entered his obi, where he quickly prayed a prayer to his chi and offered palm wine for the ancestors to drink, pouring it into a wooden bowl. Then he ran, hurrying through many hungry mosquitoes, and rushing into the darkness of Nnenna's red-clay home.

"Nnenna, wake Ijeoma, and prepare her for the consultation. Quickly, quickly, quick!"

"I have . . . heard . . . you," Nnenna said as she rolled on her mat. "Ijeọma . . . Ijeọma, rise, rise," Nnenna said while rolling onto her back; but then she felt Ijeọma patting her shoulders, and turned to see her already prepared for the morning.

"Ada of mine, you are beautiful. Go and follow your father outside."

Ijeọma obeyed and joined Ọfọdile, and the two began their journey to Igbokwe's compound. She shook her hands to greet him and wish him well, though he did not respond, as he seldom responded. So she blamed her muteness and began blaming herself, believing it to be her fault—because if he could speak with her, the way he spoke with Nnamdị, or babble with her, the way he babbled with Chelụchi, he would smile at her, and greet her, too; but then she doubted herself, her intuition and reasoning, believing her thoughts were wrong, believing that if she could greet Ọfọdile with her signs once more, he would wish her well. And so she did, signing, then signing again, over and again, signing over and again, without her father seeing her, without the one called her father knowing that she wanted to be seen; and when her chest began aching more than her moving fingers, she folded her hands and looked upon a squatting nza bird.

Ọfọdile had not seen her but spent the journey to Igbokwe's compound battling his own thoughts: the war between the gods, the one beyond human measure, causing floods and exiling sons, burdening his already burdened life. He wanted his snuff. He wanted his containers while convincing himself that Igbokwe would soon remove the curse upon Ijeọma, even if he had not seen any change in her after weeks of divination. The one called his daughter had not flown since her first consultation, and it was in that absence that he had placed his hope, planning to keep his consultations with Igbokwe until the curse was broken, saying over and again, while walking past the walls of other compounds, "No man . . . knows which, blow will break . . . the coconut."

"Ọfọdile, how are you?"

Ọfọdile silenced his whispers and turned to see the barren Ngọzi balancing a large basket on her head while greeting him with a smile.

"I am . . . well, Ngọzi. Are you off, to the market?"

"I am," Ngọzi answered, wondering at Ijeọma's falling tears. "My ground-nuts were not destroyed by Idemili and his flood. My husband was the one who helped me harvest them, and was the one who found the strength to build a good barn. But it is Chukwu and his chi that we are thanking."

"That is fine," Ọfọdile said, before scratching his leg from a mosquito's bite.

"Look at that, it is early and it seems that hunger is hungering you. Take some groundnut."

"Ngọzi. We are to meet Igbokwe soon."

"Do not worry any worries; I will share them quickly quickly quick," Ngọzi said while placing the large basket on the ground and removing the light yellow cloth that covered it, exposing thousands of gray-shelled ground-nuts harvested by her hands. She took a ceramic cup, filled it with produce, and poured it into Ọfọdile's palm.

"Is it not good?" Ngọzi said to a silent Ọfọdile. "My Ijeọma, I have not forgotten you. Give me your hands so I can give you groundnut."

Ijeọma slowly obeyed, placing her hands in front of Ngọzi and watching her fill them with a morning meal—as their fingers touched—and a wild vibration ran through Ngọzi's body.

"What is this?" Ngọzi said, dropping her cup and clutching her waist.

"What happened?" Ọfọdile said.

Ngọzi was silent, and searched Ijeọma's eyes deeply, as if they would save her from the beginnings of madness. Her breathing quickened, then slowed as she watched Ijeọma look plainly through her as if nothing had occurred, as if she had not felt the bright and wild vibration.

"What did you do!" Ọfọdile said to Ijeọma.

But she did not answer Ọfọdile's accusation.

"It was nothing," said Ngọzi. "It was nothing that happened. You should hurry and go and see Igbokwe."

Ngọzi lifted her basket and hurried to the market, feeling the shock's vibration warm her insides, relishing it and surrendering her fears to its warmth and pleasure. A nut had fallen, but she did not see it.

But Ọfọdile saw unease in the barren Ngọzi and did not believe her word to be good. There was a problem, and he believed Ijeọma was its cause. He moved to the front of her and knocked the groundnut from her hands, clutching her chin and twisting her face toward his.

"It does not concern me that a god has befriended you . . . as worthless as you are," he said through his teeth. "It does not concern me at all. If you disgrace me again in the land of my father, you will see the other side of Idemili, the part where even the alligators do not tread. It will be these . . . my own hands that will put you there. Know it today."

Ijeọma believed him. She was a child who believed what was said the first time it was said, so she believed by Ọfọdile's words that her death was more valuable than her life; it was the truth, she thought, even as an ache formed inside her, traveling through her stomach and up her chest and curdling in her throat. The ache would not leave her, even as she straightened her back and feigned an assured walk along the orange path.

They arrived at Igbokwe's compound, and the dịbịa welcomed Ọfọdile and Ijeọma as if they were children of his home, greeting them with blessings and smiles. Though when the dịbịa looked into Ijeọma's eyes, he saw hateful spirits touching her and knew in his bones from where that hate had come. But he said nothing of it, closing his mouth to prophecies and soothsaying, greeting Ọfọdile again with a touch from his hands.

And at once he began the works of his consultation, playing the music of the gods from his wooden flute and offering prayers and a sacrifice of birds to Agwụ, the healing deity. Then he began examining Ijeọma's naked body, checking it for signs legible to his eyes; his aged fingers pressed upon her flesh, reading each word the gods were humming through her bones. And when his hands returned to those of Ọfọdile, he reminded him that the power to end Ijeọma's flights dwelt in the realm of the gods—and that his work was done to help him also, to keep Ọfọdile's hope from dying.

And as he spoke, Ijeọma looked directly toward him, seeing his stout frame, and his moon-shaped hair holding specks of black; and she smiled at him, even though he was not looking at her then, eager for him to smile at her, too. And he did, somehow knowing, turning to her and smiling at her, and she smiled again and thanked him. And she thought of the dịbịa, remembering the smell of his warm breaths, breaths which smelled of honey, remembering it even as she thought, too, of alligators, and Idemili, and Ọfọdile's name; and if it were true that she was disgraceful, thinking of the two banishments and six deaths, thinking of the flood—partially true, she thought, even if truth were measured by the hairs of an ant's leg, partially true because she attracted enemies to a village that did not travel the world to find them. She smiled at Igbokwe again, but he did not see, and he did not smile at her, and she did not understand, and thought he blamed her, too, and the village, and the eight osu, with Ọfọdile, and began growing melancholy—but the vision, the vision had meaning also, and she ran from Ọfọdile's side to find its understanding.

"Igbokwe . . . have you, spoken with Chukwu? . . . Are the gods continuing their fight?"

"Two people in Ichulu know the answer to your question: me and your Ada. But I believe you, too, know the answer to the question with which you are questioning me."

"Is, there any more medicine . . . we can use to cure her?" asked Ọfọdile. "Are there . . . any more prayers?"

"No, my child," Igbokwe said, "but I will keep speaking with the gods to see if there is something that I can do again. Continue bringing Ijeọma to my compound in the mornings. I have made medicine that will protect her from bad spirits. Bring her here to my obi so that she may consume it."

"I will, bring her. But she . . . should take, some now. Ijeọma . . . where did she go!"

"Take your calm, Ọfọdile. She is there by the cashew tree playing with a stick."

"Ijeọma! Ijeọma! Come here!" Ọfọdile said.

Ijeọma heard the call and began running to the dịbịa's side, and she did not turn to the one called her father when he ordered her to drink the medicine prepared for her, but she closed her eyes as she drank the bitter liquid from a ram-horn cup—seeing the dịbịa's smile once she opened her eyes and placed the cup in his hands, then leaving him with an assured farewell and a promise to return tomorrow.

And as they left, moving away from the dibịa and toward the mouth of his compound, Ọfọdile looked at the earth by the cashew tree where Ijeọma had been playing. And below the tree's yellow fruit, he saw an image of an eye etched on the earth's skin. He did not hesitate. He hurried to the drawing, and erased it with his calloused feet, his heart stiff, his eyes threatening, his anger driving him to strike Ijeọma across her cheek.

And when they returned to Ọfọdile's compound, Ijeọma ran from Ọfọdile's side and into Nnenna's home, nearly eaten by a cave of sorrow. She fell onto Nnenna's sleeping mat and saw the one called her sister crawling atop the earthen floor, and because of it she smiled and wondered what Chelụchi's thoughts could be, knowing that she loved adventures and would escape the watch of Nnenna for the sake of discovering the compound over and again, a compound which Ichulu called modest, a compound which she thought Chelụchi deemed more vast than the village of ants, living beneath the earth.

Ijeọma watched her younger sister playing with a broom of nine sticks, and stopped her when she began chewing the broom's ends; she lifted her, and held her against her chest; she listened: their hearts sounding like the drumming at the New Yam Festival, blending with each other to make a rhythm to which they could dance; and so they did, Ijeọma shifting herself rhythmically against the hinges of her body, and shifting Chelụchi's body, too: hand to wrist, arm to elbow, waist, thigh to knee, knee to leg; they danced as their heart beats drummed more quickly, dancing in a spiral, quickly quickly quick—they were dancing—until heavy breaths escaped them—as they fell onto the ground.

And as Ijeọma held Chelụchi and felt air expanding within Chelụchi's chest, they both began laughing—as quickly as Amadiọha's lightning, her thoughts returned to the baby in the Evil Forest. She remembered her plan to help him, and so returned Chelụchi to the earth and rushed to find the one called their mother; and found her within a moment in Ezinne's home, re-shaving Ezinne's scalp.

"Ijeọma, what has happened," Nnenna said.

Ijeọma placed her right hand on the left side of her chest.

"Ehhh-heh, what of Chelụchi," Nnenna said, while sweeping the blade across Ezinne's head.

Ijeọma made rigid ovals against her stomach.

"She is hungry? Bring her here so that I can give her food."

Ijeọma nodded twice and pointed at herself.

"You do not want me to feed her with my breasts? *You* want to feed her?"

Ijeọma nodded her head three times. Ijeọma nodded yes.

"That is fine. When you feed her, remember how I have always done it. Go and boil rice and give it to the child of your mother."

Ijeọma smiled and went into the small red-clay shed where food was stored; she unsealed the wide basin of rice and measured a small portion, removing it slowly, filling the small space of her dented palm; how could this satisfy the baby for a week, she thought—so she took more rice, four exorbitant handfuls, and boiled them in Nnenna's cooking pot. And when the rice had finished cooking, she mashed it into a soft white pulp with a wooden pestle and placed it in an unused bowl. She gave some to Chelụchi, so that her word remained good to the one called her mother, then placed the bowl in a basket and hid the basket behind Nnenna's red-clay home so that nobody would find her deception.

6.

THE MOMENT NIGHT FELL, AND the members of Ọfọdile's compound fell with it, Ijeọma took the basket from its hiding place and began her journey to the Evil Forest. The paths of the village were different at nighttime, she thought—not wearing their usual deep, rich orange but a suspicious blue: the kind that says the sky can exist without the sun, or that Igwe is a different god from Anyanwụ—a blue that makes a gentle palm tree become more ominous than a threatening spirit. And she could hear small animals moving against dead leaves and dried palm branches and felt their dense aroma putting water in her eyes, hindering her vision beneath the clouded moon; and she heard, too, the voices of men, and began wiping her eyes as they came—closer and closer—she was hearing them come, the voices of two men, *why are they coming, approaching more closely, why at this time, they will know . . . and Igbokwe who curses will sacrifice me, no, no, no, it is not mine, why should I die for what is already dying?*

Her body did not move; fear had entered it; no, no, no, rang throughout her head, then fell silent to deadly thoughts and expectations—feeding the pause that comes before a surrender—as she began feeling ants gathering atop her toes, removing her from the pause, encouraging her to run behind a large tree where she prayed to Chukwu that the men had not heard.

"Who is there?"

The two men looked around and saw no one. They casually checked the borders of the path, but they did not see Ijeoma standing behind the tree as though she were stone.

"I am certain I heard a noise," one of them said.

"It must have been a grasscutter," said the other.

"Let us keep searching. Maybe we can catch whatever animal is running about?"

"Friend of mine, night has already fallen."

"But we can use the meat and bones for many things."

"You are speaking from hunger. Do you even have any traps or a blade?"

"Friend of mine, I do not."

"Then let us go to my home so that you may eat."

Ijeoma heard the two men leaving, and nearly wept from relief, and her fear-filled confession; she breathed. And she breathed again, feeling her spirit settle like the final clamors of a gong—reminding herself that she could die for the baby in the Evil Forest, then reminding herself that they could both live, and live by peace together. She breathed again, and waited for many moments to pass to be certain that the men were no longer there and that nobody had returned in their place. And when the night had become silent again, she emerged with her basket and moved forward along the blue path.

Before many moments, she reached the mouth of the Evil Forest, looking at its leaves and thinking the moon shone on them peculiarly, as if blessing them with ashes of light—believing their trees were alive, reaching and bending, confidently humble, knowing the birds did not fear the forest, flying with ease and familiarity; and the purple amaryllises, whose true color she guessed to be red, adorned the wide and leveled entrance of the village evil. She did not fear it. She prayed before entering it—asking Chukwu to protect her, asking Chineke and her chi for favor and luck; the ancestors she asked for courage, and cool wind then brushed her face.

She entered it. There were sixteen different paths that Ijeọma could see, and from the entrance of the forest they all carried the same form. She did not know where Igbokwe had left the baby, so she chose one of the sixteen, without deliberation, hurrying through it, running to reach the child before death; she ran through the first path, where sharp branches and thorny brush cluttered its thin space, and where sharp rocks cut Ijeọma's feet, and she felt the emboldened rats and grasscutters gnawing at her ankles and whipping their tails against her feet—with bats swooping low beside her to catch crawling bugs as prey as she continued down the first path, the piquant aroma of greens causing her eyes to tear; she hurried along, knowing and not knowing what she sought, imagining the baby as Cheluchi, crawling and giggling in the darkness, then imagining him wrapped in a rappa, with his skin a shade brighter than the dark of nighttime; she looked for life, any sign or sound of it, speaking in human tones, turning on human instinct, and she found by the end of the first path that such signs and sounds were not given.

Ijeọma returned to the entrance of the forest, clutching her basket of rice and water, then setting it atop the forest's earth. She ran to a tree beside her and plucked its brightest amaryllis, using one of its purple petals to mark the path she had traveled; then she chose a second path, and ran through it— quickly, quickly—searching for the little child.

The path was wider than the first, with calla lilies resting in its bushes and light from the moon sweeping through its trees. Ijeọma ran through it, fixing her eyes on every patch of earth, running to large stones and searching behind them, running to large trees and searching behind them, and finding nothing but more earth and wriggling bugs. She ran quickly down the second path, not hearing any sounds: no hisses from snakes or crunching from leaves beneath the footsteps of rats and grasscutters, no birds or bats flying about in the nighttime's air; and she stopped running, because she saw light coming from behind a bush; and she dropped her basket and ran to the light, praying as she did so, calling the names of the gods and the ancestors, sweeping past the bush's broad leaves to see if it were true.

And it was. Ijeọma looked upon one of Ichulu's four holy stones, stones that were blessed each morning. She knew that there was one in each corner of the village, one in the hunting forest, one by the compounds, one by the great iroko tree, and the last, the most precious of them, sat before her; it was as beautiful as the village thought it to be, shimmering with all of nighttime's light, and cool, Ijeọma discovered, when she placed a finger atop it; she felt heavy power from its bulk and wondered why its power could not prevent the flood from coming, and wondered if it still had power, and looked upon its luminescence and knew that it did, rubbing the stone and praying for it to guide her in the forest, then leaving it thinking of the baby and time, and returning to the entrance of the second path, marking it traveled with a petal from the amaryllis.

Ijeọma picked another, a third path, and ran quickly through it; and ran more quickly when she saw the dead corpses stretched along its sandy earth, glancing at them, looking for the baby within white cages, white teeth, white skulls—and saw one, a little skeleton tucked within the cavities of the larger, a female one, who was sent to the Evil Forest while pregnant; and Ijeọma ran out of that path, its rank odor pursuing her as she went, believing within herself that Igbokwe would not place the living child in this corner of the forest, believing that word to be good when the cool breeze had suddenly returned.

She dropped a petal, and entered a fourth pathway; she ran through it, clenching her bloody feet, tripping over large stones and large branches that cluttered the narrow path. Mosquitoes gathered around her feet when she fell, taking for themselves all the drink that spilled from her soles; the bats swooped lower, too, encircling her, flapping their thin wings against her face as she stood, and ran again through the path, looking for signs, waiting to hear sounds of life; she ran, even as she felt the blister on her basket-carrying hand, deepening and deepening and blistering enough to crack open and leak; she ran along the path's incline, its hills bearing no footholds, so when she fell again, she crawled on her belly like the alligators of Idemili, grabbing the hills' earth and pulling herself upward, looking around to see if she could see the baby; and when she reached the top of the hill, she ran again, and looked again, and fell, and bled, and saw the trees, Chukwu, and looked behind large stones, Chukwu, please, and saw the moon, Chukwu, please, the baby, where is the baby, he is not here, to understand, to understand, and go again, run again, run again, run, to see the hill, and slide along it, to roll along it, standing, standing, and having the basket, running again, running, Chukwu, running, and having the basket, the baby, where is he, again at the beginning, the petal, dropping the petal, leaving the petal and running again, to run, the earth is opening, to fall, where is the baby, Chukwu, please, let me fly again, Chukwu, please let me fly, let me fly, but my father does not like it, not to fly, running, and the petal, Chukwu, please, my legs are tired, seeing the stones, the way is dark, but the baby, running, dropping a petal, to run, dropping another, stop the bats, stop them, having the basket, and the petal, running, my feet are sore, they itch, they itch!, listening and looking, return the moon, but the baby, and the petal, going again, will run, will look, the baby, and the petal, looking, and running, and running, another petal, and the basket is still with me, and the baby, Chukwu, please, the baby, their name is Jekwu—

Ijeọma traveled fourteen of them. Fourteen of the paths held her blood on their earth; and Ijeọma labored now to breathe air into her body, preparing for the fifteenth—laboring to find power and strength. The moon's light had lost its intensity. The clouds had grown full. The darkness was thick and heavy—as if another power was conspiring against her. That was what she reasoned as she thought of returning home, no longer caring if the baby had died; and she wondered, if they were already dead, and at the way they had died, and if her journey was futile—suffering in complete vanity—that if Chukwu the Supreme Being was to defeat Ani, then Chukwu does not need the help of a child; she clasped her head at the thought, telling the Most Supreme she was sorry over and again; but finding no baby at the end of the fifteenth path, she fell upon her back, weeping.

The earth of the Evil Forest welcomed her. Its soft, cool body nestled her when she fell atop it; its smooth stones put pressure on the numbness of her arms and legs; its orange had disappeared—and its deep purple lulled her and had her wish the moon away; and she let it take her, the forest, the earth—and she closed her eyes, and closed them well, and then she heard the crying.

But she called it a lie, a hallucination, the wicked jest of the power conspiring against her. She ignored the cry when it came again, cursing the name of her enemies and cursing the name of Anị, the goddess of the earth; every path has been checked, she said within herself, it is not possible; your lie is not possible; and she cursed the goddess, calling her a goat, even as she heard the crying over and again, over and again, with a star leaping from one corner of the sky to another—her face turning upwards—with the infant's cries growing louder; as she now understood why she had not yet seen them, lifting herself to climb a tree, near the end of the fifteenth path. And she reached him quickly, lifting the covered child tucked between the space of two branches. She pulled them toward her chest, and wrapped them against her back using the black rappa that had covered them, moving slowly with each step and foothold as she carried them down the orange tree.

And once they reached the ground, she heard the infant's light breaths and saw that their cloth had been soiled; and she quickly laid them flat on the rappa, and removed a pot of water from her basket, and quenched their thirst by placing small drops into their mouth. Then she cleaned them, using the remaining water and her left hand, seeing their genitalia and believing that he was a boy, as she cleaned her left hand, and began feeding him with her right; and she saw him licking the mashed grains clustered between her fingers, but saw too that he was not eating them, and began worrying that he would not eat the rice because it was not like the milk of the one called his mother; so she thought that she had failed Jekwu, and had failed her own promises— thinking she was a liar and failure, until she saw her chi revealing her return to the orange tree and plucking from it much fruit, and squeezing its juices gently into the mouth of the hungry infant.

She hurried toward the tree, obeying her chi's revelations, then hurried to Jekwu, smiling when he showed his little teeth through a smile of his own, watching him drink the sweet juices from the oranges as she thought of playing with him, of dancing with him, of tickling him like she did Chelụchi. She kissed him on his forehead while holding his little hand, and wanted to hold it for as long as nighttime would allow; wanted to whisper in his ear: you have not been forgotten, wanted to speak it beneath the forest trees until Anyanwụ had risen again; though, when Jekwu had begun to sleep, she returned him to the branches of the orange tree, and promised that she would visit again until he was returned home.

"Ijeọma! Come here!" Nnenna said the following morning, knowing her basin of rice was emptier than it should have been. She watched Ijeọma appear within a moment, her nighttime-colored eyes avoiding hers.

"Ijeọma, how much rice did I tell you to cook for Chelụchi?"

Ijeọma put her smallest finger into the air.

"Then why have I lost so much rice, eh? Did you take more than I told you?"

Ijeọma nodded twice while twisting her left ankle. Ijeọma nodded no.

But Nnenna saw that a lie was being told, and wanted to know why. She examined Ijeọma, inspecting her firstborn daughter—her Ada—with the precision of an eagle.

"Ijeọma . . . how did you cut your feet?"

Ijeọma raised a stone from the ground, and presented it to the one called her mother.

"Ehhhh-eh. And where was this stone that cut your feet?"

Ijeọma traced vertical lines from the corner of her oval eyes using the shortest finger on her left hand.

"The stone was at the stream. Those stones that are soft like akamu cut you."

Ijeọma nodded her head three times, not seeing Nnenna looking at her quietly, waiting for silence to break deceit; and when Nnenna saw that Ijeọma remained reluctant to change her words, she flung her hands angrily, widening her eyes.

"Ijeọma, if I find that you are lying lies, you will not need to concern yourself with the warring gods. I will beat you with a thing, eh, you will you no longer remember how to sit down. Have you heard me?"

Ijeọma nodded yes, fearing the sound of Nnenna's voice as she was chastised in a manner she had not been chastised before, with Nnenna's eyes holding fury and sadness, punishing her preemptively because she had spoken a lie. And she feared what those eyes had held, and if Chukwu held it toward her, too, fearing it as she wept without the security of the good word, unprotected by truth, yet bonded still to the promise she had made to Jekwu in the Evil Forest. She called herself a failure. She called herself an abomination. And when the day had reached its hottest, she asked Nnamdị to flog her with thick branches in preparation for the beating promised by Nnenna's hands; and when she found Nnamdị's strokes to be soft and ineffective, she took from him the cane and beat her back herself, developing marks and sunburns within the heat, then covering them with egg yolk so that the wounds would heal properly.

And when the heat had left, and the day had found its dark, Ijeọma went out again to the Evil Forest, keeping her promise to Jekwu. She found him within a moment and brought him down from the orange tree, smiling with him when he opened his mouth to show his teeth; then removing the remaining rice and feeding him, and feeling his wet tongue licking the rice from her fingers, and loving that he did not cry when she was near: a sign she thought he gave to say that she was his sister.

What was that thing—Ijeọma heard a noise, and turned to see black, opaque figures growing larger and larger before the night; they have found me! They have found me! Jekwu, stay quiet . . . do not let them hear you, what will we do . . . what can, the rice and the water, we cannot hide them, what can, Chukwu, help us run, Jekwu, why are you smiling . . . close your mouth so they will not curse you . . . what are you . . . they are coming, chi . . . Chukwu, lift me! Lift me!

The plea did not raise her feet; and the forest was so thick, no paths were available; she trembled on the ground, raising one hand for Chukwu to raise her upward, clutching Jekwu with the other; and as the opaque figures moved closer, her hope of flying passed, and she thought now of punishment— floggings in the market square—flogged until her skin had peeled—until she had come to death.

"So this is what you have done with my rice?"

Ijeọma looked and saw Nnenna standing above her, feeling pleasure from the relief, wiping tears from her face and presenting Jekwu to the one called her mother.

He is beautiful, Nnenna thought, knowing she had not touched him the morning that he was born; but now, while he was in her arms, she confessed that Jekwu was beautiful; the clusters of hair atop his head were as delicate as the clouds of nighttime; his eyes, bright and wide like the moon of the New Yam Festival; his smile, as free as a miracle.

"Ijeọma, do you know what you have done? Ijeọma...do you...do you know?"

Suddenly, Jekwu began to cry, and Nnenna tried to silence him, placing her right hand over his mouth; but he cried even louder as she saw him, his hazel eyes now overcome by more light and more tears; and she quickly lowered her rappa and latched her breast onto Jekwu's lips, feeling the milk flow out of her body, her anxiety following it as she tried to think of peace; then looking at Ijeọma, then the sky, then the trees, then the infant, her eyes growing wild as if a spirit had taken her, whispering, "Sorry, sorry, sorry," into the ears of the whimpering child, until Jekwu had found true ease.

"Ijeọma, no one can know what we have done. Have you heard me?"

Ijeọma nodded three times. Ijeọma nodded yes.

"We will come here every night at this time and feed this baby so that he does not die of hunger and thirst. Have you heard me?"

Ijeọma nodded and embraced Nnenna, burying a smile against her hips. They both cared for the infant throughout the night, then returned him to the tree once Anyanwụ began rising above Amalike, beckoning the arrival of dawn.

DIARY ENTRY #952   DATE UNKNOWN

Chukwu how long will I wait for you? I am lying here in the dark, writing to you, and praying that you will break this place open and remove me from this prison. You are the most powerful, more powerful than the pastor, more powerful than my hunger, more powerful than my thirst, more powerful than my dream of touching and holding Ikemba again . . . You are the Most Supreme. Yet it has been eight days since I breathed air which was clean and fresh. It's been eight days since I've eaten anything except the hairs from my head and legs.

Where are you? I've seen you in my dreams. I've seen you even in the clouds of Igwe from my cell window. But where are you today? Did I upset you? I hope I have not upset you. I hope I have not vexed you and caused you to forget and abandon me.

But Chukwu look at me. Look at the stench. Look at my heart. What else must I do? What else must I do to be freed?

7.

IT WAS AN AFỌ MORNING when Igbokwe marched toward the Evil Forest carrying his iron staff. He had taken with him Mgboye, Nwagụ, and all of their kin; the rest of Ichulu had followed behind them. And with every step he had taken, the dịbịa had struck the ground with his iron staff, praying its bells would summon the attention of the gods. He had led them all to the orange tree where he had left Jekwu, and was now watching the infant's body lying still between two tree branches. Then he turned, and saw the moment Mgboye saw Jekwu—hearing the jagged cries escaping her.

"Aaaaaaaaaaaaaaaa-yeh-yeh-yeh-yeh! Aaaaaaaaaaaii!"

"Do not cry, do not cry," Nwagụ said as Mgboye collapsed against his heart. "Your chi has power of its own; have you heard me, *have you heard*?"

"I will see if the infant has survived," said Igbokwe, not looking at Mgboye but through the gaze of the eldest elder in Ichulu.

"Do so quickly," Ụzọkwesịlị said, "so that we can leave this accursed place."

Those who had followed expressed their agreement with Ụzọkwesịlị as Igbokwe moved to the infant, slowly climbing the orange tree, then bringing the infant down with him. The dịbịa knelt before the child and placed his smallest finger below his nose, looking upon Jekwu, knowing the power the child was holding, knowing that even a flutter of his eyelashes would make what was known no longer be known, and make the village truth an unanswered question. He exhaled, feeling his stomach trembling, feeling the infant breathing against his shortest finger, asleep, life not abandoning him; and Igbokwe believed it to be so: Chukwu and Anị were fighting a vicious battle and Anị was entering defeat. No longer would Ichulu be obligated to sacrifice its children to her, since everything she had was being reclaimed by the Supreme Being. His stomach was trembling as he knew that the goddess of the earth would no longer be a goddess, knew that Anị was going to die.

"He is sleeping. The infant is sleeping," Igbokwe said as he turned the infant toward those who had come.

"My chi! My chi has not forgotten me!" said Mgboye. "Idemili has not forsaken me! My ancestors have come!"

She rushed to Jekwu and fell at his feet, her buttocks sticking straight into the air as her lips met the forehead of Jekwu, who began to cry, and whose cries caused Nwagụ to begin tearing and thanking the Supreme Being with his hands outstretched—none of them hearing the people of Ichulu calling Nwagụ the luckiest man in the village, declaring the life of Jekwu further evidence.

"I will slaughter a cow for Ichulu!" said Nwagụ. "People everywhere must celebrate the miracle that has taken place in my household."

All the elders agreed, except Ụzọkwesịlị, the eldest among them, who turned to Igbokwe and spoke to him in fascinated terror.

"This means that we will no longer make sacrifices to the goddess—"

"That is so," Igbokwe said.

"I trust your medicine, Igbokwe, but we must have a meeting and decide if we will simply abandon Anị, lest the goddess of the earth destroy every living thing in this village."

"That is a wise decision, Ụzọkwesịlị . . . to a goddess like Anị, we are nothing more than worms."

"It is true," Ụzọkwesịlị said, watching Mgboye latching her breast onto Jekwu's lips, then teeth. "But from what I have now seen . . . if human beings are worms, love must be a merciful eagle."

Before Anyanwụ had climbed to the center of Igwe, the people of Ichulu knew that Jekwu was alive. Several people flocked to Nwagụ's compound to see the child who had escaped the machete of Anị; and they were welcomed by both Nwagụ and Mgboye, who displayed Jekwu as if he were coveted land, marveling at him; Jekwu: ten fingers, ten toes, one head, eight teeth; and they lamented their incredulity in denying the beauty of such a child, and mocked Anị's hunger for desiring a child she could not have.

But ridicule could not silence the severity of the earth no longer being deified, and before evening, the village men gathered to discuss the fate of Anị. The earth of the market square carried hundreds of men, sitting on wooden stools, with the hum of their chatter resounding like the beginnings of a thunderstorm. Nobody among them knew what the meeting would bring. Killing minor gods had happened before, but such had not been done to a god as great as Anị. Ọfọdile sat in a far corner, away from the center of the square, knowing that Ijeọma's flights made him a cause of this confusion. He greeted some of the men with rhythmic pats from his palms, and then he sat with his chi, waiting for the meeting to begin.

"Ichulu, kwenu!" Ụzọkwesịlị said.

"Yah!" said the men.

"Ichulu, kwenu!"

"Yah!"

"Ichulu, kwenu!"

"Yaaaaaaah!"

"Igbokwe, the descendant of the most powerful lineage of dịbịas, has made something known to us," Ụzọkwesịlị said. "The daughter of Ọfọdile, as many of you have witnessed, has been flying among us. Many of us did not know where the child received her power; but Igbokwe implored the gods for knowledge, and they answered him. He was told that Chukwu and Anị were fighting a war. To determine whether this word was good, Igbokwe placed Nwagụ's newborn child into the Evil Forest for one week to see if Chukwu, the Supreme Being, would sustain his life. Chukwu did so. The child is alive. Children of my mother . . . how are we to act?"

There was silence. The men held their heads low, avoiding one another's eyes, staring at the ground somberly.

"We should abandon Anị," one man said at the corner of the market, glancing at Igbokwe before continuing.

"Ichulu's dịbịa has always protected this village. Why should we not hear his words now?"

"Have you forgotten the curse?" said another. "Igbokwe was unable to protect us from a curse, a curse! My child was killed in Amalike, and now you want me to listen to his words, words of a weak man? Yes. I said it. Igbokwe might have been powerful yesterday, but what of today? The dịbịa is weak!"

"Close your mouth!" a third began. "Do you know how to talk to a god? Were your ears not working when Igbokwe told us of Amalike's curse? All of us know that Igbokwe cannot break the power of a god from another land—"

"Does Igbokwe not get his power from *all* the gods, including Anị?" asked a man while standing. "Should we then not stay loyal to her? What will happen if the other gods discover that we have rejected their sister and wife? What will Igwe, Anị's husband, do?"

The men began to chatter loudly, each expressing his opinion on the matter. Friends became opponents. Brothers became boisterous. Then a man wearing a cloud-white beard, and an eagle's feather needled through his domed red hat began rising. His name was Nnabụenyi, and he was the second oldest man in Ichulu.

"It is enough," Nnabụenyi whispered, as he brought the room to silence. "I know more of these things than any of you, maybe even more than Igbokwe himself. I have worshipped and served Anị all my life. Do you know how many children I have lost to the Evil Forest? Eleven. Eight boys and three girls. And I know many of you have lost children, brothers, sisters, fathers, and mothers to the forest. I am not blind to the changes that are happening in this village. A girl can fly; a boy has lived. If anybody ignores these signs, let him call himself a fool. If anybody forgets our ancestor Solomto, who flew across an ocean greater than Idemili, who flew to Ichulu after he was taken to be a slave ... let that person call himself a fool. We are the ones whom the gods should fear. Without our sacrifices, they would starve in the heavens, lonely and powerless. Without the blood of our children, they would perish. Answer me, what has this child done, except be born with teeth? Did his father say that the teeth made him appear like a wild animal? Did his mother complain that he was biting her in the womb? Is his mother, or any woman who has given birth, here to speak for themselves? No. My brethren, my children, the time has arrived, and we must meet it at its face. Now is not the moment to fear a dying god—but to heed wisdom as wisdom."

Nnabuenyi eased onto his stool—softly, like the wind—and the men received his words as if they themselves had said it. The assurance of the elder, his shrewd audacity, drove fear from their eyes. Their hearts lightened. Their minds gained clarity. Their unspoken truth had been spoken: Ani could not be worshipped. Slowly, each man expressed his agreement, beginning in whispers, then rising to the tones of fired guns. They had prepared to finalize their growing consensus when the bearded Okoye began rising.

"Men of Ichulu, the words of Nnabuenyi are indeed very good. But we have forgotten to examine one possibility. How do we know that Nwagu and his wife did not go to the forest and nurse their child? Do you—"

"Eat shit!" yelled Nwagu, who was sitting at the very front of the crowd. "I will break your neck for accusing me of tampering with the work of the gods."

"If you did not disturb Igbokwe's plans, then you and your wife should not be afraid to swear your innocence upon the Stone of Ani."

"My wife and I will take the oath this moment!"

"Someone go and fetch Nwagu's wife." Okoye smirked as he turned his eyes to Igbokwe. "You must lead the oath. The rest of us, let us go to the stone."

All the men began scurrying. And Okoye was happy to see it while dwelling in thoughts against Ọfọdile—knowing Anị's demise would bring glory to the one called Ọfọdile's child. "It will never be," he thought aloud, while walking boldly among the men, using law to stop love from finding its way toward his enemy, demanding over and again that the oath be taken, reminding them of their honor, reminding them of their devotion to the gods and the trickery of the desperate and the lies of the wicked, among whom he counted Ọfọdile.

The good word traveled throughout the village and soon all in Ichulu gathered around the Stone of Anị. Ijeọma and Nnenna were there, too, with their lightly colored rappas and their tightly plaited hair; because of the fear of the Ichulu noting their absence, they came, and neither could look into the other's eyes; and neither could stand steadily, questioning which gestures would inculpate them. They were both guilty. They had both deceived. And if Igbokwe exposed their evils while in his state of possession, they would both be killed.

And Ijeọma looked at the one called her mother, with her eyes wide, with her mouth open, with her hands pulling at Nnenna's rappa, tapping her waist, then pulling her rappa, then tapping again, worry taking her, fear taking her, then feeling Nnenna's hand touch hers, pulling it upward and taking it past a little tree as they watched the beginning of the oath away from Anị's jagged, gray stone, avoiding the dịbịa as he chanted ancient chants and moved fiercely before the people of Ichulu.

"Alaaaaaaaaaaaaaa-ay-yay-yay-yay-yay-yay-yay! Alaaaaaaaaaa-ay-yay-yay," Igbokwe sang as Ichulu watched in silence.

Igbokwe struck the sharp stone with open palms, his hands wide and red, blood coloring his arms—his wounds reminding everyone that Anị was a fearsome goddess. He showed his blood to Mgboye, who stood beside Nwagụ with tears falling from her eyes as she cursed Okoye for throwing Jekwu's life into greater jeopardy.

"Nwagụ . . . Mgboye . . ." Igbokwe said in a voice high and heavy, swirling like the waterspouts of Idemili. "Put your hands on the Stone of Anị."

The husband and wife obeyed.

"Nwagụ and Mgboye, do you swear upon the Stone of Anị that you did not aid your infant child while he was in the Evil Forest, that you did not send anyone to aid him, that you did not use any medicine to sustain his life?"

"We swear," they said.

"The goddess has heard you. If it is that you are lying lies, let your bodies betray themselves. May sickness and disease fall upon your household so that you may be punished and shamed. Let Anị cause your stomachs to swell and your hearts to burst; may she cause you to crave madness. And then when you have faced all suffering, may a merciless death fall upon your heads."

The couple removed their hands from the stone, with innocence resting on their faces: the village had seen the truth, but the truth could not be pronounced within themselves or within the market square until a year had passed. No one in Ichulu, except Ijeọma and Nnenna, could declare the good word with certainty: that in a year's time Nwagụ, Mgboye, and Jekwu would be alive, and Ichulu would cease to worship Anị.

8.

SEVERAL WEEKS AFTER MGBOYE AND NWAGỤ took their oath, Ichulu held a thanksgiving for the gods. The preservation of their lives from Idemili's flood had compelled them to show gratitude to the pantheon. Every neighboring town, except Amalike, received an invitation to the feast, though a few from the eastern village, using disguise and deception, entered through the market square. Ichulu had not known of it. The village was filled with joy. There were heaps of gold-colored pounded yam sitting next to pots of every kind of soup—soup that was ruffled and browned like egusi, thick and green like onugbu. Four cows and twenty goats had been slaughtered for the occasion: they were cooked and seasoned with ụzịza, salt, and black pepper. The sweetest palm wine filled hundreds of gourds. The sounds of the drums lifted thousands of spirits. Young dancers dressed iridescently as if shot forth from heavy rainbows—then danced the dance of the Atịlọgwụ, shaking their bodies like the beads of the ụyọ—kicking and turning to greet each cardinal direction, vibrating along the flute's light tones to build human pyramids that reached the top of mango trees.

And the ancestors left their anthills that day, adorned with bells and colorful feathers. They paraded the orange paths, chasing anyone who stood idly before them, reminding everyone of their power—power residing not in their canes or machetes, nor in their pristine fans, but lying in their swelling voice: the risen dead, crying that nothing is forgotten.

Some women sang songs of praise, as some men drank and ate until they became tired, as many children ran and played in the fields of the market square, raising dust to the heavens, to the belly of Igwe. And many said that the earth of the market square could have sunk from their weight, so that when Ijeọma and her family arrived, there was no place for them to rest. Ijeọma saw Nnenna placing Chelụchi on her back with her purple rappa, and saw Ọfọdile pulling Nnamdị closer to his side. She looked around her, growing amazed at the festivities that lay before them—watching some girls atop a hill playing a hand game that was popular in Ichulu, seeing one pat the other's hands to the rhythms of a song being sung—and watching the others sing the song faster and faster, so that the two might fail to meet their hands and another pair could have their turn. Ijeọma could hear them singing:

> Mgbeke and Okeke went to the market.
> Mgboye and Okoye sold a loom.
> Mgbafọr and Okafọr caught a rat.
> Mgbankwọ and Okonkwọ made some soup.

She began mouthing the playful lyrics to herself—smiling at the rhymes opening and closing each phrase.

"Why not go and join them?" Nnenna said.

Ijeọma nodded her head twice.

"Ijeọma . . . I said go."

Ijeọma refused again.

Nnenna gave her a sorrowful stare, thinking of how the one called her daughter did not have any friends her age; *she will not survive my death like this*, Nnenna thought, as she turned to look at the group of girls, examining their faces, then recognizing one as Mgboye's third daughter. She seized Ijeọma's hand, leaving Nnamdị with Ọfọdile, then walked along the hill to the group of girls, abruptly interrupting their game.

"Chinwe, how are you?" Nnenna said to Mgboye's daughter.

"I am doing well," Chinwe said.

"That is beautiful. I see you are playing our game."

"Yes! Me and Nkiru are winning," Chinwe said while smiling.

"Ehhhh-eh. That is beautiful, too. Would it not also be beautiful if my daughter joined you?"

Ijeọma saw the girls turn toward her, some with ridicule resting in their eyes; and she wished Nnenna had respected her desire not to join them in their game.

"It is beautiful," Chinwe said. "She can join us."

"Thank you, my child! Where is your mother so I can greet her?"

Chinwe slowly pointed to the western end of the market square, then watched as both Nnenna and the baby on her back left them atop the hill. She turned to Ijeọma, and let out a fearsome laugh.

"Why do you look so afraid," Chinwe said.

Ijeọma's head was lowered, and her eyes were fluttering wildly.

"What is your name?"

Ijeọma squeezed her eyes and softly signed her name by inverting two fingers and resting them on her left hand's palm, then brought them to her heart, then to her palm, over and again.

"Come," Chinwe said. "You can play with me."

Chinwe took Ijeọma's hand and told the other girls to sing, knowing that some did not like Ijeọma, knowing, too, the words many said of her: that the mute girl may not have been thrown into the Evil Forest, but she was surely not a girl for them to befriend; she knew they hated the way her hair was plaited, the presence of her muteness, the fact that she could fly—and that some were now turning their eyes away from her, passing grins to their friends to remind them of those things they said of her yesterday.

Ijeọma saw what they were doing, and her heart began trembling and her eyes began to tear, until the touch of Chinwe's hands made her turn from her loathsome thoughts. She took those hands, and became deaf to what their eyes were saying: ugly hair, ugly mute, ugly bird, ugly fool; and she watched Chinwe ask the girls to sing, patting and clapping Chinwe's hands to the rhythm of the song, striking her hands with a forceful speed as the others sang faster and faster, their hands beginning to burn, the words of the song welding onto one another.

MGBEKE AND OKOYE WENT TO THE MARKET.
CLAP CLAP PAT PAT PAT CLAP
MGBOYE AND OKOYE WENT TO THE BUSH.
CLAP CLAP PAT PAT PAT CLAP
MGBAFỌR-AND-OKAFỌR-CAUGHT-A-RAT.
CLAP-CLAP-PAT-PAT-PAT-CLAP
MGBANKWỌANDOKONKWOMADESOMESOUP.
CLAPCLAPPATPATPATCLAP

They fell on the grass laughing together, clasping their hands as their eyes faced Igwe, not noticing the others staring and whispering at how they lay on the ground. Ijeọma turned to Chinwe, her heart racing from the thrill of the game, feeling Chinwe's palms against hers, the child who could not speak, me, the mute who now flies; she smiled, wondering if Chinwe would remove her hand, come and visit me, come be my friend, and she smiled and smiled because their hands were still joined, even when Chinwe looked into her eyes, we will play until tomorrow, we will, even in the morning time, we can take our baths together, in Idemili, and even go to paint uli, but we cannot, not by ourselves, not on our thighs, but we can climb the other hills, keep my hand in yours, keep it, please keep it, so that we can be friends—and not blame me, please, do not blame me—but, you are still seeing me, are you still seeing me, you are, you are, keep my hand, keep my hand, love me always—and she let the idea stop, and thanked her muteness for keeping it unsaid; she averted her eyes, seeing now the mango-shaped birthmark sitting beside Chinwe's ear, and feeling the presence of Chinwe's eyes on her; and when she felt new pressure squeezing against her hands, she sighed, believing Chinwe had not ridiculed her.

"Do you hear that?" Chinwe said, as she released Ijeọma's hand, as Ijeọma began raising herself to look down at the market square, seeing more than fifty very young men with bushy, unkempt hair walking into the thanksgiving festival. She recognized one to be Ụzọdị despite his pale skin and sunken eyes.

"What are the osu doing in this place!" asked one of the girls, one who had not seen Ijeọma's eyes growing insecure and silent.

"I do not know. Let us go and hear what they are saying."

Chinwe, Ijeọma, and the rest of the girls ran down the hill and stood amid the crowd where the ones called osu had gathered. They heard many people anxiously cursing at them, demanding that they quickly leave the market square.

"We have chosen not to leave," said a person called osu. "We know that the gods are battling, and that even Igbokwe does not know which gods are living and which are dead."

"You animal!" barked a freeborn man, with his brow highly raised, turning from the muscles of the very young men. "How do our affairs concern you!"

"If you do not know which gods are alive or dead, how can you say that we are dedicated to gods?" continued the person called osu. "What if the gods to whom we are bound are dead? We admit that some who live among us want to remain as they are. For them, we do not speak. But for those of us who have been forced into this slavery at the hands of our enemies, we seek to return to the land of our ancestors. You—all of you who challenge us—name the god. Name the god to whom I am bound, and I will hold my tongue."

Nobody in the market square answered the tall, fair-skinned person. And Ijeọma, who did not care for the words being spoken, left the side of

Chinwe—and moved closer to the ones called osu—wanting to be near Uzodi—moving through the crowd—pressing through the spaces between people taller than her—hoping that Uzodi would not leave the place where she saw him—moving and moving until she walked into the legs of Uzodi's mother, Ezinne, who was standing next to Ofodile and Nnamdi.

"Ijeoma, where are you going?" Ezinne said.

Ijeoma pointed at Uzodi.

"Stay here," Ezinne said. "You cannot go to him. Nnamdi . . . come." She beckoned to Ijeoma's younger brother.

"Nnamdi, go to that table and get me those groundnuts."

"I will go," said Nnamdi.

Ijeoma saw Ezinne patting Nnamdi's head before he began running toward the table. She looked upward and saw Ezinne's quivering lips and could hear her whispering curses at the people challenging those called osu, then praying for Amalike's death and condemning Ichulu's prejudice. She knew that Ezinne wanted to be with Uzodi—that from the terror in her voice, Ezinne wanted to hold him as if tomorrow would never show itself again, as if the moment would last for the duration she wanted—for it to last, as sleep is wished to last before confronting a burdensome day.

"We will not go until the good word is spoken," said another called osu.

"The good word can *never* be given to a slave!" said another freeborn man.

"Please, people of Ichulu . . . listen to us."

Ijeoma began jumping over and again as Uzodi began to speak.

"Please, listen, list—"

"Shut your mouth, you animal!"

"Please, please. We do not want to make trouble with you," Uzodi continued. "All of us know that something is changing in our land. We have witnessed events that even our ancestors could not have imagined . . . We have seen miracles. Everybody gathered here, you know how I became an osu. I was made one by those wicked people in Amalike. I became one when I chose to serve our village. Now I am here, in my father's land, welcomed not with jubilation but with insult. Do not become blind to the signs the gods are sending you. Do not . . ."

The eyes of all in the market square faced the sky. Ijeọma's feet pointed toward them, and her arms were opened as though embracing Anyanwụ and his sun. Ichulu and its visitors stood dazed—stuck in their disbelief and fascination. No one could deny Ụzọdị's claim. They had all become witnesses to his words. They saw his good words and they were beautiful. They saw Ijeọma and she was beautiful. And Ichulu looked upon the one called their daughter, many seeing her flight for the first time, and began praising Chukwu for what Chukwu had done, and smiling at Ijeọma, each heart and each spirit, expecting her to send their joy up and through the sky.

And as Ichulu looked upward, Ọfọdile's hands began shaking. He looked about himself, hoping nobody had recognized him as the titleless man called father of the mute, deciding unequivocally that he would return home, turning to take Nnamdị, but Nnamdị was not there, and Ọfọdile began searching throughout the festival, looking for the one called his son, checking through the bushes and inside the market sheds, still he could not find him, wanting to scream his name, but fearing Ichulu would see him and shame him and his chi.

There: next to Ijeọma's foot was a branch of a cashew tree, and on that branch was Nnamdị. He had climbed the tree so that he too could join Ijeọma in the heavens. And when Ọfọdile saw him, he rushed toward the tree, hoping he could reach it quickly—running, before Nnamdị decided to leap off the branch. There was a moment when those watching Nnamdị in the air believed he, too, possessed the gift of flight. But the faith which sustained that belief quickly vanished—and within the moment, Nnamdị laid unconscious on the market square's ground.

"Move from my way! Move from my way!" Ọfọdile screamed as he rushed to Nnamdị's side. Blood was oozing from the side of Nnamdị's head, and his arms were limp when Ọfọdile lifted them. "Where is Igbokwe? Someone call Igbokwe!"

The message traveled that Igbokwe was wanted, and only a few had noticed Ijeọma's return to the earth. Nnenna was among them—seeing

Ijeọma descend—as she pushed through people to get to Nnamdị's side. And when she saw Ijeọma moving toward Ọfọdile, she moved into Ijeọma's path, stopping her, the root of Ọfọdile's frustration, from entering his path.

"Ijeọma," she said, "come with me. Let us allow your father to take care of Nnamdị himself."

Ijeọma obeyed, not understanding—but heeding the wisdom of the one called her mother—even as she heard bells ringing, and saw Igbokwe walking toward Ọfọdile and Nnamdị.

"Igbokwe . . . I have died! I have died! My enemies have come for my only son!"

"Ọfọdile, there is still life in your child. I will heal him."

Igbokwe asked two very young men to carry Nnamdị to his compound as he and Ọfọdile followed behind them. And Igbokwe tempered the anxious spirit in Ọfọdile, saying over and again, "For us it will be beautiful. For us it will be beautiful."

Nnamdị was laid before Igbokwe's obi when they arrived, and Igbokwe entered his obi to retrieve some medicine. And Ọfọdile was left with the body of the one called his son, tears capturing the oil and sweat dripping from his face; and like a man seized by the rapture of every god, he raised his hands as if to thrash the sky.

"Chi of mine! Chi of mine! Is it me that you have forgotten? I have prayed to you every day of my life. I have never asked you for the impossible. You have given me a family, and a harvest, but this child . . . this child of mine. I do not know! I do not want to know! I have fed her, played with her, loved her . . . but I cannot tolerate the curses my enemies have made. They mock me . . . they have called me a failure because I have won no chieftaincies or titles, and now look at my son! If this is because of Chukwu and Anị, tell them to resolve their quarrel. I am an innocent man. I have not harmed any person in my life. Why should this happen? What have I done? Chi of mine . . . if there is anything I did to offend you, please turn your eyes from it. But if this misfortune has been caused by a common man . . . let him never see a good day. Let his children die. Chi of mine, I beg you. Give my son his life. I love my son. I love the name of my son. Please, please, give my son his life."

Ọfọdile cast his arms by his sides and returned himself to Igbokwe's compound. Then, within a moment, a smile found its way onto his lips—and a breath came into his heart. Nnamdị's eyes had opened.

PART II

ANOTHER
TOWN

1.

"JESUS IS . . ."

"Lord!"

"Jesus is . . ."

"Lord!"

The pastor of Precious Word Ministries called the Son of God's name so loudly, his congregation thought the church louvers would burst and shatter. To prove its faith was no less fervent, it, too, screamed with force—matching his tones as if crying hip, hip, and hooray—as though their chests held bombs.

The pastor was Innocent Nwosu: a bona fide man of God in the congregation's eyes, one who was tall and slender, with fair skin and a bushy mustache and spectacles balancing on his arrow-shaped nose. Those spectacles often slid down his face when he contorted his body to bring emphasis to his preaching, as he bent backward to support his guttural amens, tilting to his sides as stiffly as bone, marching forcefully in his lord's army; and when he was finished, he pushed his spectacles up the hill of his nose, and cried out again, amen.

In this service, as in any service, Pastor Nwosu paced before an altar covered in purple linen, bearing a portrait of a Jesus whose hands were cued for benediction. He clutched his microphone tightly, avoiding the large speakers that flanked the altar, refusing to have any feedback interrupt God's power on him, and his power on his congregation.

"My brothers and sisters, do you feel the presence of the Living God, here, in this room?"

People nodded their heads in agreement, some raising their hands in jubilation, others finding tears moving along their faces, as one woman began speaking in tongues, making sounds which were not understood.

"I SAID BROTHERS and SISTERS! DO YOU FEEL THE PRESENCE OF THE LIVING GOD, THE EL SHADDAI, THE ANCIENT OF DAYS, THE UNSHAKABLE SHAKER?"

"YES! YES!"

"Then let us pray in this moment. PRAY for yourselves and your children. Matthew 7:7 says, 'Ask and it shall be given unto you.' So I command you to lay your needs before your Father, *in the name of Jesus*. Anything that your heart desires, ask it of Him. Petition your God in the name of the Blood of His Only Son. GIVE Him all the glory! PRAISE Him with all your strength! CLAIM your portion! I SAID CLAIM YOUR PORTION IN THE MIGHTY NAME OF JESUS! You are the children of Abraham, the HEIRS of God's kingdom! Ask Jehovah Jireh what it is you need! Ask it, *in the name of Jesus! In the name of Jesus!* In the name of . . ."

"Jesus!"

"IN THE NAME OF . . ."

"JESUS!"

"PRAY! PRAY! PRAY! PRAY! *In the name of Jesus*, I command you to PRAY!"

The people gathered began. The church was a collection of loud murmurs and the occasional scream. From the altar, Pastor Nwosu inspected the aisles, moving his gaze from the scaffolding of the church edifice and examining the avidity with which his congregation spoke to its god. He saw the excitement on their lips, lips muttering electrically—lips praying in lighter tones, then heavy ones—praying in crescendos rising more quickly than the town's steepest hills; the congregation was enraptured, praying heartily and with feeling until their closed eyes pressed tightly against their sockets, and their lips stretched back against their teeth; and when most began leaning atop their chairs, moving their weight from one leg to the other, Pastor Nwosu believed their prayer was acceptable.

"AMEN!" said Pastor Nwosu.

"Amen!" replied the congregation.

"Now that we have offered our prayers to the Lord, it is time for praise and worship. Sister Grace . . . come forward and lead us in the hymns we shall offer Jesus."

A short, stout woman, wearing a blue dress and a red kerchief, moved toward the altar. She took the microphone from Pastor Nwosu and gave a long bow in his direction; then, placing one hand atop her abdomen, she let out a D flat in a lush contralto.

"Praaaaaaaaaaaaaise the Lord!" sister Grace said.

"Aaaaaaaaaaaaalleluia!" said the congregation.

"I said, PRAAAAAAAAAAAAAISE THE LIVING GOD ALL YE PEOPLE!"

"AAAAAAAAAAAAALLELUIA!"

We are praising, praising, praising our Jesus;
We are praising the wonders of His name.
We are praising, praising, praising our Jesus;
We are praising the wonders of His name.

The congregation began exploding in music: the drummers were pounding their sticks and fists atop their drum sets and drum skins; the pianists were striking their keys, joining Sister Grace's voice with wild rifts and runs; the bassists were playing chords that echoed in the chest cavities of everyone singing, pushing the songs into and out of their bodies. White Precious Word Ministry fans and handkerchiefs were rising into the air as people danced to the rhythm of the music, shifting their bodies along the floor, as if they were joyfully sweeping.

Two hours passed before Sister Grace returned to her seat—knowing the congregation was energized, eager to hear the sermon of its pastor—knowing, too, that Pastor Nwosu was pleased with her, once he turned to her and gave her a smile.

"My brothers and sisters . . . Sister Grace has done it again!" said Pastor Nwosu. "Sister Grace has received the grace of God and has shared it among us! Amen?"

"Amen!" said the congregation.

"Let us now prepare ourselves to receive the word of God this Sunday. Bow your heads as I lead us in prayer . . . Lord Jesus, let the word that comes forth from my mouth touch the spirits and minds of those before me. May it put them on the path of salvation and invigorate in them the righteousness that You seek. May it bestow on them revelations and truths to be used for Your greater glory. Let them accept Your Word this day and sow it into their hearts. May their hearts be fertile ground. May their souls be Your spiritual ground. I ask this in the mighty name of Jesus."

"Amen!"

"Brothers and sisters . . . today I will preach on the necessity of loyalty. Every Christian today must be loyal to his church, loyal to his pastor, and above all loyal to God . . . to Jesus. I want you to turn your Bibles to the Book of Ruth. Why do you look surprised?" the pastor said while chuckling, "How many of you have read this sacred book before?"

He looked around the sanctuary and saw few answering affirmatively.

"Well, it is a book that tells us that GOD abundantly rewards those who are loyal! It begins with three widows: Naomi and her two daughters-in-law, Orpah and Ruth. Yes, they were all widows and remained that way for a long time; so, all of you YOUNG WOMEN chasing men like chickens, you better WATCH OUT!"

He heard laughter spreading throughout the congregation as he pushed his spectacles along his nose.

"They also had no children . . . Naomi's sons Mahlon and Chilion died before they could give Orpah and Ruth any children, so all of them, Naomi, Orpah, and Ruth, were childless widows. These women had been living in Bethlehem until a famine descended upon the land. That was when they decided to leave ALL their property to travel to the land of Moab. They stayed there for ten years . . . TEN YEARS! until they heard that a flood had come to their homeland, and that the famine had ended. Naomi told her daughters-in-law to return to their fatherlands. Naomi, who was an elderly woman, encouraged her daughters-in-law to remarry so that they may know the joys of having children. Orpah honored the suggestion, and left her mother-in-law . . . but Ruth, RUTH! stayed with Naomi. My Bible says on chapter one, verse sixteen, that Ruth told Naomi, 'Do not ask me to abandon or forsake thee! For, WHEREVER YOU SHALL GO I SHALL GO, WHEREVER YOU SLEEP I SHALL SLEEP, YOUR PEOPLE SHALL BE MY PEOPLE, AND YOUR GOD MY GOD. WHEREVER YOU DIE I WILL DIE, AND THERE BE BURIED.' LOOK AT IT! WHAT LOYALTY!

"RUTH STAYED WITH NAOMI. SHE CRIED WITH NAOMI. SHE SUF-FERED WITH NAOMI. SHE REMAINED LOYAL. AND THE LORD, THE LIVING GOD, THE EL SHADDAI, REWARDED HER FOR IT. When RUTH! and Naomi returned to Bethlehem, a very fine man named Boaz asked Ruth to marry him. And RUTH! agreed to marry him because she would be able to stay in the town and care for Naomi. So RUTH! and Boaz married, and together they gave birth to a bouncing baby boy named Obed. Obed gave birth to a son named Jesse and Jesse gave birth to a son named David . . . KING DAVID . . . WHO DOES THE GOSPEL OF MATTHEW SAY THAT JESUS IS THE SON OF?"

"DAVID!" the congregation said.

"I SAID WHO DO THE GOSPELS SAY JESUS IS THE SON OF . . ."

"DAVID!"

"WHO?"

"DAVID!"

"Yes! THAT IS CORRECT," said Pastor Nwosu. "Brothers and sisters, do you not see it? You must remain loyal to Jesus the same way Ruth remained loyal to Naomi. Why? Because it is your faith that justifies! Your faith, not your work, is what redeems you before the throne of God. Your faith is what makes you a loyal servant of God. When some of you face hardship, you come to me asking, 'Pastor Nwosu, what will I do? How will I take care of my children? How will I eat?' Today I am telling you to remain loyal to God and he will reward you abundantly! Do you not see how he has provided for me? Do you not see the wonderful suit I am wearing, imported from Dubai! I tell you, he is an unchanging God! He holds yesterday, today, and tomorrow in the palm of his hand. Let your loyalty to sin, to mammon, to adultery, to fornication, to greed, to blasphemy, be consumed by Holy Ghost fire! Give your loyalty to Jesus, and not the principalities of this world! Does the first commandment not say, 'I am the Lord your God, who brought you out of slavery, you shall have no other God besides Me'? The first commandment says that we must be God's loyal servant! If you obey it, your children will be like the children of Ruth—heads of their households and kings of nations! Some of you are hearing me, some of you are not. I said if you do not give the Living God all your loyalty, everlasting damnation will be your portion. Is that what you want? Do you want to burn with Lucifer and his dark angels?"

"No!" the congregation cried.

"Then listen to what I am telling you! My brothers and sisters, you must express your loyalty to God by being loyal to His messenger, the pastor. When a pastor says pray, says tithe, says sacrifice . . . you must trust in him, because you are loyal to him. When a pastor says he can heal any sickness and lift any burden you must trust in him because you are loyal to him. If I, Pastor Innocent Nwosu, say that I can raise the dead in the name of Jesus, you must trust in me. To be loyal to the Living God means that you are loyal to me, your pastor."

Pastor Nwosu looked about his silent congregation. Some were nodding in approval. Others were wiping tears from their eyes as he heard the first set of amens, then the second, louder and louder, before he nodded at two large men standing by the sanctuary door.

"Bring in the children from the Manifestation Quarters," he said. "The ones who have been possessed by evil spirits."

The two large men left the sanctuary, and returned pulling several children bonded by a heavy rope—watching some fall as they walked toward the church's altar—many dragging their bruised feet while wearing gray and tattered clothing. They were the children of the Manifestation Quarters: a blue bungalow sitting near the unfinished church edifice, keeping tiny cells with iron bars that guarded its windows and padlocked doors. They were under the guardianship of the church, and were clothed and fed and prayed over by Pastor Nwosu and his attendants—attendants who believed the pastor could expel every demon dwelling in the children, believing it when he prayed on them in the Manifestation Quarters—believing it now that the children stood before him, lined along the steps of the concrete altar.

"Brothers and sisters . . . I will show you how my loyalty to Jesus allows me to do great things. As you know, these children live in our Manifestation Quarters and have been brought to Precious Word Ministries by their families because they have been possessed by dark angels, and evil spirits! TODAY, BY THE ANOINTING GIVEN TO ME BY THE BLOOD OF JESUS CHRIST, I WILL REMOVE THESE EVIL SPIRITS. I WILL DO IT BECAUSE THE LORD HAS MADE IT SO! AMEN?"

"AMEN!"

"Bring her forward!" Pastor Nwosu said, pointing to one of the girls on the rope. The two large men untied her and brought her closer to the altar.

"This girl has been possessed for eleven years, ELEVEN YEARS . . . Her uncle brought her to me because there was nothing else he could do! Doctor oh! Medicine oh! Nothing worked! So, he brought her to me . . . expecting a miracle. Today . . . GOD HAS TOLD ME THAT THIS EVIL SPIRIT WILL LEAVE HER BODY!"

"AAAAAAAMMMMEEEEEN!" sang the congregation.

The drummers began drumming. People began dancing throughout the room. And the one called the girl's uncle was running toward the steps of the altar, his Precious Word Ministries fan, falling from his hands the moment he reached Pastor Nwosu and fell near his feet.

"Is it true?" the man said.

"WHERE IS YOUR FAITH!" said the pastor. "DO YOU NOT BELIEVE IN JESUS, THE GOD OF WONDER, POWER, AND MIGHT . . . THE ONE WHO CAN DO ALL THINGS?"

"Yes! I do! I do!" said the uncle.

"THEN YOUR NIECE WILL BE DELIVERED FROM THIS DEMON. BRING HER TO ME."

The girl was taken to Pastor Nwosu, as the one called her uncle heard her screaming in a terrifying treble. He looked on despondently, watching as the straps of her gray gown fell from her shoulders, exposing her breasts, wanting to cover her but not knowing if he had such authority. He looked to Pastor Nwosu, but the pastor was praying beneath his breath with his hands pressing upon the young girl's head.

"JESUS!" Pastor Nwosu said into the microphone, "DESCEND UPON THIS GIRL WHOM I HAVE LAID MY HANDS ON. BY THE POWER OF YOUR PRECIOUS BLOOD, I COMMAND THE SPIRIT POSSESSING THIS GIRL TO COME OUT! COME OUT! COME OUT! I COMMAND THAT THIS GIRL BE RELEASED IN JESUS' NAME! I RELEASE THIS GIRL FROM THIS EVIL SPIRIT IN JESUS' NAME! I RELEASE YOU IN JESUS' NAME! LET HOLY GHOST FIRE DRIVE OUT THIS DEVIL AND LET IT BE CONSUMED BY THAT FIRE! LET THIS SPIRIT . . . WHETHER IT IS OGBANJE SPIRIT OR MAMMY WATER SPIRIT—LET IT COME OUT OF THIS GIRL NOW! I DRIVE YOU OUT IN JESUS' NAME! COME OUT! COME OUT! COME OUT!"

The girl fell to the floor, rolling in many directions, screaming as though Pastor Nwosu had pierced her with a blade.

"Leave me!" she screamed, closing her eyes, knowing it would beckon the mercy of the pastor.

"I WILL NOT LEAVE YOU UNTIL YOU COME OUT OF HER!" said Pastor Nwosu.

"Please! Leave me! Leave me!"

"I WILL NOT! GET ME THE HOLY WATER!"

Pastor Nwosu directed his command at the two large men, who then left the altar and quickly returned with water in a bucket and a wooden cane. He was given the cane before he placed it in the bucket, soaking it in his holy water; then he removed it—and began beating the girl—whose screams rose—and seared the walls with its aching—piercing through the microphone with one strike then the next—over and again—her body twisting like a worm dying in sunlight—as she looked upward—staring at Pastor Nwosu—her eyes bright and red—pleading and threatening before she closed them—until more quickly than a gasp—she stopped.

"I SAID COME OUT IN JESUS' NAME! COME OUT IN THE MIGHTY NAME OF JESUS! COME OUT!" the pastor said, now noticing her closed eyes.

"What is her name? Quickly! What is her name?" said Pastor Nwosu.

"Nonso. Her . . . her n-n-name is . . . Nonso," the uncle said.

"Nonso, I release you in Jesus' name. Do you hear me? Do you hear? I release you in Jesus' name."

"Please leave m—I hear you," Nonso said through a whisper.

"GOD IN HEAVEN! SHE IS HEALED!" said the uncle.

"She is healed indeed," said Pastor Nwosu.

And the congregation began yelling praises to its god, thanking him for his infinite mercy, and thanking him for bestowing power onto their pastor. Sister Grace began leading the congregation in a song, while Nonso and the one called her uncle were escorted to a back room—away from the church's jubilation.

"Have you seen it?" Pastor Nwosu said. "Have you now seen what the power of loyalty can do?"

"WE HAVE SEEN IT!" yelled one worshipper standing in a middle row, his hand waving happily in the air.

"WE HAVE TRULY SEEN IT!" said a woman, shaking her body as the rest of the congregation joined in her professions.

"Now, there are more remaining," the pastor said, "more who are still possessed. They require more spiritual deliverance than that girl, and will be returned to the Manifestation Quarters for more prayers and heal—"

"PLEASE, PASTOR! WHAT OF IKEMBA! HOW ABOUT IKEMBA?"

A woman was crying in the center aisle. The one called her son was tied to the rope, and his possession, to many, seemed to be the most diabolical. His skin was black. And some had believed the evil spirits within him made him darker than charcoal—wearing both marks of Ham and Cain.

"I-I-I will heal him in God's time, my sister; and if I cannot, I will send him to our brothers in London City who will procure his deliverance at our Christian school abroad. Remember what I said about loyalty. Return to your seat, and turn your fears over to Jesus. *Pray for your son. Pray that he may be healed.* In short, let us all pray for these children. Everyone rise to your feet and stretch your hands toward the front of the altar."

They did as they were told. Arms shot forth like the bracts of pineapples, and the congregation bowed its head with esteem.

"Now pray! Pray that possession will not be their portion! Pray that the great El Shaddai, the great Ancient of Days will deliver them! Pray that they will see salvation! Pray that they will drink from the cup of good health! Pray that they will no longer know suffering! Pray that they will return to their families! PRAY! PRAY! PRAY! PRAY!"

Pastor Nwosu's congregation obeyed him, praying fiercely, petitioning the one called their god for the spiritual deliverance of the children, and asking for their own steadfast desire to move to London City, praying, still, with the rigor its pastor commanded, and clutching toward its loyalty to Jesus and the pastor which Jesus had given them.

"In JESUS' name!" the pastor said.

"Amen!" said the congregation.

Pastor Nwosu commanded the two large men to return the children to the Manifestation Quarters. And the men pulled firmly on the rope, taking the children out of the sanctuary as the congregation sat down and turned again to its pastor.

"Remember that today, the Living God has moved me to speak of loyalty, and you have now witnessed what the power of my loyalty can do. Amen?"

"AMEN!"

"Every single one of us must develop a *personal relationship* with Jesus, and Jesus alone. Everything else is evil! Those children, do you know how they became possessed by evil spirits? They engaged in those demonic rituals our people are so fond of. They danced with masquerades. They witnessed libations. *And upon all of that*, THEY PRAYED TO IDLE GODS! THAT WAS IT! THAT WAS THE PROBLEM! THOSE CHILDREN DID NOT KNOW HOW TO BE LOYAL TO THE LIVING GOD. *There are principalities in this world* . . . and those children followed them like fools. Tell me, how can anyone call themselves Christian today, when tomorrow they turn their backs, and do libation to their ancestors, pouring palm wine onto the ground for a spirit to drink? That is an abomination! Who will drink that wine? The ants? Let me tell you something, when you die, you will not have life until Jesus comes in glory to judge the world. *That is written in our Bibles!* Turn to Ecclesiastes, chapter nine, verse five . . . Have you found it?"

The congregation nodded while replying in loud yeses.

"Good, good; let me read it . . . 'BUT THE DEAD KNOWETH NOT ANYTHING, NEITHER HAVE THEY ANY MORE A REWARD; FOR THE MEMORY OF THEM IS FORGOTTEN.' Have you heard it? THE MEMORY OF THEM IS FORGOTTEN! So you people who defy the Living God in the name of culture and tradition, I warn you that peace of mind will not be your portion! You will end up more possessed than the people you have seen today! I have said it before and I will say it again, you must be loyal to Jesus! He alone will answer your prayer! He alone is the true God! He alone is the Way, the Truth, and the Life! Every other god is a devil! Every other god is waste!"

Pastor Nwosu fixed the microphone onto its stand, and sat in his seat at the altar while hearing the blasting applause. The service continued by the leadership of church elders and deacons. Tithes and offerings were collected. Testimonies were shared. More hymns were sung, and the service ended with a prayer from an elder.

"Jesus in heaven. We thank you for giving us another service. We ask that you continue to bless us and grant us our hearts' desires. I ask this in the mighty name of Jesus. May the grace of our Lord Jesus Christ, the love of God, and the sweet fellowship of the Holy Spirit, be with us now and forevermore. Surely . . ."

"Goodness and mercy shall follow us," said the congregation, "all the days of our lives, and we shall dwelleth in the house of the Lord forever and ever . . . Amen."

Pastor Nwosu shook the hand of the church elder who had prayed, then walked along the church's center aisle toward the back of the edifice near the sunlit entrance, where he would wish his congregation a blessed Sunday. He turned, and saw many flocking to meet him—and he greeted them, with handshakes and hugs, laying his hands on many, invoking the fire of the Holy Spirit.

"Pastor Nwosu! Please come! Something is happening at the Manifestation Quarters!"

It was John, Pastor Nwosu's administrative assistant, who was approaching the pastor's back when the pastor turned to him, abruptly ending the pastor's blessing on a large woman wearing a large hat.

"John, what is it? What is happening?" the pastor asked.

"It is Ikemba, the possessed youth . . . the one with black skin. He has escaped his cell and now he is causing trouble in the quarters."

"What do you mean? How did he—Follow me! Follow me quickly!"

Pastor Nwosu left the large woman and the rest of his congregation, and marched along the gravel path leading to the Manifestation Quarters—not seeing John following behind him. The young assistant feared the pastor, partially because the pastor was a man of God, but mainly because the pastor employed him. Any mistake, and John was both damned and sacked. He knew he could regain salvation by joining another church, but finding a new job in his native country was nearly impossible. The young assistant did not tell Pastor Nwosu that it was he who was responsible—that it was he who had lost his set of keys by the cells in the Manifestation Quarters, allowing this disturbance to happen. When they arrived at the Manifestation Quarters, John left the pastor, hurrying into a very far corner, avoiding any further interactions with this man of God.

"What is happening here?" asked Pastor Nwosu, looking about the Manifestation Quarters, seeing that the potted plants had been turned over, leaving dirt scattered across the floor, with papers flying in midair by the thrusts of twirling ceiling fans. He moved farther along, following a noise he had been hearing from the entrance, then saw Ikemba jumping toward the high fans, slamming his feet against the old wood of a table, his black muscles glistening under the fluorescent light, standing half naked with eyes stretched wide like an open palm.

"It is Ikemba! Pastor, it is Ikemba!" an attendant said.

"My Lord and my God," said another attendant with a cane, "he is possessed! My Lord and my God! My Lord and my God...Jesuuuuuuuuu uuuuuuusssssssss!"

"SHUT UP!" said the pastor. "HOW DID THIS HAPPEN!"

"We don't know," implored the first attendant, as she slapped her hands atop each other.

"Give me that cane!" the pastor said, snatching it from the attendant who had screamed, then banging it on the wooden table.

"Ikemba, I am warning you," Pastor Nwosu said, "come down from that table right now!"

Ikemba ignored the pastor, and continued jumping over and again, looking through the black of the pastor's eyes.

"Ikemba, I said come down now!"

"DAH-DAH-DAH-DAH-DAH-DAH-DAH DAH-DAH-DAH-DAH-DAH," Ikemba sang.

"I will break you to pieces if you don't come down this instant!"

"This is my revolt!" Ikemba said. "THIS IS MY REVOLT! You have kept me here in your church for two years . . . YOU STUPID MAN! IS THIS THE WAY OF YOUR GOD? IS THIS WHAT YOUR BIBLE TELLS YOU TO DO? It is time for me to leave this church by force and by fire! Do you hear me, stupid man . . . BY FORCE AND BY FIRE!"

Ikemba heard the pastor banging the cane on the table, but the sound of it only excited him, moving him to jump on the table with more weight and power.

"If you have a gun," Ikemba said, "now is the time to shoot it."

Pastor Nwosu fell silent, then struck Ikemba on his arm; but the boy of sixteen protested more loudly and jumped harder on the table, putting fear in the attendants, and without warning, began unloosing his corduroy pants and aiming his genitals toward the pastor.

Urine erupted on Pastor Nwosu's face, some of it mixing with his mustache, some of it passing through his lips; and it was enough to make the pastor howl, jump onto the table, and bombard the teenager with blows from his cane, enough to make the pastor kill with a strike to the temple, if not for the commandment of the one called his god—which he recalled while sharing the tabletop with the other—one disobeying church authority, one disobeying no law of Amalike, both disregarding the fact that the table could not hold their weight—and when it began collapsing, the pastor landed on his feet, and the child on his right ankle.

"NOOOOO!" Ikemba screamed, as droplets of blood widened from where the cane had opened his skin, as his ankle began swelling to the size of a garden egg.

Pastor Nwosu ordered the attendants to pick him up from the floor and return him to the cell in which he was kept. And as they followed his orders, he dropped the cane and went to the staff restroom to wipe his face clean with water and soap. He saw himself in the mirror and saw that the urine had stained his red silk shirt, and he began cleaning the stain with tissues, roughly—roughly, until he saw the composure and authority he expected from his reflection, keeping himself from thinking of things he could name as sin. Then he opened the bathroom door, and moved through the corridor to where the children were kept, yelling, "AAAAAAAAAAAY!" for their attention.

"Let this be a WARNING to each of you! If you try and cause trouble in this HOUSE OF GOD, you will have me to answer to! I will make sure that you are SEVERELY DEALT WITH! Possessed or not possessed, INSUBORDINATION will not be tolerated! If you try it like this BASTARD among you, your penalty will be high."

Pastor Nwosu marched out of the corridor, as quickly as he had entered it, and did not notice that his assistant had not been following him. John left his hiding place when he saw the pastor leave the quarters, and went toward the cells to look for his missing keys. John kept his eyes low, searching the wet concrete floor for the sparkle of gray metal, avoiding the many children residing in those cells, with their scab-ridden skin and pale faces, with their jaundiced eyes more yellow than their growing teeth. He did not want to see the children of Precious Word Ministries, and stood in the middle of the corridor, flanked by the caged cells, avoiding the children's skinny arms reaching toward either side of him.

"Sah, sah . . . please, we are hungry, give us bread."

"Sah . . . give us bread."

"Sah, I want water to drink."

"Sah . . . sah . . ."

And John left the cells and ran out of the quarters, abandoning his search for his missing keys. He returned to the second floor of the girdered church edifice—rushing to the pastor's door—hurrying to fulfill the pastor's requests.

Quickly he knocked on the pastor's door and waited for a response, and when he was told to come in, he entered and saw the pastor by the window, lifting a curtain to let the sunlight in, then watching as the afternoon light spread across the oak desk, spanning the large room, touching the burgundy chairs and a picture frame bearing the pastor and the ones called his wife and four children, touching a mirror that reflected the light onto a painting of the child Jesus teaching the elders of the temple.

"Would you like to eat your afternoon meal now, sah?" John said.

"Yes," said the pastor. "What did the cook prepare?"

"Rice and stew with goat meat."

"That is fine."

John set off to the church kitchen and returned with the pastor's meal set on a ceramic tray; he left the room again and timidly waited by the pastor's door—tapping his feet and pressing his knuckles, bearing solicitude, thinking of the merits of death over unemployment, and outpacing his own thoughts of the lost metal key—before being ordered inside the office again, to remove the pastor's plates.

"Pastor sah . . ." said John, returning the red-stained plates to the ceramic tray.

"Yes, what is it?"

"I wanted to inform you of today, your scheduled meetings."

"Yes, yes," said the pastor. "Go ahead."

John put down the last plate, then removed from his pocket a notepad filled with names, times, and dates. He turned to the page bearing the day's agenda and read out the schedule to the pastor.

"At three o'clock you have a meeting with Mr. Anyaọkụ regarding the Christian Men's Association. At five you are scheduled to bless the new house that the Nwanka family has built. And I moved your six o'clock meeting with Obi Iroatụ to one thirty p.m., because of your upcoming travels to Nnewi City."

"What time is it now?"

"One o'clock."

"OK. Take these plates away, let me prepare for my meeting with the king."

Pastor Nwosu did not see John leaving when he began stretching over his desk to organize his work area, discarding some papers and arranging his Bible, his office ledger, and the red notebooks he used for drafting sermons. And when he believed his desk was in order, he walked to his window and pulled his curtains farther back, and saw people from his congregation gathered beneath the scaffolding of the church edifice, discussing matters he hoped were for the benefit of his church. He wanted to go to them and give them counsel—but he heard, instead, a knocking coming from his office door.

"Come in," Pastor Nwosu said.

"Pastor! Pastor!" said Obi Iroatụ, as he entered the room, gold hanging from his neck as yards of cloth streamed down his back. He extended his hand to the pastor, and his pastor accepted it with a smile before they both began moving toward their newly imported chairs.

"Obi Iroatụ, welcome!" said Pastor Nwosu, sitting down.

"Thank you, my pastor. How has your Sunday been?"

"To tell you the truth . . . it has been hectic," Pastor Nwosu said, bringing his hands to his mustache. "It is just as they say, the work of God's servant knows no end."

"That is very true," the king said while grinning. "It is very true indeed."

"In any case, the great king of Amalike has come to my office. What have we to discuss today?"

"Pastor, I have come to make another donation to the church. My businesses have been doing well. My profits have been tripling, and it is because of how you tend to this church. The Almighty is working wonders through you and I must thank him!"

"That is well. That is well indeed," said the pastor. "You have not forgotten Jesus amid your success. It is a mistake so many others make."

"I know. That is why I am gifting fifty million toward the construction of the church."

"That is a generous gift!" Pastor Nwosu said. "It will bring us closer to our goal; but, why so much? You have already taken so many children to London City to study at your brother's Christian school, and now you are giving me millions to continue building this House of God . . ."

"Pastor Nwosu, it was you who told me that when one has faith, a donation to the church is an investment. You invest in God, and God will in turn invest in you. Here . . . take this check and deposit it when you are ready."

The king gave the pastor a blue slip of paper as the pastor remained silent—grinning while morose as he lifted his falling spectacles.

"Thank you very much Obi. On behalf of Precious Word Ministries, I thank you. We will use this money to continue building this House of God. I was even thinking of purchasing property to expand the church grounds."

"*Purchasing?* Pastor, I am the Obi of Amalike. If you need more land, just tell me, and I will give it to you."

"Surely God will bless you, Obi Iroatụ."

"Of course, my pastor . . . yes, yes . . . my pastor . . . there is even an important thing I wanted to ask you."

"Yes, what is it?" said Pastor Nwosu, after darting his eyes from the unfinished edifice.

"Today, I did not understand what you said about libations. How did you manage to call *offering libations* to our ancestors an evil? I couldn't understand it."

"Obi, it is not me calling it an evil. It is the Holy Bible. I read the verse in Ecclesiastes that speaks to such matters. When someone has died, he has died. There is no more life in him. If you pray to him, it is like praying to an idol. That is what makes it an abomination in the eyes of the Lord."

"Pastor, I know, I know, but it is one of our traditions. We have been doing it for centuries."

"And it is time that I put an end to those sinful habits. I am the pastor of this church, and I will not allow my flock to engage in acts of Satan in the name of *tradition*. If they do, they cannot be members of Precious Word Ministries, and they will be condemned to the suffering of eternal hellfire. And if you want those financial blessings to keep flowing by the hand of God, and his servant the pastor, you must abandon those heathen practices yourself. Remember, our God does not like sharing His glory!"

Obi Iroatụ fell silent, believing the blessed assurance which had come through the pastor's hands saved him from the gloom of high-risk business choices and protected his investments living within the Manifestation Quarters; and his fear of losing those investments outweighed any desire to pour wine onto the earth—for any ancestor, regardless of their resting place—regardless of their name.

"You are right, pastor! You are right! If you want, I can even outlaw the practice of libation in Amalike."

"In due time, Obi. Let us first work on converting these hearts to Jesus."

"If you are speaking of converting the hearts of your congregation, there is something you must know."

"What is it?"

"Many members of the congregation have been traveling to Ichulu in secret."

"WHAT! That heathen, backward village! Why are they—I should have wiped that place out with Holy Ghost fire years ago. Nothing good can come from Ichulu. *It is caged.*"

"It is true," the king said, thinking of loyalty, thinking of another investment.

"I have warned them!" Pastor Nwosu said. "They are not to travel there, not for any reason!"

"I know," said Obi Iroatų, "but they are going anyway. There is a young girl there . . . Many believe she has been blessed with the gift of flying. They have seen it with their own eyes. They say that the girl has been given this power by the Living God."

"What? That is impossible!"

"That was what I thought, until one of my personal aides, Madụka, confirmed it for me. Pastor Nwosu, this girl can fly."

"She must be a witch! That is it! She must be a witch, and now she wants to compromise the faith of my flock. God will not allow it!"

"He will not," the king said. "Pastor, let me make a suggestion."

The pastor nodded his head.

"Why not bring this child here to the church and keep her in the Manifestation Quarters. Since she is a witch, her witchcraft must be broken by the blood of Jesus. You must heal her, pastor."

"Obi Iroatụ, that is an excellent idea. I must bring this child here—I'll send my assistant to Ichulu, to escort her to the church. Yes, that is what I must do. John! John!" the pastor said from his office.

"Yes sah," said John as he entered.

"Prepare your bags! You are making a journey to Ichulu."

DIARY ENTRY #958   **DATE UNKNOWN**

but Chukwu is not a fool i know that Chukwu the Most Supreme Being is not a fool but how Chukwu how could you do this to me please please remove me from this prison you've seen me you see that i haven't eaten. you see that i haven't slept only pure water i can smell everything sitting in that metal bucket everything that has come out of me but Chukwu is not a fool so take me out of this prison remove me i need to eat. Please. anything give me to eat i've been counting with these marks one eight thirteen nothing to eat for these thirteen days where is the time? chukwu where is it? when did prison become home.

and my father my old father solomtochukwu solomto please solomto you flew like me i flew and sang your songs in my heart tell that god to get me out tell chukwu to get me out chukwu isbut i can never say it. i didn't say it when they roped me up then beat me like a goat that day i flew in the sanctuary i didn't say it when they burned my lips chukwu is not a fool not listening to me after every good thing i did all the things please please tell the most supreme remind that god i went up each day up i never cursed when others cursed did i steal when others stole i didn't lie when they told me lies never never always the truth chukwu remove me, take me up, what have i done, what have i

i hear them the children. they say it to but me me Chukwu! mercy! it cannot each believe, for it too be separate, even separately.

2.

TAME WATERS FROM THE RAINY SEASON, and gentle winds from the dry, had visited Ichulu and left—so, too, had a passable harvest—and the Stone of Anị rested amid the towering necks of slender grass and reeds. A year had passed since Nwagụ and Mgboye took their oaths before the village, and as they moved throughout Ichulu, filled with health and joy, nobody doubted the goodness of their words. Jekwu was a son to be kept, a son for his parents, and a son for Ichulu. He was saved on the fourth day from his birth, and was circumcised on the eighth, and was given ichi so thin his scars healed in twelve days. He was sung to by many women before Anyanwụ had risen, and was sung to many times before Anyanwụ set in the evening time. And after being washed by Igbokwe on the banks of Idemili each night, he was given those blessings that only Igbokwe's prayers could give.

But there was a lingering fear among many in Ichulu: how could Anị be lost? The promise of no longer losing loved ones to the Evil Forest was enticing, but not enticing enough to erase the memory of last year's damages. The flood had eroded much of the village, making it difficult to rebuild red-clay homes and red-clay obis, making it difficult to trust the days when Igwe, the husband of Anị, sent his rain. The harvest of that year had troubled them, as it had not been as bountiful as those of the past, and it caused the people to wonder if the goddess of the earth had made it so—cursing them like the eight osu—because her death had come through the life of a little child. The village slept disquietly—knowing that a goddess whom they served from their remembered beginnings was now dead—murmuring, "How can Anị be lost . . . How can the great Anị be dead?"

It especially bothered the bearded Okoye, who was carrying his cutlass to the Stone of Anị. He moved with the desire to upkeep the sacred grounds, and to give life to a thing which had fallen. And upon his arrival, Okoye saw Igbokwe standing above the stone, wearing a look that betrayed the dịbịa's confidence.

"Even the great Igbokwe is doubting this decision," Okoye said.

Igbokwe looked at Okoye with disinterested eyes, then turned again to the jagged stone.

"If you are certain that we should kill a god whom Chukwu has rejected— why do you stand over Anị's stone with sorrow?"

"Okoye, what is it that you want," Igbokwe said.

"I want you to deny what you have told Ichulu! Tell them that your word was not good! Tell them that Anị is not dead, but alive! We have worshipped her since the first day our people could even know a god, and now because of children we abandon her? Igbokwe, what you are doing—it will anger the goddess who provides us with harvest and posterity and will anger our ancestors who speak to Chukwu on our behalf."

"Okoye, it is not so. I have read my shells, and you . . . have you not seen the power these children possess? A child has survived the forest. A child is flying to Chukwu."

"That child is an abomination! She should have never been born!"

Igbokwe's near concession was a silent one; and as he looked through the black of the bearded man's eyes, he remembered how Okoye was once engaged to Nnenna, how the two enjoyed a romance, to which the children of Ichulu crafted songs, dancing a dance of passion that left the others in the village troubled with envy. Nnenna would wash Okoye's clothes at the banks of Idemili, erasing their dirt and stains with the pruned touch of a zealous lover. Okoye would catch hordes and hordes of game, hunting tirelessly, demonstrating that he could care for Nnenna and the family they both wanted. Names of children were already decided. The first boy was to be named Ifeatụ, and the first girl Adaakụ, and the remaining children were to be called from the dead, given the names of ancestors.

They planned to marry. And their plan to marry bore no threats, until the day Okoye and Ọfọdile had an argument. Okoye had gone to see if his traps had yielded any game when he found Ọfọdile moving away from his traps with a carcass strung across his shoulders. He hurried toward the man whom he thought to be a thief, and quickly seized the dangling animal.

"Ọfọdile, you have now become one who steals?"

"Steals? What are you saying?" Ọfọdile said.

"You have stolen an animal from one of my traps!" said Okoye. "I saw it with my eyes!"

"Are you steering madness? This is the game I caught from my own trap."

"Are you saying that I am lying lies?"

"No," Ọfọdile said, "I am saying you are a fool!"

The accuser dropped the carcass; the carcass was still dropping when blows were exchanged, the first blows coming from Okoye's fists—with blows being returned by Ọfọdile's stout arms—the betrothed too slow and too close to dodge the bachelor's fists—both fighting with the volatility of a growing flame—Okoye tackling Ọfọdile to the earth—using his body to press him down—but Ọfọdile finding his way upward, delivering more vicious strikes—even as Okoye tackled him down—he rose again, even when tackled again, he rose over and again, until he was subdued—and Okoye scratched his tired face—stealing from him, dark skin and beauty. He let out a scream and released himself from under Okoye's body as the people moving around them asked what had caused this terrible fight.

"It is enough!" Ọfọdile said, blood moving down his cheek. "Okoye— you have accused me, an innocent man, of stealing from you; then you found the courage to attack me as if I were a wild animal. But let these people be witnesses. You, all of you . . . mind your ears. If I stole game from Okoye, let my eyes go blind and never see the morning light, and the land of my father. But if I did not steal from this man . . . Okoye, if I did not steal from you, let everything that you cherish and that you love abandon you; I swear this on the head of my chi!"

Okoye watched Ofodile depart without game, and watched as the morning light glistened upon his back. He did not fear the curse, believing Ofodile was a thief and that in time he would lose his sight and become an outcast. But by the fourth week, Okoye believed that it was he who had experienced much sorrow and hardship. The one called his father had rebuked him for not improving his compound, the one which Okoye was to inherit as the firstborn son. "If you do not repair these crumbling houses," the one called his father would say, "you will never inherit my obi . . . bush animal! You are not my son, but a titleless bush animal." Then, as Okoye began repairing the houses to appease the one called his father, the ones called his younger brothers despised him, as he was to inherit their red-clay homes; and they insulted him without shame, calling him a selfish dog, a selfish dog that would rebuild the compound's houses while his younger brothers still lived within them.

The insults continued; the isolation broadened; and like the others, Nnenna ended her affection. When Okoye asked her what he had done, she said that she hated his shaven face. When Okoye grew a beard, nothing changed in her; and when he heard her call him the man whom she used to love— incapable of satisfying her affections—and saw her flee to another—the one whom the village said spoke to her, and listened to her, and filled her with the powers of romance and zeal—hearing that he held her like a hunted animal trapped in a corner, which made her acquiesce to lust—watching her accept the lashes of the scandalous affair, saying after four rousing weeks that she would keep her betrothal to Ofodile—Okoye swore himself to a life of righteousness, forever tending to the gods for protection against human wickedness.

"Igbokwe," Okoye said, "because of that thief, I do not have a wife, or children—*but I have my gods.* If you respect what is holy in Ichulu, you will resurrect Ani."

"Okoye—my power is not to resurrect the gods. I am their messenger. I am not their leader. If you want to worship Anị again, then you yourself, go ask it of Chukwu."

The dịbịa moved away from the stone, though doubt had flown into his mind, shaking it with vigor. *How*, he thought, *will we survive*—the reality of declaring Anị dead striking him like a blow, disturbing him as it disturbed all he was to protect; even with the evidence of Jekwu, and the evidence of Ijeọma, how would Chukwu provide the way Anị had provided, bearing children through divine fertility, holding the bodies of our people dead, forging the boundaries of evil and good, producing crops for eating and sacrifice, will it be the Supreme Being who will tend to the affairs of the living, when the harvest of this year was not as bountiful as those before it, when eight of our sons have been cursed, six of them shot dead—

Igbokwe let out a mournful sigh, and another one, over and again. *Why have they done this*, the dịbịa thought, *why have the gods gone to war?*

3.

NWAGỤ AND MGBOYE WERE APPROACHING the four-home compound
of Jekwu's deliverer, with offerings of yam, palm wine, and palm oil stacked
atop their heads. They considered the discomfort of their load remuneration
for all they owed the household, because if not for the flying one, Jekwu
would be dead. The year-old infant was fastened to the body of the one called
his sister, with a thick, purple rappa tied tightly around Chinwe's back. His
head bounced with each of her steps, until he saw the clouds and trees spinning in uneven circles, until he vomited upon her sweaty shoulders, and let
out a piercing sigh.

"Chei!" Chinwe said, quickly peeling Jekwu from the curve of her back,
then using the purple rappa to wipe them both clean. "Jekwu—I will beat
your buttocks if you vomit on me again!" she said before her irritation paused,
fleeing from her, when she looked at his plain face, watching him laugh at
clouds gleefully.

She was amazed—realizing how quickly he had grown in a single year. He was taller than the distance between her foot and her knee, and was heavier than a basket of mangoes; his head was as proportionate as a garden egg, and his voice had begun making soft sounds as if made from the purest metal. Chinwe lifted him and placed him again on her back, warning through a joke that he would eat his own vomit if he vomited on her again. And at once, she heard him laughing a laugh—as if acknowledging that he had understood.

When they arrived, Nwagụ, Mgboye, Chinwe, and Jekwu were waiting at the mouth of Ọfọdile's compound, waiting for a response to Nwagụ's call, listening for an answer to, "Compound of Ekwueme, the family of Nwakaibie has come."

"You have arrived?" Ezinne said, after sprinkling river water on the ground; after standing to Nwagụ's call, as she prepared to sweep Ọfọdile's compound.

"Yes, we have arrived," Nwagụ said, smiling.

"Welcome, all of you welcome. Ọfọdile and Nnenna are in their homes. I will go and call them for you."

Ezinne walked toward Ọfọdile's obi and then to Nnenna's red-clay home, her smooth scalp playing with the sunlight as she went. And within the moment, she returned with her in-laws near her side, and continued sweeping the compound.

"How are—"

"Ehhhhhh-ehhh! Ehhhh-ehh!" said Nnenna with a smile, interrupting Ọfọdile's words. "Is this the one who has birthed eight children, and is still looking like a young woman! Where are the others?"

"They are at home cooking food," said Mgboye. "A woman with five children is not to be in the kitchen, or you did not know?"

The two laughed together and moved toward Nnenna's red-clay home, after putting aside the yam and other gifts. Ọfọdile had asked Nwagụ to break kola in his obi, and as they moved, Chinwe and Jekwu remained close to Ezinne.

"Our mother," said Chinwe, "do you know where Ijeọma is?"

"She is on the other side of the compound, near her mother's home."

"Thank you," Chinwe said, while moving to meet Ijeọma.

"Chinwe! Chinwe!" Nwagụ's voice was coming from the mouth of Ọfọdile's obi.

"Make sure you take care of Jekwu. Let nothing happen to him! *Have you heard?*"

"Yes." Chinwe said.

"No, no, give him to your mother. That is greater in beauty . . ."

Chinwe nodded, and Nwagụ watched as she entered Nnenna's home with Jekwu on her back; and he watched as she emerged without him. Then he entered the obi and sat across from Ọfọdile—not seeing the unease of his host, but speaking the purpose of his visit once the two had broken kola.

"Ọfọdile . . . even the sky! above us! cannot hold the gratitude I have for you and your family . . . If you could hear the joy of my chi! or the exclamations of my forefathers! then you would know the extent to which I am indebted. Without your daughter, there would be no hope, no peace, no balance in my household. I would have killed all affection for my newborn son, and would have been forced to refuse the affection he has for me. Do you know what would have happened if he died in that forest? I would have cursed the goddess who brought him into the world—only to remove him from it days later. I would have cursed the woman who I call my wife for birthing a child who is an abomination to our people. I would have cursed my own chi for not obeying my will, for if a man says yes, so must his chi! ỌFỌDILE! I know Ichulu has called me lucky—my traps are always full, my harvest always abundant—never have I lacked; but this thing called luck only exists if a village makes it so, if a man's chi makes it so—"

"Nwagụ . . ." Ọfọdile began, "you should not, be grateful to me . . . or any member of my household. It is true, that my daughter is the reason . . . your son is alive today . . . But the very fact . . . that she flies . . . like some animal, makes her an abomination, whether or not Anị is dead. Anị is no longer worshipped ... and the people of Ichulu, now see the results. Look at how people ... complained of their harvests."

"What are you speaking? The harvest was acceptable."

"My yams, that used to be ... the size of large stones, were smaller than my forearm," Ọfọdile said.

"But my yams of this harvest were the same as my yams of last harvest," Nwagụ said.

"So you, do not see? That, too, is a problem," Ọfọdile said. "If Chukwu ... the Most Supreme ... has taken the place of Anị ... should our produce not be, greater in beauty? And what of ... the children? Were there not less born ... this year, than the last?"

"Ọfọdile, I have listened; but have you not heard what Ichulu is saying?"

"What, are they ... saying?"

"They are saying that they do not know; whether we will survive without Anị, whether Chukwu will govern the harvest, whether your daughter is to blame ... Ichulu does not know."

"Can you say ... that there have not been, men ... who have blamed ... their misfortunes, on our names? Can you, say it?"

"Ọfọdile, let those foolish men continue their gossiping. Do you know how many of them have committed abominations against Anị? The harvest is still growing, and the children are still being birthed. The people of Ichulu know in their spirit that what our children have brought is good. Even if it is not said, all of us, from the greatest man to the smallest child, know it."

"Nwa—have you become foolish! Ichulu is great because it has never changed! Great because we have followed every tradition, given by our fathers, all of them without failing."

"Your word is not good," Nwagụ said. "Ichulu's greatness comes from how we move with change and difficulty—just like our god Idemili. We honor our traditions, but when they can no longer serve us, we drown them in the deepest river."

"But, if we continue, to discard our traditions ... what will remain, for our children ..."

"My friend, I do not know, but our children and their children will uncover it."

The two men sat in each other's company, bearing their discord. They could hear the laughter of their wives jumping across the compound, and they wondered if the women, too, discussed the meaning of their children's lives. Neither knew what to do with the silence. They barely noticed the sounds of goats bleating at the mouth of the obi. Nwagų stared at his host. Qfǫdile suppressed his irritation, wanting to douse his nose in a container of snuff; the two were neither enemies nor friends.

Ijeǫma and Chinwe were not the same as the ones called their fathers. Since last year's thanksgiving festival, Chinwe visited Ijeǫma as much as she could, bringing with her stories that Mgboye told and songs which the older children composed. She learned to speak Ijeǫma's language, partially through her own intelligence, and partially through the intelligence of Nnenna's teaching: raised eyebrows and endearing gazes—arms swinging and motioning in the air—all of them now bore meaning to Chinwe; and, as she sat in the middle of Qfǫdile's compound, savoring the company of her friend, Chinwe used her eyes to listen.

"Ijeǫma, I like the color of your rappa ... It is as if they dyed it with the brightest palm oil."

Ijeǫma smiled, and clasped her palms, presenting them to Chinwe.

"Even your father's rappa; I like his, too ... It is even redder than yours."

Ijeǫma presented her hands again.

"Do not thank me, my friend! Because of you, Jekwu survived death. My youngest brother would have died if not for you."

Ijeǫma fell rigid—guilt pulling at her insides—knowing that Chinwe's profession was true in two ways. Her friend knew of the flights—but did not know of the second: bold secrets, hiding in the Evil Forest; and it became for her a terrifying fear—speaking the good word—even if good words were true, *even if they are,* she thought, *good words can kill friendships, and if Chinwe knew that Jekwu's survival was not from the gods, she would cast me away*—your brother was saved by my hands—she thought loudly—thanking her muteness for keeping it unsaid—*he licked rice from my fingers—and drank milk from my mother's breasts—but you would not understand, if I told you, you would not like it, and you would tell me to go, and befriend Chukwu and the gods, and cast me away, like the girls in the market square; can you hear me? Is that why you are looking at me in that way . . . why are you, I am sorry, I am sorry, I am nodding, three times yes, two times no . . . I am pointing to my stomach, I am sorry . . . do you understand, I am pointing to my stomach.*

"Yes, I would like something to eat," said Chinwe. "What is it that you would like to give me?"

Ijeọma quickly took Chinwe's open right hand and led her to Ọfọdile's orange tree. She plucked one of those golden spheres and handed it to Chinwe, and watched her tear the orange peels with her teeth—letting the juices wash through her mouth and chin—consuming it voraciously—while the plump goats ate the dirt-covered peelings—as they bleated—in uneven tempos.

Chinwe recoiled when a goat whipped its black tongue against her feet, the wet on her skin thicker than mucus, sticky like peeled okra.

"Go from here! and leave!" Chinwe said, as she reached toward the dust—to dry her feet—and her gaze met two skinny legs—walking in her direction.

"Nnamdị!" Chinwe said, as she began standing, seeing Nnamdị walking toward her in the middle of the compound, thinking him to be ill. But when she looked more carefully, she saw that his body was just as she remembered; it was his limp which had fooled her into distorting his sprightly chi. So she turned from his gait, and began calling his name again, this time in the tune of song, seeing Nnamdị smiling at her as he walked slowly toward the orange tree.

"How are you, Chinwe?" Nnamdị said, his left hip curving away from his body's center.

"It is well," Chinwe said. "Ijeọma has been feeding me your father's oranges."

"That is beautiful . . . These oranges are the best in Ichulu!"

All of them began laughing as Nnamdị reached for fruit of his own, stretching his curved body as far as he could stretch it. He plucked the orange and tossed it between his hands, then began peeling it and staring at Chinwe frankly—curiously.

"Do you think that Jekwu is ugly?" Nnamdị said. "I heard a man say his teeth made him ugly. He said they looked like those of a crocodile."

Ijeọma glared at Nnamdị, but he ignored Ijeọma and continued asking his questions.

"What do you think? Do you think that it is true?"

"How can it be true, Nnamdị? If Chukwu saved Jekwu, how can he be ugly?"

"But how can it be true that Chukwu is better than Anị? Look at how beautiful the earth is. Who can even see Chukwu?"

"Truth is not something you see at one time. You cannot pour it into a single cup and say, 'It is my own.' What we see . . . and do not see, from yesterday until tomorrow, they are not greater than the Most Supreme."

"Nnamdị! Are you disturbing Ijeọma!" Nnenna said from inside her red-clay home.

"No, mama of mine, I am not!"

"Ehhh-ehh . . . come here! I want you to fetch some water for me."

Ijeọma watched Nnamdị as he went—watching him limp forcefully toward Nnenna's home, then watching him leave the compound with a clay pot on his head. Her heart pulled open within her chest, relieved and happy and thankful that both she and Chinwe were with themselves, and would not be bothered by the meddling of their families. She glanced at Chinwe and smiled a bit, afraid that yesterday's loves would no longer be continued—and saw that Chinwe had been smiling, too, and now, wrapped her hands around hers.

They pulled their arms—together, and forward—and began speaking of new things, new songs, new dances, new growths that sprung through their plaited hair, pondering on Idemili and his river, Igwe and his sky, pondering on the marriages of three men, and the chieftaincies of four women, and the little girls whom no one knew had tapped wine from a palm tree. They talked—until the sky was less bright—talking until they began chasing each other around the compound—dashing within the dust—forming clouds beneath their feet—running to the rhythms of circles and other patterns—along the paths—that the chickens etched upon the ground; everyone in the compound could hear the noise of their steps and the wonder of their laughter; and after many moments—they collapsed on the earth—drenched in sweat and thanksgiving.

"I love you, my friend," Chinwe said.

Ijeọma pointed to her eye while smiling.

"Who taught you how to play so well . . . What has made it so that you are not wording words? Tell me, who taught you?"

Ijeọma raised her hands to her head and began ruffling them through her hair.

"Have you not seen him since the festival?"

Ijeọma nodded her head twice.

"That is terrible! You cannot see your own kin because of a curse! Why can they not break the curse on Ụzọdị and return him to this village?"

Ijeọma could not say; and she thought of Ụzọdị quietly, morosely, remembering her love for him, a love which she thought greater than that obliged by family—since they loved each other—with her tearing eyes, she began weeping—wanting him returned to their village, praying that somehow the gods would offer their mercy—and that Ụzọdị would forgive her for her influence in his banishment—professing all her prayers, as sunlight gave her long tears shine.

"Ijeọma, it is enough. It is enough. You ought not cry."

Her weeping continued despite Chinwe's words. She sat motionless, not signing any signs, not looking to her friend. Then, quicker than Amadịọha—her tears gathered heat—blood, rushing—heartbeats clapping like rain—violently, violently—thinking of the men exiling Ụzọdị, and Igbokwe sending Ụzọdị to Amalike—and the village, doubting every sign that Chukwu had given—every sign Chukwu had sent; Anị had died, and flowers still grew; Igwe was still offering his rain; children were saved; children are saved, but still they doubt—Ijeọma screamed.

"Ijeọma! Ijeọma!"

Ijeọma screamed again—the breath passing through her, emptying into the air—leaving her with biting sorrow.

"Let us see him. Let us go and visit Ụzọdị."

Ijeọma signed nothing, not believing Chinwe's words.

"Ijeọma, let us go and visit your kin. We will go at a time when no one will see us . . . in the darkness of nighttime . . . You will do it?"

Ijeọma nodded three times—wondering what spirit had given Chinwe courage.

"Yes, this will be simple. We will leave our beds when Ichulu is most quiet, and the moon is not too bright; then we will meet under that giant tree, beside the river, and walk to the place where the osu stay."

Ijeọma nodded two times.

"What is wrong with my words?"

Ijeọma pointed to the sun.

"You want to go in the morning?"

Ijeọma nodded three times.

"That is beautiful. We can tell our mothers that we are going to fetch water, but we will go and see Ụzọdị instead. Let us travel tomorrow."

We will travel tomorrow—Ijeọma signed—before leaving Chinwe—with an embrace.

4.

IJEǪMA THOUGHT THE MORNING WAS bright—bright enough to hide the moon forever, bright enough to burn any residues of fear dwelling within her chi. She rose that morning longing to see the one called her kin. And after clearing her mat from Nnenna's dark floor and cleaning her mouth with a frayed chewing stick, she told the one called her mother a borrowed lie: that she was going to Idemili to fetch water for the compound. And when Nnenna said, "Go, and return well," Ijeǫma rushed to her pot—and hurried off into the morning, justifying her dishonesty by remembering Ụzǫdị—who taught her that one's word must always be good—even in the smallest affairs. So, she planned to return—with water from Idemili—but not as quickly as Nnenna assumed. She lifted the blue water pot atop her head—balancing it—then walking in the northeast direction, along the orange paths, and toward the market square, meeting Chinwe by the large tree next to Idemili, greeting her above the ebbing waters, wrestling with the wind.

"Are you prepared to travel," Chinwe said.

Ijeọma nodded three times.

"Then let us fill our pots with water, so that we can offer it to Ụzọdị."

Ijeọma nodded three times, and the two quickly began filling their pots with the gift of Idemili. They squatted beside those vessels and lifted them atop their heads once those vessels were full. Their necks were firm, and their hips were swaying to the rhythms of the oscillating water shifting inside their clay pots—both looking like thin cashew trees pivoting before a storm. They moved quietly and cautiously, trying to avoid being seen. But it was terribly difficult, nearly impossible, because Ichulu was unabashed in its ways. One could be sought for a greeting or for gossip even if one's path were covered by trees.

"Ijeọma! What are you doing at the market, without your mother," said Adaọra, biting on a chewing stick beneath her shed.

"We are taking a longer path to my father's compound," Chinwe said.

"*Is madness within you?* Why are you carrying these heavy pots on a longer path?"

Ijeọma did not know how to respond, and glanced at Chinwe, whose mouth had fallen open.

"Our mother . . . the water is not heavy," Chinwe said. "We are very strong!"

"Chei! Children born in these days! Continue with your journey home, and be certain to greet your mothers for me."

The girls promised to do so, and turned and left Adaọra, releasing anxiety from their breaths. And when they believed that no eyes were watching them, they rushed into a nearby shed and made it their place for hiding. They placed their water pots atop the earth, and gave their journey the benefit of strategy—regarding the different possibilities of finding Ụzọdị. They knew the Place of Osu was east of the village and also knew of two ways through which a sojourner could arrive. One was a wide path filled with many people, a path where the young composed songs for new occasions and created dances for the village's festivities. The other was not a path at all, but a thick forest of linking trees, bearing dry and stony earth.

"We must travel it."

How, Ijeọma signed.

Chinwe put her hands on her waist while thinking of making a path in the Forest of Nta. She looked back at Adaọra, who was sitting in her shed, and watched as she bit on her chewing stick and sorted through her greens. Chinwe saw that a machete lay in the corner of her shed.

Chinwe tapped on Ijeọma's shoulder, then pointed. They both said nothing. It was against Ichulu's moral code to steal, forbidden by every measure. Children were told stories of ill fate befalling thieves. The elders declared proverbs warning of taking what was not one's own, and Ijeọma and Chinwe were waiting for the other to sign a name from one of those stories, or share the wisdom of those many proverbs to remind the other in their hiding place of keeping the good word. But they did not: Chinwe did not want to be considered a coward; Ijeọma did not want to lose a friend.

They waited patiently for Adaọra to visit the shed of another market woman. They knew they would not wait long, since the women were still preparing their sheds for the beginning of the market day; and once Adaọra had left, they rushed into her shed and stole her machete, then hurried into their hiding place, praying for forgiveness, asking every god to not combat their immorality; then lifting their water pots atop their heads, they continued with their journey—swaying past the market women and their babies, quickly and casually—before entering the pathless forest with the women to their backs.

It became dark after they pushed beyond the forest's thick barrier. Its intertwined trees blocked any sunlight from resting atop the earth, waning the rules of the ordinary as though in a foreign world, as the tree branches did not spread outward—but curved inward, toward themselves—nearly caging the forest's visitors—and caging the beast rumored to be living there. Ijeọma and Chinwe remembered that Nta had eaten children who did not know their boundaries—curious children—who were too stubborn to obey the wisdom of their elders. They were told it was fiercer than any wild animal, with teeth as long as a tall man's arms—possessing the power—and the strength—of one hundred—crazed bulls.

Ijeọma began falling as she thought of Nta—fearing what the beast might do, how it could devour her body with its fearsome teeth, dragging her ruthlessly into the caged forest; it was hidden behind the trees, she knew, moving swiftly like a lion, waiting to pounce on her chest and break open her skull, waiting to consume her fully in its jaws. But if she smiled at it, she thought, or sang to it, giving it kindness, it might show her mercy, and spare her from dying. She searched for fear on Chinwe's face as she began standing and adjusting her pot, but Chinwe's face was unwavering; her eyes were determined; and Ijeọma could not understand: they could both be found; they could lose their direction; they could both be eaten by the vicious Nta; and her water pot felt heavier; heavy enough to force her through the stony ground, even if she continued walking and praying to her chi, while following the path that Chinwe was making.

"Ijeọma, does your father like my father?" Chinwe asked, cutting through the trees with the machete, then turning around.

Ijeọma quickly nodded three times; Ijeọma nodded yes.

"He does not like my father, Ijeọma. I could see it in his face when we last visited his compound."

Ijeọma's eyes began fluttering as she recalled what Chinwe had recalled— knowing within herself that Ọfọdile disliked Nwagụ, but also knowing that the one called her father despised her more than anything in the village. It was her flying that gave Jekwu an opportunity to live while threatening each of Ọfọdile's traditions. It was she who made Ọfọdile the unluckiest man in Ichulu—believing that if Ọfọdile disliked Nwagụ it was not because of anything Nwagụ had done; it was because of her: his firstborn daughter, the one called his Ada.

My father respects your father, Ijeọma signed by tapping her head, then her chest, then her head again.

"I know he respects him. All Ichulu men are to respect one another. Does he *like* my father?"

Yes, Ijeọma nodded, but it was a lie; and though she attempted to find solace in it, little thoughts stole her ease: a common beast had her fearing the end of their friendship, because Nwagụ and Ọfọdile were not men who danced the same dance, or sang the same songs; and she believed that very soon, Ọfọdile would forbid her from being Chinwe's friend; the thought of it brought tussling to her heart—not wanting to be separated from the one whom she loved—knowing from the prickling atop her right arm that she was to speak the good word, placing that arm beneath her rappa to enlarge her stomach, and seeing that Chinwe immediately understood.

"Pregnancy. Pregnant woman. Baby!" said Chinwe.

Ijeọma nodded three times. Then she pointed to Chinwe and again at her stomach.

"Do you mean Jekwu?"

Ijeọma nodded three times.

"What happened to him? What of Jekwu?"

Ijeọma spread her arms about her, then touched the trees and the ground, lifting the dirt then letting it fall through her fingers.

"Dust? Anị?"

Ijeọma nodded twice.

"What is it that you are saying?"

Ijeọma kept pointing at the interlocking trees and spreading her arms about her while hearing Chinwe say "air," "leaf," guessing incorrectly until she placed Chinwe's hand atop a tree.

"Forest. Do you mean forest?"

Ijeọma nodded three times.

"Jekwu and forest . . . Jekwu . . . Do you want to tell me of when Jekwu was in the Evil Forest?"

Ijeọma nodded three times, then pointed to herself, directing her fingers toward her mouth and beginning to chew.

"Eat . . . eating food . . ."

Ijeọma nodded twice, then emphasized her fingers, pointing toward her mouth.

"Feed."

Ijeọma nodded three times, then pointed to herself, lowering her head, knowing that Chinwe would soon know what was true.

"You fed Jekwu . . . do you mean that you fed Jekwu in the Evil Forest?"

Ijeọma could not look toward her face, shame and discomfort both rising within her.

"You defied the gods to save him?"

Ijeọma kept silent, and heard Chinwe's breath moving closer and closer, keeping her face low—hearing Chinwe moving closer, then feeling her hand—the squeeze coming forth growing tighter and tighter as if both their fingers would shatter, as though the entire earth would quake—and its warmth made shame flee—from Ijeọma's body—as she raised her head—smiling, and taking Chinwe's other hand—hearing Chinwe scream as they both held each other and looked at the strip of sun, shining through the trees—both thanking the Most Supreme for what they were each given.

And Chinwe began—to sing—and scream—and sing: *The one who flies, the one who Ichulu does not hear, the one who I can hear, the one who saved Jekwu, the one who freed Jekwu. Freedom! Freedom! Praise Idemili! Praise Idemili! Praise Idemili!*—and she thanked the god of the river; and thanked, too, the Most Supreme, and through a trembling voice thanked her friend with screams of jubilation.

"I love you! Ijeọma! Ijeọma, I love you!"

Ijeọma began to smile, wanting to tell her friend that she loved her also. So she pointed to her eye, hoping Chinwe would understand the fullness of her speech—and when she saw her smiling, too, watching her face brighten with the sincere and guileless, brighten with the honesties that love requires, she knew it was accepted; and she believed those words which Chinwe blessed her with, as the two put their water pots down and fully embraced.

And when they released their arms, they lifted their pots and began swaying their hips as if drummers were playing beneath the stony ground, as if the ancestors were whispering within the leaning trees, laughing together and walking quickly to reach their destination with timeliness, cutting new paths with the blade of the machete, laughing together as they burrowed through the dark forest of Nta.

AND SUDDENLY THERE WAS MORE LIGHT. Ijeọma and Chinwe had reached the end of the forest and the beginning of the Place of Osu. They could both see them—in wild hair, and tattered clothes—as they each felt their stomachs quivering slightly, but keeping it unacknowledged, reminding themselves that the ones called osu were people, too, remembering through pointed signs, that they were each somebody, that they were all somebody. Do not fear, Ijeọma signed to Chinwe; and they both began nodding their agreement, even though the stories of Ichulu had them judging the osu: the madness of weak gods reflected on their wild hair, the disgust of hopeless poverty written on their tattered clothing; but there was nothing to be feared, they said over and again, now smelling the sour scent of ụkwa carried by the wind—believing that there were women cooking appetizing food—women who most likely birthed the children before them, playing calmly with old tree branches.

"Who are you?" said one of the children, who had stopped his happy game—and looked plainly at the sky, then the girls, his eyes rolling softly as if counting the many threads of the wind—as if there was never yesterday, as though tomorrow were not to come.

"You are both freeborn," said the child. "Is that what it is?"

Yes, said Ijeọma and Chinwe through sight and sound.

"Then go as you go, and come as you come."

"But we are looking for a person," Chinwe said. "Will you help us?"

"If you are to be helped, help will come."

And the boy turned away and continued playing with the others, as Ijeọma stood waiting—unnerved by the child's words, upset that the children began erupting into laughter—irritably watching them clutching their bellies and revealing their missing teeth—feeling insulted that they did not assist them, angry at the child, angry at the osu, believing that they all deserved to be cast out for not helping her find Ụzọdị—then regretting the thought, with remorse and uncertainty, yet feeling insulted still.

"What of this person walking before us," said Chinwe, "Perhaps they know where we can find Ụzọdị."

Ijeọma nodded three times and hurried to the person timidly, then began tapping on their bare back.

"Who has come?" the person said, turning downward, knowing by Chinwe's plaited hair that she was a foreigner.

"We are looking for someone," Chinwe said, having followed behind Ijeọma. "His name is Ụzọdị."

"I know a man they call Ụzọdị," the person said.

"She is his kin! She wants to see him . . . We have brought him water from Idemili."

The person stood on his toes. And he looked down into the girls' water pots, watching the water move, right to left, knowing where it was from as the light danced upon his undulating face. He had forgotten the taste of Idemili's water and had forgotten, too, how it touched the skin; and as he looked into the girls' pots, and then looked back at them, a single desire moved his heart.

"I will show you where he is, but give me water to drink."

"Yes, we will do it. We will give you water."

Chinwe brought her water pot down from her head, then watched the person kneel to the pot's height—watched him dip his cupped hand into the water, and bring it to his face—drinking the water slowly, as if it yielded pure hope. He was from Ichulu, and as he drank, he recalled his time in Idemili, remembering how Idemili's water would cleanse him in ways other water could not. And as he drank, he prayed to Idemili, thanking the river god for returning to his lips.

"In the morning time, the one they call Ụzọdị farms," the person said, lifting his face to Chinwe, "Begin your search there, at the farms. It is not far from your hands. Move along this path and take it all the way, until you see the farmland."

"We thank you," said Chinwe, as she reached for her water pot and returned it to her head—joining Ijeọma in leaving the person with assured farewells as they continued their search for Ụzọdị, as they moved down the path—passing the ones called osu, watching what they thought to be harrowing eyes sternly following them. And as they moved through the Place of Osu, enduring the thought of feeling menacing stares, they dared not speak—not by tongue nor by actions—seeing the ones called osu as they, too, were clearly seen, watching them heating spears and sharpening machetes within their homes, believing them to be in forced restraint, subdued by ancient laws and hierarchies as they walked quickly, in a gait of subordination, appealing to the mercy of the osu and praying for the mercy of the gods, reaching cleared earth with fewer eyes upon them—then putting their hands in their water pots and rubbing the water on their chest and legs, hoping for Idemili's protection.

They continued walking while searching docilely for the farmland and found the man's promise to be true. The farm was not far. It was not long before the heaps of earth lay beneath their feet. And in a distant corner, Ijeọma and Chinwe saw a man tilling the soil with muscles protruding from his body like large stones. They saw no one else on the farm, so they reasoned that this man would know where Ụzọdị could be found; and they walked closer to him, his muscles growing larger to them as they walked closer still, until their footsteps brushed against the weeds and reached the ears of the farming man.

And he turned to them, with Ijeọma nearly weeping, not knowing what words to sign or think, trembling at what stood before them. What has happened, thought Ijeọma, what has happened to him, wondering at the stories that made his face forlorn. Sadness has followed him . . . has pursued him . . . *And it has changed his eyes:* and she saw them to be even gloomier, duller, than when she saw them at the thanksgiving festival, with the hair about his face much wilder, bushier than that atop his head, with his lips no longer pink and wet like moist kola, but dry and gray and cracked.

And they cracked again as his mouth stretched open—Ụzọdị feeling uneasy that they had violated Ichulu's creed, traversing the border between free and slave to come to the Place of Osu—wanting to chastise them for disobeying a law that would ensure both a beating and exile. But he did not do it. He turned to Ijeọma with gratitude overtaking his dark red eyes, and kissed her on her forehead; and turned to Chinwe, and kissed hers, too.

"You have put yourselves in trouble by coming here," Ụzọdị said.

"We desired to come," said Chinwe. "Ijeọma wanted to see you!"

"I wanted to see her, too," he said, kissing Ijeọma's head once more. "Let us go. I will take you to where I live."

They followed him and watched him move. His way of moving had not changed: it was as calm and measured as it once was. And Ijeọma began believing that beneath the walls of his brawny frame, Ụzọdị was who Ụzọdị had been: his chi had remained within him. Though she wondered at the cause for his body's change, and feared it somewhat—wondering if the curse of osu had truly changed his being.

She trembled from the thought as she followed him inside his home. It was a small home, made with crumbling clay and discolored palm leaves. Its color was dull, paler than a dead goat's tongue. And she saw that Ụzọdị was not only an outcast, but a poor man, too; he did not have very much in his little home. There were no mats, no pots, no art; and Ijeọma wondered if he tilled the earth relentlessly to erase the presence of such poverty—looking through the black of his eyes—wondering if that was why his body had become what it had become.

"Ijeọma, you now see how I live," Ụzọdị said, reading the signs she did not sign. "You have seen it. *I am an osu now.* The one who was to earn titles of chief and restore honor to our family is now an outcast to those in Ichulu. Every child that I conceive will be a slave. There is no hope for a man like me. So I farm. I farm fifty rows of yam because what am I to do? I will never be remembered in Ichulu as anything . . . not a hunter, a chief, or an elder . . . but if anybody were to come to this land of outcasts, and see my rows of yam, they would know that a powerful man has lived here."

Ijeọma looked at Ụzọdị. She saw the way he rubbed his dry arms, up and down, up and down, the breathy sounds of it whispering those things he could not say. And Ijeọma began to sign how sorry she was that he could not return to the village; and she began to sign how sorry she was that he would never become a chief or an elder. And she was going to sign how sorry she was for being a reason he was sent to Amalike, when Nwabụeze, one of the eight emissaries, walked into Ụzọdị's home.

"Chei! What are my eyes seeing?" said Nwabụeze. "Ụzọdị, you did not tell me that these people were coming. What are the two of you doing here?"

"Nwabụeze, keep your calm. They are only small children."

"Lie! Was it not this small girl who put us in the hand of our enemies? Is it not because of her that we are here? And this one . . . What is your name?"

"It is Chinwe."

"Yes, this Chinwe, she must be a fool if she thinks she can simply enter the home of an osu without punishment."

"Nwabụeze, friend of mine, you know that the story is not as you say. Many things happened that even the great Igbokwe could not understand. Now, do not give my kin trouble . . . for if a person attacks a child, they attack all to whom that child belongs."

"Ụzọdị, you are not an elder or a dịbịa! I do not want your proverbs! I only came to your home so that I could collect the snuff that I forgot here yesterday."

"It is there," said Ụzọdị, pointing to a small pouch sitting against a wall and watching Nwabụeze walk toward it and collect it.

"I will return to see you," said Nwabụeze as he left Ụzọdị—saying nothing to Ijeọma and Chinwe; ignoring the westward flying birds singing toward Ichulu.

"Do not heed your ears to him," Ụzọdị said. "None of this is because of you, Ijeọma."

Ijeọma did not sign any signs, believing within her chi that she was a culprit, believing that she was to be blamed, for everything, she was to be blamed; that all which had failed, had failed because of her; because she was mute, worthless, as Ọfọdile had said.

"I am not an osu because of you. *Do you hear me?* Or are *you* the person who cursed yourself and made yourself a mute? It is nonsense!"

Ijeọma nodded three times. Ijeọma nodded yes, hoping to believe him, hoping not to be the cause of his fiery voice.

"Nwabụeze is always talking and talking and talking," Ụzọdị said. "He is angry because he has not learned to live with his wife."

"Nwabụeze has married?" Chinwe said.

"Yes, he has married an osu woman . . . and he keeps giving her trouble, because he has not accepted that this woman is not from Ichulu. His wife does not live as Ichulu lives. She is from the Place of Osu, and so lives as though she were a cloud, or the wind. Though I believe Nwabụeze will learn. He will learn, even, how to shut his wide mouth."

Ụzọdị saw the girls laughing, and began laughing himself—feeling as if he were traveling to a different day, one where he was not enslaved, one where he would always believe that Ijeọma loved him—calling it love if she left the compound of the one called her father to find him.

"Ijeọma, does your mother know you are here?

Ijeọma nodded her head twice.

"Do you know the kind of trouble you will see when she discovers you have visited the Place of Osu? And your father . . . he will give you a serious beating."

It is not my concern, Ijeọma signed.

"She loves you, Ụzọdị. She loves you more than she fears punishment. She loves you, and that is why we are here."

"Ijeọma . . . I love you, too."

Ijeọma smiled at him, remembering her memories, shattering the lie that the person before her was not Ụzọdị and wondering why she had believed the lie at all. He was not the Ụzọdị of yesterday, thin and plain and youthful; and then she remembered—yesterday is not the king of truth; yesterday has its lies. And she looked at him—seeing beauty and life, both from Ichulu, both from outside of it—seeing him—and not looking elsewhere, even as Ụzọdị looked through the black of her eyes.

"Ijeọma, I want you and Chinwe to visit me when you want to visit me. You can even call this small obi of mine your home. But I do not want you to be punished by anyone in Ichulu because you have come to see me. What lie did you lie to leave the compound of your fathers?"

"We told our mothers we were going to fetch water for the compound."

"That was not a clever lie. It does not take this kind of time to fetch water."

Ijeọma and Chinwe both sighed, knowing that their parents would not believe their words.

"Here is what you can do. Break your water pots and tell your mothers that you feared coming home because they were broken. That will keep your word good."

"We will do that," said Chinwe.

"You must now go because I do not want your mothers and fathers to begin looking for you. You have already taken much time to arrive at this place, and it will take you time to return."

Ijeọma agreed, pointing to her heart, then to her mouth.

"And when you come again, tell your mothers that you are going to care for Nwabụeze's grandmother, Mgbeke. She lives in the compound of Nwabụeze's father. She is very old and her memory has left her. Do you see? Tell your mothers and fathers that you are going to take care of Mgbeke. Then go to her house and care for her for a short time, so that your word is good. Mgbeke will not know when you have departed because her memory is lost. Only come on the day of Nkwọ because that is when Nwabụeze's father travels north, leaving Mgbeke with her chi."

The girls nodded, letting Ụzọdị know that they both understood.

"That is what we will do!" Chinwe said.

"It is good. Now you must go. I believe that your mothers are already searching Ichulu for you."

The girls agreed, nodding their heads, and leaving Ụzọdị with smiles and assured farewells. They moved quickly, running down the path and cutting through the Forest of Nta, knowing that Ụzọdị was right in saying that Nnenna and Mgboye would not believe that they had only fetched water. So they broke their water pots as he told them to do—letting the water of Idemili spread across the dry earth of the Forest of Nta. And once they left the forest and returned to Ichulu, and the roads leading to the compounds of the ones called their fathers no longer stretched together, they left each other with assured farewells.

And Ijeọma walked atop the yielding path on her own, then walked through the mouth of Ọfọdile's compound. It was silent. Only the goats and chickens seemed to be in her company. She walked around Ọfọdile's obi; and saw the burning firewood; and saw the black pots sitting atop them; and knew that Nnenna was cooking. And she lamented that she had returned when Anyanwụ was west of Idemili—nearly tucked beneath the brim of the glistening river.

"Ijeọma. Where have you been?"

Nnenna was coming around the obi with logs of firewood mounted atop her head; and she saw Ijeọma signing to her, that her water pot had broken and that she was afraid to return home after breaking it, because she did not want to be punished.

"Ijeọma. It does not concern me if you have broken ten water pots. I can make one hundred more with these hands of mine. I have told you many times to come to the home of your mother even if the world is at war. I was here cooking ọgbọnọ soup without my Ada to help me."

Ijeọma nodded three times.

"Where did you and Chinwe go *after* you broke your pots?"

Ijeọma pretended not to have heard the question.

"Ijeọma, have you lost your hearing? Answer me. Where did you go after you broke your water pot?"

The compound of Chinwe's father, Ijeọma signed.

She saw Nnenna grin, and did not know what it could mean—considering that her smile could now have many meanings: joy at her new friendship, satisfaction with her independence, memories of their secret in the Evil Forest. Ijeọma did not know, and she looked closely at the one called her mother—watching as Nnenna began stirring the large pot of soup.

"Ijeọma, when I was young like you I played with a girl named Yọbachukwu . . . I would call her Yọba and she called me Nne, and everybody thought that we were sisters, from one mother and one father."

Where is she? Why have I not seen her, Ijeọma signed.

Nnenna's eyes watched the bubbling soup, not needing to discern Ijeọma's signs.

"She found a lover. She found a lover, and he gave Yọba a baby before giving Yọba's father a dowry. It was an abomination, and they banished her from the village."

Nnenna stopped stirring the soup, and turned to her daughter, gazing at her fearfully.

"Every day I see you, Ijeọma. You are becoming more and more like a woman. Your eyes have lost their apple shape; they are now narrow—so I must warn you. Never give to a man that which you cannot retrieve. You must be a woman of sense, not one that runs about like a fool because she wants to fornicate. You are my Ada. Remember that you have a mother, one whose greatest hatred is against those who abandon integrity. I am the one who carried you in my body. Never disgrace these breasts you have suckled."

Ijeọma swallowed the saliva rising behind her lips, and listened to Nnenna—now knowing that she considered her to be like a woman, and trusted her with womanly things. And she stood before her, not wanting to defile this trust, not wanting to make it the kind that could rot, the kind she sometimes saw between Nnenna and Ọfọdile; but wanting to keep it, and have it turn into greater secrets and finer sensibilities. But then her heart remembered: it loved Ụzọdị; and she told the one called her mother that she and Chinwe would be taking care of Mgbeke on Nkwọ days, and was not surprised when Nnenna said it was a beautiful thing for her and Chinwe to learn from the elderly, and not to treat them as outcasts.

She smiled. And Nnenna smiled, too; and she kissed the one called her mother, then took from her hands the stirrer and began mixing the bitter leaves, and crayfish, and palm oil in the boiling ọgbọnọ soup and watched a large bubble—expanding—in the pot—pop, from the fire beneath it.

DIARY ENTRY #919   31 JANUARY 2000

Chukwu, tell me what is true? Please, whisper it in my ear. Is it not I who has come from a village that murdered its own, one which declared those murders as being in the name of a god? And from that village, did I not learn that a person can be told NEVER to walk upon the land into which they were born? This, after Uzodi put his life in danger to protect the village from the greatest calamity it knew. They discarded him like filth, threw him away like trash! Even to be born into the village with teeth, simple, small, and straight, meant death; then saving Jekwu meant death; then loving him meant death.

Then Amalike, AMALIKE, who has held so many of us as prisoners, with many others disappearing as though they had never existed. They beat and burned me as a child, and now I witness the same horror as they desecrate another set of young ones. In the name of Jesus, is what they are declaring, in the name of another god. Yet, somehow, they have read through ink and paper to see nothing except nothing, and make the smallest of children prisoners and slaves by the misapprehension of their holy bibles.

Chukwu what is true? Tell me what is true. For whether it is in Ichulu or whether it is in Amalike I see falsehood, so much falsehood, leading us all into suffering and death. It is as if the one who commits them has no sense that he has killed another, as another will have killed him by his very sensibility. For if I tell a child, "You will not eat," that child would die within the night. And if that child dies, what recourse will I have to her ancestors? And if I speak to a child crassly, that child will not know of the joy of the Most Supreme. And what recourse will I have to you, Chukwu?

Then what is true? Are you true, Chukwu? I learned of you from the place of an error-ridden Ichulu. Are you a lie like the other lies? For I must say of what is keeping me from disowning you as my god is the simple joy which comes when I am risen to the sky

5.

ON NKWỌ DAY, ỌFỌDILE DID NOT SPEAK to the one called his daughter. Things had become as they had been when she had lost her voice. He heard many in Ichulu say that Ọfọdile's household should be sent to the Evil Forest if Anị was not truly dead; that Ọfọdile had produced a child that threatened Ichulu's prosperity; that Ọfọdile's words were no longer good—that he no longer does what he says. And he blamed Ijeọma for it all—not wanting to speak to a mute and the murderer of a god, hating that she kept flying in the market square and in his compound—flying even in the middle of Idemili while the village children bathed; and he swore that he would fix her, taking her each day to Igbokwe's compound, hoping that the dịbịa's medicine could cure her so that one day he would earn a title.

But Ijeọma, too, was silent—no longer hoping for Ọfọdile to love her, but wanting instead for him to remember Chukwu—and the vastness of the Most Supreme. She prayed for him to remember it since she was told that

Chukwu had taken her to be Chukwu's own. And she walked through the foggy path—knowing that she was given a vision, a vision greater than the people who wanted her removed from the village—greater even than Nnenna, and Chinwe, and Ụzọdị. She knew her purpose to be true, and examined that truth thoroughly—like the lines from a new tale or the patterns on a mottled butterfly; examining it—until the labor of her mind found new ease.

And she remembered Igbokwe, and she believed that in all of Ichulu Igbokwe most understood the gifts Chukwu had given her. While the people of Ichulu worshipped Idemili and the other gods of the pantheon, she and Igbokwe gave what they could give to the Most Supreme. She smiled—when she remembered the prayers he taught her—prayers that he prayed to Chukwu, prayers that she prayed every night, giving thanks to Chukwu, giving thanks to Chineke, giving thanks to her chi in the warmth of Nnenna's red-clay home, reciting those words the dịbịa had given her: "If the word of Chukwu is not good, then whose word is good? Who does one believe? Who can one believe," mouthing the prayer, over and again, as the dịbịa asked her to remove her rappa—then traced her nakedness with his thin, dark fingers—breathing warm breaths as he searched for the message of the gods.

And as she felt Igbokwe's touch that Nkwọ day, on the day she planned to visit Ụzọdị, she began thinking of the words spoken at the thanksgiving festival, remembering the challenge of the one called osu—the one who demanded that Ichulu name the god to whom they were bound. If Chukwu has killed Anị, Ijeọma thought, perhaps the gods enslaving Ụzọdị, and the seven others, have also died.

Return them, Ijeọma signed to Igbokwe.

"Who?"

Ijeọma brushed her fingers against her hair.

"I cannot."

Why?

"Because I do not know where Amalike gets their power. It is dangerous."

No. Return them—return them.

"I cannot."

You must!

"I cannot."

You must!

"Ijeọma . . ."

Suddenly Ijeọma's body began to ache; her head spun wildly; her stomach began quaking, as if filled with tumbling stones.

Return them—return them!

Her body shook again, her legs vibrating as if filled with seeds from the ụyọ; her eyes lost their focus; her stomach rumbled as if holding the mighty waterspouts of Idemili.

And then she saw the blood—moving down the inside of her thighs, and then dropping—leaking onto the earth of Igbokwe's obi; she watched it, placidly; looking for words, one at a time, to name what she was seeing: *injury*, she thought, *who has injured me*, she thought, *sacrifices for the gods, a sacrifice for Chukwu . . . inside of me*; she faced Igbokwe, then turned her eyes and saw the blood gathering atop the earth like palm oil, knowing that it would continue falling until the trickling against her thighs had stopped.

"My daughter can now bear this village children."

She looked at him again.

"That is what the blood is telling you, Ijeọma. You can now have a child."

Her eyes began fluttering—not knowing the child—or its name—or whether it would have teeth or talk or fly like me; who will be the father—or who will be my husband—and if our child will have a chi—or ichi, and how long their marks would go—or would they come from the gods—from the good word of the Most Supreme—

"Ijeọma, Ijeọma. There is nothing that can happen in your life without Chukwu first permitting it. Chineke has brought you to womanhood . . . Do not fear it. Do not mourn it. You, my child, will become a mother of this village; and your children will bless you, just as you will bless them."

Ijeọma smiled at the dịbịa so that he would know that she believed his words; then she sat with her back along the obi's walls—watching as Igbokwe left his obi and returned with a mound of orange earth in his left hand, and a cluster of broad leaves in the other. Her heart was pulled by an unnamed heaviness, a heaviness which had her believe that she was to be blamed for the bleeding—seeing Igbokwe covering the blood while feeling the weight still: gloomy, shadows from a growing doubt, wanting to take the blood with her and not abandon it there on the floor, beneath the orange earth. And Igbokwe gave her the leaves—and told her to wipe herself—and place some in her garments; and she obeyed—placing the leaves firmly in her garments, then collecting her rappa from Igbokwe—to join him in meeting Ọfọdile outside.

"Has she been cured?" Ọfọdile said.

"We have already known the answer," said Igbokwe—while thinking of telling Ọfọdile that Ijeọma had begun to menstruate as he watched them both turn and leave. Her entrance into womanhood would make him more hateful, he thought; so he chose not to follow him or tell him anything, but told Nnenna of what had happened later that day. And when he did, he watched her throw herself into her own excitements. "The time has come!" Nnenna said. "My daughter is now a woman!" Nnenna said. "Let us praise Idemili!" she bellowed over and again. "Let my family praise Idemili!"

And after being hugged by Nnenna incessantly, Ijeọma met Chinwe at Nwagụ's compound. It was one of the largest in Ichulu, bearing within it twelve red-clay homes: five homes for each of Nwagụ's five wives, homes for the ones called his children and the one called his mother, an obi, and spares for visitors, and storage—all of which came from him being a titled man.

"Friend of mine!" shouted Chinwe.

Friend of mine! Ijeọma signed by tapping her wrist, then her eye.

They embraced—eager to be with each other—eager to begin their journey again to the Place of Osu.

Have you told your mother of Mgbeke? Ijeọma signed.

"I have told her. Let us go."

Machete?

Chinwe nodded, and pointed to the wooden handle protruding from her knotted rappa. Ijeọma smiled as they both left Nwagụ's compound and traveled to the compound of Nwabụeze's father. It was very close to them—five compounds from where they stood—and emerged along the orange path leading to the market square. Upon entering it, they saw Mgbeke—lying flat atop the compound's earth, not reacting to their presence—but watched her eyes: gray, and dimly lit, as she lay at the mouth of her red-clay home with fat flies sitting on her yellow-toned skin.

"Who has come? Who has come to watch me die?" Mgbeke said—within a whisper.

"Our mother, it is us . . . Chinwe, the daughter of Nwagụ, and Ijeọma, the daughter of Ọfọdile."

"Ehhhh-eh. The daughter of Nwakaibie, and the daughter of Ekwueme, have come to watch me die. You think because I am old, I do not remember? I was present when your mothers gave birth to you . . . Have you not brought goat meat for me to eat?"

"Our mother, we do not have meat," said Chinwe as she moved closer to Mgbeke to better hear her words. "We came to care for you."

"Who is that talking? I said who is that? Who is speaking to my mother?"

"Who is that? Who has come to watch me die?" Mgbeke said.

"Our father," Chinwe said, "it is us; Chinwe, the daughter of Nwagụ, and Ijeọma . . . the daughter of Ọfọdile."

"Children of my mother, why have you come?" asked Nwabụeze's father, as his eyes rolled softly with the wind.

"We came to care for our mother," Chinwe said.

"Because of what?"

"Because we were told that it is a beautiful thing."

"That is well . . . I am traveling north to Etuọdị today, and I usually leave her with her chi . . ."

Nwabụeze's father looked toward Mgbeke as he spoke and saw that her illness was worsening, and that she could benefit from the help of Ijeọma and Chinwe.

"Mother of mine," he said, "I am going to Etuọdị . . . Ijeọma and Chinwe will care of you."

"Why?"

"I know you have always cared for yourself . . . but today the children will care for you."

"Who are you," she said, looking at the girls.

"They are our daughters," said Nwabụeze's father.

"Who has come to watch me die . . ."

"Do not be afraid, Ijeọma and Chinwe. She forgets what is happening because her memory is sick. Care for her as you can."

The girls nodded twice and watched Nwabụeze's father leave his compound. And Ijeọma saw that he still walked as confidently as the other men in Ichulu; and wondered if he mourned the loss of Nwabụeze as an outcast; and wondered the same of Mgbeke, when she turned to face her—watching her lie on the earth—wondering, if Mgbeke bled, in the way she had, that morning, in Igbokwe's obi.

Suddenly there were knocks behind her; and Ijeọma turned to see two rams running into each other's heads. She believed they were finished when the white rams had turned again, huffing beneath their tired breaths; but the two rushed again, colliding, turning, then colliding again, turning and colliding, over and again; until the rams soon enclosed themselves—following each other, head to rear, head to rear—forming engraved circles with their pattering steps.

"How much time should we remain here?" Chinwe said.

Let us feed Mgbeke, Ijeọma quickly signed, believing the quickness came from the dictates of her chi.

"What should we give her?"

Ijeọma signed for the cashew tree on the path to the compound.

"I have heard."

Chinwe ran from the compound and returned to the path where the cashew tree was swaying. She grabbed the handle of the machete at her waist and pulled out the hidden blade—knowing that she was not allowed to climb the trees in the village and pluck the fat, maroon-colored fruit at the top. Such allowances belonged to the boys and to the men. So she settled for the greener fruit on the lower branches and cut two branches down with the machete's blade before quickly returning to the compound of Nwabụeze's father.

"Here they are," Chinwe said.

Ijeọma nodded three times, then removed five of the cashew fruit from the first branch and placed them in front of Mgbeke with a smile, signing for her to eat. And she saw the elderly woman take one fruit and softly devour it—eating quietly, as Ijeọma plucked more fruit from the second branch and placed them by Mgbeke's hands.

"Let us go, Ijeọma," said Chinwe.

What of Mgbeke?

"We are only here so that our word is good to our mothers and fathers. We must go to Ụzọdị quickly."

Ijeọma knew within herself that she was to stay longer—that her chi had obeyed Chukwu's words: to stay longer and nurse Mgbeke. But she nodded three times and followed Chinwe—leaving with a piercing heaviness.

"My daughters, where are you going?"

"Our mother we must go," Chinwe said.

"Who has come to watch me die?"

And the girls did not answer but left the elderly woman with the fruit—wanting to believe that she would not recognize their absence. They traveled slightly northward, toward the market square, then eastward, and soon they were again in the Forest of Nta. And as Chinwe swung the machete against the interlocking branches, Ijeọma placed a finger on her thigh, searching for any residue of blood from the morning. There was none. And she took her hands and rubbed her stomach—pushing it to see if there was more pain hiding, or if her stomach would rumble again. It was quiet. But she thought it would return, a thought both she and her chi could not carry; so she turned to Chinwe, and tapped on Chinwe's shoulder.

"Ijeọma, what is it?"

She signed for blood. She signed for blood leaving the space between her legs, and Chinwe understood.

"You are becoming a woman," Chinwe said.

I do not like the blood, she signed.

"Yes, the blood may seem bad, but anyone with sense knows that it is a beautiful thing."

Why?

"When was the last time you saw blood? Was it not when someone was injured and hurt or crying? This one is not of the same kind. This blood is for jubilation—some women, the very, very old, pray for it; some dance when it finally comes. It is blood which the strength of our bodies can know, and every elder in Ichulu honors it."

Ijeọma looked around her—wondering if the stones and trees would agree with her friend—wondering if they would give her those secrets every woman in Ichulu seemed to be keeping; when they would say, "This is not for children," or "Return to your sleep," when they would share those secrets that made their ways seem mature. She thought of them, and wondered if that was why they bathed at a separate time from the children in Idemili, and if that was why they argued with the ones called their husbands—loudly, loudly, then softly—retelling their secrets in the nighttime, between the firm walls of red-clay obis.

What else will come? Ijeọma signed.

"You will grow breasts like those of your mother, and hair will sprout from your body."

I already have hair, Ijeọma signed, pointing to her head.

Chinwe smiled, and loosened the knot of her rappa—unwrapping the cloth from around her legs. And Ijeọma now saw where the hairs would grow, and became nervous and unsure of where she was going—turning her face from Chinwe's body—understanding that Chinwe's hairs and breasts and her own bleeding were signs of womanhood, and trusting, with hope, that she would be guided through them all, and welcomed as a woman of the truest kind.

What of the other girls, Ijeọma signed.

"Whom do you mean?"

The ones from the thanksgiving festival in the market square.

"They know of the bleeding, too. Many of their bodies have already begun changing . . . But why do you ask of them?"

Ijeọma nodded three times, too embarrassed to tell Chinwe of her shame, as she remembered the girls laughing at her atop the market square's hill; too afraid to ask Chinwe why she had befriended them, when they had treated her with such cruelty. She simply nodded three times, then nodded three times again, promising herself that Chinwe was a good friend, promising—because of Chinwe's kindness—because why else . . . she is here, is she not? because of what else—leaving Chinwe with a grin, then a smile.

They continued to cut through the path as Ijeọma doubted quietly, and soon they again found themselves in the Place of Osu.

"You, are you the kin of Ụzọdị?" a person said—moving toward Ijeọma, after rushing from their home—carrying a dead fowl in their hand.

Ijeọma nodded three times as Chinwe answered, "Yes."

"We did not know who you were . . . when you came before. And why were you being so fearful then? Was someone chasing you?"

Ijeọma and Chinwe both looked at each other, nervously, shamefully.

"I saw you flying in the market square when I went to support the protest of my siblings, but I did not recognize your face because you were so high in Igwe . . . I wanted to speak to you when you descended, but when that little child fell, the market square became too wild."

"We thank you," Chinwe said, as Ijeọma sighed from the thoughts of Nnamdị's accident—wanting dark clouds to hover and consume her.

"It is well, children of my mother. My name is Chika, and these ones . . ."

Chika waved their arms—bending them in the direction of their clay home—until four small children appeared.

"These ones are the ones with whom we grow. All of you," Chika said, kneeling beside the four little ones, "whenever you see these girls—welcome them. They are beautiful just as you are beautiful. Have you heard?"

"We have heard," the four little ones said.

"And this fowl . . . we sent it away for you, with our machete. We use our tools to send the animals away, when the waters begin speaking their names. This one is Iro. It is for you."

"Thank you," Chinwe said, "but we cannot—"

"Know that you have died," said the youngest of the four little ones. "Anyone who resides in the Place of Osu has died."

Chika saw through the black of their youngest child's eyes before standing and hugging Ijeọma and Chinwe—keeping the fowl named Iro, and praying for Ijeọma and Chinwe's protection. And they watched the girls continue toward Ụzọdị, as more people greeted and welcomed them on the path to Ụzọdị's home, having learned who the girls were; the girls now recognized that the people now looking at them looked with no maliciousness, receiving smiles sent brightly toward them—filling them with a peace they had denied themselves when first visiting the Place of Osu.

And when they finally arrived, Ijeọma and Chinwe saw Ụzọdị and Nwabụeze sitting in front of Ụzọdị's clay home; and they soon saw Ụzọdị stand then greet them with an embrace—as Nwabụeze scoffed at the sight of them, hearing him wish they had not come.

"Ụzọdị, I must go. I do not want to mingle with these freeborn children."

"Nwabụeze, friend of mine, dance the dance of the Place of Osu. Why not stay?"

"Stay for what?"

"Friend of mine, do you not know that these girls have visited your grandmother?"

Nwabụeze turned to Ijeọma.

"Is it true?" he asked.

Ijeọma nodded three times.

"How is Mgbeke?"

"She can remember things from long ago," said Chinwe, "but she cannot remember the things of today."

Nwabụeze fell silent, his eyes wandering toward the earth, his legs weakly leading him inside Ụzọdị's clay home.

"Have you eaten?" Ụzọdị asked Ijeọma.

Ijeọma nodded twice. Ijeọma nodded no.

"Then you must eat with me."

Ụzọdị led the girls into his clay home. Then he lifted a bushel of yellow garden eggs and a bowl of water resting on an iron table. After washing his hands and sharing the bowl with the girls, they began eating the eggs— chewing them quietly.

"Ụzọdị . . . I want to question you with a question," Chinwe said.

"What is the question?"

"When you went to Amalike, to ask them to lift the curses, how did you speak to them?"

Ijeọma flashed her eyes toward Chinwe—wanting her to quickly close her mouth.

"What are you saying," said Ụzọdị.

"Someone told me that the people of Amalike do not speak like the people of Ichulu. I wanted to know the difference, but they did not tell me."

Ijeọma's eyes grew more severe, and she began signing for Chinwe to stop speaking when Ụzọdị waved his hand.

"There is no trouble, Ijeọma. Amalike has given me many nightmares, but I can still speak of it . . . I spoke to them kindly, Chinwe. They spoke Igbo like us . . . except for the obi's gateman. I had to speak to him in *English*."

"Engurrish?"

"*English*. You know it. It is the language they have told us never to speak again."

Chinwe nodded, as did Ijeọma, who now believed Ụzọdị was unbothered by the question, so began pointing to her mouth and ear, then to her left eye.

"How do they call it?" asked Ụzọdị.

Ijeọma nodded three times.

"They call it *eye*."

Eye . . . *eye* . . . It was a sound that she had not heard before. *Eye*, she thought, what is a word that is like it? Ijeọma could think of none.

"How did you learn English?"

"My father taught me, and his father taught him. When the white man came to Ichulu, our grandfather learned English in their schools before the Igbokwe of that time destroyed—"

"My grandmother is dying!" Nwabụeze said, tears falling flatly from his eyes. "My grandmother is dying and I am in exile! And these wicked, foolish men of Ichulu are preventing me from seeing her?"

They are afraid, Ijeọma quickly signed, then heard as Ụzọdị began interpreting her words to Nwabụeze.

"What are you saying," Nwabụeze said.

"Igbokwe is afraid of Amalike," Ụzọdị said in translation.

"Why?" said Nwabụeze.

"Igbokwe does not know how Amalike overpowered the medicine used for Ichulu's protection."

"Coward!" said Nwabụeze, "Igbokwe is a coward!"

"He is a coward," Ụzọdị said as he turned his gaze to Ijeọma. "When you return to Ichulu, tell Igbokwe that I will curse him. I no longer care for his power. My chi has power it has learned."

Ijeọma fell silent at the threat—knowing Ụzọdị held his words with high conviction, leaving the Place of Osu carrying their weight—feeling them shift her faith in Igbokwe's wisdom. Her journey back to Ichulu was a silent one. No signs were signed to Chinwe to say anything of Ụzọdị's words or of returning to the Place of Osu when Nkwọ morning came again. She was afraid, fearing the audacity of it—carrying a threat for the great dịbịa of Ichulu, a threat that came from the one called her kin. And she feared, too, the response Igbokwe would give, praying to her chi to cleanse her memory of Ụzọdị's words—entering Ọfọdile's compound so unsettled by it all, she did not know Nnenna had been waiting.

"Ijeọma . . . I do not know where you have been. And I do not care to know. I see now that you are becoming a woman. You have become bold, you are keeping secrets . . . I will not ask where you have been, even though I know that you were not with Mgbeke. And I will not fight it. Ijeọma, I will not fight. You are no longer the daughter of yesterday. You are becoming a woman, a woman who even Chukwu has taken."

Ijeọma kept silent, looking at Nnenna as Nnenna looked through the black of her eyes.

"Be certain that your father does not see you."

Nnenna entered her home to tend to Cheluchi, and Ijeọma was left with her chi in the open compound, bearing the shame of being exposed—wishing she could tell Nnenna that her accusations were unfounded, yet suppressing a delight in the admittance to her knowing things of which Nnenna did not know.

Four days passed, and Nkwọ came again. Four consultations passed, and Ijeọma could not tell Igbokwe that Uzọdị would curse him. She only informed the dịbịa, over and again, that she wanted Uzọdị and Nwabụeze returned to Ichulu; and when her imploring was denied, she, too, felt the temptation to accuse Igbokwe of cowardice.

She met with Chinwe, and after cutting through the Forest of Nta once more—hearing whispers in the wind, which they thought were masquerades—the girls found themselves in the Place of Osu. And when they arrived, they were greeted fondly by those gathering around them—hearing, "How are you, you daughters of Chukwu," as each one of them erupted with laughter and with smiles, sharing a brightness that made the sun seem small; holding community; bearing one another; as nobody was left unwelcomed.

And after eating the pounded yam and ọgbọnọ soup that they had cooked throughout the day, and drinking small cups of palms wine, night fell; and Ijeọma and Chinwe laid atop the open earth—resting with the children with whom they had eaten as the moon glowed more thoroughly than the smoke from a sacrifice.

"Do you want to hear a story," Uzọdị said.

The children immediately lifted themselves, screaming, "Yes! Yes!" as Ijeọma nodded excitedly, remembering how much she loved Uzọdị's tales.

"Then I will tell you a story of how Tortoise received its shell."

They suddenly fell silent, and waited for Uzọdị to begin.

"When Chineke, the God of Creation, was creating the animals of the earth," Ụzọdị began, "Chineke did not know how they should look and what kind of bodies they should be given. Chineke sat for many days asking, 'How should these animals appear to the world? What should their bodily forms be?' One day, Chineke decided to call upon the spirit of each animal to question it and to let its answer determine the kind of body it would have. Chineke first called the spirit of Lion. The formless spirit appeared and Chineke asked it, 'Lion, who do you think that I am?' And Lion said, 'You are Lion, the most powerful being in the world, for you created me.' And Chineke acknowledged Lion's answer . . . and gave Lion a body that wielded much power. Lion's teeth were large and sharp, and Lion's strength was mightier than one hundred wrestlers. Then Chineke summoned the spirit of Snake. The spirit appeared, and Chineke asked . . . 'Snake, who do you think that I am?' And Snake said, 'You are Snake, the most ambitious being in the world, for you created me.' And Chineke acknowledged Snake's answer, and gave Snake a body that could satisfy its ambitious eyes . . . the kind of body which could consume animals larger than Snake by one hundredfold. Chineke continued summoning each animal's spirit, and used their answers to fashion their bodies, but the God of Creation remained dissatisfied. After creating quieter things, like trees and stones, Chineke returned to creating the animals . . . and finally Chineke called upon the spirit of Tortoise. Chineke asked Tortoise, 'Tortoise, who do you think that I am?' And Tortoise paused . . . and Tortoise thought of the question very carefully. Tortoise was thinking and thinking, and believed that it could not truly know who this being was, because the being was the one who created it. So Tortoise cried out, and said, 'You are the one that stands beside me! You are my creator, and I am the created thing!' And Chineke smiled and said, 'Because you have answered well, I will give you a special body. The power of Lion will not overcome it, and the ambitions of Snake will not subdue it. I will give you this shell so that your body will be protected. I will make you shrewd so that your thinking will be clear. And I will give you this memory, so that you will not forget that I, Chineke, created you.' And Chineke gave Tortoise its body, and Tortoise descended upon the earth.

"After living upon the earth for many years, all of the animals built many villages and towns. They had chiefs, elders, even a market square. And after many more years, the animals began asking themselves, 'Who should be our Obi?' Every animal said that they wanted to be Obi, except Tortoise, who was the only one among them who remembered that Chineke was their creator and ruler. Tortoise said, 'None of you can rule me, because Chineke is my creator.' The animals became angry and began threatening Tortoise. But Tortoise, who was very shrewd, knew that the insults were the beginning of violence, and immediately drew its body into its shell. Lion boasted, 'I am the most powerful animal in the land! I will break the shell of Tortoise open!' Lion used its paws, its arms, and its large teeth to try and break the shell, but all of those failed. Finally, Lion decided to use its large head to open the shell—but when Lion hit its head against the shell . . . its own head split open and it died. Snake then said, 'I am the most ambitious animal in the land, surely I will be able to destroy Tortoise.' Snake then opened its mouth, as wide as it was able, and attempted to swallow Tortoise. But Tortoise's shell was so strong that it broke the jaw of Snake, and Snake, too, fell over and died. All the animals who were foolish, by not learning from the errors of Lion and Snake, perished in trying to destroy Tortoise. The wiser animals saw Tortoise with its chi and noticed that its once-smooth shell had become jagged from the attacks of the other animals. And they told Tortoise, 'Tortoise, come out and see what they have done to your shell!' And Tortoise came out; and when Tortoise saw its shell, Tortoise laughed and laughed and said, 'I do not mind these damages, but the rest of you will repay this debt.' The other animals became confused and asked each other, and then asked Tortoise, 'How will we repay you?' But Tortoise laughed . . . Tortoise laughed and laughed, then put its head into its jagged shell."

The children laughed aloud, as did Ijeọma, who began patting her hands against the dark earth and smiling at the wonder of Tortoise's wisdom. She wondered who taught Ụzọdị the story; and so she moved closer to the one called her kin, asking for an answer—then saw him looking through the black of her eyes, saying, "It was my father."

His name was Olisa, and he was a man who had won all the titles a man in Ichulu could win, with the entire village calling him the Great Eagle. Then a time came when he could not stand from his sleeping mat: sickness had entered his legs. For many weeks, he would watch Ezinne—the one called his only wife—enter his obi to feed him and to clean him, even after Igbokwe's bleak pronouncements. She was possessed by their love, was what the people of Ichulu would say, because nobody could understand why Ezinne would enter Olisa's home—cleaning him and feeding him, even when the pink lesions appeared—and the large bumps covered his face and lips, and shut and then sealed his eyes. Nobody could understand their love. And when it was time for the men of Ichulu to fulfill their decision and take their leper chief into the Evil Forest, nobody could understand why Ezinne covered him in her nakedness—swearing upon it, daring any man to touch the Great Eagle—while her breasts pressed against his body. The women were called to peel her from the one called her husband; and the women stayed, too, to shave her head as was done to every new widow. And Olisa was taken into the Evil Forest, and died there six days later.

While the child Ụzọdị lived in Olisa's compound after Ọfọdile had become its steward and had secretly claimed the compound as his own, he would tell Ijeọma that Ichulu should not have treated its Great Eagle like an animal. And now that Ijeọma was reacquainted with the wisdom of Tortoise, amid the exile of the one called her kin, she understood more fully the goodness of Ụzọdị's words; and as it began to rain, she saw beyond the little children removing their clothes and bathing themselves with the falling rain; as she felt Ụzọdị—snatch her—into his arms—then lead her into the refuge of his pale-clay home.

6.

Ọfọdile was in the northern forest, where the hunters go to find their prey, where the village begins its end and Ụmụka speaks its boundary. He was checking his traps when he saw the long—thick chord—emerging from his trap—to his foot, nearly denying that he had caught a python, feeling his stomach turn and fall. He moved closer to examine his trap and found that this one did not have any bitter kola seeds to repel the sacred snake; and he nearly howled—recounting that he was to report this to Igbokwe so that the dibịa could remove his abomination from the village.

"I, will . . . bury . . . it," he said.

And as he spoke, he did. He raised his machete—and cut the long python into many pieces; then began opening the earth with his machete, and with his hands, to bury the mutilated snake.

"Cheeeeeeeiii! Come and see it! Come and see it!"

Ọfọdile did not move. He heard the scream coming from the mouth of the forest—from the path next to the Stone of Anị. He quickly buried the python, and left the forest and his secret, to rush to where the screams were originating from. It was Ngọzi, and she was surrounded by almost all the women of Ichulu—all of them moving toward the market square, singing, over and again:

Ngọzi you are so beautiful, mgbo, mgbo
Ngọzi you are so beautiful, mgbo, mgbo
Whoever chi has appointed, let them rule
You are so beautiful, mgbo, mgbo
Whoever chi has appointed, let them rule
You are so beautiful, mgbo, mgbo

Ọfọdile could see Ngọzi—dancing as if a spirit had taken her, seeing her through the forest's trees—as she held onto the knot of her rappa, not letting it fall onto the earth—not holding any groundnut in her hands. He moved closer, closer, before the crowd had grown larger, seeing then what had caused her joy, seeing her stand from her low, undulating dance to reveal that she was pregnant. And he heard Ichulu break into chant and song; the woman who had not conceived a child carried a stomach larger than a whole melon; the woman who had sacrificed to Anị until she had reached her own impoverishment was now pregnant; the woman who had hidden a secret no longer hid her growing babies.

And Ọfọdile smiled—almost forgetting the abomination he had committed—believing that Ngọzi's pregnancy provided goodness to the word that Anị was dead in the village. He did not know how else to explain the pregnancy of a barren woman when the goddess of earth and fertility was dead; esteem might return to his household, he thought, and his reputation in the village might improve; shame might depart from him; he smiled, and he hoped; though both quickly left him when he saw Ijeọma walking toward the crowd from the east, with the Forest of Nta to her back. He quickly moved to her path—moving through the growing crowd, then standing before a girl whose shifting eyes revealed that she was holding secrets. He grabbed her arm—and pulled her body through the crowd—and through the market square—and down the orange paths—into his empty compound.

"Where were you coming from!"

Ijeọma signed nothing.

"Where were you coming from! *Answer me!*"

She did not sign one thing while looking past his face and into the sky above.

Ọfọdile slapped her. He slapped her, over and again, until her face turned hot and her body began to shiver.

"Lie down," Ọfọdile said, not caring if she obeyed, leaving then returning with a thick branch from his orange tree. He flogged the air—testing the cane's pliability, then flogged the air once more—firmly, assuredly, quickly beginning the same on the back of Ijeọma, beating her, as if it were the cure he was after, beating her as if the blood he saw popping through her skin, healed his anxieties—relishing it—feeling the cane—fit well in his hand, letting the flexing of his arm and chest give him ease. His heart thumped; his mind became excitable, lost in its aggression; he entered into it wildly, readily, with nothing to pull him out—no gasps, no screams—and when the branch from the orange tree cracked—then broke, his rage did also; and he left Ijeọma, in the middle of the compound—still and red as an old rose.

The sun gave her thin lines of heat. The welts gave her more. So she stayed on the ground, fearing those heats would swell and grow if she moved; turning her head to the earth beside her and seeing specks of blood sinking into its orange, as the sight of them made the welts feel larger, feel deeper, than the river channels feeding the village farms. And she dared not move, not with the many sounds preserved in her head, preserved in the way salt preserves raw meat; and those sounds were not the sounds of the cane against her back, but the sounds of Ọfọdile's beating litany: *bush animal and fool! Ichulu's destroyer! root of this family's shame! thief! title killer! they no longer call me Ekwueme because of you, thief of the titles I would have earned, cause of Nnamdi's impairment, near-assassin to my only son! prostitute for the osu! Ani's poison, you think I do not know you fed Jekwu! deceiver, jeopardizer of the promise I made my brother, did I protect Ụzọdị, animal! flying animal! flying animal that does not talk!*

She lay atop Ọfọdile's compound exposed—back bleeding, with no rappa to cover herself; feeling the ants crawling along her legs, along the line of her buttocks and her back; and she did not move, letting the ants stay and take what they wanted, hearing Nnenna's footsteps, and asking her not to come beside her, not to cover her and ask how she was doing, not to do for her trite things adults proclaimed children needed, not to take from her any more secrets that she owned.

"What have you done to our child!" Nnenna said, breaking into Ọfọdile's obi as he snorted snuff atop his raffia mat.

"Are you now deaf! What have you done to our Ada!"

Ọfọdile remained silent, shaking more snuff out of his container as Nnenna rushed to him—slapping his face over and again, then falling on him—secretly praying to crush him dead.

"Lift, yourself from me!" Ọfọdile said, pushing Nnenna's body away.

"If you are a man, you will tell me, the mother of your children—what our Ada did to be beaten close to death!"

"You bush animal. You come into my home, with foulness, and shit on your mouth. You knew that your Ada, was with the osu!"

"Hear how you speak. You cannot even talk like a man! Yes! Yes, I knew it! I knew it! And what of it? Is she not becoming a woman? Is Chukwu not protecting her?"

"So you support it? You support your disgusting child, running about this village, spoiling my name, and the name of my father?"

"May Chukwu burn your name and the name of all of your fathers! You abomination! You foolish man who wants the love of the world before the love of his own child! Our home is burning. Our home is burning and you do not even see it! You do not even see. Does Ichulu not call me mother of the mute? Do they not call me that? But have I let it kill me! You weak, titleless man! She is my daughter, and my daughter will be free! My daughter will be free, AYY! If you could only speak with her! If you could only speak to her, as you speak to our other children—but if you touch her again, it will be me who will take your life from you . . ."

"You stupid woman! Ijeọma will remain, where I say she will remain."

"You are more foolish than I believed," said Nnenna, unknotting her rappa and tossing it on the floor. "Come and touch our daughter again. Come and try it! But on these, these breasts of mine, on these breasts that nursed your children I swear it! Touch any of our children again, and death will fall on your head!"

Nnenna quickly walked out of Ọfọdile's obi—and with her rappa in her hand, she approached the mouth of her red-clay home, hearing Nnamdị's voice beside Ijeọma's body.

"He will love you one day," she heard Nnamdị saying. "I know that you despise him now. But one day he will love you, and our mother, and Ụzọdị, and everybody again. When I wanted to join you in the sky, and fell hard on the ground and broke my leg, I saw nothing at all. But then someone told me to open my eyes, and I did, and I saw our father doing something which I have never seen. He was crying, Ijeọma. Our father was crying, because he thought he had lost his child . . . *Ijeọma, he loves us.*"

Nnenna watched Nnamdị stand from Ijeọma's side and limp toward her red-clay home. And as he stood beside her, she saw him looking within her eyes—knowing he was seeing them be tired and dim.

"I love you, my father," Nnenna said—as Nnamdị enclosed her within his arms—both unable to say even the smallest word, as Nnenna began weeping terribly.

DIARY ENTRY #964   DATE UNKNOWN

*ofodile you put me in this prison how? how? fathers don't send their
children away fathers don't abandon what chukwu has given them even
when you beat me down until my back tore open i managed to find a way
to understand you i gave you everything that a child can give. i gave you my
heart. was there more i could do?*

*the day my mother told you I could fly you didn't sit with me and talk
with me or ask me what the gods were doing when I gave you your dinner
that day you brushed me away. you told me i did not matter to you without
having to say it. maybe you thought i wasn't worthy of being spoken to. all i
wanted to hear you say was "My Ada I love you."*

*but you are evil. cold-hearted and evil. evil like the pastor who wants
me dead. evil like the gods who condemned me evil like the god who has
abandoned me every time I pray on my knees and offer up my blood and
tears i want to damn all of you. i want to curse all of you, like uzodi willed
himself to curse the dibia i will not do it. but I will not lie and say that
hatred has not taken my heart, to you, to the pastor and his workers, to
chukwu, even to you chukwu.*

*AH! I wish you dead Ofodile! I wish you dead! Every pastor and every
attendant! I pray you burn in the everlasting fire of which you preach!
Chukwu you, Chukwu you are hurting me, you are hurting me so badly
that my wounds, my blood, my pain, my broken heart. They are too much.
I gave you my entire being and you've only ignored me Hatred is taking my
heart Chukwu and your name is close to it*

*Remove me from this cell today! If you are Most Supreme, do it, I want
to be freed today! Today! Today! Free me today! Today! Or else how do
you dare call yourself a god!*

7.

QFQDILE'S COMPOUND HAD FALLEN ASLEEP to a ruptured home and had awoken to a dark and silent morning. Nnenna had left the compound very early to bathe herself in Idemili, and the ones called her children lay quietly on their raffia mats, waiting for the cocks to crow. The chickens tended only to their chicks, and the goats ate their grass wearily; and the silence was then crudely broken by the presence of a rumbling noise.

Nnamdị stood from his mat and hurried toward the noise—boldly, curiously—seeing a man on a vehicle at the mouth of Qfọdile's compound and knowing that he had not seen the man or his vehicle before—one which looked to him like a metal ram. And as Nnamdị began limping toward the unfamiliar, he thought of how he would greet this man—agreeing within himself to smile.

"How is it that you are doing?" Nnamdị said.

"Good morning," the man responded, his Igbo sounding bizarre to Nnamdị; stiff and inflexible, like his metal ram.

"I am looking for a man named Ọfọdile. Does he live here?"

"Yes! He is my father."

"That is fine . . . My name is John. What is your name?"

"My name is Nnamdị."

"Is your father here," John said.

"Yes. He is there in his obi. Follow me, and I will show you where he is."

Nnamdị took John through Ọfọdile's compound, grabbing his right hand and pulling him to the mouth of Ọfọdile's obi.

"Father of mine, a man from another place has come to see you!"

"What is it!" Ọfọdile said, coming out of his obi, thinking of how early in the morning it was.

"How are you, Ọfọdile? My name is—"

"Where are you from?" Ọfọdile said.

"I come from another place," said John, "a place that we call a house of prayer."

"And where is this house of prayer?"

"It is in Amalike."

Ọfọdile widened his eyes—leaving his visitor, then quickly returning with a machete.

"If you do not remove yourself from my compound and my village, I will cut off your head!"

"Please, please . . . listen to me," John said, waving his hands fearfully.

"Do you think I am a man of idle words? Get out, or I will kill you!"

"It concerns Ijeọma! The man who leads the house of prayer knows of Ijeọma and he wants to cure her! He wants to cure her!"

"What!"

"*He can cure her!*"

"What?"

Ọfọdile dropped his machete and looked deeply into the man's eyes, searching for any sincerity—but by the promise of a cure he believed John's word to be good, and he invited him into his obi, watching him enter it with slight hesitation, sitting down timidly and refusing all his offerings, even that of kola.

"What did you, say . . . was your name," Ọfọdile said.

"My name is John . . . and I am a servant to a very powerful man in Amalike."

"What . . . is, the man's name?"

"His name is Innocent Nwosu."

"What? Nwosu? How can, an osu's child . . . be a powerful man . . . in Amalike?"

"Nwosu is a slave to a powerful god, the most powerful god, that cures any illness and answers any prayer. The god's name is *Jesus*, and he is a god that does whatever Nwosu asks."

How is this possible, Ọfọdile asked himself, trying to find meaning in the words of John—trying to understand why this most powerful god had favored an outcast named Nwosu instead of a freeborn?

"He knows about your daughter flying," John said. "He has sent me here to tell you that he can cure her through the power of his god."

"How, will he do . . . it?" asked Ọfọdile. "How will, he cure her?"

"He wants your daughter to come with me, back to the house of prayer . . . and there he will cure her."

Ọfọdile remained silent—thinking of the daily consultations he had been having for more than one year; recalling that Igbokwe himself stated that he did not have the power to stop the flights. Now the gods had presented him with a man whose master guaranteed that he could heal Ijeọma.

"You have spoken, good words Jọn," Ọfọdile said to John. "My people say . . . 'Hot soup, must be eaten slowly.' Return tomorrow . . . and I will answer you."

"That is good, sah!"

"Sah?"

"I wanted to say elder of mine."

The two men stood together, then slapped their hands in rhythms to exchange their farewells. Kola was not broken, but each felt at ease with the other; and when Ọfọdile heard the bold sounds of John's vehicle driving away from his four-home compound, he could not help but wonder at the promise of this foreign god.

On the day that followed, there was no consultation. Ọfọdile left Ijeọma in Nnenna's home and journeyed with his chi to the compound of Igbokwe. He walked through the thin orange paths connecting the compounds of Ichulu, and he arrived at the compound of Igbokwe before the roosters had broken their cry. Ọfọdile could hear the dịbịa singing in his obi, chanting prayers to their holy pantheon; and as he stood at the mouth of his obi, waiting for the singing to end, he could hear the words, from an ancient song, more clearly than he had heard them before:

> Let the man who calls the woman 'fool'
> Forget the name of his Mother.
> Let the woman who calls the man 'fool'
> Forget the name of her Father.
> And let the one who forgets the name of their chi
> Never see the coming Home;
> For if one forgets that they are as the Other
> They have begun to perish.

A rooster crowed, and the singing ended; and when the dịbịa saw his visitor, he bellowed from within his obi, "Ọfọdile! Come and greet me!"

"How are you, Igbokwe?"

"I am well, child of mine . . . Where is Ijeọma?"

"She . . . is not coming."

"What? Who has made that so?"

"Igbokwe, a man came and visited me . . . yesterday. He told me that he knows a man, who will cure Ijeọma."

"Ọfọdile . . . this man who said he can cure Ijeọma, did he tell you the name of her sickness?"

"Igbokwe, what kind of question is that! The girl is flying! That is her sickness!"

"That is what *you* have called it . . . I have told you each day that Chukwu has favored your daughter. You came to me, not because you thought I could stop her flying. On many days I told you I could not stop it. But you brought your daughter to my compound, month to month to month . . . because of your fear—to prevent your hope from dying. Qfǫdile, my child . . . why are you afraid to love this child?"

"Igbokwe, I do not want to hear your nonsense! You have not, been able to heal my child—so I must send her, to this man who promises he will."

"My child . . . I have heard you. Before you remove my daughter from the land of her ancestors, and the outer realms of her chi . . . let me tell you of the dream that has visited me for three weeks. I was in a land with no trees, no grass, only the pale eroded earth like that which came after the flood. And in this land I saw yam, soft and white, falling from the sky. *Yam was falling from the sky,* feeding me in this barren land! Qfǫdile, I have told you of the war between the gods. I have told you of the mighty power wielded by Chukwu. *And I have seen the power of your daughter.* Do you not know that before Ngozi announced her pregnancy in the market square, she came to me and told me of the origins of her pregnancy? She told me that one morning, the morning after lying with her husband, she saw you and Ijeǫma on the path to my compound. She said that she was carrying groundnut, and when she shared some with Ijeǫma, she felt something like fire enter her body and settle in her stomach. Ngozi told me that she felt the fire move the seed of her husband . . . but did not want to tell the village of any of it, even when her bleeding stopped . . . because of the possibility of there being a miscarriage. She did not want any evil befalling your name. Do you not see? *Your daughter is saving this village.* Without Ijeǫma, the flood that came would have destroyed Ichulu; my divinations have told me so. *Do you not see?* Your daughter has done these things because Chukwu has made it so. Keep her where she is. Allow Chukwu to finish what Chukwu has begun. Let those who curse you and speak against you drown in their foolishness . . . because if they do not accept Ijeǫma, they can never be free."

"Igbokwe, I have heard you. And you, have said nothing . . . You cannot cure Ijeǫma."

Igbokwe watched as Ọfọdile turned and left him, knowing that he might never see Ijeọma again, heaving a groan to release his sorrow. He had not understood Ọfọdile's fear. The gods had given the village enough signs, he thought, to make Ijeọma's flight a blessed thing; the infant Jekwu had been saved from the Evil Forest; a woman who could not give birth was now many months pregnant; Ichulu was changing, and Igbokwe believed that nobody should be afraid. Chukwu was protecting the village. The war between the gods had ended—how else could he explain the peace in the village; how could there be a war when the sun, and the rain, and the earth, and the wind all worked with the rest of creation to sustain Ichulu; when the cowrie shells predicted no more floods, or wars, or calamities, but showed the death of a goddess, and the peace of this village? The world was indeed well, and the dịbịa sang his ancient song, hoping it would reach the heart of Ọfọdile.

And as Igbokwe sang into the day—watching Anyanwụ, traveling from east to west toward the undulating god, Idemili—the people of Ichulu continued with their affairs. Nnenna had finished fetching water from Idemili and began returning to Ọfọdile's compound; until she saw the bearded Okoye approaching her, then sliding around her front and back.

"Nne! How is the mother of my future children?"

"Okoye, you are a foolish person!"

"Ahhh, Nne! You know that we were once betrothed when Ichulu sang of our love. Return to me, so that we can enjoy ourselves like in those times."

"Okoye, move from my way; Ọfọdile and I are doing well."

"So he has not told you," Okoye said, looking at Nnenna perplexedly.

"What? What has my husband not told me?"

"Ijeọma..." Okoye said, falling silent, reading Nnenna's eyes—and having them reveal that she did not know of what he was speaking. He held her hand, then felt her quickly remove herself from his grip, feeling then his own moroseness in preparing to tell her of that afternoon.

"Nnenna... some of us saw Ijeọma on a vehicle with a man who is not from Ichulu. He was traveling east. We tried to hold him; but he said that he was sent by Ọfọdile. You know that Ọfọdile and I do not speak, so I gathered the other men, and we went to Igbokwe to consult with him. He told us that Ọfọdile sent Ijeọma to a man who would stop her flying."

Nnenna pushed through Okoye—and began running home—the water pot on her head shattering to pieces as she went—the orange dust behind her heels—rising to Igwe in the heavens; she rushed through the mouth of the compound—and cried, "Ijeọma! Ijeọma!" She cried, "Ada of mine! Ada of mine!" but heard nothing. The compound remained silent, and remained dark—then more silent, until the sun was hidden beneath Idemili—and the children were told their stories beneath the moon.

8.

ONCE THE VEHICLE'S ENGINE CEASED rumbling and John's feet touched the dusty ground, Ijeọma knew it was time to dismount his motorbike. She memorized his paths—believing that if she wanted, she could run from him—and head westward—returning to where she came—leaving this new town to itself; but remembering then—that she could no longer return to Ọfọdile's compound—not wanting to accept that word, nor call it good—shuddering: still despondent and weak—thinking no more of Ọfọdile. She was looking around and about her—searching for the familial, searching all about—believing—she is coming . . . she is coming . . . but there was no face resembling Nnenna's, and she did not want to believe it—continuing her search—waiting for Nnenna's face to appear from within the busy streets of Amalike.

There were people moving through the streets in their vehicles: metal rams and gliding pots—which Ijeọma believed, cooked their foreign clothes—she watched them move on paved roads, and in newly styled hair—seeing no one look down to help her, giving neither recognition nor greeting—believing they mocked and sniggered—Chukwu, please . . . Chukwu, come, please, please . . . but there she was still, in the town of foreign things; in the town which smelled of diesel, with its open sewage filled with thick-green waste, smelling of corpses and sulfur; in the town she felt abandoned, considering those things she was unable to do: no speaking; no signing; no journeying to the river god; nor holding onto Chinwe's palms; no dancing with Chelụchi or resting with Nnenna—keeping her search for the one called her mother, but seeing only vendors selling groundnut and green bananas—hearing only music playing from small shops: no Nnenna, no home—as tears began falling.

"Pastor Nwosu will not like that you are crying. Stop it," John said, "Please, stop it now."

But Ijeọma did not understand him, as her tears continued falling.

"*It is enough Ijeọma; it is enough,*" John said in a hushed Igbo.

But Ijeọma chose not to stop, ignoring the commands of John, which felt as senseless as asking the wild beast Nta not to hunt its prey—or telling those six dead emissaries not to mourn their deaths; she continued crying—yielding tears, and scalding pain—revealing that hope was in jeopardy of leaving her eyes, opening her heart to the morose, to the rejection of her existence, weeping and crying that she was no longer home, and that how could it be that Nnenna did not come, how could it be life, how could it be . . . trying, then punished like a worthless animal, trying to please Chukwu, then beaten like a fleshless rat, how could it be so, working each day to the love the Most Supreme, to love my mother, to love my father, then to be punished with this punishment—weeping as though dying from the fire in her tears.

And John was confused. When adults spoke he thought children obeyed; and at once he realized he had forgotten his own childhood's sensibilities—he chose then to squat next to Ijeọma, and to accept that she would stop crying whenever she would stop crying. He checked his watch for the time, and checked it again; and after two minutes he began watching her wipe her eyes with the back of her left hand, then took that hand and squeezed it softly before leading her inside the church edifice.

They walked into the large cement building, entering first the church sanctuary, seeing its wooden benches aligned in neat rows with its green streamers thrown from one end of the wall to the other, and with its altar adorned in purple linen and a picture bearing a portrait of Jesus the Christ.

"*This is a holy place,*" John said in a hushed Igbo, "*And it should be revered by anyone who enters it.*"

Ijeọma nodded her head three times; Ijeọma nodded yes, but she listened to very little of what John was telling her; and wondered how the face of a human being could remain more still than a corpse—staring at the picture and the person within it—thinking of its long, brown hair as the veil of a masquerade—noticing that as she walked behind John—its gray eyes seemed to follow her, and as they did, she wondered why the head of a white man— lay at the center of the holy place—monitoring it—haunting it like a spirit.

And when she saw the dark rectangles—resting in midair, appearing to her to be vessels—through which she could go to where she wanted, she thought she would pass through them, and reemerge in Ichulu on the other side—staring at their softly dappled corners—expecting their power to transport her to Nnenna's red-clay home.

"We call them *speakers*," John said less quietly in Igbo. "Those are where our voices come out loudly."

And he recalled within himself that Ijeọma was from a foreign place and began explaining all that lay around them: the light fixtures hanging against the church walls, the fans spinning beneath the church ceiling; and as they passed the center of the sanctuary's back wall, he explained the wooden cross that hung upon it.

"Ijeọma, this is the cross of our Lord and Savior Jesus Christ. He died on a cross like this for you and me . . . to save us from our sins. If you believe in His cross you will not perish, but will attain everlasting life. I know you will have questions about what I am saying . . . Do not worry, do not worry at all. The pastor will help you understand and believe."

Ijeoma did not know what John was saying; and did not know the meaning of attaining everlasting life, as if Ichulu did not already have it; and could not understand why a man had died for people who had not asked him to die. She looked at John—knowing his words were strange, feeling each one of them carry her further from Idemili—as she was led out of the church sanctuary and along a set of stairs emerging up to the office of Pastor Nwosu.

"Ijeoma, sit here," John said in English, while pointing to a chair next to the office door. He knocked on the door, and upon hearing a response, he entered the office quickly, leaving Ijeoma to herself. Her body was shaking from the cold; her bare feet—not used to the cool of marble tiles; her arms—not liking the winds of the ceiling fans; and she rejected the smell of Amalike, which smelled neither fresh nor green but bore a strong odor from burning fuels—fuels from the cars she deemed gliding pots, and the metal rams, and the fluttering generators—fuels from many running things, *when will it go*, she thought, *this thing that smells, when will it go*; and she stopped asking and buried her nose inside her green rappa—inhaling what remained of her village, breathing into her rappa deeply—remembering from where each smell had come, seeing the round, black pots—atop Nnenna's firewood—the honey-smelling, honey-colored brown of Igbokwe's palms—the ebbing waters of the god Idemili—filling her deeply—blocking the smells of Amalike, and allowing her to remember home.

Her prayers emerged as she began rocking her body before the pastor's office—praying to many gods for many things—an undivided will, and her belief in the Most Supreme—Nnenna's arrival and Uzodi's, too—please, Chukwu, and my friend Chinwe whom I love: Chukwu, answer—Chineke, answer—so that Cheluchi and Nnamdi may grow to know me—and my mother's heart, may it carry her to this place—may they journey soon—so that tomorrow—he may love me.

"Ijeoma, come," said John in English, opening the office door and beckoning her with his hand.

She rose from the chair and met John at his side; and she could see the pastor rubbing his eyes, then saw his large eyes flickering when he lowered his hands, before covering them with a thing she deduced was for the blind.

"So this is the little girl who is stealing my flock from me," Pastor Nwosu said, while putting on his spectacles. "I have been told that you cannot speak. This, of course, does not surprise me, since the witchcraft of your people is very dark and evil. You should consider yourself lucky that the good Lord only deprived you of one of His many gifts. Tell me, would you like to speak one day?"

"Pastor Nwosu . . ." said John. "She does not . . ."

"I know that she does not understand English! But I will not speak any Igbo to her, and neither will any of you. I'm sure you know that it is against my regulations."

"Yes, yes . . . I do," John said.

"Good," said Pastor Nwosu, inspecting Ijeọma from behind his spectacles—watching her as if disinterested but relishing her appearance as a skinny girl who seemed more nervous than a sinner confessing her sins—believing that the demons living within her were trembling at his authority. And he smiled at her because he wanted her to receive the peace of his Christ—seeing her nodding—as if already touched by the fire that he believed his growing church would deliver.

"Now, Ijeọma . . . I have also heard stories about how you can fly in the air. Tell me, are you a witch or a human being? Are you a demon, or are you human like us?"

Ijeọma did not know how to respond, but from the way the pastor spoke she knew she was asked a question; and she believed it was the kind of question one could not directly answer, like the kinds in old dirges and distant proverbs; and she believed it could not be, not exactly as the two, as he was neither singing nor speaking Igbo; and she believed that she was to sign something in response, then looked upward, and saw his eyes sitting behind his spectacles, more fully than before—knowing they were the kind of eyes which had not brightened in very long, as if they could no longer be surprised or enthused or happy—believing that such eyes saw contempt throughout the world.

The pastor had asked her another question, but she did not answer—carrying fear, not trusting his eyes nor words. She did not know the sounds of

English, and the language appeared aggressive to her—as if it were meant to provoke a war—there is no music in it, she thought, no rhythm to which one could dance—and her eyes began fluttering as she stood by John, knowing only to nod her head when the pastor had finished speaking, hoping that he would finish his speaking soon.

"As far as I am concerned, you are nothing short of a witch," Pastor Nwosu said, "and in the name of Jesus, I will remove every demon ravaging your body so that you will grow into a God-fearing woman. As of now you are a daughter of darkness and a child of evil spirits. When the prayers I have prayed over you have settled, you will surely become a child of God."

The pastor stood from behind his desk and came to where Ijeọma was standing. He laid his right hand atop Ijeọma's head and raised the other into the air.

"John, join me in this prayer."

"Yes! sah!"

"Heavenly Father," the pastor began, "we thank you! for this day, and for all of the blessings you have bestowed upon us thus far. We thank you! for bringing your lost daughter into our care . . . so that we may bring her back to you. We ask that she loosen herself from the grip of Satan! and that she follow the commands of JESUS! I said we ask that Satan leave her, and that JESUS YOUR SON enters her soul! As she partakes in the fruits of Precious Word Ministries may she never hunger! May the enemy never find her! And may the world come to call her a child of God. In the MIGHTY NAME OF JESUS we pray."

"Amen!" said John.

"Now, it is time for Ijeọma to settle in at the Manifestation Quarters. John, go and escort her."

"Yes, sah!"

John removed Ijeọma from the pastor's office, then the church edifice, and led her along the gravel path that led to the Manifestation Quarters. He wondered what Ijeọma was thinking—not knowing that she thought now of the path's unusual lack of color, which bore little resemblance to the warm orange of Ichulu's earth and instead looked as Ichulu did after the terrible storm—with the feeling of the gravel beneath her feet not bearing the smooth of Idemili's river stones; and as she kept walking, she fell from the pain of the rough gravel and cut her leg against its jagged edges, wondering if the wound would now bleed; there was no blood as she felt John lifting her upward and saw him smiling as he put her in his arms—as they began walking again on the gravel path.

Ijeọma nestled in John's arms as he carried her, then looked at him and began examining his features. She thought his nose was stout and wide— and his lips plump and thick, almost like Ụzọdị's—with his face looking as innocent as the infant Jekwu. She liked John, and thanked the gods for making him a kind man; and when the gravel path ended at the mouth of the low, blue bungalow, she knew they had reached the place where they were going. She climbed out of John's arms and looked at the blue house—holding on to John's right hand, seeing the bright blue of the building, the metal bars on the window, the rusty zinc roof sloping downward; and immediately believed that Amalike was a hateful place that could not build a building.

"Ijeọma, this is where you will be staying," said John in English, while leading her along the bungalow's steps.

He used his left hand to try to sign his words, and knew that she understood when she let go of his hand and entered the blue bungalow.

"Remain next to me," John said with a smile. "I am making arrangements for you to stay here in the quarters."

Ijeọma smiled with John's smile, then saw him tapping on the shoulder of a female attendant wearing a pink-checkered dress and wondered why they began whispering to each other when she could not understand their words. She watched the attendant glance past John's shoulder, then look at her with disgust on her lips—and immediately turned her eyes and began staring at the marble floor with a design of tiny blue and black dots, waiting for the two to finish speaking.

"Okay, Ijeọma, it is time for me to leave you," John said. "Be a good girl . . . I will see you soon."

He patted her head, turned toward the doorway, and returned to the gravel path—leaving Ijeọma with the attendant.

"So you are the one who can fly . . ." the attendant said, looking at Ijeọma hatefully. "Let me tell you now, I will not have any of that demonic activity on the premises of this holy church. If I catch you performing any of that witch-craft, I will flog you to pieces. I will beat you silly! Do you understand?"

Ijeọma did not look at the attendant as she spoke; she was entranced by the ground, tracing the pattern on the marble floor with her eyes: the dap-pled black and the dappled blue, crowding atop each other like sleeping gnats, bounded by the deep crevices between each tile. She ignored the harsh tones being spoken at her and watched only the tiles, waiting for the sleeping gnats to fly again from where they came.

And as she heard the attendant's voice still, she thought of John; and wished that John had not left; and remembered how John carried her in his arms; remembering his care; remembering his smile, his advice; the story that he told, the farm, the lie, the new sound: the new word: eye; remember-ing his kindness, his face; wide nostrils, wide lips, his home, his laughter; him playing by Idemili before the sun had set; him saying, "If you whisper into a goat's ears before they die—you will not like the taste of their meat," his love and hope for greater things while being an osu, while having his father dead, his—SLAP—SL-SLAP—SLAP!

"*I said do you understand me,*" the attendant said, while striking and squeezing Ijeọma's face.

"All of my questions require answers! I don't care if you are mute, and I don't care if you cannot understand my language! Once we are done remov-ing these demons from your body, you must understand . . . *stupid child!*"

And the attendant—swiftly raised Ijeọma's head and slapped it again, and began dragging her—through the main corridor of the Manifestation Quarters—without Ijeọma knowing what she had done—believing she had offended the woman, as she raised her own hand to her cheek; feeling the dull heat from the slap, then quickly turning her head; preparing for another strike, but meeting instead the stench of the hallway; and being carried by its smell—odorous, like the Evil Forest, where festering carcasses seized night-time's air.

"This is where you will be staying," the attendant said, as she opened a squeaking door and shoved Ijeọma into a cell. It was a tight space—smaller than the shed where food was stored—with very little light passing within it. She saw rusted iron bars blocking the narrow door, and saw the narrow window appearing across from it—with the ground more seared and stony than that of the forest of Nta.

"When you are tired, sleep on the floor. When you have to ease yourself, use the small bucket. The large bucket is for bathing."

When the attendant shut and locked the barred door, then moved away from the tiny cell: Ijeọma understood. She saw rats scurrying atop the cell floor, one of them slow and heavy and sitting by her foot; she watched it lifting its large body and gnawing at her ankle, tugging at her smooth-dark skin; then she lifted the rat before pushing it through the metal bars of the window—not seeing if it had survived the little fall, and praying it had not—wishing it dead, and wishing for it to become an ancestor to its rat brethren—wishing for it to send them strength and power from the land of spirits, as she prayed: looking toward the black ceiling of her prison cell and asking Chukwu for courage, for the strength to peacefully live in exile—for a stronger devotion to the Most Supreme, and Ụzọdị—what of his loss of freedom, that to be forced from home and become an outcast is a death—and to be forced from home is to be a corpse and a slave.

Old proverbs filled her heart as she prayed for Ụzọdị, praying that he and the other osu would find refuge in Chukwu—that both he and they would one day be free, for Chukwu to show it, reveal it now, Chukwu—and believing a sign was given when the wind blew inward—past the bars, and into the cell—smelling of Ichulu, smelling like the roasted yam Nnenna would cook for the evening meal—smelling like Igbokwe's obi where the ancient medicines were kept—smelling like home. And in it, Ijeọma found solace to lie on the stony cell floor, and close her eyes, gently, gently, gently, to sleep.

DIARY ENTRY #927   14 FEBRUARY 2000

Why have I not been taken? Chukwu, tell me; why have I remained? It is a
fact. Night after night children disappear. I've seen it many times how they
go at night and take some children, then lead them into a car and drive
away. We do not see them again.

Where is the pastor taking them Chukwu? When will they come back?
Still I want them to come back, even if this is a terrible place.

Then what of me? Please do not consider me selfish for asking, why am
I still here? Why have I been selected to stay like those very few others? I do
not know. I don't know; and my heart says that it shall not be permanent.
My heart is thumping like a rusty generator. I'm finding it difficult to write.
I'm finding it difficult to breathe. I wish I could be given palm wine a whole
jug of palm wine, so that I might consume it all at once and go to sleep.

Perhaps it must be that I believe as Ikemba believes, that all of
Precious Word is good and that all of Amalike is good. It would be a lie. Yet
there are those who attempt to live within the emptiness of a lie. And
perhaps this lie will give me more peace than I already lack, or allow me to
sleep when it is time to sleep. For I do not know what my life has become or
where it is going. I fear Chukwu, I fear; and I am afraid of a thing I cannot
name those many uncertainties which lay in the tomorrows yet to come
those uncertainties which carry the certainty that I must suffer, that I must
truly suffer and never survive it, and that will be my end. And yet, Uzodi
taught me the difference between a wanted truth and the good word. The
difference, he said, is that the good word first arrives with sorrow more
bitter than the greatest kola nut, but a wanted truth comes only with
vanity, and vanity alone. If now is the time for bitterness, let it quickly pass

away. Though my mind and heart know of something true: it is unusual and unfair that I was not taken like the others, and something will be done to correct this

9.

IT WAS NOT THE SOUNDS of cocks crowing that awoke Ijeọma but the blast of a deafening bell, rung to precede dawn's sky.

"Get up! Get up! It is time for you to rise!"

A large female attendant in a pink-checkered dress walked through the corridor with a long cane and bell—her loud voice, and louder bell—disrupting the children sleeping in the Manifestation Quarters—especially Ijeọma, who had not known of a sound so crass. The gongs used in Ichulu bore a timorous sound, which made Ijeọma revere the message of the clinging metal. The sound of Amalike's bell seemed irresponsible, and Ijeọma covered her ears with both hands—not getting up, but lying on the floor—waiting for quiet to return—clutching her ears, still hearing the noise—but remembering her dream: Nnenna was cooking soup and asked her to feed Cheluchi, as Ọfọdile sat with visitors in his obi and Nnamdị danced a dance with other boys. Ụzọdị was somewhere she could not remember, while

Ezinne, the one called his mother, sang as she swept the compound's earth. It was a wondrous dream, and Ijeọma refused to rise from the floor until such dreams returned and pulled her down to sleep.

"Did you not hear me! I said get up!"

The large attendant quickly raised her cane—and beat the legs on Ijeọma's body. She raised it again, and beat Ijeọma for not promptly rising from the floor—beating her as she recalled this to be the cell of the flying witch, the cell of the girl most diabolical, and she refused to show any signs of fear but beat Ijeọma—until her cane cracked in two, shouting "Holy Ghost fire! Holy Ghost fire!" beating her then with a wooden beam—then a plastic-covered chain—beating Ijeọma until her hands were weak, exorcising demons before dawn—even as she shivered from the beating, on the ground she shivered and waved her hands for the beating to stop, and screamed and screamed for someone to hear, and felt the prickly sides of the wooden beam piercing through her back, and the dense weight of the plastic-covered chain, bruising and breaking what had been bruised and broken before, and she nodded her head, three times and then three times again, surrendering over and again, but the beating continued, and she remained on the cell floor— clutching the brim of her metal bucket, then letting it go—and when the beating stopped, quickly rising and watching the attendant pointing to two buckets and feeling the attendant force the buckets into her hands.

She was pulled out of the cell and into the corridor, and she saw the other children who were kept in the Manifestation Quarters—seeing that they stumbled, painfully shifting their weight from one leg to the other—seeing that she, too, was doing the same: a consequence from the beating; a consequence from the stony floor on which she slept at night; a consequence of Ichulu fading from her footsteps—all of which began dwelling in her heart as she moved through the lightless corridor—following the children outside, all with two metal buckets—following them as they led her to the church bore-hole behind the Manifestation Quarters.

And as she waited with them by the rusted pipe to fetch her share of water, she saw some emptying their defecation buckets—with green specks falling on their arms and lips and murky waters plopping onto the ground. The bucket she held was empty, brought through hateful coercion; and not wanting to think of that morning's attendant, she looked down to her throbbing leg and found it to be reddish in color, with no broken skin, but behaving as though blood would burst forth from its swelling.

"Who beat you," she heard him say, hearing bright conviction in his voice.

Ijeọma looked upward to see the one who had spoken, and saw it was a boy; whose skin was as the night, whose stature had her believe he was a warrior in groom.

"Will you not answer me? I asked who beat you?"

Ijeọma remained silent—staring into the boy's narrow eyes, eyes which made him seem wiser than many—not knowing how to answer him, so tightening her hold on the bucket handles—and moving away as she began looking upon the borehole. She could feel his gaze: it pierced her back, and she swallowed into her chest as she filled the bucket with the water falling from the borehole, as she turned from him—praying she had the courage and ability to ask the boy with black skin his name.

And when it had been filled to the brim, she placed the showering bucket atop her head; and put the second bucket in her hands; and made her eyes avoid the boy with black skin while following a young girl to the clearing where the other girls were bathing. She could see the boys showering from where she stood; their penises limp; their buttocks firm and plain; and she saw, too, the girls' developing breasts; and did not want to be naked within their sight. It was not Idemili. The water was not the body of the divine—and the other girls bathing were watching her, she thought—even with their dull and expressionless eyes—and if she could see all of them—they could see me, too—and they would laugh in the way, the other girls laughed—those girls on the hill at the market square—those girls whom Chinwe had named as friends; so she stood by the buckets—staring at the purple mud through sad and fluttering eyes.

"*Girl! YOU! Girl! If you do not begin your shower eh, I will flog you to pieces!*" said one of the attendants, who began shouting more threats at Ijeọma and began approaching her with his cane—who watched as she quickly removed her rappa with terror seizing her face, who smiled a smile and left Ijeọma once she squatted by the bucket, and cupped her hands, and began cleaning herself like the other children did, washing under her arms, and behind her neck, and inside her mouth, not caring if the other girls noticed her, or spoke to hear, not hearing the clanging of the metal buckets, or the splashing of water hitting the grass.

And after showering, Ijeọma and the other children were returned to the cells and began dropping their buckets at the command of the barking attendants—hurrying out of the cells, walking quickly because the attendants pointed their canes—to the center of the corridor. She made a line with the others—and they were led to a parallel corridor within the Manifestation Quarters—where the pastor had built a chapel for the building. They walked through a dark hallway and veered right toward the chapel's iron door; and once the door was opened and the line passed through it, Ijeọma walked through the door's frame and saw red and green cloths hanging from the chapel's walls, and orange flowers pinned to the corners of the chapel's windows and benches. And she followed the line to the first row of benches and sat at the command of an attendant speaking through his cane—then heard soft footsteps coming from behind the chapel's door.

"Good morning," the person said as they opened the door—smiling at the children, revealing the gap in their front teeth—as they moved to the front of the chapel, wearing a blue cotton dress with white lace sewn about its edges and a small blue cloth resting atop their head.

"For those of you who are new and do not know who I am, my name is Mrs. Phyllipa Nwosu, and I am the wife of the pastor. I am here to pray with all of you this morning. Please, bow your heads and close your eyes."

Ijeọma did as the other children did, bowing her head, then closing her eyes, and wondering at the meaning behind the gestures. She heard the person wearing the dress say many things in English, and when the person coughed a light cough, Ijeọma raised her head and saw that all the heads were still bowed, save one: the boy with black skin, the boy from the borehole. And she did not think that he had ever bowed his head, believing the boy with black skin to be stubborn, knowing he was defiant to the traditions of Amalike and its god; and she continued looking at him, wanting him to turn around so she could see his narrow eyes once more. Though he did not, and when Mrs. Nwosu finally ended her prayer every head had been raised, and the children were herded directly to the quarters' dining hall to eat their morning meal.

An attendant told Ijeọma to sit at a wooden table, where metal bowls and silverware were placed before her. By her left hand was a girl who smelled of fresh dung, and by her right hand was a boy with missing teeth—one too old to have them missing through childhood. And as she looked to her left hand and watched the girl and began wondering how her stench could be after bathing, she saw the smeared stains on her rappa and understood, watching then as an attendant came to where she was sitting and placed a ration of gray yam and a spoonful of stew on her plate. She almost screamed when she saw the attendant leaving with the remaining food, seeing the rations given to the other children and signing softly in the air: abomination, abomination; more was given to Ichulu's goats—signing while turning to her plate and watching the gray yam—one no bigger than a tiny river stone—not knowing what to do with the silverware as she watched the other children cutting their tiny yams in half. The meal was not sensible neither did it honor reason; and her thoughts had refused to thank Chukwu for the yam, as she lifted it with her fingers, before swallowing the gray lump.

"Ikemba! Ikemba!"

Ijeọma heard a crashing sound, and saw an attendant screaming at the boy with black skin.

"You satanic animal!" screamed one of the attendants, as Ikemba threw another plate against the ground, bringing the entire room to silence. The attendant used her heavy cane to strike Ikemba on his head. And when her continuous beatings caused him to collapse onto the floor, she dragged him toward the cell, hearing the other attendants order the children to continue eating, warning them that Ikemba's insubordination would not be tolerated should any of them dare repeat it.

"The church pays for your food!" they said.

"You must respect what you eat!" they said.

"You must not give in to your evil inclinations!" they said. But Ijeoma did not hear them as she thanked the gods, and thanked Chukwu, for letting her learn the name of the boy with black skin.

She was returned to the dark cell in which she was kept; dark because the morning light was blocked by the full, thick branches of an ngwu tree shielding the cell's window. And she sat in the darkness, thinking of Ichulu, wondering at Ichulu's affairs, and if they had forgotten her, hoping that Igbokwe convinced Ofodile to allow her to return home; yet somehow hearing, too, the words of a dwelling thought: you will never again touch the earth with your feet, or drink water from Idemili, or fly in the market square, or see the face of Chinwe, or the love of your mother, it will be so, it will be, I know it will be so—and she sat trembling in the darkness, with anger and with melancholy—believing the whispers of those words.

She quickly denied the music of Ichulu within her: the light tones of morning greetings and evening farewells, the trebles of an accolade when elders say, "Well done," the rising and falling and rising and falling of a single word, a single sound, heard in the music being played when Ichulu spoke its Igbo.

And she could not pray; she tried, over and again, to pray for herself and the others but could not lift her hands to speak of hopeful things, to ask for their survival in a hateful place; she could not find strength to do it, after hearing that dwelling thought; to return home to their families, for Chukwu to protect them; she could not do it, to protect Ikemba who was beaten that morning; to dive into supplications, and forget where she was; to ask for food and water and more food and more water, asking for a chewing stick to wipe her mouth clean for a river; for the sun, for those things that make a place holy, that day she could not do it; and she touched her skin, holding it, feeling its smoothness, grabbing a fold, and feeling how it snapped: slipping through her fingers and returning to the bone; and she wept in the darkness, ignoring the rats scurrying on the floor, knowing her reality to be true.

The bell rang again.

"It is now time for the afternoon prayer!" an attendant said as the doors to each of the cells were opened.

She and the others were moved to the chapel to pray a prayer led by another attendant. She bowed her head and closed her eyes with the others, learning the traditions of this new place; trying to survive it, bowing her head, and listening to the sounds coming forth from the attendant's mouth, reluctantly discerning their tones and patterns, irritably trying to understand.

"Amen," said the attendant.

"Amen," replied the children.

Amen, Ijeọma mouthed, bitterly tasting the textures of new speech.

"Now form a line!" the attendant said. "You are going to eat your afternoon meal!"

Ijeọma and the others obeyed the attendant, scuffling into a line and moving to the dining hall, where their rations were even smaller than that of the morning. She winced at the spoonful of white rice on her plate, knowing it would not be enough; watching the other children take their spoons and put their rice into their mouths, ending their meal as quickly as it began. And looking for more food, and finding none, she ate as the others did, then took her metal cup and filled it with water kept in a pitcher on the dining room table.

And after drinking water that was filled with dust, she realized that the boy with missing teeth was no longer in the dining hall. And as she began searching the hall for him with her eyes, she saw Ikemba sitting a few tables from her and thought he might throw his dish in protest again. But he was sitting peacefully, uttering not a sound; and she smiled, wanting to be near him; finding courage, then lifting herself to the soles of her feet; when suddenly all the attendants and children began standing alongside her.

"Children of the Manifestation Quarters," Pastor Nwosu said, once he fully entered the dining hall. "I hope that you are receiving your portion of the Holy Spirit today, and that our Lord and Savior *Jesus Christ* is moving within you. If not, it means that those demons are still in control of you. If you are allowing evil to possess you, you are not only an enemy of God, *you are an enemy of this church.* You must know that none of you shall be released until you change your ways and join in the redemption of God's Word. *Until you accept Jesus as your personal Lord and Savior,* you will never be free, whether or not you are in the Manifestation Quarters. I have come to remind you that this coming Sunday, I will attempt to remove the demons which have possessed some of you through the blood of Jesus. But if any of you want to repent now, the road is clear. All you must do is speak."

The room was silent, and Ijeọma was not sure if any of the other children understood what the pastor had said. She looked about her and saw many heads wavering as if preparing to fall, and saw many eyes puffier than a tall man's thumb; with lesions marking ashy-white skin, mottled with blood stains and pus.

"You, mistah man of God . . . you are a fool!"

Ijeọma turned her head and saw Ikemba rising.

"No demon has possessed me," Ikemba said. "*It is you who are possessed.* You say that you worship Jesus? It is a lie! Would Jesus lock children inside cages? Would he? . . . Ehhhhh, no answer? Your god is evil, but my God is good. My God's name is *Christ Jesus.* My Jesus is the God of Life, whereas yours is a devil."

Ijeọma saw Ikemba continue speaking—even when the pastor walked to where he stood and slapped him over and again, and seized an attendant's cane to strike him on the head—striking him until he fell to the ground. And she sat tensely, wishing she could understand what Ikemba had said, wishing him no pain, wishing Ụzọdị had taught her more than one English word.

"I will not tolerate blasphemy in this house of God!" Pastor Nwosu said. "All of you have been sent here by your families because of your evil. It is by the power of my Lord and Savior Jesus Christ that all of you will be set free. If you choose to believe the blasphemies spoken among you, you will never leave this place. Have you heard?"

"Yes pastor!" the children said.

"Good. Now, finish your food," the pastor said, leaving the dining hall as the children were hurried into the cells, including Ijeoma, who sat in a corner of the dark space, recalling what had transpired. If Ikemba was injured, she did not know, and she prayed for the ability to speak to him through the bars of the cell. He would answer her, and the two would be able to converse, and laugh, amid the great darkness of the Manifestation Quarters. But she believed it to be an untenable prayer, one which she doubted in the grave silence of the Manifestation Quarters, where neither the songs of birds, nor the hum of mosquitoes, nor the whisper of a prayer were listened to among the children waiting in the darkness, some with knees pulled to their bowed heads, waiting for the silence of Manifestation Quarters to numb the bitter aches slowly forming within their chests.

And then the bell was rung, and the evening prayer was prayed, and the evening meal was served. The sun went down, and the bell was rung, the sun rose; and the bell was rung again. With showers came the bell; and the bell came with eating and solitude and giving thanks to God. And after three days of these repetitions, Ijeoma knew what the day would be—not requiring a bell to remind her.

10.

SHE WAS THINKING OF CHUKWU when she rose that morning, waiting for Chukwu, waiting for the Most Supreme to carry her home like the nza birds that left her window; or like Solomto, who returned to Ichulu after being taken to a foreign land. She lay on the floor of the tiny cell, waiting for her chi to remove her from it, patiently waiting—dismissing each discontentment that said her waiting was prolonged—not knowing which threats the attendants had barked to her that morning; not knowing why the borehole's water was colored in blue; not knowing the name of the ONK! ONK! sound coming forth from the metal rams and gliding pots echoing throughout the church parking lot; wondering why there were so many of them that day parked haphazardly in the clearings where she showered; not understanding the music of the guitar, the keyboard, or the drum seeping from behind the sanctuary door when the ekwe made hollow knocks; and the ogene joined with its metallic timbre and weight; when the udu grounded it all, through its deep and spirited bellows; not knowing that the day was Sunday morning at Precious Word Ministries church.

And as Ijeọma and the other children waited outside of the sanctuary door, waiting for Pastor Nwosu to give them permission to enter, they could hear the pastor's muffled voice rising behind the door, reminding Ijeọma of Ichulu's masquerades grunting proverbs behind masks and fabrics. So she stood, wanting to see the works that lay behind the gold-colored wood, looking upward but being afraid that she would be punished for wrongdoing, turning her face; not wanting to be blamed; and seeing that the attendants who escorted them were no longer there—that instead there were two large men in a corner, speaking loudly and handling rope—and she wondered if they could tell her what the muffling was, whether if she listened carefully she might hear them speaking Igbo, and hear them speak those things that lay behind the door.

"Pastor Nwosu says he would like them to enter," said an usher who had come in from the sanctuary.

Ijeọma saw the two men approaching her and the others with their rope—and felt them tying it around her waist before they opened the sanctuary door and led them toward the front of a room—where she heard the silence of the people gathered and saw their disapproving glances before she turned her face to the ground; not wanting to be seen; or to exist; or to want anything from being anything; not to fly from being a bird; not to burn from being a sun; not to be a child whom Chukwu had taken; not wanting to follow the pull of the rope—leading her to the stairs of the altar—where Pastor Nwosu had been standing.

Ijeọma felt the rope tightening around her waist, and she tried loosening its hold by slipping her fingers between the rope and her hip, but it failed. Again, she tried pulling the rope to loosen it but met resistance since the others had been doing the same—each one looking for a way to find ease; and she kept pulling the rope—until a few had lost their balance, and all of them found themselves on the sanctuary floor—falling as though their brittle bones had lost their rigor.

"It is time for a deliverance!" the congregation began saying, raising their fans within the large sanctuary.

"It is indeed time," said Pastor Nwosu. "You see them . . . these witches and wizards . . . You see how they have no reverence in the house of Almighty God . . . tumbling down like drunkards and fools!"

"We see it, Pastor! We see it!"

"So then it is time that we raise our Bibles and pray for these children, so that they may know the name of their Maker. Prrray for them! So that they may know the name of Jesus!"

Ijeọma turned her neck while on the floor and watched the people of Precious Word Ministries stand with their Bibles, seeing as they closed their eyes and forced words out of their mouths aggressively; as if their tongues had become machetes used to fight a vicious beast like Nta, watching as their bodies swayed back and forth; and hearing them make sounds in a language spoken so quickly, she did not think anyone could ever understand it. The conviction with which they prayed reminded her of Igbokwe's prayers to the gods in the mornings, before her daily consultations; except these prayers held different tones: more audacious, more entitled; and like their English, she did not understand the Igbo that Igbokwe had spoken. It was older than her, ancient and enigmatic; and she began to smile as the rope tightened again, realizing that Igbokwe did not scream to the gods like they were very far; that he seldom screamed at all, and she supposed it was an assurance that came from being consumed by the Most Supreme; and the rope tightened more and more, and the greatest god changed him, the work of the Most Supreme, and now he gives those things which others deny, it does not have a name, a complete name, but I see it . . . look at it there in Anyanwụ, maybe Igbokwe has seen it before, and that is why he gives those things . . . those nameless things, as he lives, and she began smiling within the falling sunlight, the rope tightening more and more, pulling neither left nor right.

It was not known that Precious Word Ministries had ever stayed so silent. It looked toward Ijeọma as she rose powerfully toward a second-story beam with some of the roped children ascending with her; and it looked at Pastor

Nwosu for direction on what to do, and what to believe, not having seen its witches and wizards practice their occultism in its holy sanctuary before, with those who had taken secret trips to Ichulu being amazed that Ijeọma could fly in the house of this god, smiling at her ascending body, admiring her beauty and gall.

"PULL HER DOWN!" the pastor said to the attendants. "I COMMAND YOU TO PULL HER DOWN!"

And Ijeọma, whose gaze was fixed on a vision of faces, smiling at her with a wholesome eye, was pulled down to the tiled floor of the sanctuary as murmurs spread throughout the large room; with fear and confusion spreading quickly, too, as the congregation turned to its pastor, waiting for him to act, watching him push his spectacles along the hill of his nose, not looking at all toward the face of his congregation.

"Bring her to me," Pastor Nwosu said to the attendants.

And she felt the two large men grabbing her arms—and loosening the rope around her waist—causing her to return to herself and see the looks of disdain among those in the congregation, seeing, too, the wielded disgust of those dragging her to the pastor. But she was happy she rose; she smiled as she rose; she could not focus on the conceit of those despising her, not fearing their scoffs nor heeding their grimaces, but feeling the soft, soft whispers of the one called her chi moving within her chest; tumbling behind her belly, singing a song for the Most Supreme; one of joy, one of hope, one of unrelenting beauty—*if a river cannot reveal your face—or a neighbor cannot hold your heart—or a lover cannot wipe the water of your eyes, listen to me, listen me, listen to my whispers, listen to my thoughts—I have listened—chi I have listened—chi-Chineke-Chukwu I have listened through the good word.*

"Members of Precious Word Ministries," Pastor Nwosu said, looking at the green streamers hanging from the unfinished walls. "Somehow . . . the principalities of this world have found their way into the house of the Living God. I would like you to stretch your Bibles toward this possessed girl, as I lay my hands on her . . . to cast out this demon. As you stretch out your Bibles, pray for this child . . . that she may know our Lord and Savior Jesus Christ, that His Blood may purify her . . . and wash her clean."

The congregation erupted with voices heard beyond the walls of Precious Word Ministries. It had not known an act so unabashed; and so it prayed as though bearing witness to a war, or seeing a crazed man enter a shop; knowing its possessed girl could fly, and expecting from their prayers the power to remove her evil; as its pastor believed the same—reminding himself that he was divinely ordained to cleanse Ijeọma and bring her to Christ; clenching his right hand on Ijeọma's skull and praying more rigorously—shouting his prayer into the microphone, making the speakers blast at full volume, applying more pressure onto Ijeọma's head——squeezing it as though he could pop her devils out—like pus from a boil—hearing his congregation yell, "Holy Ghost fire! Holy Ghost fire!" then releasing her head from his grip with great propulsion; and watching her fall backward into the arms of the attendants.

"THE WITCH HAS FALLEN!" a man said.

"GLORY BE GOD!" a person said.

"GLORY BE TO GOD!" the congregation kept saying.

"HALLELUJAH! HALLELUJAH! HALLELUJAH!" the congregation kept saying.

"You see what prayer can do?" said Pastor Nwosu. "Do you see it? Return that child of God with the others. Do not tie her very tightly, because I pronounce, as the Man of God in this church, that many of those demons have already fled from her body."

"AMEN!" the congregation said.

"Amen. Amen," said Pastor Nwosu, looking now at his congregation. "There is still work left to be done on that girl, but today is the beginning of her breakthrough. Do not fear Satan, you children of God . . . Do not fear him! Jesus is our Master and He has already overcome every principality that would keep us away from the Living God. Do not be fooled by Lucifer, the Father of Lies. Do not be afraid of him! All of us standing here, we are serving the one true God!"

Music began playing, and the people in the sanctuary erupted into song and dance, trusting the words of their pastor; all of them, except the children on the rope, who were dragged down the red-carpeted aisle and then returned to the cells of the Manifestation Quarters, where they were ordered to sit quietly until the afternoon prayer.

But the children did not stay quiet, rejoicing at what they called a miracle and a sign from God that they would one day be free. They did not know her name, so yelled, "Flying girl! Flying girl!" from inside the cells, wanting to speak to her, hoping she would respond to them from within the darkness; and when no response came, they chattered among themselves, asking if they had truly seen what they had seen.

"You saw it!" Ikemba said. "All of us here, we are witnesses!"

"So she can really fly," asked a little boy.

"Yes! Yes! She can fly," said Ikemba.

"Believe it, you must believe!" said a teenage girl.

"Yes I believe, I believe!" said another.

"Me too! I believe!" said another boy.

"I believe! I believe! I believe!" was the song of the children.

"She is a living saint!" said Ikemba. "Never believe this foolish pastor! This girl has real power, holy power that comes from God."

And the children believed Ikemba's words, and continued with their praise and chatter, professing that they believed—over and again—believing in both wonder and truth.

And as they sang their praises, Ijeọma sat with her chi, nursing the joy she had received from the flight, hoping she would soon fly again. She expelled the doubt of whether Chukwu was with her in exile, believing now that the Most Supreme had not left her—a small grin growing—with Chukwu, she could do the impossible; with Chukwu she would survive her imprisonment, and live a life with happiness; she unraveled her rappa and placed it atop the cell floor, lying prostrate, praying to the Supreme Being, asking for peace and assurance—the kind she saw in Igbokwe when she visited him each morning—the kind she thought opened the world—as wide as Nnenna's pots—and filling them with all the love and mercy the Supreme Being had given her.

Quickly the cell door was opened. Ijẹọma was pulled from the cell, hurrying to put on her rappa as she was led along the corridors to the chapel where Phyllipa led them in a prayer. She was ordered into the dining hall with the others to eat the afternoon meal; and she ate a small ration of beans without any fear, finishing her meal with no concern for tomorrow's hunger. And as she reached for the pitcher of water in the middle of the table, she heard footsteps coming from the entrance of the dining hall and saw Pastor Nwosu entering with great force, holding a large cane in his hand.

"YOU!" he said, pointing at her violently—using his large, wooden cane. "COME HERE AND LIE DOWN!"

But Ijẹọma did not understand him, and looked at the pastor in amazement, watching his eyes grow livid—not knowing he believed her to be insubordinate, feeling one of the attendants seizing her right arm, then pulling it forcefully toward the pastor's feet.

"YOU WITCH!" the pastor said, striking Ijẹọma's thigh. "WHEN I SAY LIE DOWN, I MEAN LIE DOWN."

He dragged Ijẹọma by her hair and kicked her until she was fully prostrate, until her back lay flat against the floor. And he began beating her with the cane—his wooden stick landing across her back and buttocks—as he cried, "YOU WILL BE RELEASED IN JESUS' NAME! YOU WILL BE RELEASED BY HOLY GHOST FIRE!" watching Ijẹọma trembling from each blow, seeing her curling atop the floor; then ordering two attendants to take her hands and feet—beating her until he was tired and turned to the door— flogging her with more than fifty strokes as he approached the door's handle, believing now that his assurance had returned.

But Ijẹọma was on the floor. She could not move and she could not weep—strapped between the thoughts of flying, and the sores from the wooden cane—thinking she was not to cry since she had heard the songs of her chi—and knowing the pastor had beaten her because she had flown before his people. Fear was the cause, and Chukwu scared him, she knew, Chukwu scared him so greatly, he thinks he can erase the good word, bruising a body that is already bruised, wanting to kill what has already died, one that is waiting to die again, Chukwu, am I to weep, because I will weep when my body bleeds, and the sores become painful, and my flesh is opened for the flies, I will weep even after hearing your melodies, and being taken toward Igwe and his clouds, because I must weep for my body and the one who has given it this pain.

She pitied him as she cried. And the other children pitied similarly— pitying the pastor since they knew her levitation made his confidence fail, and made his power seem small. They had not seen the man of God look so contemptible, so void of his usual authority—with his spectacles sitting unbalanced, and a corner of his shirt left untucked; and what they reasoned to do with those revelations was laugh—laughing and laughing, all were laughing, hysterically, maniacally, lifting their heads and spreading their lips—cackling as the pastor was preparing to leave the dining hall.

"COME AND SEE!" Ikemba said while cackling. "THIS BIG PASTOR IS AFRAID OF A SMALL CHILD! WHY, PASTOR? ARE YOU AFRAID SHE CAN PERFORM BIGGER MIRACLES THAN YOU?"

The pastor turned to Ikemba and said nothing.

"THIS PASTOR IS A FOOL! HE DOESN'T EVEN KNOW THE POWER OF THE GOD HE SER—"

"Ikemba, sit down and close your mouth," Pastor Nwosu said.

"HE DOESN'T EVEN KNOW THE POWER OF THE GOD HE SERVES. THAT IS WHY HE THINKS HE CAN LOCK US UP AND FEED US NOTHING BUT HIS LYING GOD."

"I said sit down!"

"YOU DON'T EVEN KNOW HOW YOUR OWN GOD SPEAKS, MR. MAN OF GOD. YOU DON'T EVEN KNOW...A NUN IN MY VILLAGE TAUGHT ME ENGLISH, MATHEMATICS, AND THE NAME OF A SAINT WHO COULD FLY."

"I will not warn you again! Sit down *or I will pieces you!*"

"HIS NAME WAS JOSEPH...FROM CUPERTINO...JOSEPH OF CUPERTINO! AND HE COULD FLY. NOW YOU HAVE THIS GIRL FROM ANOTHER VILLAGE, WHO IS DOING THE SAME, AND YOU CALL HER A WITCH. CHEI! YOU ARE A FOOL MR. MAN OF GOD, A GREAT FOOL!"

Pastor Nwosu dropped his cane, then lunged at Ikemba, quickly wrapping his hands around the boy's neck, wringing it to break and kill, waiting for Ikemba's eyes to redden and roll backward, for the breath moving through his neck to cease. They did not. He released himself from the pastor's grip, and with his available hand punched the pastor in the temple, before watching the pastor lose his balance and stumble about within the walls of the manifestation's dining hall.

And the children looked on in awe, laughing at the pastor, hoping Ikemba would strike him again. But before Ikemba could punch him a second time, the attendants descended on him with their canes and dragged him to the cells.

The room became silent again. After many moments of lying on the ground, Ijeọma was told to rise by an attendant. She lifted herself and began returning to her seat, walking stiffly as she went; not wiping her own tears, looking for Ikemba's face among the children; and finding that it was not there. She knew he was being punished, and as she looked around, she noticed all the children staring at her and sending smiles and soft laughter as greetings. And she did not want them to look at her in such ways—not wanting any prideful attention. But the children gazed at her anyway, wanting to be acquainted with the flying girl.

"I want to fly like you," she heard one girl say as she sat down beside her. "If I could fly like you I would go home to my parents. What is your name?"

Ijeọma did not answer, and the girl gave her a perplexed look.

"Why won't you answer me? Do you not speak English? What is it that is your name," said the girl in a hushed Igbo.

And Ijeọma turned, and looked at the girl, putting a hand over her own mouth, and shaking her head: signing that she did not have the ability to speak.

"It was only this that I wanted to tell you . . . if you want the pastor to stop beating you . . . *close your eyes.*"

The girl quickly turned her head, and Ijeọma thought she might have upset her; she wanted to ask the girl for forgiveness and understanding, wanted to ask the girl to be patient with her muteness. Though it could not happen; and she moved her eyes, and saw the pastor talking with a group of attendants; and she wondered what he was telling them, wondering if she should prepare herself for another beating; watching as the pastor separated himself from the group and stood at the very front of the dining hall.

"I will not tolerate any insubordination from you children. Any of you who disobey my authority, and follow the example of that devilish boy, will be dealt with seriously! I am sure I am making myself clear."

"Yes sah!" the children responded.

Ijeọma watched Pastor Nwosu begin walking toward the bench where she was sitting, his spectacles resting on the tip of his nose—exposing his bloodshot eyes—as he snatched her arm, pulling her up from the bench.

"This flying witch here does not have the power to speak! She is dumb. Do you see now what your satanic practices lead to? Her witchcraft has made her dumb! But my God is a Living God. He will restore her. He will give me the grace to teach her written English. Know that I prophesied it . . . When I am through with her, the whole world will know her testimony."

Pastor Nwosu quickly dropped Ijeọma on her seat and left before the children were ordered to the cells. They all were all inspired by Ikemba, allowing his defiance to fill them with glee, some calling Ikemba a prophet and understanding his words since the pastor had confused miracle for mistake, believing a young girl could never be given the gifts of holy men. They had not known Ijeọma, but they did not believe her to be a witch; and they had forgotten their evening meal to agree with Ikemba—whispering of how the pastor did not know his own god, agreeing with Ikemba, and professing that Ijeọma, too, was a saint—regardless of whatever it was the pastor had believed.

DIARY ENTRY #929   18 FEBRUARY 2000

How can this be Chukwu! How can this possibly be! Can the world be this broken? Does it truly have no heart! Answer me, Chukwu; answer me! What does this mean! the king's wickedness the pastor's wickedness! What does it mean! When I have tried to love when all of us have tried to love and yet you allow the king and his pastor to ruin us as slaves. ~~Most Supreme for what.~~ *Answer me! Chineke! Answer me! Because what does it mean that a person whom you created, whom you can destroy within a single whisper can kill and siege and sabotage without immediate consequence! Have I done something to you? What, WHAT, have we done to you?*

    For, what does it mean that I must be pregnant. Chi what does it mean that the world will believe that I am carrying a child within me can you be god?? can you be real? is anything which I now SEE and remember REAL For I should now fall into the madness beckoning my mind since to accept you, the Most Supreme, as REAL is to place a merciless affliction into my life.

    It may be better, to live and die, than to say that you are real. It may be better, to build a temple to Ani and remove the food that once sustained Jekwu, killing him, destroying him in time, than to say, "Chukwu is Most Supreme." For how am I to believe this? How am I to believe that this is what you have allowed my life to be?

11.

IJEỌMA WAS UNAWARE OF WHAT her flight had brought to the Manifestation Quarters. She had been residing with her chi, listening to its voice as she watched the rats moving within the cell, some of which she had given names. And when she would hear her chi's whispers of good fortune and possibility, she would pray to the Supreme Being to take her home. Lying prostrate on the ground one evening, giving herself fully to Chukwu, diving deeper into her supplications, the door of the cell was opened. She lifted her head to see who had come, hoping to her chi that it was not an attendant with a cane; she stood slowly and saw the lace-covered hair of Phyllipa, the wife of Pastor Nwosu.

"Come with me," Phyllipa said, stretching out her arm, then drawing her sliding handbag.

"I would speak to you in Igbo but it is not allowed. Come," she said, eyeing the attendants in the hallway. *"They will not hurt you today."*

And Ijeọma approached her, taking Phyllipa's hand and following her through the long corridor. She was at ease when Phyllipa led her into a room she had not previously entered—a room filled with many wooden benches facing a blackened wall. And she looked at Phyllipa, wondering, then, why she had brought only her into this room, thinking she had committed a grievance and pleading with her eyes for Phyllipa to pardon her offense.

"It is all right, Ijeọma . . . This is your classroom," said Phyllipa in a softly spoken English. "This is where you will join the other children for lessons. Because you cannot speak, you will have special classes with me where I will teach you how to write English. Those are your red notebooks." Phyllipa pointed to a column of books by a window. "Pastor Nwosu bought them for you and will be inspecting them every week to review your progress. Should you do well, he will believe that you are an obedient child."

Phyllipa smiled at Ijeọma, and watched her look out of the window morosely.

"I have another thing for you," Phyllipa said in Igbo, as she pulled out a large, green book from her bag and began flipping its blank pages before Ijeọma.

"This is a *diary*," Phyllipa said. "It is a book where you can write whatever you think and whatever you are keeping in your heart. Take it, and do not let anyone see it."

Ijeọma nodded three times and took the large, green book from Phyllipa's hands, keeping it closed as she wondered at its pages; sitting with it as Phyllipa introduced her to the English alphabet, letter by letter, through symbols; writing foreign characters on the blackened wall, wondering if they would scurry onto the diary's pages; sitting with it when she returned to the cells; wishing she could fill it with those symbols she had seen so that one day the other children would see her words. She smiled then, because only she was given this gift from Phyllipa; and as new memories came, she was sitting with it still—staring at its green cover and thinking of cassava petals, and Ani, and Idemili's weeds, staring at the green, until the night had quickly come—and covered all the color away.

Ijeọma joined the children for their lesson the following day, with much anticipation in learning from the pastor's wife. She sat on the wooden benches of the Manifestation Quarters listening to Phyllipa teaching them English, and though her private lessons were to begin after the other children were dismissed, she sat attentively in the back of the room, watching the others reciting words written on the blackened wall, wondering if she could make new signs for the new sounds the children were making.

They often looked back at her—twisting their white necks, in wonder of whether she would fly again—wondering if she would always be their saint. And Ijeọma could see that their eyes held hope; and believed it to be because of her flight, and Ikemba's rebellion. No longer were they dull and spiritless; but they were growing brighter and more earnest, glistening with the belief that she was never meaningless coincidence, but sent by God to set them all free; so she began looking through the black of their eyes as they were being taught—seeing them looking back, and carrying the belief that she would bless them again—with an ascension to the sky.

And then she turned her gaze to Ikemba, watching as he sat with his head resting on a table—remaining silent as Phyllipa was teaching the lesson. She intuited that he was bored—learning a language that he had already mastered; remembering how confidently he had spoken to Pastor Nwosu— remembering his speech being swift and clear; and she believed he should be the one standing before them; declaring within herself that his boredom was unjust, wanting Ikemba to be the one to teach her how to write; wanting, for a moment, to see the black of his eyes.

"Ijeọma, come to the front of the classroom. It is time for your lesson," Phyllipa said. "The rest of you, the attendants will escort you back to your cells."

Ijeọma watched the other children being quietly led to the cells—when her eyes were pulled to Phyllipa, pointing to the column of red notebooks sitting by the afternoon window. And she stood from her chair and began walking to the window, thinking of Ikemba's skin.

"Only take one," Phyllipa said, as Ijeọma turned to see her. "One," Phyllipa said, raising a single finger.

Ijeọma nodded her head three times, understanding the gesture, and took one notebook from the column. She hurried to a bench in the front row, and watched Phyllipa raising a small piece of chalk before writing English characters on the blackened wall.

"Ijeọma, I want us to return to the English alphabet," Phyllipa said, pointing to the wall and writing on the air with her other hand above Ijeọma's notebook.

Ijeọma understood and began copying the letters with a pencil Phyllipa had given her. Her hands were shaking when she began, and the wooden pencil continued slipping between her fingers; and the letters she wrote did not resemble the ones on the blackened wall, especially after her first page had torn. Still, she continued writing the alphabet, over and again, until her wrists and eyes began to memorize each curve, and stroke, and dot; until she learned the kind of force to use to prevent the notebook's paper from tearing. She copied the alphabet, over and again, grateful that Phyllipa had not come to aide her; believing herself to be capable as she pondered upon each letter's groove, waiting to see if the words she had written would make the sounds the people in Amalike habitually made; or make the sounds of Ichulu, or make any sound at all.

And after three hours, Phyllipa asked an attendant to return Ijeọma to the cells. She kept Ijeọma's red notebook and smiled at the pages bearing the smallest and most legible print of the alphabet she could remember seeing. She smiled and planned on teaching her elementary words during their next lesson, believing Ijeọma to be intelligent, more so than the other children she had taught. She liked the belief, somehow knowing Ijeọma to be a girl whose intelligence could be used for the benefit of many things; things like the words of her Jesus, and the great pragmatism of his love.

Though Ijeọma knew very little of Phyllipa's Christ, believing that she and the rest of Amalike served a perilous god, a god whom they asked to heal the children locked in the cells, a god who was partial to them, and partial to them alone, a god, like most other gods, Ijeọma had discerned; one who had her cringe from the thought of being beaten, one whom she thought was much less desirable than her own; so she turned to hers—the one who brought her to the sky, the one who brought her to the cells; and asked for an end to Amalike; and asked for their traditions to disappear, believing she would never go free if they continued to remain—believing the Most Supreme would soon abolish every cell.

And she thought of those things that night on the cell floor, desiring an answer, wanting to know what force could break the customs of Amalike and allow all the children to be freed, remaining awake throughout the night; searching, thinking; arranging ideas to formulate an answer, when she heard rattling coming from the cell door's lock—trying to see the person's face, but the corridor was unlit—and the door kept rattling—and she knew within herself that it was an attendant, and she heard the sound of keys—*they have come for another beating*—and she heard them jingling in the night—*I am not awake, your cane is very powerful, you are entering, why have you entered, what did I do, please, go, let me sleep!*

"Do not be afraid. It is only me, Ikemba."

She looked upward and could see the outline of his face, and stood; she nodded her head perplexedly, waiting for him to speak again.

"What is it that is your name?" he asked in Igbo.

Ijeọma signed her name—inverting her middle fingers, and pointing them to her heart—doing so, over and again, but Ikemba did not understand.

"Can you not speak?"

Ijeọma nodded her head three times.

"I did not know that you were mute . . . Do you want to know how I was able to open your door?"

Ijeọma nodded, and watched him display a single key in his palms.

"This key belongs to the pastor's assistant. I stole it from him many months ago. There is a story in why I stole it, and it is why I have come to visit you this night. Many of the others and I are planning to escape from the church very soon. We want you to join us."

Ijeọma kept silent, not nodding her head or signing a word, but listening intently, making sure she understood what Ikemba had said.

"Did you hear me? We want you to join us and leave this place, since you, too, have been targeted by the pastor. Follow us in going home to the places from where we each come."

Ijeọma nodded; and she could see Ikemba's large, white smile—beaming in the darkness.

"I must return to my cell before the attendants see me. We will be leaving in two days so be prepared when I come again. Have you heard me? Be prepared."

Ijeọma nodded her head again and watched Ikemba leaving, softly rejoicing that the one she admired had left a cell to see her. She could not sleep for the rest of the night, feeling a tightness pulling within her chest; nursing her first memory of ever speaking to him, and relishing that his good word pertained to an escape; he was brave, she thought; brave enough to argue with the pastor, and brave enough to plan their escape from the Manifestation Quarters; she would escape with him—then return home to Ichulu, to tell Chinwe of the boy with black skin—and she would describe him with much appeal, and they would laugh together at their lust—and she could not sleep; crafting all her ploys—thinking of fanciful things in the playgrounds of her mind.

And when morning came, her back was stiff, since the rough cement floor yielded no comforts. And as she tried stretching the pain from out of herself, it refused to leave. So she kept to the ground, waiting for the morning bell to be rung; thinking again of the night, and wondering if Ikemba's visit was a dream. The promise of going home seemed untenable, and even if she could return to Ichulu, she wondered if her arrival would be welcomed. The one called her father would punish her for returning without being healed and would send her again to Amalike and the pastor's church. Her heart tightened as she stopped her thoughts from understanding Ọfọdile to be an evil man— but her pain was pressing: *he is senseless*, she thought, *afraid of things dying when things have their time to die, afraid of things being born yet hoping for life among the ancestors; it was cowardice*, she sighed, believing that she did not hate Ọfọdile, but wanted desperately for courage and truth to reside in him—praying to Chukwu, that the one called her father would not cower in senseless fears, and senseless lies, and the common senseless practice: another opposing another while forgetting that they are another.

When the morning bell had finally rung, she turned from her thoughts of Ọfọdile and slowly rose from the floor—putting both buckets in her hands and joining the other children on the moving line—increasing her pace and straightening her skinny back, then walking to the pit and emptying the metal bucket. She waited at the borehole to fetch water for her morning bath; and once the bucket was filled, she headed to the field where the other girls were bathing; soon placing the bucket firmly on the ground—and tossing aside her rappa, not crouching behind any metal to hide herself—but standing openly—cleaning her body without shame.

"Girl who flies! Girl who flies!" said a girl in a loud hush. "My name is Alison . . . What is your name?"

Ijeọma kept silent and moved her eyes to one of the attendants monitoring them.

"I understand, but I must say what I must say. Ikemba told me to tell you that we are leaving this night. One of the attendants became ill this morning, which means there are less people watching us. Prepare yourself."

Ijeọma saw Alison moving away, and noticed the white patch within her hair as she felt her own chest quivering from wanting her to stay and continue speaking, and not abandon her by her bucket, wanting answers to questions as she gazed toward the grass: *when did Ikemba decide that this would be the day of escape, how did they plan to leave the quarters without being seen, why did you select me to escape with you, why did you select me and to which home would a person go if a person had no home*—and Ijeọma wanted to speak with the girl, but that was not allowed; so she washed herself, more roughly, more firmly; and, when finished, joined the other children being escorted to the cells, to return the metal buckets to the molding cell corners.

They prayed their morning prayers and ate their morning meal and soon a bell began ringing for their classroom lesson. They watched Phyllipa entering the room once the bell had finished ringing, and watched her stand in front of the blackened wall, wearing a purple dress and holding a small cane in her left hand. One of the children began banging a rhythmic beat atop a table, as all the children began standing and greeting Phyllipa in unison; and they were told to sit down by the one called the pastor's wife, and watched as she put down the cane on a table beside her; then, taking a piece of chalk, she began writing a word on the blackened wall.

"Children, today we are going to learn the word *opposite*. Do any of you know what an opposite is?"

The room remained silent, and after a few seconds, Phyllipa decided to answer her own question.

"An opposite . . . is when a person *believes* that one thing is incompatible with another. Let me give you some examples. It is said that the opposite of *tall* is *short*. It is said that the opposite of *big* is *small*. It is said that the opposite of *fat* is *skinny* . . . Are you beginning to understand?"

"Yes ma," some children said.

"OK, who can tell me what the opposite of light is called," said Phyllipa, as she saw one of the children raising his hand.

"Go on, Ọgọ, tell us . . ."

"The opposite of light is called dark," Ọgọ said.

"Well done, Ọgọ. *That is what is believed.* So, who now knows what the opposite of up is called?"

"Down," said some of the children together.

"OK. Now what is the opposite of black called?"

The children were silent. They knew that black was a color, but were not certain of which color could be its opposite.

"Yellow!" said one child.

"That is not it," Phyllipa said with a smile. "The opposite of black is called white."

Phyllipa continued reciting a list of words while looking through their eyes and asking them all about opposites; and she looked through the class window when telling them all that the opposite of girl was boy, that the opposite of happy was sad, that the opposite of night was day, that the opposite of nothing was something.

"Children, you are beginning to understand this lesson. Now let me give you another word . . . Who can tell me what the opposite of Christianity is called?"

Again the room became silent before Phyllipa.

"Christianity has no opposite," Ikemba said, looking at Phyllipa with determination in his eyes.

"What do you mean," said Phyllipa.

"I said Christianity has no opposite. It is only one religion out of many."

"That is not it, Ikemba. The opposite of Christianity is called Paganism."

"Why is that so?" Ikemba said.

"Because Paganism is said to be a dark religion, and Christianity is said to be a religion full of the light of Jesus."

"You are wrong!" Ikemba said.

"Ikemba, you have started with this again. Keep quiet before the pastor comes."

"I will not!"

Phyllipa moved to the table where her small cane lay, and continued moving to where Ikemba was sitting.

"Let me see your hand," Phyllipa said, before slapping Ikemba's open palm with the cane; and when she saw him looking through her eyes plainly, she told him not to speak for the remainder of the class, for his own sake— and the sake of the other children—and continued with the lesson, teaching the children many other words considered to be opposing.

And Ijeọma wondered what Ikemba had said to be touched as though he were a goat. She looked at him while he was struck and saw that his face remained undisturbed by the stroke, believing that it was his plan for that night that made him so defiant—and made any punishment seem irrelevant. And Ijeọma believed the same of herself, and so did not give Phyllipa her attention when it was time for her private lessons; neither did she notice the English words she was beginning to write—bitterly turning her eyes from: cat, dog, north, and south, written on her notebook's paper, believing that she would never use the language called English once she left Amalike; Igbo, signs and sounds, would be enough, she thought, and Phyllipa, who had beaten a boy as beautiful as Ikemba, could never teach anyone anything useful, or give anyone any wisdom for honoring their life.

And when she returned to the cells after the evening meal, her thoughts had gathered to Ichulu. She would return home to the village, even if Ọfọdile did not consent, since nothing except Chukwu would prevent her from touching the orange earth; and bathing upon Idemili's clear skin; and rolling down steep hills, playing with Chinwe in the market square. It would come soon, she knew, and as the hours passed, she did not grow tired at all, but stood by the window of the cell, eagerly waiting for Ikemba's arrival—not thinking of the bars or her defecation bucket, but the movement of the westward sun resting softly above her village.

The sky was purple and black when she suddenly heard the lock on the cell door rattle. She knew it was Ikemba, but felt somehow that the attendants had learned of their plan; and began doubting as the lock was rattling, and continued doubting as it rattled even more—believing that she would be beaten, and die—all of the children—beaten and killed—and buried in a cursed forest—hidden in Amalike; but those doubts fell apart, once the cell door was opened and she saw Ikemba's face appear more fully, his lips asking her, "Are you ready . . ." as she nodded her head three times. She moved toward the door with him—watching as Ikemba opened the cells of the other children—before gathering with the others in the long, dark corridor—unable to see their faces, but feeling the excitement passing through her toes.

"Crawl to the main door. Make sure that you are quiet. Don't make a single sound."

They obeyed Ikemba, and followed him silently toward the main door. They would have walked, if not for the attendant sleeping at a desk near the door, one who was snoring loudly, letting the children know her sleep was of the heavy kind. They crept past her, one child behind another, knowing that the snoring woman would not awake; and she did not, allowing the children to crawl out of the main doors and onto the gravel path which lay outside.

And as Ijeoma felt the night to be warm, and saw the moon to be bright, she thanked Ikemba for leading them out of the cells, clutching his palms and holding his wrists, clasping her palms, then presenting them to Ikemba, seeing the gravel path running to the gate of the church—and moving toward it—returning to Ichulu—thanking Chukwu for Ikemba—praying that he be blessed for unlocking the cell doors—then feeling a descent, from the piercing scream—shattering her heart.

"I don't want to go! I don't want to go!"

One of the children began crying and screaming at Ikemba, even as the others began hushing him, and whispering, "CLOSE YOUR MOUTH!"

"Are you stupid?" Ikemba said. "You will wake up all the attendants!"

"But I don't want to go! I don't want to go! *Pastor is my home!*"

The boy began screaming, until the children were surrounded by seven attendants in pink-checkered uniforms, who were surprised to see the children out of the cells and quickly grabbed each child and threw them into the cells, while pulling out their canes—beating those who did not obey, watching some of the children run down the gravel path, toward the iron gate—hunting them, and throwing them, too, into the cells; and the children were all thrown into the cells at the hands of those seven attendants.

And Ijeoma could not understand why that boy had destroyed their plan; and wanted to beat him for what he had done, for crying out and denying her a reunion with home; Nnenna was home, and she was not there; Nnamdi was in Ichulu, and here she was, close to home, near home, angry at the world for not giving her what she wanted—angry at her chi for not guiding the children out of Amalike—because the foolish boy could not be silent, *chi . . . chi, where did you go, how many times . . . give me hope and take it, love, and take it . . . you are needed, chi . . . but you give sadness, only sadness, are you not from Chineke, and is Chineke not from Chukwu, and is the Most Supreme not good?*

She could not sleep in her cell, not when her thoughts troubled her and troubled her memories of home; not when those memories were becoming fainter and fainter, each sense of comfort blurring against the other. She barely remembered the aroma of Nnenna's soup, or the games she played with Chinwe, or the taste of Idemili's river water; and she could not sleep that night, raising herself many hours before the morning bell was rung; not signing any signs during bathing, or prayer, or the morning meal; not wanting to remind herself of the tragedies from the night before; not wanting to hear a single word—until Pastor Nwosu entered the dining hall, and placed a bucket and a pair of rubber gloves on a wooden table.

BAM-BAM! BAM BAM BAM!

"Good morning, Pastor!" said the children as they rose.

"Good morning . . . S-Sit down, all of you," said Pastor Nwosu, watching each child obey.

"This morning I was informed by my assistant that there was an escape attempt last night by the children of the Manifestation Quarters. I was told that the devil has found his way into my church . . . Apparently you all have started growing wings. When I flog you with my cane, it is not enough for you to learn your lesson. But I am not worried. Today I have come with a better punishment. Stand up, and form a line."

The children all stood from their seats and formed a line along a wall, closing their eyes as they faced the pastor; wondering if he would still punish them, and wishing for the attendants to stop raising their wooden canes.

"Ikemba, you foolish boy. I know that you were the leader of this nonsense."

"You are correct, Mr. Man of God!" said Ikemba, looking through the black of the pastor's eyes.

"I don't know how you opened the cells, but *you especially* will be punished this morning. Quickly! Come to the front."

Ikemba moved closer to the pastor, keeping his eyes on the pastor's lowered gaze as he went to receive whatever punishment awaited him.

"Tie him," said the pastor to the attendants.

Two attendants obeyed, hurrying to a back room to "get the rope; once they had returned with it, they tied it tightly around Ikemba's wrists and ankles.

"Open his mouth," said Pastor Nwosu.

The two attendants grabbed Ikemba's jaw and held it open.

"G-G-Give me a metal cup."

A cup was given to the pastor as he put on the rubber gloves and dipped the cup into the bucket's fluid. He did not have to tell his attendants the fluid's name once they saw how it burned Ikemba's tongue as it passed through him, watching him wince, then scream and shake with pain, some looking away as the blood, dripping from the corners of his mouth, fell into the cup of acid held beneath his chin.

And the other children were punished in the same way, bound by rope and forced to consume the acid; and when it was done to Ijeọma, she prayed for the pain to be swift and easy; but the pain could not be, as the acid in her mouth began scratching the back of her throat, like the beginnings of a cold, quickly eating her insides, sharp beaks of vultures gathering, and cutting the delicate pink turning white; she could not breathe as the acid lifted layers of skin, taking it, slicing it narrowly, as she screamed a scream, screaming over and again, until the attendants heard the pastor's command and let go of her shaking jaw. And when she fell atop the floor, shivering like an animal decapitated, she was forced onto her feet to be seated like the others.

Their mouths were open. It was too painful to keep them closed. Some of them were crying, and others who wanted to cry could not find the strength. Ijeọma sat in her seat quietly, praying that Chukwu would remove the pain, praying that Chukwu would allow her to fly to Ichulu, away from Pastor Nwosu. And when she looked to Ikemba, thinking that he would speak, thinking that he would challenge the pastor as he had typically done, he was silent; not looking at anything, or anyone inside the dining hall; not looking like the person he had been before consuming the acid; but pressing his eyes closed; wailing from the sorrows of his heart.

DIARY ENTRY #960   DATE UNKNOWN

you put me in a godless world and I am alone. why did you do that
Chukwu nobody is supposed to struggle like I have struggled nobody is
meant to live as a fatherless child and a prisoner and a mute. did you give
me a friend chukwu did you give me a sister did you give me anyone who
could talk like me or fly like me i am not ungrateful but I am not a fool
cheluchi was my sister from the same mother and the same father but how
can an infant understand this even chinwe, who befriended those girls who
hated me, the ones who scoffed at me and mocked me in my face i should
have told her, that day in Nta that she had killed my spirit, since it was
those girls who chinwe had befriended. and Uzodi,not even ikemba
understands they do not know who I am, and maybe it's because they are
godless too. if they believed in you the way i believe in you, wouldn't they
have flown to the sky with me? but they did not, and i am isolated in every
way a person can be isolated every song was in vain every wise proverb that
the elders used was wise only for that moment because nobody truly knows
or cares and nobody truly believes in the most supreme chukwu, if you
made it so that i would be alone forever take me to a place where loneliness
is a beautiful thing if you made it so that i would be alone forever, kill me
quickly, mercifully.

*   i did not think correctly, when you carried me to Igwe up to the sky i*
did not know and I am sorry. i am disgraceful see the things coming out of
me. i know you smell them since you're most supreme my bucket is full and
i've not cleaned my body. i did not think correctly this place has made me
see it, i am a fool, and I am sorry who am i chukwu who am I my skin
smells more bitter than the dying smell me how dirty i am you see it

chukwu you see it i know that I am worthless i know it. don't look at me.
even those children have done more, at least they speak too when they are
hungry and when they are angry

who am I, even to write the most supreme i know that i am useless they
hate me look at what they say, all of them even ikemba even uzodi and
chinwe they did not come. i did not see them we have spoken of their pain i
carried it in my heart they will not come i know that i am worthless: who
comes to see me in this prison? when I hear them unlock the door i think it
will be uzodi running to take me, or i think it will be you chukwu coming
from your Obi to take me home again, that you will never do it i am sorry
please i am sorry i wrote to you i am sorry i prayed to you i am sorry. i
called your name and i am sorry. please i beg you i beg you please please i
am sorry i was born a mute i am sorry i did not remain fully muted i made
a mistake chukwu ofodile i made a mistake nnenna I made a mistake
please forgive me. who am I please i will go i won't bother any of you again
please please forgive me

PART III

MERCY

1.

NOBODY IN ICHULU KNEW THAT Ijeọma had been sent to Amalike with-out any intention of returning. No freeborn person had been known to leave Ichulu without stating when they would return. Such stories could not be recalled; they bore no song, no dance, no memory. It was a reason why every farewell was assured, and every departure was no departure at all—not even the one of death. The elders often said, "Nza, nza, nza can fly through the wide bowels of Igwe, but it has only one nest to which it returns." And those were words that Ichulu honored—words which the village could not deny, believ-ing them when the ancestors rose as masked spirits; and believing them still when it learned Ijeọma had been moved from the village, believing that the one called their daughter would soon return, and that Chukwu would not punish them if any affliction befell her. She had not been living in Ichulu, but the village awaited her return—casually, patiently—knowing within them-selves that her return was inevitable.

Though nobody in Ichulu understood why Ọfọdile had removed Ijeọma. After the announcement of Ngọzi's pregnancy, there was little doubt that Chukwu had won the war against Anị. The goddess of the earth was now dead—and the village had turned from her orange breasts, and looked toward the magnificence of the heavens, as if they, too, would someday fly—or at least have visions of what lay above the clouds.

They said among themselves, "The Supreme Being has always been Most Supreme," while no longer whispering their gossip concerning Ọfọdile and his compound, but rather praising the man who gave life to Ijeọma: the girl who saved them from sacrificing the innocent among them, the one who refined their senses to what truly was, the one for whom their hearts were refusing reticence, as even the bearded Okoye confessed that Ichulu was changing by the divine, no longer trekking to the Stone of Anị to cut its unruly grass but abandoning the once-sacred stone, believing Chukwu to be Ichulu's sustainer—professing his enemy's child to be wondrous and holy.

But Ọfọdile did not know these things before dismissing Ijeọma. Notice is seldom given to a reputation revived. And unlike the rest of Ichulu, Ọfọdile could neither trust nor forgive the Supreme Being—cursing the Most Supreme, while snorting from many containers of snuff—Chukwu had mocked his family, a family that he had labored in making presentable to the village—allowing enemies to make Ijeọma a mute, creating a spectacle by causing her to fly, taking Nnamdị's ability to properly walk, causing his family to disrupt a village with well-preserved traditions, causing him to be a title-less man; what future could be expected from the one called Most Supreme; what light could there be in tomorrow's tomorrow, after receiving no honors or titles from Ichulu, after enduring the gossip of this judgmental village, one that would curse his name once it met with any hardship—the outbreak of disease, another flood, a gruesome famine—it would blame him and his household for all its calamities; and he would be angered, and mocked, and shamed. So he sent Ijeọma out of Ichulu—demanding that she never, on any day, be returned.

He made his decision, believing it to be true, reasoning that Ijeọma was an aberration, and was his greatest opposite. He who was normal—had endured the most abnormal of things, white cloth and palm oil—the two could not mix; the two were irreconcilable; the two were at war. So he dismissed her from Ichulu to become the headache of another man, carrying with him a belief of which he was certain: as long as Chukwu existed, Ijeọma would fly; and as long as Ijeọma flew, she would destroy his father's name.

Yet only he in his household accepted such reasoning. Nnamdị ran after Ijeọma and the metal ram the morning they had hurried away, limping as he went, not understanding why Ijeọma was leaving, pleading for Ọfọdile's reconsideration. And when he heard Ọfọdile's harshly spoken "No," he began limping into Nnenna's red-clay home and seeing Chelụchi crying on her raffia mat. He looked at her and wondered if she knew that Ijeọma had been removed from the village, then placed her in his arms—soothing her with old songs composed in the market square, wanting, too, to cry or scream or engage in the most cathartic of things—wanting to openly mourn the departure of Ijeọma. But he did not mourn. He did not indulge in his own emotions, because he was the one soothing a crying child.

He held her along the curves of his arms until evening came, leaning against the inner walls of the red clay home—rubbing the back of her infant neck, slowly succumbing to the weight of his drowsiness, closing his eyes, closing his eyes, until he heard the loud cries of the one called his mother, demanding Ijeọma's appearance. *How is it that she does not know,* he thought, as he placed Chelụchi on her sleeping mat, soon running to meet Nnenna outside.

"Mama of mine, why is it that are you calling for Ijeọma?"

"Nnamdị, have you seen her?"

"Yes. She was taken by a man on a metal ram, but I do not know where they have traveled . . ."

Nnamdị had not seen Nnenna this way before—with sweat gathering on her face, with quivering lips, with worry taking her eyes; and he could not recognize her without her strength, as a being so small and ordinary. He watched her turn and leave him, then enter Ọfọdile's obi—and he immediately heard shouting, the shrill and authoritative voice of the one called his mother consuming the entire compound. And he could not tolerate what soon became the harsh sounds of the ones called his mother and father—so he ran into Nnenna's red-clay home, covering Chelụchi's ears with his shaking hands—thanking the gods that she was sleeping, and praying—that she would not then tussle—or awake.

And within a moment, Nnenna joined him—entering her home in silence. He could see the many bruises on her face—the prominent one on her right cheek—and knew that they were causing her pain, yet caused her face to reveal not a thing except fury; and he wanted to ask questions concerning her face, and her pain; but knew he was too young to be told the truth of such things. So he exhaled and lay on his sleeping mat, waiting through dreams, for the morning to come.

And as he heard the chirping of nza birds, and the bleating of the compound's goats, he opened his eyes and saw that Nnenna was not there, and believed she had been reconciled with Ọfọdile. So he lifted himself with the strength of his heart—thinking of his many responsibilities as he took his frayed chewing stick—while moving toward Idemili to take his morning bath. And while on the path to the river—he heard a woman's screams coming from the market square, and began running toward it—running toward the market square—to listen to the words hidden beneath those screams—to hear the words—to which the one called his mother wanted Ichulu to bear witness.

"Cheeeeeeeiii! Chei! Chei!"

Nnamdị saw Nnenna entering the market square—screaming to the village unclothed, her breasts oval and flat, her rappa flaying about in her left hand, her pubic hairs as dark as the bruises that colored her face.

"Cheeeeeeeiii! Chei! Chei! Come and see what he has done! Mind your ears and listen to what he has done!"

Nnamdị and the market square listened to the words of Nnenna—seeing her nakedness, and preparing themselves for the person's name, readied to watch another's destruction through the power of vengeful words.

"That man whom you call *Ekwueme*. That man whom I used to call my husband—*that wicked man*, he has taken my daughter from me. *He has taken my Ada*—stolen her! *And now she is with our enemies in Amalike.*" Nnenna fell to her knees, and the people at the market square gathered around her.

"Last night he was telling me that my Ada is not returning to Ichulu, *that my Ada is not returning!* I asked that fool of a man, I asked him to return my daughter to me, and he said I will never see my Ada again. He said that he has dismissed her, *never to return to Ichulu*. He, Ekwueme, this fool of a man, told the mother of his children that she would never see the child whom she carried for nine months—*the child whom I birthed with my own blood.*"

"If we knew Ijeoma was going to Amalike, we would have quickly removed her from that vehicle!" said many men who were present when Ijeoma left the village.

"So what did I do?" Nnenna said, not looking at the men who had spoken. "I went to his home and I took his machete, and I held it to his neck—*I held his machete to his neck*, to kill him the way he has killed my Ada. He lifted himself and his hand caught the blade of his machete. I prepared to strike again, but he seized the machete from me and beat me—beat me like a wild animal. Ichulu, come and hear what he has done. Come and listen to what Ekwueme has done. He has taken my Ada from me. Me! The mother of his children. I swear it on my nakedness, I swear it. Ofodile, the son of Nwankwo, will lose his peace and his chi will drown in Idemili. *I said his chi will drown in Idemili! I swear it on my nakedness.*"

Nnenna began weeping against her knees, and all of the market square became uneasy. How could Chukwu's vessel be exiled from the village, they asked, knowing within themselves that it would anger the Supreme Being— believing that punishment would befall all of Ichulu. They gathered around Nnenna—lifting their voices and hands, begging the Supreme Being to have mercy on them and punish the culprit and his chi for their deeds.

"Ofodile was the man responsible for removing Ijeoma," they said, "let him eat all of Chukwu's wrath!"

"Let him burn as a sacrifice!" a girl said.

"How can a man be so foolish?" asked a man.

"I will pray to my chi that Ọfọdile never knows peace!"

"Let his compound burn with the rage of the gods," the boys whispered among themselves.

And Nnenna continued cursing the name of Ọfọdile—her voice trembling as she heard the sympathies of Ichulu. And it pleased her that she had gained the support of her village—but she grieved still, knowing that nobody could retrieve Ijeọma from Amalike—remembering that those who last crossed the town's boundary returned as outcasts; and that six did not return—not even as masquerades. Who would sacrifice their life and their eternity, she thought, who would fight a war without their opponent's kind of gun? And she believed that there was nothing to be done to retrieve Ijeọma, except destroy—with much haste—the name of Ọfọdile.

And Ichulu looked upon her bruised body; mourning with her, pitying her; and when all became somewhat settled, the bearded Okoye ran toward Nnenna and took her rappa from her hands, before using it to conceal her body and watching as Nnenna's face turned to his.

"Thank you, Okoye."

"It is nothing," Okoye said.

"What will I do, Okoye? What will I do?"

"You will come and live with me. Bring your remaining children and come and live with me."

And Nnenna returned to her knees weeping, not resisting when Okoye knelt beside her and held her the way he did many harvests ago. And she let the feeling of his heat consume her—staying in his arms atop the orange earth; until Anyanwụ began moving again—and the breeze began shifting Igwe's clouds; and after many moments, the people dispersed; and Okoye accompanied Nnenna to her red-clay home.

And once they arrived, they gathered all they could gather, collecting pans and water pots and the wooden masks decorating Nnenna's walls, with Nnenna carrying every rappa she owned and Okoye using her bright blue one to tie Cheluchi against the curve of Nnenna's back. And they both told Nnamdị to walk beside them as they prepared to leave; watching the young boy remain quiet and obey, as the four of them walked onward; toward the sight of Ọfọdile emerging from his obi.

"Where are you going?" Ọfọdile said.

But nobody responded, even as he looked about them, watching Cheluchi suck her thumb; quickly glancing at the darkness surrounding Nnenna's cheek, seeing the one called his son looking at him in silence; discretely ignoring Okoye's cruel eyes.

"Will you not answer me? I said where are you going?"

"Will you close your mouth!" Okoye said. "After sending your holy daughter to our enemies in Amalike and beating your wife now beside me, you think we should now answer your questions? Eat shit!"

Ọfọdile kept silent; even as he wanted to strike Okoye's face, he did not. He was unprepared to fight Okoye again, desperate in his silence for anyone to answer his question.

"Ọfọdile, I am leaving—I have been too patient with you. I have watched you hate our Ada since she lost the gift of speech, and now you have taken her from me. You have stolen my child—and will never be forgiven. I am leaving the compound of your father, so that you alone will be punished for your theft."

"Then go!" Ọfọdile said, wanting to bruise her other cheek; but turning to enter his obi, as he heard the voice of the one called his son.

"Father of mine . . . fasten yourself to power."

But he did not turn to the voice of Nnamdị, but entered his obi— supplicating to the ones called his ancestors, and the ones called his gods—to kill his enemies for destroying the goodness of his home. And he did not know that all in Ichulu had learned that he had exiled Ijeọma until he saw children running into his compound and excreting heaps of shit around his red-clay obi; and watching women throw snaps of disdain at him as he fetched along Idemili, feeling some spitting on him; feeling some hurting him with their slaps, as he dared not speak to the other men, fearing their threatening eyes; believing that if he spoke to any of them, they would kill him quickly—without remorse.

The anger of Ichulu had landed on Ọfọdile's head, and he carried it with his chi in his quiet compound. No longer were there sounds of anyone calling him family, or the sight of anyone calling his home good; there were no visitors; there were no consultations; so he sat with himself in the company of his misfortune, drinking palm wine; then gulping it, snorting snuff, then shoving it against the walls of his nose; not eating hefty meals, as there was nobody there to cook the animals he had hunted or the yams he had uprooted; but plucking oranges from his compound's trees, until there were no more oranges to be plucked; he had not learned to cook because he was told it was an act of women, and as his stomach pain pushed him near the memories of Nnenna's pounded yam; he savored his saliva, and began praying for his stomach to be merciful.

And still, his thoughts wandered to the memory of the one called his brother: Olisa—The Eagle of Ichulu—the leper—the one for whom he did not speak when illness had appeared on his body. "The man is an abomination" was what Ọfọdile had said when he learned that Olisa developed leprosy. "He must leave the village; I am his only brother, so I promise to care for his only son, Ụzọdị. But as tradition states, the man must leave the village." It was Ọfọdile's words that made it less difficult for the elders to banish Olisa to the Evil Forest. "If his brother honors the tradition," they said, "who are we to contest it"—and now as he sat with his chi in his obi, drunk from palm wine and filled with snuff—he believed that he could hear the voice of Olisa asking, "Which tradition taught you to hate your brother"; he believed that he could hear him—his voice, firm and plain—but said it was the wind—saying it was only air—until he found more snuff, and put it inside his nose.

He was with his chi, fully abandoned by his family—exposed to the ridicule resounding throughout Ichulu; there was no more will to make what was said, an act to be done, to make an incredible dream, a thing to be touched, and heard, and seen; he had broken his vow—the one which he had made when his brother became ill, the vow that said he would never again be ashamed—the one that he renewed when Ijeǫma was born; and as he sat in his obi, he was growing more fearful—finding little solace in his memories— who taught you to hate your brother, who taught you to hate me—firm and plain—who taught you, Ǫfǫdile, that a title was greater than one's home, that hearsay was greater than one's own daughter, that wealth reaching Igwe's sky is greater than your obi, do you envy me, do you envy Ijeǫma because Ichulu praises her—was I to love a leper was I to love a leper—and yet you left your compound to reside in mine, the compound of a leper, and called my obi your own, was my home not good without many houses, was Ezinne not smiling, did Ụzǫdị not laugh—YOU WERE AN ABOMINATION AND YOU HAD TO DIE AND DID I NOT RAISE YOUR SON AS I PROM-ISED YOU BEFORE YOUR DEATH DID I NOT DEFEND YOUR SON BEFORE ICHULU'S MEN ỤZǪDỊ WAS OUR HOPE ỤZǪDỊ WAS OUR HOPE ỤZǪDỊ WAS TO MARRY WOMEN AND WIN TITLES THE BLAME IS FOR YOU AND YOUR GODS AND YOUR CHI NO MAN IS TO LOVE A LEPER EVEN IF THE LEPER IS HIS BROTHER GET OUT OF THIS OBI BEFORE I SEND MY CHI TO BURN YOUR SPIRIT AND BURN THE GROUND THAT YOU HAVE MADE YOUR HOME WHY ARE THEY LAUGHING AT ME IS THAT IJEǪMA, IJEǪMA WHY ARE YOU HERE IT IS YOU WHO HAS CAUSED ALL OF THIS YOU AND YOUR ABOMINA-TIONS WHAT MAN CAN LOVE AN ABOMINATION FLYING LIKE AN ANIMAL SILENT LIKE AN ANIMAL THEY NO LONGER RESPECT MY NAME LEAVE MY OBI BEFORE I SEND MY CHI TO PUNISH YOU IJEǪMA WHY ARE YOU DANCING IJEǪMA WHERE HAVE YOU ESCAPED TO OLISA I HAVE TOLD YOU I WAS NOT TO LOVE A LEPER I AM EKWUEME TRADITIONS MUST BE HONORED YOU WERE AN ABOMINATION IJEǪMA WHY ARE YOU SMILING WHY HAVE YOUR EYES GROWN NARROW AND THIN—

He was knocking; he was knocking his fists against the floor of Olisa's obi, attempting to expel the many spirits, over and again, knowing it was time to leave the vexing obi; wanting to visit Idemili to cleanse his body, cursing the name of Ijeọma once more as he drank his palm wine; and snorted his snuff, calling for the gods to end her life.

And when he lifted himself—he fell down; fear and wine had toppled him—with his gourd empty as he was now thirsty—he left his obi when the night was as black as Ijeọma's eyes, and began trekking to Idemili, where he would drink from the river water—and it would heal him—and it would make every pain flee, beyond and away, that was what he knew—as he walked haphazardly along the path—balancing himself on nearby trees, the voice of Olisa following him—the face of Ijeọma pursuing him—alongside the gossip of Ichulu, as he became fearful—while hoping for beyond and away.

But Idemili was still when Ọfọdile arrived, as if unwilling to heal him; and he saw himself in the river; the moon's light had made it so. He had become thin, and his red rappa wrapped across his legs as if swaddling a baby. He could no longer hear the voice of the one called his brother, or see the face of the one called his daughter, or feel the gossip of Ichulu; and he was happy— happy to the point of abandonment, removing his rappa—and with the moon so bright, seeing his full self—his arms rising from his sides—his back bending downward, swaying, as his hips were shifting—gliding with his feet lifting upward, patting the ground the way drummer hands pat drums—his knees bending with grace and jubilation—unlocking themselves to the happy and blithe—his back curving, curving, like potent river waves—no longer hearing those voices—but dancing like in his youth, slowly, then quickly—then violently—dancing like in his youth again—beginning to smile, beginning to dance more violently, as if pursuing a dream.

And the following morning, when the people went to Idemili to fetch and to bathe, they found Ọfọdile's red rappa and feared that he had committed suicide. And once they saw Ezinne—the one called mother of the osu—they gave her the cloth, and began asking if she knew where he was.

"I have not seen him since I left his compound many weeks ago."

"But he is missing!" said the people gathered, thinking of Nnenna's curse.

"Then let it be," Ezinne said—rubbing the entirety of her bald scalp— then leaving the people gathered to themselves.

The word of Qfodile's disappearance quickly entered the ears of the village, and soon it resided upon the eyes of Igbokwe. He sent four very young men to look for his body in Idemili, though after many days of swimming to its depths they did not find his corpse. So the dibia, not knowing whether Qfodile was dead or alive, threw his sacred cowrie shells to determine an answer—but saw that no answer was given by the gods, and decided that if Qfodile did not appear in four days, he would pronounce him dead throughout the village. Igbokwe quickly thought of the fate of Ichulu and the uncertainty made from the gods not answering his cowrie shells—wondering if Qfodile's disappearance was the beginning of Ichulu's demise, wondering, too, if it was a sign of Chukwu's anger because Ijeoma was no longer living in Ichulu. He could not answer these questions, not with his cowrie shells; he wanted Ijeoma's body, but it was no longer available to him. So he prayed to Chukwu, praying for mercy on his village—and after four days had passed— praying for mercy on Qfodile's corpse, even as he was unsure that Qfodile had truly committed suicide—pronouncing him dead to a spiteful village, one that was grateful for the death of Ekwueme.

Nnenna, too, was grateful when she was told of Igbokwe's pronouncement. She smiled a smile believing that she would no longer see Qfodile—not when she went to Idemili, not when she visited the market square. She had told the ones called her children that Qfodile was nothing to them, nothing more than evil—that he neither cared for them nor loved them, that he used them only as instruments to boast before the village; that he was selfish— and when Nnamdi and Cheluchi seemed to disagree, she reminded them that they had a new father, a good father, one who loved them as they were. And on the day of Igbokwe's pronouncement, she swept that father's compound while awaiting Igbokwe's visit, preparing herself to be a widow receiving the news of a husband's death, staying in Okoye's compound to make herself available, cleaning its earth, cooking large meals, then hearing soft ringing coming from the bells of Igbokwe's staff.

"Igbokwe, welcome," Nnenna said.

"My daughter, how are you?"

"I am well . . . What will I give the great dibia of Ichulu?"

"My daughter, I will drink the water of Idemili."

"It is no problem. Nnamdi, Nnamdi! Go and get water from Okoye's obi!"

Nnenna and Igbokwe both heard Nnamdi's faint yes—and watched him appearing from the back of the compound, then into Okoye's obi—then watched as he gave Igbokwe a cup of river water.

"Nnamdi, thank you," said Igbokwe, as he began sipping from the cup, as Nnamdi nodded in his direction, before turning to move away.

"Do not leave, my child. I have news that concerns this entire household."

"Igbokwe, what is it?" said Nnenna.

"Where is Okoye?" Igbokwe asked.

"He is hunting," Nnenna said.

"That is fine. I will say what I must say, and tell Okoye another time." Igbokwe lifted the cup and took another sip of water.

"It is Ofodile. He has died."

"What," Nnamdi said.

Igbokwe turned to Nnamdi—and watched terror seize him.

"Great dibia, what do you mean? What do you mean . . . my father has died?"

"Ofodile is dead!" said Nnenna. "Are your ears not working?

But Nnamdi did not answer, quickly turning to the one called his mother.

"Igbokwe, thank you for giving me this word . . . but are you surprised? That man was a useless man. What did he do for this village—nothing. What did he do except cause problems? He was an abomination! We should have exiled him years ago or taken him to the Evil Forest, we should ha—What is this . . . Nna . . . *is madness within you!*"

And Nnenna wiped the saliva that Nnamdi put on her face, looking at the one called her son, not knowing why he had defiled her. She lifted herself to strike him, but Igbokwe held her waist; and she sat down, watching Nnamdi moving away—seeing Igbokwe not looking at her at all, but hearing the dibia's assured farewell—then hearing nothing, for many moments—until the CLINK, CLINK sound of someone sharpening their machete—pierced through the air, as she felt the sticky residue on her face, and felt the anger still, then the grief, not from loss, but from realizing she had been—for a very long time—what she hated most in the world; and she ran toward the sound, quickly, quickly, quick—running as if death stood behind her neck—running to her neighbor, and seizing his machete—and using its blade to cut off her hair—running it through each lock—cutting through each bundled strand, while asking the startled neighbor for a knife—and when one was given, she moved it through her scalp—shaving her hair low, toward skin and blooms of blood; praying to the gods, to the ancestors, for atonement, for wisdom, for the spirit of Qfǫdile, the handsome face of Qfǫdile, the one whom Ijeǫma resembles, their children, their baby Chelụchi, Nnamdị and his crass reminder that she would soon return, that she would soon come home come home come home: sweet Ada of mine.

And Igbokwe, too, prayed for Ijeǫma to come home, praying for the return of Ichulu's daughter, their only vessel to the Most Supreme. He sensed the emergence of a thought: to send some very young men to Amalike, to return her to the village; but he immediately recoiled, remembering the murders of the eastern town and their wicked divination; *the lives of Ichulu's people would not be risked a second time*; but Chukwu will destroy this village if Ijeǫma is not within it; and the thought came again, over and again; sending men, fields and fields of very young men, who would be strong and protected; *but the divination is failing, since the holy stones had not protected Ichulu*; and the cowrie shells were not being answered; what of making sacrifices to the Supreme Being, a sacrifice of one thousand chickens, one hundred goats and rams, and fifty cows, and if Chukwu is not satisfied a child could appease the hunger of the one Most Supreme; *Igbokwe does not make sacrifices to Chukwu: the Most Supreme is Most Supreme*—but which Igbokwe has seen the gods at war, and a girl who flies, and a child delivered from the Evil Forest, no Igbokwe has communed with Chukwu through the flesh. And as the dịbịa sat in his red-clay obi, lifting his goat-horn cup to divine which sacrificial name the cowrie shells would reveal, he heard commotion building near the path to the market square.

Ngozi you are so beautiful, mgbo, mgbo
Ngozi you are so beautiful, mgbo, mgbo
Whoever chi has appointed, let them rule
You are so beautiful, mgbo, mgbo
Whoever chi has appointed, let them rule
You are so beautiful, mgbo, mgbo

And then he heard sounds that astonished him, the cries of many little babies at once; and he hurried to the path of the market square, and bore witness to the reason the people had been singing their song—seeing Ngozi—and seeing that she had given birth to four children: two carried in the folds of her cradled arms, two carried in the arms of the one called her husband—as all were dancing, and dancing—to the melody of the singing, as the people began shouting the names of the infant children: Chukwuka the first child, Chukwuzatam the second child, Chukwudịmma the third child, and the fourth, the only female child, they named Ijeọma. And Igbokwe believed that Chukwu was alive and was not angry with the village, as he felt his ease return with his reason, as he began weeping among Ichulu's jubilation, accepting the good word that the sacrifices would never occur again.

2.

IJEỌMA SAT IN THE BACK of the classroom, leaning on her desk with her red notebook to her side—attending to very little of what was being taught. Her thoughts had been lingering in the past: to when the pastor had said, "Now that I have punished you wizards, you will turn your wretched backs from evil," hearing the pastor saying, "You children will receive the Lord, and it is me and my church who will give Him to you"—seeing him holding his cane, and adjusting his spectacles—smiling as they raised their cries— feeling her own back tightening and aching, remembering, with the pastor screaming, "YOU MUST STUDY THE BIBLE! AND KNOW THE WORD OF GOD! UNTIL EVERYTHING IN YOUR MEMORY IS WIPED!"; and Ijeọma sat in the back of the classroom shivering—moving her tongue across her eroded mouth, not listening to Phyllipa talk of Precious Words Ministries, not listening to her say that they were made in God's image and likeness and did evil because a snake had seduced their ancestors into temptation. She sat, instead, with her gaze fixed on the black-ened wall, pondering the questions that they had asked as children: "Why did God, who has all the power in the universe, take rest on the seventh day?" "And if Cain and Abel were the only children of Eve, how did they bear any children?" "And if Jesus was begotten of God, they were separated . . . and if they were separated why did they still love each other?"

"It does not mean the two cannot love simply because they were *separated*," she recalled Phyllipa telling Ikemba.

"You are right ma . . . you are—you are right," Ikemba had said, though Ijeọma still recalled the urgency with which he had whispered into her ear when he had told her that separation meant it was possible for them not to love. "The Son could have seen the Father with bitterness in his heart . . . by the very fact that he now existed apart from his daddy." That was the phrase she recalled, and she recalled nodding her head when he had said it, as she was nodding her head now, against the palms of her hands; then looking beyond the past, feeling echoes of Ikemba's whispers—their growing heat, and tender sighs—wondering if he would touch her with his urgency—wondering if he could sense those hums of freedom—moving softly along her heart.

And she sat in the back of the classroom, looking for Ikemba's hands among the rows and rows of hands that sat atop metal desks, holding translu-cent pens. She had not found the pair that belonged to him, while remembering her words; remembering, then, her many lessons with Phyllipa, how scripture had been plainly taught before the language called English; and how she had wanted very much to comprehend those new words, wanting to write in her diary; wanting to understand the things that the other children had under-stood, wanting to feel among; without any attention given to the fact of her muteness. And she began rolling her pen when thinking of how she had stud-ied again, over and again, the words Phyllipa had written on the blackened wall: *dog, cat, apple,* and *rat,* studying again, until she had slowly known them; believing herself foolish for struggling to have read words like *cat,* turning her eyes against herself when she recalled the Christian books she had been given to read; books written for children much younger than her, ones which she had labored to read each day; having read them in many incorrect ways, for as long as she had been reading them—studying them again, because she had forgotten exactly how the studying had begun—as she had moved to sentences—and then to larger books—writing small paragraphs in her red notebooks with handwriting small and fine, and showing those paragraphs to Pastor Nwosu, who had commanded her to continue improving.

And in time, she learned more words and wrote longer sentences, and read the works of Dwight L. Moody and Henry Venn and William Wilberforce and Fanny Crosby—all at the orders of the pastor—studying their sentence structures, and uncovering the meaning of their words in church dictionaries and encyclopedias, then putting those works aside to practice and write in the quiet of the cells. And when Phyllipa had said, "Recite the alphabet," Ijeǫma had written the alphabet before twenty seconds. And when Phyllipa had said, "Write an essay on the story of Noah," Ijeǫma had written an essay, whose closing line was quoted by the pastor during one of his Sunday sermons. And when Phyllipa had said, "Write a poem," Ijeǫma had written:

The Father took me from my mother's home,
The Father brought me off my sinful road
The Father loves his name, loves his Son's too;
The Father turned, and made my life anew.

Ijeǫma had written for Phyllipa, had written for the pastor, and, in her green diary, had written for herself. And after nine years of continued writing, she had become fluent in the language called English, crafting and seeing those things which the tongue did not make, writing in red notebooks to communicate with others in the church, writing of personal matters in the diary Phyllipa had once given her—as writing became her music; her sentences gave her reasons to dance, as she could now release the noises of her thoughts through her body in a different way—carefully, openly, in the bright pages of her notebooks.

And like her writing, many things had changed through the nine years, since many of the children with whom she had been held were now attendants of the Manifestation Quarters. Very few were returned to the families who had sent them, while the others who had been taken from Amalike's streets were moved throughout the world, traded by the hands of foreign people; and Ijeọma was uncounted among them—for a reason she had wanted to know—assuming it was because the pastor believed her demons had not been excised.

And her assumption was not incorrect from the gaze of Precious Word Ministries. Ijeọma still rose from the ground as an attendant of the church, doing so in secret, in the privacy of her bedroom, not looking upon her wooden desk, or her open mirror, one she had once thought would take her back to Ichulu—as the light that passed through her morning window, beckoned her with its pull—drawing her toward the warmth of its soft orange whenever she faced the sky—whenever she felt her wholesome body—rising into the air—feeling the touch of her chi's vibration build something within her more cathartic than a scream; then in the sky she saw those persons, those many persons, smiling and beaming, blessing her with the love they beheld, watching lilies pour forth from their eyes, as the lilies sang songs bemused by laughter, as trees waned in a dance of sunlight and serenity, stretching their branches beyond each person's eyes, laughing at incurable things—shedding antidotes of antidotes through leaves and petals and bursting seeds, as the crowns of their heads bore gems and rocks, sitting across each person's head, glowing like the hope before a fire ignited, summoning lost things, summoning forgotten things, summoning the plenty: the infinities and forevers within a moment, as cruel patterns began to flee, as cruel thoughts began to flee—imprisoned by the horizon—with clouds descending like valleys—plain as their upper lips—each person's lips—as birds sang newer songs, in newer ways, chirping before their minds could know, as tears trembled, waiting in their eyes—each eye—each person's eyes—undulating through smiles made by spontaneous forces—the kind before a chuckle, the kind before a laugh—roses resting on their tongues, moonlight passing through their lips—bearing the soft enunciations of a lantern—blue, black, red, green, dancing like gnats across the bridges of their noses—across the wide of their eyes beneath the stories of their souls; and Ijeọma did not forget that she belonged to the Most Supreme, and did not underestimate the weight of Chukwu's power.

For nine years she was persuaded to become a Christian, and for nine years she secretly dismissed Christianity—pushing to the farthest corner the Bible sitting on her desk, when she pronounced in her room that Amalike's Christ could never be her own—knowing of his death on a cross, and his resurrection from a grave: a story like many she had heard before, where the gods were called several things—powerful, awesome, mighty in battle, the one who grants wealth and riches, and cures every kind of disease—an ordinary Christ, a man and god of many things, she confessed, things which by themselves make no kind of god exceptional; and she would forget the drunk exclamations of the titles of Precious Word before rising to the air, where human praise was inconsequential.

Ijeọma was induced by Phyllipa to worship the Christian god; and she felt much sorrow in refusing a person whom she found to be benevolent; one who would secretly sing to her in Igbo by the church edifice; one who had given her roasted yam when food had become scarce. She could recall days when Phyllipa had placed paper notes inside those unauthorized food flasks. *This is the day which the Lord hath made*, one read, *Try and rejoice and be glad in it*. And Ijeọma would quietly discard those notes once Phyllipa had departed, then focus on the food she had received, smiling before the yam, and eating it as though it were more precious than her chi. And when Phyllipa would return to say, "I love you by the grace of God," Ijeọma would write, *I love you too*—not wanting to disclose the secret she thought would devastate the one she admired, so avoiding matters concerning conversion and faith, even while sitting in the back of a Precious Word classroom.

"Today we will be returning to the book of Exodus," Phyllipa said, beginning the lesson for that day's Bible study, watching as all the attendants opened their Bibles and waited for further instruction.

"I want you to turn to chapter three, verse thirteen. Have you found it," she said as the attendants began nodding their heads.

"Good, good. Now, in this chapter, Moses is speaking to God. He is asking God how the sons of Israel should address him. And God in the form of a burning bush says, 'I am who I am.' Now . . . what do you think God means by this?"

Ijeọma clutched her red notebook as she turned from her memories, latching on to the words of Phyllipa's question—how could a bush on fire speak with such frankness, she thought, or name itself more assuredly than the common person—and what could stop such a bush from becoming a tree or a python or an infant child, and say that it simply was.

"It means God has named Himself to be whoever God says He is. It is not man's place to question God. It is man's obligation to obey God's will."

Ijeọma heard the conviction with which Ikemba spoke, and her heart began lowering in her chest.

"That is correct, Ikemba. The name that God gives Moses is at once a mystery and a definite thing. 'I am' is the name he has chosen to give us. What other names can we call God?"

"Yahweh," said one attendant.

"Jehovah Jireh," said another.

"El Shaddai," said one with glee.

"Ijeọma, what of you? What other names can we call God?"

Ijeọma wrote something quickly in her red notebook and watched Phyllipa move to where she was sitting, then showed Phyllipa what she had written, thinking somehow that she would accept it.

"Ijeọma what you have written is inappropriate. Chukwu is not another name for the God that we worship. Chukwu belongs to a different religion, one that has no place in this classroom. What if the pastor were to have seen this? Speaking Igbo as well as attempting to write it are prohibited on these premises. *Do not fail to remember it.*"

Ijeọma nodded her head and closed her red notebook, acknowledging that she had nearly exposed herself as a Pagan; but acknowledging, too, that the word Chukwu best translated the word God in Igbo. Just as God reigned supreme above all creation, revealing himself in mysterious ways, so did Chukwu; and now Phyllipa argued that such thinking was unacceptable, and perhaps she was right, she thought, lowering her eyes to her own reasoning—recalling her own unbelief in the Christian god, while recalling her faith in the Most Supreme. She stared into the rust of her metal desk, shamefully waiting for the Bible study to end; and once it had, she began returning to her bedroom to place her Bible on the wooden table, keeping her eyes lowered as she nursed her own regrets, turning her eyes against herself once she glanced at the pimples in her reflection; then she left her room again, and took with her her green diary before checking the calendar for the date and heading toward the large ngwu tree that once stopped light from entering the cell in which she was kept. She sat beneath its broad, waxy leaves, and began writing:

DIARY ENTRY #907   1 DECEMBER 1999

Chukwu I have come to write you again. I hope you are well. I know you are well because Anyanwu is shining brightly and the clouds in Igwe are whiter than the teeth of children. I know you are well because you lifted me from the ground this morning and brought me closer to you.

Chukwu how is Ichulu? Does Igbokwe still pray to you in the mornings? I know he does. Does my mother still remember me? Are Nnamdi and Cheluchi getting along? Yes, yes I know it. I miss them Chukwu, all of them, even my father. I know I was not his favorite child, but I do miss him somewhat. I hope he's still hunting, and has learned to get along with Chinwe's father. That girl, sweet Chinwe, I know she is married and pregnant by now, and still taking trips to the Place of Osu, visiting Uzodi, and hearing all of his precious stories.

When will I leave this place Chukwu? I hope that my exile will soon end because I do want to leave Amalike and go back to my home. Today I said that the Christian god could be given your name. I know now that I was being foolish and not thinking properly. Phyllipa was right. I cannot translate you into a different language any more than I can become a Christian. Never again will I write my way into a church. No being can have a name like yours. You are above all created things. Never forget me Chukwu. I am yours.

"IJ, WHAT ARE YOU WRITING?"

Ijeọma closed her diary and kept its pen within it, not fully recognizing Ikemba's voice when he spoke; but then she turned toward him, raising herself from the ground as he moved toward the ngwu tree; kissing his cheek, then softly touching his finger; and not resisting when he firmly wrapped his hands around her waist. They stood behind the ngwu tree and closed their eyes to begin their silent prayer—a prayer that had their heartbeats quickening with joy—both believing that nobody on the premises could see them. And when the moment passed, Ijeọma sat atop the shadowed ground and pulled Ikemba toward her knees.

"Why do you always keep your writing a secret? Is it because of this Y2K?"

Ijeọma turned her eyes from Ikemba's smile, and revealed a new pen and a new page in her red notebook.

Diaries are meant to be secret.

"You are right, my love . . . Anyway, I meant to tell you immediately after Bible study that I thought you were correct in calling God *Chukwu*. Never mind the things Phyllipa says. Her husband is the true Bible scholar."

Ijeọma remained silent, neither signing nor writing a word.

"Are you beginning to doubt yourself? Let me tell you, IJ . . . I was thinking the same thing. Chukwu is the way we Igbos call the name of God. It is a matter of translation."

Ijeọma returned to her red notebook.

No, my love. It is a matter of belief.

"We have had this discussion before. You think we believe in different gods . . . *but our gods are the same . . .*"

Let's not talk of this.

"No, Ijeọma. I want to talk about what we have been talking about. *Why do you keep avoiding this conversation?*"

What exactly am I avoiding?

"Ijeọma, we have been in love for nine years now. And for nine years we have been dodging this topic. Ijeọma, I love you, but I am also a follower of Jesus . . ."

Then follow him, Ikemba; except do not expect me to forget what is mine. I do not mean to be stubborn, but I cannot (and will not) follow Jesus and Chukwu at the same time.

"Yes you can, IJ. Our ancestors did not know the name of Jesus because he had not revealed himself to them. If he had shown them his many signs, they would have called him Chukwu's son. Ijeọma, it is as simple as this . . . Chukwu is God the Father, and God the Father is Chukwu . . ."

No, my love. They are different. Is Chukwu male, or elderly, or white? Does my religion not have power of its own, or do I have to conquer every corner of the world before Chukwu's name has meaning? Look at what is happening in the name of your god. Look at those children; or have you forgotten? These children are being kept under the orders of the pastor. You all have made Mr. Nwosu your god. Follow your god, and I will follow my own.

"Ehhh so you want to follow the gods now? What of Anị? Ask any Igbo person and he will tell you that people not fit to live are given to the goddess as a sacrifice. Is death not worse than slavery . . ."

Anị is dead in my village.

"Really? And what was it that killed her."

I saved a child, and it killed the goddess.

The two fell silent——becoming unsure of who they were becoming.

"I love you, Ijeọma . . . I have always loved you . . . And I want you to marry me . . ."

I love you, too, Ikemba, but we must both be careful about what we are ~~doing~~ saying.

"Why is it that you are not believing my good words?" Ikemba said in Igbo.

~~Listen~~ I have my beliefs and you have yours. I understand what you have said, Ikemba; but I have seen my own signs. I know that I love you, too, and that fact will endure.

"Don't you know we will one day die! I don't want my beloved to perish in hellfire because she did not believe in the word of God . . ."

Ikemba, when did our ancestors start perishing?

The two fell silent again, ending the argument as they typically had as Ijeọma turned to her diary without resolve, writing in its pages—not wanting to watch Ikemba return from where he came, yet watching him still—both reminding themselves that they loved each other as fully as they knew how. And though their love did not convert one to the other's most sacred belief, it sustained them through the years, and created for them a place of refuge—a place to where they could escape when they thought of going home, giving them security when Pastor Nwosu threatened them with punishment— having them hopefully in the morning's survival; and they remained with each other despite their conflicting beliefs; and they kissed each other with pressing lips, remembering their own love, remembering that it began when he found her looking at him in secret, and when he asked why she did so, he saw her growing more mysterious; and began perceiving those things he knew had laid beyond her eyes—since he was pulled toward her, too—drawn up by her beautiful frame, drawn up by her nighttime-colored eyes—as they spoke to each other, sharing their hearts during the evening meal—falling deeply, then more deeply, attending to those things more precious than a church's name.

It was their love which transformed Ikemba, who believed such love came from the hands of Pastor Nwosu. So he protected this love, obeying the will of God as was determined by the teaching of his new church. He had not known that something had changed within him the night he was given the pastor's acid, and fell silent at memories of that night, when he thought the pastor cast out his many demons—refusing to fight Pastor Nwosu, and beginning to obey the pastor's words—believing that any follower of Christ was an actual follower of Christ—falling silent as the pastor bruised and burned the newer children—apologizing to the pastor for all his sins, for urinating on him, for attempting to escape; and he was forgiven after he promised to reject any temptation toward disobedience, and to become truer to the ways of Precious Word Ministries.

It was with such conviction that Ikemba led the children of the Manifestation Quarters into the church sanctuary on Sunday. He had tied them together using the church's old ropes, and was leading them toward the front of the altar, not hearing them dragging their feet as they went, not seeing their heads swinging low as if too heavy for their bodies.

"BRING THAT BOY TO ME!" said Pastor Nwosu.

Ikemba quickly untied a little boy from the rope and led him to the side of the pastor.

"TODAY! ALL OF YOU GATHERED HERE WILL WITNESS A MIRACLE!" said Pastor Nwosu.

"AMEN!" cried the congregation. "HOLY GHOST FIRE!" cried the congregation.

"This boy here has been possessed by evil spirits, and TODAY! I will remove every single one of them. BRING ME THE HOLY WATER!"

Ikemba left the altar and then quickly returned with a bucket of water and a thick palm branch, leaving them all near the pastor's feet.

"WHAT IS YOUR NAME?" said Pastor Nwosu.

The little boy looked upward and gave no response.

"AM I SPEAKING TO THE SPIRIT OF DEAFNESS? I SAID WHAT IS YOUR NAME!"

The boy gazed into the pastor's eyes, unmoved by the pastor's yelling; but stood before him, silently engaging in his protest, which vexed the pastor; and led the pastor to begin shaking a boy who was tired of being hurt and touched, who recoiled his head and spat onto the pastor's face—with mucus-coated saliva running down the pastor's spectacles, all the way to his lips—as the angry boy frowned, as Ikemba grabbed the boy and threw him onto the sanctuary floor, seizing a cane from an attendant—and beating the boy, watching him quivering at every stroke—hearing him screaming as he was beaten, not feeling satisfied, not feeling satisfied, until the lashes would break his skin—beating the little boy, lashing the reddened child—until his blood became blood which the church gathered could witness.

"My sso—it is enough, Ikemba," Pastor Nwosu said. "It is enough."

And Ikemba dropped the cane and moved away from the child, looking upward as he went—seeing the silent congregation—noticing the amount of people who had attended the church service that day: the elderly men of the first few rows, the widows sitting near the main entrance, the choir, the many families, the hundreds of families, holding the hands of the ones called their children as he saw bewilderment in their eyes, as he moved away from the children on the rope, toward a far, back corner, to stand within its crevice until the church service had ended.

And when it had, he found himself on the gravel path heading toward his bedroom—walking quickly, wishing not to be seen—then feeling a soft tap, and turning to see Ijeǫma holding a sheet of paper.

How could you beat that child?

"He spat in the pastor's face. He was to be punished . . ."

Who, with true authority, says he was to be punished? And if such were the case, why must the punishment come from you?

"What are you talking about? Haven't you ever struck these witches and wizards before . . ."

No, I have not. How can you possibly call them witches? It has not been long since we were held in the quarters against our will.

"Yes, but we do not live in the quarters anymore. We have been promoted . . ."

Promoted to what? Pastor Nwosu has not given us anything except uniforms and a place to live. We still belong to this church just like the children.

"I am no witch or wizard, Ijeọma! I am a child of God! And maybe if you were to abandon your pagan ways, you would agree with me. Do you not wear the pastor's uniform also? You've come to chastise me, but aren't you dressed in pink and white? If you don't like this church, leave. If you do not like the man of God, leave his house! No one is holding you anymore!"

Ijeọma turned to move away from him, but he held her by her shoulders and produced an apology; but she did not think it enough—flexing her shoulders, then hurrying away from him—running up the gravel path—until she looked above the roofs of the cars in the parking lot to find another, a large black other, whose wheels were tall and whose windows were wide—one whom Ijeọma remembered as the greatest of the metal pots, whose body bore the letters J-E-E-P—driving quickly onto the lot and producing a person who collected from an attendant's arms the boy whom Ikemba had beaten—throwing him into the back of the idling car before hurrying away from the lot. And Ijeọma thought she knew what she had seen until she remembered Ikemba's words and reminded herself that she was nothing like the others, not like the attendant whom she now saw—moving along the gravel path—rubbing the skin on their arms. She was kind, she thought, a kind attendant, a benevolent attendant, it was Ikemba who had changed, recalling nine full years at once: nine years of resisting Pastor Nwosu and his church, nine years of professing something they had both been calling love; and although acid, and starvation, and beatings had changed their bodies, she did not think they had changed Ikemba's mind, seeing him beating that child, remembering, doubting that he had ever loved; doubting their years of loving had been true; knowing for years that love would be difficult; but not knowing how difficult that love would be; and wanting, somehow, for their love to be easy; then sobering to the truth that love must only be what it can be as she returned to her room, and opened her diary to write:

DIARY ENTRY #911   8 DECEMBER 1999

Chukwu what has become of Ikemba and me? I love him and I believe that
he loves me too. But when he beat that boy today, I saw him as something
else, ruthless, even a monster. I couldn't believe that a man whom I love so
dearly could hurt another person so.

    Chukwu are all men like that? Are all men full of anger and hatred? It
seems to be that way. Look at my father. Look at the pastor. Perhaps there
are exceptions. My cousin Uzodi has always loved me and he is a man. But
after all this time that could have changed. Perhaps there are exceptions, I
have now remembered Igbokwe; but who else?

    Chukwu I love Ikemba. Give him back his heart. Bless him with a
kind spirit. I want to kiss him, and feel as if you were pulling us into the air.
Perhaps you can lift him up and show him the vision. Perhaps you can
raise us both, and take us back home, or somewhere else that is not here.
Chukwu don't leave me.

IJEOMA CLOSED HER DIARY, AND spent the rest of the afternoon at her post in the Manifestation Quarters. She walked along the corridor, watching the children in the cells, pitying them as they sat in dark corners, silently waiting for the day to pass. And she wished she could open the cell doors and have them run through fields, and wanted to feed them until they grew full and stout, until their spines stopped protruding from their curved backs—not wanting to beat any of them—but desiring for them all to be freed from the cells—and to fly to their truest home.

And on quiet evenings, when the night was at its darkest, she would take old fruit from the kitchen and give it to the children to eat, finding that she could become acquainted with the younger ones, and learn their names, and offer them to Chukwu in prayer, hearing them say, "Thank you ma," without caring that she did not audibly respond, without caring that the fruit was nearly rotten as they devoured each piece and yelled out their names, as she raised a finger to her lip, reminding them of silence. And they would smile at her, in the cells and in the dining hall, and she would nod to them, refusing to forget that she had once been as they were, whether in those times of touching the palate of her mouth, or of descending from a flight in the privacy of her bedroom, Ijeoma recalled it—through the eyes of memory—that she had been a child of the Manifestation Quarters.

And that evening, as she ate her meal in the dining hall, she felt Ikemba sitting next to her, then holding her right hand.

"I am sorry, my love. I did not mean to speak to you in such a manner . . ."

Do not worry, Ikemba. I am not upset.

"I want you to understand something. Do you not know that it is because of you that I have become like this . . ."

So, I have become the root of this problem?

"No! No! God has blessed me with you, IJ! And I am afraid that if I offend Him, he will take you away. I cannot live with such a thing—so I obey Him, with all that I have, so that we will remain together . . ."

Ikemba, it is like I said, I love you. Though you must understand that if you touch any child in the manner that you did this morning, I am not sure that I can continue to remain with you.

"Okay, you have my word. I will not flog them anymore . . ."

Are you sure of it?

"I am sure."

They nodded at each other, and Ikemba joined Ijeoma in finishing their evening meal. And when their plates were empty, they stood from the wooden bench and returned the children to the Manifestation Quarters as Ijeoma walked behind the bobbing line—wearing her pink-checkered uniform, and holding a small cane—leading the children into the cells, then closing the barred doors, watching some collapse onto the cement floor as others began picking their wounds and as many began begging for more to eat. And she turned her eyes; closing the doors; quietly thanking Chukwu to be no longer in the cells; covering her nostrils as foul odors rose; looking past the mottled red sprinkled across the zinc roof.

And when she heard their voices begging as she turned her metal key, she wanted to tell them she would take them home. But there were no homes to which she could return them, since some were taken off village paths and village roads and several others were sent by their families; and Ijeọma understood, locking the children in the cells because it was her assignment, those were the laws of the church, and the church and the children were now bigger things, and this was the time for survival. And as she slept in her room, seeing a black ocean in her mirror and blue squares streaming along her mounted clock and bedroom floor, her justifications began peeling like the skin of the children pleading in the cells—not letting her go, but encircling her and moving inward—and asking her and begging her and why, why treat us like monkeys, why Ijeọma, why you call us witch, Ijeọma, no give us bread, why not give us bread and yam, let us go, Ijeọma, please, please leave me, leave me, don't come around me, please, get up from me, get up from me, go to the home of your mother . . . the world is at war, please I can't breathe, please go, go, go, as she awoke to the silence and sweat, weeping from a guilt pronounced within herself, condemning her life and her abomination, knowing Ikemba's words to be good, wondering if Chukwu condemned her, too—and reviled her, too, and rejected her, too—pleading for the leniency of the Most Supreme, pleading for Chukwu's mercy.

And she thought of releasing them. She had her own set of keys, and permission to move about the quarters; but there were other attendants who stayed awake each night, patrolling the church grounds; and if they were discovered, they would all be forced to drink acid: a punishment she did not want another person to bear again.

She began fingering the taut skin around her lips, using her tongue to feel the cavities and bumps of where her mouth's palate was once smooth, sitting atop her bed and thinking of any name, any face among the attendants with whom she could tell secrets and make plans. But there was no name. Not even Ikemba would understand, she thought, as all the ones with whom she had been kept were now transformed by Precious Word Ministries; there was no dịbịa to speak of new things; Nnenna was not there to help feed the children once the night had grown to its darkest; help of that kind was no longer with her. And she remained in her bedroom, residing with unseen things: Chukwu, Chineke, and chi, and memories of faith, and those responsibilities that did not ask to be given, yet each moment required the most precious care, mercy, love and mercy, life and mercy, rejecting the responsibilities, but watching them return, pleading and pleading for them to go, to let the children fend for themselves, to let them value denial, defeat and denial, deny, since I did not build the prisons, I did not make this church, so accept it, please, please, accept it, you children, what, *what,* is there between you and me—

DIARY ENTRY #917   18 DECEMBER 1999

Have I become a monster? Have I? Look at what I have done. I have grown into a woman who locks innocent children into prison cells. I thought I was good. I thought you chose me to fly because I was good. But how can someone who is good do evil. Shouldn't I leave Precious Word? But where will I go? I don't have any money. I can't even utter a sound. Chukwu stop this. I ask you to stop it. But it is like I have become like those hateful men. I have become just like my father.

I do not want those parts of him that are in me. What am I supposed to do? How can I reject him for those things he did? I am doing the same, almost the same. Who is above evil? Perhaps I was never good; but you raised me to the sky . . .

Protect those children Chukwu. There is very little I can do for them. Why don't you protect them? If you want them free, they will be free. But this is not Ichulu.

IJEQMA CLOSED HER DIARY AND placed it under her pillow then turned to lie flat on her bed. And when she opened her eyes to a knocking at her door, she saw John forcing his way into her room, with terror in his eyes and a lantern in his hand.

"Ijeqma, you must listen, and listen well. By the orders of the king and his pastor I have c-c-come to rape you."

Ijeqma had not sat up when John had entered, and was now clutching her rappa, remaining still and flat.

"Keep y-y-your clothes . . . on," said John, "There is much more you must know." John brought his kerosene lantern to Ijeqma's desk and turned its small knob to bring more light into the room.

"Ijeqma . . . I am someone . . . I am someone too," John said, looking back to Ijeqma's bed and seeing that her face was a darkened silhouette, with two eyes for moons.

"Obi Iroatụ, the king who now reigns over Amalike ... H-H-HE is my uncle ... he is a wick-k-ked man. A very wicked man. Do you know those boys from your village ... who came to this town ... and were murdered ... My uncle, after shooting them dead ... plucked out their organs, and sold each one for millions. That is what he does. That is how my family has been making money for years. They sell bodies, especially those of the children here in Precious Word ... They won't saw or pluck out their body parts, unless they die on the road to the people who have come to purchase them. Haven't you seen them? ... in the big Jeeps ... when they throw the children inside of them, and we never see them again? And what of your boyfriend Ikemba; he has remained in the church simply because he is the pastor's first son, birthed before the pastor was married to any woman. And what of you? ... Do you know why the king and his pastor have commanded me to rape you? It is because the king has now fully corrupted the pastor, and has said that the ONLY way the church will finish construction is if you, YOU, produce off-spring who can fly. My uncle wants to sell your children to people around the world, so that he can continue making his billions."

Ijeọma remained still; not signing or writing or moving; not knowing if anything were truly happening; not knowing if John had died and this was his ghost; or if she had died and this afterlife was the consequence of working for Pastor Nwosu.

"But I know what to do, Ijeọma, I know what we can do!"

Ijeọma tightened her legs.

"I know of your diary—the green one with many pages. That will be your baby. Three months ago, I told the pastor that I had come to your room and had performed my duties to him, but in those three months I also learned of your diary. Use this rappa ... and tie your diary around your stomach, so that people may believe that you are pregnant—so that the pastor and the king may believe that I have done what they have commanded me to do.

"Have you heard?" John said, speaking a soft Igbo, then handing Ijeọma a dark brown rappa. "If you do not do this, they will ship you away to a place much worse than the Manifestation Quarters!"

Ijeọma prayed for death as she took the dark brown rappa from John's hands. She prayed for Chukwu to end her life as she stood by her bed after John had left, waiting for her chi to suffocate itself, or drown itself under the rivers in her veins. But when dying had not come, she found herself writing her 929th entry, with fury against the Most Supreme burning against her knuckles and wrists—wanting all the betrayal seizing her heart to be exposed and be evidence for Chukwu's eyes—but keeping those pains within, bury-ing them within, because how dare she write an accusation against the Most Supreme; with what audacity? with what authority?

So she buried those pains as one buries an ambitious dream, praying that their allurements never reappear again; and once her tears had tired her to a sleep, she was awoken to a steady knocking at her door, to a room with no black ocean or moonlit squares, and she waited fearfully atop her bed before permitting her feet to touch the sunlit floor; though the knocking continued as she turned the metal knob to see Phyllipa standing with a food flask and a rainbow-colored bag.

"Ijeọma . . . how are you?"

Ijeọma quickly nodded four times.

"Do you know," Phyllipa said, while watching Ijeọma hurrying to her desk, "it is like I am your mom . . . You can confide in me and tell me if your morning is not well . . ."

I am fine, ma. I'm faring well.

"Then I will thank my God," Phyllipa said, turning from the notebook and looking past Ijeọma's eyes. "How old will you be turning this year?"

I will be nineteen.

"Then surely you have grown since you first arrived at this church . . . I was exactly your age when I chose to marry the pastor."

Ijeọma turned her head—lowering her gaze, through and through—as though seeing beyond the floor.

"My husband . . . Innocent . . . he has purchased something. I want to give it to you," she said, while handing Ijeọma the rainbow bag. "It is a Christ-mas present."

Ijeọma kept her gaze fixed through the floor, asking again for dying and death.

"Do you know . . . whether you can believe it or not, Innocent was not always as you see him now. There was a time when his heart was supple and kind. There was a time when he would give his very life to help the neediest people in this town. But the world is a wicked place, Ijeọma. If you are to survive within it, you must never be truly kind or truly generous—but be kind and generous when it seeks to benefit you. Take what is to be taken, and protect your life by any means . . . *Are you hearing me?* Now, take what the pastor has purchased."

Phyllipa maneuvered the handle of the colorful bag into Ijeọma's closed fists.

"You must understand, Ijeọma, sometimes a person may not have the strength to overcome what has happened in their life, or in the lives of their forefathers . . . Sometimes the grandchild of an osu might always see himself as an outcast, and might do anything to include himself among the most powerful. Do you understand?"

Ijeọma shook her head, looking at the brown rappa lying on her bed as an angry melancholy passed through her—hoping it would drive Phyllipa to the outside of her room, seeing that Phyllipa was now eyeing the dark brown rappa with moroseness resting beneath her eyes and lips.

"It will be well," Phyllipa said.

Ijeọma said nothing in return.

"I have brought food for you . . ."

Ijeọma saw Phyllipa place the black food flask on her desk, and watched her frown as she turned and closed the bedroom door. She opened the rainbow bag—and saw a lavender rappa, with threads of gold webbing outward along its length; then she opened the food flask, and saw a mound of yam porridge, with a written note tucked beneath the food flask's lid: CALL NO MAN FATHER, NOR WOMAN MOTHER.

And Ijeọma rushed out of her room with a red notebook in her hand—searching the grounds for Ikemba—running out of the living quarters—then searching behind the gray walls of the church sanctuary, and not seeing him—running to the Manifestation Quarters, then searching through its classroom and dining hall—and he was not there; then entering its small chapel, and seeing him in the back pew; watching him pray in deep meditation, his body bent low; though not low enough to conceal from her the division between his hair ending and his neck beginning; knowing that division, knowing his shades of black, and wanting to sob into them, and weep into them—wanting to call his name from the sorrows festering within her gut, but believing she was to be silent—crafted to be silent.

"Ijeọma, what is it," Ikemba said, after an hour had passed and he turned his head. "Were you watching me pray?"

Ijeọma looked along the hill of his downward-pointing nose, and thought it resembled that of the pastor.

I was waiting for you to finish.

"Well, I am finished now. What has happened . . ."

My life has ended.

"What do you mean . . ."

Ijeọma quietly turned her notebook's page.

John, the assistant to the pastor, came to me last night and said that he was ordered by the pastor to rape me. He gave me a dark brown rappa and told me to tie my diary around it so that others will believe I am pregnant. ~~Then he tol~~ that all of this has happened because the pastor and the king of Amalike want me to give birth to children who can fly so that they can make money.

"It is a lie. John is a liar."

Are you true?

"I know the pastor. He is a Man of God. He would never do such a thing . . ."

Bastard

"What?"

Ijeọma wrote nothing back.

"Ijeọma, what do you want me to do? Believe that the person who has brought me to everlasting life is a liar? Are you sure that you heard John

properly? And it could be that you were having a nightmare. There are principalities in this world—"

Ijeọma began hurrying away, as she felt a stillness tighten the air around
her, making the entire world seem like it was trapped behind glass—to be
believed, to be honored, to be alive, of what use was it; to be well, of what
consequence—when she was not seen as she saw herself or others; or seen as
she saw the world; or seen as Chukwu saw her—but understood no differ-
ently than a farmer understands their livestock, or a judge understands their
crimes before calling forth a criminal; and if this were the world, and if this
were its reality, in what good was she to hope; and if marriage could blind
and imprison a woman like Phyllipa, why would one ever marry; that perhaps the time had come to cast away the elders' proverbs, and the fastening
of oneself to power; and to hold, as a singular truth, that in all is dying: in
everything is death; and that to hope in another's understanding is among
the greatest foolishness—

She was to be at the front desk of the Manifestation Quarters by three
p.m. So she was there, thinking of Ikemba while sitting in a plastic chair,
unable to monitor the main entrance as she saw herself beating Ikemba to
the ground; then feeling the desire to ask for his forgiveness; but leaning
into the thought of brutalizing him alongside the pastor and the king; no
longer believing he was ever committed to her; no longer trusting the memory of him once planning their escape or whispering into her ear Igbo
proverbs of freedom; it was the foolishness of their past, she thought, no longer wanting to believe that they prayed in ways that hastened the attention
of the ones called their gods, or that he truly read her words or desired to
wait for her to write as much as she would write before acknowledging her
ideas and making his own sounds; it was not love but playful vanity, she
thought, foolish, wasteful vanity.

And she pulled herself away from her thoughts; and once it was seven
p.m., she led the children out of the cells, thinking of them while escorting
them to the chapel for the evening prayers. And when the prayers were finished, she led them to the dining room to eat the evening meal, sitting away

from Ikemba, not thinking of Ikemba at all but wondering about the children, watching them eat, then not eating at all, seeing them lick their bowls—too fearful to beg for any more than they were given. And when one smiled at her, she nodded at them, wondering if Chukwu would feed them, wondering if Chineke would give them yam and fill their stomachs with anything more.

And when she finished her own meal, Ijeǫma entered her second-story hostel, sitting to the right of the Manifestation Quarters. And when she entered her room, she removed her diary and used the dark brown rappa to tie it around her stomach. She felt the diary move and shift as she lay on her bed; and as she stood up to tighten the rappa around her navel, she began feeling the gloss of the diary's surface cool the heat seeping through her skin; and she began falling asleep with thoughts of dying—wishing she and death could rest more closely, hoping they would one day share a bed: a more perfect bond—believing it all as she wished her life away; not hearing the whimpering sounds of the children beneath her—praying never to bear children of her own, praying for the one called the Most Supreme not to bring her past tomorrow.

3.

IJEOMA AWOKE TO THE MORNING light unprepared to receive her blessing. The rays of Anyanwụ were filling her room and she knew to whom Chukwu was calling. So she stood by her window and watched black doves darting through the cloudless sky, recalling the lonesome melancholy of the weeks that had come and gone, the burdens begotten from the unrelenting labor of Christmas Day; the hopelessness that appeared in celebrating the coming year without any resolution of the preceding year's problems, frowning toward the birds as she returned to the light, feeling its heat against her face, and against the rappa that held her written words, feeling the light touch her legs, then her toes; touching her entire body until she found herself lifted into the air, gazing upon the sky, seeing again a vision to which she grinned, and welcomed; and praying with her chi to greet each person properly; then closing her eyes and reopening them, over and again, to see whether the vision would leave and abandon her.

"Ijeọma, I have come to—What is this! What is this! WITCH! WITCH! WITCH! WITCH!"

Alison, one of the female attendants, with a pink-checkered shirt and a patch of white hair, had entered Ijeọma's room, and saw her levitating; and as Ijeọma began hearing the frantic tremors in her voice, she turned to Alison's face and fell to the ground, as the room grew darker, as clouds appeared suddenly to cover the sun.

"COME AND SEE, OH!" Alison cried. "COME AND SEE THE WITCH!"

And Ijeọma's room was soon filled with attendants wearing their pink-checkered uniforms, whose sweaty bodies prevented her from seeing her clock for the time or her calendar for the date, as the clamoring attendants tried to make sense of the commotion; seeing only the room, and a room's typical things: a bed, a desk, a mirror, a Bible.

"What is the matter? What is the matter?" they said.

"I saw Ijeọma flying!" Alison whined, pointing her finger at Ijeọma.

"What? Ijeọma, is it true?" said the eldest among them.

"Why are you asking her!" cried Alison. "She is a witch!"

"Are you sure you saw her flying?" said another attendant.

"I saw it with my two eyes. If I am lying, let God come and strike me!"

"Eeeehhhhh!" the attendants cried together.

"We must take her to Pastor Nwosu!" the eldest said.

"That is what we must do," two other attendants said.

And the others agreed, and they began dragging Ijeọma out of her room, then dragging her down the stairs of their living quarters, then across the gravel path; watching her slip and fall as they pulled on her and spat on her; kicking her to the ground; then dragging her upward against cement stairs to the second floor, shouting prayers in the church edifice to gain protection for Christian blood, as one attendant knocked on the pastor's door, crying, "Emergency, Pastor! Emergency!"

"Come in," Pastor Nwosu said.

The band of attendants entered his office, holding Ijeọma out like a captured thief.

"What is this? What is going on here?" said the pastor.

"It is this witch that calls herself a worker of this church!" cried Alison, "I saw her flying in her bedroom! She is a devil! A friend of the dragon of 666! The cause of Y2K!"

Pastor Nwosu remained quiet as he pushed his spectacles along his nose, looking at Ijeọma, seeing the protrusion along her stomach.

"When did you see Ijeọma flying?"

"It happened this very morning, Pastor," the eldest among them said, "before the morning prayer."

"I see. Thank you for reporting this. All of you may go and say your morning prayers. I will deal with Ijeọma alone."

The young women threw Ijeọma onto the floor as they left the pastor's office, but they stood behind his closed wooden door, waiting to hear him punish their witch.

"Stand up!" they heard him say. "How long have you lived on these grounds? How many years have I spent preaching the Word of God to you? How many times have I laid my hands over you in prayer . . . and still you will not repent! Are you a fool? Are you? I should curse you naked! You are a wicked girl! An ugly child! After I have clothed you, fed you, given you everything you need to live . . . still you disobey me and follow the ways of the devil. There is no hope for you! No hope at all! You are a disgrace to this ministry."

And as he spoke, he heard the clamors of the female attendants still standing behind the door, and so he seized Ijeọma's arms while pulling off her blue rappa, only to see another one wrapped around her stomach—seeing her closing her eyes, he began seizing the second rappa—not yielding to his conscience nor his cane as he forced his fingers through the rappa's knot, and suddenly heard the sound of a book falling onto the floor.

"WITCH!" the pastor screamed as he began punching Ijeọma's lips, then eyes, then open mouth.

"YOU WILL NEVER BRING SHAME TO ME! YOU WILL NEVER BRING SHAME TO THIS HOUSE OF THE LIVING GOD! I KNOW HOW I

WILL DEAL WITH YOU! YOU ARE NO LONGER AN ATTENDANT OF
THIS CHURCH. FROM NOW ON YOU WILL LIVE IN THE CELLS WITH
THE OTHER WITCHES AND WIZARDS. YOU WILL NEVER BE GIVEN
FOOD! YOU WILL HAVE NO VISITORS! YOU WILL REMAIN THAT WAY
UNTIL GOD HAS TOLD ME TO RELEASE YOU. IF YOU WANT FIRE, I
HAVE GIVEN YOU FIRE! JOHN! JOHN!"

"Yes, pastor . . ." said John as he rushed into the office.

"TAKE THIS WITCH STRAIGHT TO THE SOLITARY CELL AND
LOCK HER UP!"

"Yes, pastor."

"AND BE CAREFUL! SHE IS A DANGEROUS ANIMAL! A LOATH-
SOME BITCH!"

"Yes, pastor. I'll be careful."

John took Ijeoma by the arm—after collecting her pen, rappas, and open
diary—then led her out of the office and the church edifice, knowing that the
pastor had learned of her flights and false pregnancy; and as he looked upon
the zig-zag angles making her plaited hair, he wanted to tell her that she
would not be shipped to a foreign country; but remained silent, knowing the
empty promise was what he evaded each day he traveled to work; and nearly
wept at the many sorrows he saw plaguing her face: her languished eyes, her
melancholic lips—as he walked her along the corridor of the Manifestation
Quarters with a guilt pulling at the center of his throat; having found the
cell farthest from the children; and locking her in it; leaving with an explana-
tion for the two buckets beside her; and the distant whisper, "Y-you . . . you
are brave."

And Ijeoma watched him leave through small metal bars embedded in
the fastened iron door, as she stood in the silence, wishing for someone to
return and be with her, praying that someone would reopen the iron door.
She could feel the heat again, a stream of light flowing into the cell, and wondered if someone would truly come, raising her thoughts to a dire
expectation, ignoring the good word as she raised her head to the window to
see if the sun was there; and saw some of its body, muted by the clouds,

glowing as an orb behind their gray as she stretched forth her legs to make herself prostrate, praying, as she stretched herself onto the cement floor, praying for Chukwu to remove her from the cell and remove the pain from her swollen eyes and lips, lying on the ground for hours in prayer, waiting for the cell door to be reopened, thanking Chukwu for her life, praising the Most Supreme for all that was given to her, and asking for an open door, as the stream of light became faint then disappeared, as she prayed through unwept tears and a blackened sky, until her desire for an open door had broken for the day, and she closed her eyes to hope in tomorrow's answer.

And when the morning came, she lifted her head from the dark brown rappa and adjusted the blue one wrapped around her body. She had awoken to hunger. And the hunger had joined with the biting disbelief of still being behind the iron door. The union had quieted her mind, slowing it to the pace of a crawling infant, but she opened again a hopeful thought and prayer as she heard an attendant in the corridor ringing the morning bell, and heard, too, the locks of other cell doors opening, and the screams of many children as they were flogged and beaten as she was smelling the odor of their defecation buckets moving along the main corridor. She stood along the cell wall—believing that the iron door would soon open—then hearing the attendant approaching the cell push a water pouch between the bars while saying, "Why give pure water to a witch?" And Ijeọma rushed to the floor, taking the pouch of pure water and breaking the plastic bag with her teeth; she thought of rationing the water, not knowing if another bag would come, as she thought that more water would be given in the afternoon, but not truly knowing, as she drank the water slowly, feeling the warm liquid flowing through her tumid lips, then through her throat, and through her chest, and into her stomach; and although the water quelled her hunger for a little while, the void in her belly returned—even as she unwrapped her blue rappa and removed the diary to read her words through the light rays entering the plastered cell.

DIARY ENTRY #930 DATE UNKNOWN

Chukwu I'm writing to you again. They've called me a witch and put me into the prisons again. Why? I'm thinking of many things, and keeping them, but I know that you will provide for me. You will quickly remove me from this place.

Chukwu send my love to Ikemba. I know I insulted him, but please forgive me. Let him know that I am sorry, and that I love him. I didn't tell him that you were still pulling me upward. I was a coward, and didn't tell him because I didn't want him to call me a witch like the others. Perhaps if I told him, he would have believed me. I know he would have believed me. The fault is mine. If my insults and lies are why I have been put into this cell, forgive me Chukwu. I love him Chukwu. I love you most Chukwu. Surely you will protect my life.

SHE CLOSED HER DIARY AND counted the passing day with a tick, knowing that it was past noon because the bell for afternoon prayers had been rung.
She heard the metal clanging from the other cells being opened, and the
silence of hers remaining closed; and she sat with little tolerance for patience,
before being given water and being called a witch, drinking some of what
came forth from the pouch, and saving what remained for the next moment
of hunger. And as she laid herself on the floor, feeling its rough cement, pro-
voked by the memory of the clanging metal, she thought of memories within
a time moving slowly, and saw the face of Ikemba suddenly unveiled, recalling her reasons for loving him: the way he spoke, a way she had heard from
the mouth of Ichulu's dịbịa, one without the fear of being right or wrong,
his strength, his voice, his black skin, the other thing blacker being her
nighttime-colored eyes: so she began tapping them, her lidded eyes, over
and again, sending a message to the one whom she said she loved, hoping

somehow that he had received it, believing that the message was flying through the iron door.

And she saw the sun again—a little part of it—and waited for the world to move, waiting for all to leap from their holds, and accelerate wondrously toward the sky; and when they had not, she began writing to Chukwu to show her those things she saw while in the air; writing as steadily as her hands would allow; forgetting her dreams of a levitating world; writing as legibly as her hands would allow; until her fingers ached; until her palms were sore; and she laid there waiting; feeling her chest heaving up and up; hearing her rumbling bowels as she closed her eyes; and saw the sun's red turn yellow then blue as her daze grew colder and her thoughts felt the world unmoved, stuck in the place where yesterday had bruised it.

And she rested her head until the evening came, along with more water; and she drank what she could drink, as the hunger was taking her, as her want to see Ikemba seemed less and less vital than her hope for eating bread. Still, she thought of him, and prayed for him, and waited for his message to be delivered through her eyes, praying for Chukwu's forgiveness as the water became settled and streams of vitality began growing. And when she believed that Chukwu's touch was raising the hairs on her neck, she asked for strength, and asked the Most Supreme to bless the one whom she said she loved; and when the water had passed from inside her body, her prayer began slowing, and her strength began slowing; and her thoughts wandered to the food which she could not have: the yam covered in seasoned palm oil, the pounded yam dipped in ọgbọnọ soup, the roasted corn, yellow and black, spiced with salt and smoke.

DIARY ENTRY #941   DATE UNKNOWN

*Chukwu how are you? I know you are well. I know Ikemba is well, because
you are watching us. Chukwu my hunger is growing. How will you feed
me? There are rats running in the prison. Am I supposed to eat them?
Should I pray for these pure water plastics to become oranges? My stomach
is empty. I would like food. There are so many things I would like. Chukwu
provide for me. You haven't lifted me up above the ground since I have been
in this place. What again have I done wrong?*

*I am stronger than this prison Chukwu. I will stay strong in you. It is
because you are Most Supreme. What else?*

SHE PUT DOWN HER WRITING pen and stopped thinking of food, believing that her hunger was not allowing her to sleep; and she used the metal bucket away from the dark rappa, thinking of those things which lay past the metal bars, knowing that they would never come as she battled with reasoning which said the children snoring meant Uzọdị and Chinwe were coming; or that since she had once fed them, she was entitled to be released; or that because they had not been beaten by her hands, the iron door would be unlocked; as such reasoning was just, and such reasoning was sensible. Yet the defecation bucket had been filled with her waste, and the iron door had not been unlocked; and Ijeọma quickly removed from her heart the false hopes and vain fantasies that came shackling her further in the prison of Precious Word.

And so it was: with no dreams came no comforts; with no dreams came no deception that things were better than they truly were, and when she opened her eyes she knew she would have the very same things, and be in the very same place as when her eyes were closed. Though no comfort or no deception, she did not know which one harmed her more as she spent many nights without sleep, thinking of Ọfọdile, blaming him for her being in the cell, not seeking the gull to curse his name, but stopping her heart each time it sought to pray for his destruction, for rejecting what Chukwu had given him—parting her lips to breathe—outwardly, outwardly—releasing any hate which had emerged.

And she would not say if Ikemba still loved her, or ever loved her at all—a man foolish enough to love a flying mute; an ugly mute; a voiceless dog—every thought made before strictly professing that such a man could never exist; and she did not want to think of Ikemba any longer—even as thoughts continued coming deeply, deeply, until she was hearing him say things she believed he had said before, calling her witch, reporting her to the pastor—he was the one who sent the attendant to open the bedroom door; Ikemba deceives; Ikemba corrupts—and she rushed to her diary, opening its pages, hating Ikemba—praying for Amadịọha to strike him dead.

DIARY ENTRY #945   DATE UNKNOWN

~~I hate Ikemba!~~ *Chukwu what has become of my life? I don't even know if you can hear me. Am I not a fool for believing that the flights were good? They gave me joy. But what good is that joy when all I am left with now is growing bitterness.*

I have prayed Chukwu. I have prayed for you to give me peace. I am unconcerned if that peace is in Amalike or elsewhere, I simply want it now.

Who do I have? I have lost everything; when have I created trouble? Now people have called me witch, and have treated me like an animal because of what you have done.

I have prayed Chukwu for you to please answer me. Where have you gone? But you are the Most Supreme, and I've asked for you to hear me and I am praying to you Chukwu. You are the one who takes care of me. Give me peace. Please, that is what I am asking.

A DAY HAD COME. ANOTHER had passed. And Ijẹọma lay on the cell floor counting the number of water pouches around her, reading their fading labels, then crumpling them and shoving them into her mouth— remembering old sensations of chewing as she spit them out, bits of plastic lodged deep inside her mouth as she saw the rats scurrying around her head, one then two, running about her, four then six running through the cell wall as she watched their gray bodies squeeze past a hole and knew that the hole was too wide to warrant any squeezing, because they had eaten, and had eaten well, she thought, as she began making new observations of their food being nearby: inside the hole, behind the plastered cell wall.

But she left the thought to itself and turned to her diary, writing through each slow-moving day, etching each letter softly to disallow hunger from overpowering her, writing to Chukwu and asking to be free, and asking what else she could do to have her prayers answered; not calling Chukwu a fool, not calling the Most Supreme a fool, but reminding Chukwu of her charity; praying for her isolation to flee; asking for a friend and for a sister and doubting that she truly had one; wondering why Ụzọdị and Chinwe had not visited, and wondering, too, if she had loved them too generously; then hating them all, condemning them all, the pastor and his church, the feeble-minded attendants; the one called her father: the evil one who had abandoned her.

And as days passed, she grew too tired to write, and lay in the cell, no longer counting the ticks or drinking the pure water but remaining still and quiet, blinking her eyes and breathing light breaths as days passed without her praying a prayer. And days passed, and she had forgotten whom or that which she loved. No songs, or words, or memories of sprightly things as she laid quietly in the cell, not moving to pass her urine or to resist within herself any craving to die, blaming herself for it all, that if she had not gone to the Evil Forest, or worked as an attendant, Chukwu would not have punished her, that if she had obeyed every tradition honored by Ọfọdile, and treated the osu as osu, she would have been honored, welcomed, it was you who disobeyed Ichulu, born mute so that Ụzọdị could be exiled, and now while in this prison cell you must be ashamed since you are more shameful than the one whom you said you loved, the one whom you foolishly pranced about, saying he loved you, and now look at the blood and shit piling high inside your cell, you stupid bitch, every stroke that the pastor gave you is one that you deserved, you should have been beaten to a pulp as evil as you are, as wicked as you are, who can say that they truly love you after you imprisoned all those children and worked for the pastor, who will ever say that they will hold you and remain with you until you grow older and uglier than you already are, *oh my god, oh my god,* you stupid witch, more stupid than Ọfọdile could have ever believed, it is no wonder that Nnenna never came and Ụzọdị never came and Chinwe preferred the other girls to your dumb and rejected voice, you ugly bitch, why not rid the world of your ugly self, why not fall to pieces and die, why not die and stop inconveniencing us, you dumb and wasteful shit—

And she believed that those words were good words; and despised herself, while weeping for herself; and noticed the rats again—seeing them moving slower than rats should move; and knew each one of them was eating—that their food lay within the dark hole. So she thrust into it; fingering the hole; pounding the concrete wall to break it open; hitting the wall over and again; against a cement that was too thick to break, beating the wall until the overfed rats began fearing and flooding out from behind the wall, flooding into the cell, dozens and dozens, bringing no food as they went, as she slipped her hands through the passing stampede with the rats all slipping through her fingers, their wet feet, their thick tails giving nothing except the itchiness running through her mind's skin: a million caterpillars were squirming as she heard the ringing of the bell, and the cell doors unlocking, and the children walking through the quarters' halls, as she began pulling strands from her plaited hair and putting them into her mouth, pulling strands from her arms and from her waist and putting them into her mouth, hearing quick footsteps as a water pouch was falling, and "witch, bitch, witch" was being sung by an attendant near the door, as she took the pure water and threw it into her defecation bucket, then the metal bucket, then the metal bars, then her old rappa covering a dozen pouches among a dark green lying on the stony cell floor.

Look at what you did to me. YOU LIED. CHUKWU LIES. All that I gave you. I loved you and look at what you did, Chukwu. All those people eating, rejoicing, who don't say a word to you and look at what you did to me. ME! Even those rats, but ME! Never come near me again. Stay where you are and never put your hands on me. Never call my name. Never send me any gifts or blessings. Never lift me up again! Stay where you are and never harass me or I will curse you and tear you down.

She pushed her diary against the cell wall and thought of nothing; no ideas or memories or insights were what she could hold: an unignited mind. And the rest of her, those parts unconcerned with thinking, lost every hopeful expectation.

The days moved stubbornly across her sunken eyes. Her body was thinning; her defecation bucket was not emptied in a cell bearing the odor of her waste; her lips were cracking; her thighs were growing damp and moist at their crevices; her limbs were barely moving as her head kept spinning and spinning and spinning until she vomited bile; she had become cold, silent and cold, with few thoughts among those which convinced her to die, as she lay with her chi believing them, then not believing them; in the deadly silence of her isolation, as she watched the sun and heard her breath and saw her diary, she reconsidered it all now that there was very little left, now that she was dying, and understood it to be so—now that she had seen those things buried within her, with tears trembling in her eyes—as she opened her diary, silenced by what she could believe—preparing facts in her spirit, truthful facts and belief—*i'm sorry chi. chi forgive me chi. i lied, moving through this world believing i was most innocent, most holy; and yet in your justice, i have failed. for i thought i was better than those who've sought to kill me; truly we are each within the same. for my wrong was done at my level of responsibility; my wrong was done through ME. where was i when i was to remove those little children from prison? and now that i have returned, how dare i ask any soul to come, and rescue me. can it be the ones whom i hated within the walls of this prison? uzodi forgive me! chinwe forgive me! because if it is as i wrote, that a person who does wrong should receive immediate consequence, chineke must strike me down, and whisper my life away, today or many years ago or when i saw that little boy being forced into the Jeep, knowing that his life was in peril, but shamelessly denying that it was so. and so i am preserved, preserve also the pastor whose heart is broken and beating in broken ways. and if i am preserved, preserve also the king, who kills from the hated illness he has yet to overcome. and phyllipa, are we both not in the same? making false concessions, distorting the truth out of our loneliness and failing esteem. was i not to stay longer to feed Mgbeke, because I knew within me that I was? preserve us Chukwu; and even still, with what audacity do i write this? after cursing you, and dishonoring you, and telling audacious lies. because if you chose to wipe away the world with a whisper, who could arrest you, the Most Supreme. is such in my control? is it in the control of my words, or the words that any human being can utter? for you are the one who carries the world; you are the one who possesses us: Olisa. and it is by your gracious providence that i have come to see.*

She turned to Chukwu, rolling herself on the cement floor like cowrie shells, giving her sufferings to the Most Supreme in prayers with no antipathy—not against the attendants, not against Ọfọdile—but for essential things like patience and pure water. And when it was that neither came as she had imagined—no prickly dots against her tired skin, no pouches pushed between the iron bars—she began doubting; doubting after many days of waiting; doubting if she had ever flown; despite her chi whispering, over and again, doubting is deadly, doubt is deadly; but still doubting whether she had ever written, or had known the wisdom she had come to understand as she believed that a mute could never know any of anything; and so she no longer wrote, but lay on the cell's ground blinking her eyes; not lifting her arms to get the tepid pure water; not encouraging herself to pray as she lay on the ground and acknowledged that she was dying; that what was now true, was that she was now dying; as she counted the ticks, counting an imprisonment of three weeks; counting the thought that she would never be released from the cells; knowing within herself that she would die a prisoner, with no witness to her final sigh, not even among those whom she had come to love again; so she gave them permission to forget, impassively, assuredly. She gave it to Ikemba and Ụzọdị; she gave it to Nnamdị and Cheluchi, and gave it to Nnenna, and Nnenna's words and hugs and understanding, giving it to Ọfọdile, and the love he had or had not, the love she truly wanted, whispering it to the mango-shaped birthmark resting behind Chinwe's ear, giving it to Ngọzi and Nwabụeze and the elderly Mgbeke, to the girls who had sniggered, to the girls who had laughed, from Nwagụ's stare to the six osu who died, giving it to them all, letting the home she called Ichulu thoroughly dissolve, and praying that Ichulu would forget she ever was.

She closed her eyes and stopped her breath, preparing to surrender herself, waiting for it to come; waiting for the darkness of that night to take her home as she opened her mouth then quickly closed it shut, sealing her face with trembling hands—gasping then sealing her face again, covering her nose and mouth—waiting, waiting, trembling as the waiting failed; and she tried over and again: sealing her face and stopping her breath—sealing her face and stopping her breathing as the waiting failed and she felt the dark brown rappa—thinking of another way—laughing, chuckling—while unwrapping herself from the rappa's hold—coiling it around her neck— pulling at both ends without hesitation—with all her strength—feeling the air inside her throat escaping—and the popping in her ears and neck growing louder—pulling at the rappa until her oval eyes began fluttering and the room began spinning—and the rats on the floor began scurrying from a new light in the prison cell as she chuckled from the glee in taking her books— going to wherever it is the ancestors go

ijeoma . . . what are you doing

"I am"—Ijeoma held her mouth, feeling the texture of the air above her tongue, hearing her voice sound bright like new metal, as she saw and heard that of another, one whose voice was making letters formed like clouds.

"I am choosing to end it."

why

"Because my life no longer belongs to me."

but i am here

"And who are you?"

i am the one who brought you to the sky

"Are you Chukwu?"

i am—i am

She leapt to her feet—quickly dropping the rappa then lifting it again— to clothe herself as she began wrapping herself, not believing that she could stand as she was standing—not believing that power had found its way into her body as she looked toward her feet but could not see them—as the smoke entering the cell stopped her from seeing the cell floor—as she tried remembering things: her voice and the voice she heard and saw, or the rattling and shaking coming from the cell door as its lock was being unlocked; and its door was finally opened.

"I'm sorry I didn't believe you! I'm sorry I didn't believe!"

She rushed toward him, and embraced him, and opened her mouth to speak but did not. And with soft melancholy, she shifted the brim of her rappa, then took her diary and began running through the smoke-filled corridor behind Ikemba, and heard the children screaming, each one of them, all of them, shouting behind their locked cell doors as Ijeọma pulled Ikemba's arm and pointed.

"We don't have time!"

She ripped a page from her diary and wrote, then put the page in Ikemba's hands.

I will burn with them, he read as he pocketed the page, and reached into his bag to remove his set of keys and a lavender rappa, giving to Ijeọma what Phyllipa had once given her before hurrying to each cell, then unlocking them, releasing each child, and shouting that they must leave through the backmost door since the fire was coming from the front. And they listened to Ikemba's words, rushing from their cells, not hearing the church attendants running from their quarters and into the streets, carrying their belongings in their panicked hands and shouting that the one called their god had forsaken them, that he did not stop an enemy from destroying their holy church, as they blamed their witches and wizards and presumed them all dead when none were found among them in the streets of Amalike.

But the children were all following Ikemba still, rushing out of the cells and through the dark corridor as the smoke was growing thicker and thicker, as those who had come out of the building began inhaling the charcoal-smelling air as they watched the church edifice burning brightly in the nighttime, with nobody there to save it. And Ijeọma followed, too, running behind the line of children—until she turned and saw pink checkers near the front of the quarters—rolling beneath the churning smoke. She thought they would move in her direction to reach the same refuge she was reaching, but the fire approached the pink checkers as she ran back toward the flames, rushing to remove the attendant—letting the quickness of her feet glide through the smoke and ash until she reached a person whose eyes were filled with the panic of the night, who was coughing and then collapsed at the weight of it all

as Ijeọma shielded their bodies with the lavender rappa, as flames began licking their covered shoulders: succumbing gently to the ecstasy consuming
them both as they were lifted, near the moon they were lifted, through the
black-colored walls and the crumbling roof where they found the most merciful love—and felt its *sorrows* let them be.

EPILOGUE

HE SAW IJEỌMA DESCEND TOWARD the earth like a star and followed her trajectory, running toward it until he could read her eyes. There was a light in them: a brightness he had not seen before. And he held her—then raised their linked arms—trusting the person who began walking as though the night were an afternoon, leading them out of Amalike and into another place beyond unpaved inclines and grassy hills—through the middle of paved streets that soon became dusty roads—atop paths running through small deserts which soon revealed forests which could have been named as evil—then through dark trails, and trees, now making space for many feet.

And when Ijeọma finally stopped and signed for their arrival, Ikemba saw homes no longer built with zinc or cement, but wearing clay and raffia as their material. He thought of which home Ijeọma would now awaken, until he saw her clapping her hands near a dark entrance, summoning a shirtless person whose muscles consumed her in an embrace; and when the embrace had parted, she came to be in search of something which he came to understand, as he removed her green diary from his bag, as she smiled and then kissed his wood-scented hands.

This is my cousin Ụzọdị.

And Ijeọma saw Ikemba smile and greet Ụzọdị with an embrace as she left the two to see the children sitting on the ground and speaking to each other breathlessly, rejoicing in the powers which had released them.

"Ijeọma, leave the children to rest; come into this home of mine."

Ijeọma smiled to herself when she heard Ụzọdị's Igbo, and felt tears pushing against the back of her eyes as she entered his home, seeing Anyanwụ filling its darkness with a lightening blue.

"What is happening here?" a young woman said.

"My kin has come to see me. Ijeọma, this is my wife, Ụlọchi. Ụlọchi, this is Ijeọma and her friend Ikemba."

"Welcome," Ụlọchi said. "Is there anything you all would like to eat? I can cook yam and akara for you."

"Leave it, Ụlọchi. It is too early to eat."

"Then I will come and join all of you," Ụlọchi said, moving near Ụzọdị and caressing her belly.

"Ijeọma, where is it that you have been?" said Ụzọdị. "You have not come to see me in so long. Tell me, why is it that your hair looks like that of an osu . . . and why is it that you are so skinny?

Ijeọma opened her diary and began writing in English, then placed the book into Ikemba's hands.

"Ijeọma says that her father sent her to Amalike, where she stayed for many years."

"Is that where you learned to write?" asked Ụzọdị.

She nodded her head three times.

"I do not understand," Ụzọdị said. "Why did Ọfọdile remove you from Ichulu?"

Ijeọma began writing more words and passed her diary to Ikemba, who read, "He removed me because of my flying."

"You can fly?" Ụlọchi asked.

"Yes, she flies," Ụzọdị said, smiling. "If I had known you were in Amalike, I would have come to see you. Amalike does not know me as an outcast."

Ijeọma looked through Ụzọdị's eyes and nodded three times, nearly weeping that she had doubted that such words could be good.

"If you were staying in Amalike," said Ụlọchi, "what prevented you from coming here?"

"We were prisoners," Ikemba said. "And if not for Filipa, a woman of integrity, who had given me a set of keys, gasoline and matches . . . we would have remained as prisoners."

They all became silent as Ijeọma wrote again in her diary.

"Ijeọma wants to return to Ichulu," said Ikemba.

"There is not a problem in that," Ụzọdị said. "But what of the children? I think they can remain with us. There are families here with big homes, and there is enough land to build more houses."

"Ijeọma wants the children to come with us to Ichulu. That is what she has written."

"When do you want to go to Ichulu?" Ụzọdị asked.

Ijeọma pointed to the ground over and again.

"Today?" asked Ụzọdị and Ụlọchi at the same time.

Ijeọma nodded her head three times and watched Ụlọchi stand and leave the room, then heard her rummaging through groaning pots in preparation of the morning meal. And within a moment Ijeọma smelled the aroma of fried akara filling the air—as she walked with Ikemba and Ụzọdị to a nearby stream, after having asked Ụzọdị where she could bathe herself. And she carried in her right hand the lavender rappa, and smiled when she placed a page into Ikemba's hands with the words: *Uzodi's home is now red.*

When they arrived at the stream, Ụzọdị and Ikemba left Ijeọma and began conversing as they returned to the red-clay home. And as they moved away, Ijeọma stood by the water, hearing it spill over the rocks and stones, then stripping herself of her old rappa and lunging into the stream. She remembered the voice in the cell and could not help but wonder what she was meant to do with such a memory, since the voice left her with a feeling, too, great to ponder alone with her chi; perhaps if she gave the memory to Ichulu, then they would understand; perhaps if she gave the feeling to Ikemba, then he would truly know—can god not see, she sighed and breathed as she dipped beneath the water, allowing herself to be cleansed by a serenity, feeling the cool water heal her deepest hurts and winnowing pains, believing the worst of them gave her this dream of precious water, hearing the water whispering, *"What has god made that could never see?"*

She left the stream cloaked in the lavender rappa, and thanked Chineke for Phyllipa's cunning before returning to Ụzǫdị's home, where the children were running in circles, and eating groundnut, and playing an old game she remembered from her childhood. And when passing them, she returned each of their nods with smiles—and some of their smiles with hugs; then kissed their foreheads—and walked into the home of the one called her kin.

"Ijeǫma, the children have already eaten," said Ụlǫchi, with a hand resting atop her hip. "The remaining akara is for you and Ikemba."

Ijeǫma nodded three times, then took one of the brown akara and put it in her mouth, eating it slowly, letting its oils and flavor remind her that food is a wondrous gift. And when she saw that Ikemba had been watching her, she turned to him and smiled at him and lifted her diary from where she had left it.

Do you know what I would see in the sky each time I flew?

"What would you see . . ."

I would see an eye, the most beautiful eye, with faces appearing within its pupil, as if it were the entire world.

"Did you ever see my face?" said Ikemba, keeping his eyes low.

I did, many times.

"What do you think it means, the vision . . ."

Play with it. Play with the word 'love' in Igbo as I have, as anyone who cannot speak has played with it. You cannot say 'love' without saying 'eye'.

"Because the eye sees itself last . . . then first . . ."

Then last again; and how else can love be?

Ikemba, I love you. I do not know whether I loved you before, because there were things, many things, that I had yet to understand. Though as a truth, I know that I love you today. I couldn't have reached this virtue of freedom without your being in my life.

"I love you, too, Ijeọma . . . at least . . . I am trying . . ."

Then let us be partners in raising those children, as they will have been partners in raising us too. Let us, together, be chaste and free.

He fell silent reading the words, then their letters—space, then silence again.

"I understand you, Ijeọma . . . but what of our beliefs . . ."

chineke and jesus came from separated land; but what could i call them before i was?

Ikemba smiled. Ijeọma smiled, too. And they remained that day within Ụzọdị's red-clay home, watching the children with whom they came; and soon the good word traveled out of the Place of Osu and into Ichulu that Ijeọma had left Amalike; and the people of Ichulu left their pots and prayers and hurried out of the village—rushing through the Forest of Nta, carrying the ones called Ngọzi's four children ahead of themselves—seeing shadows of nza birds stretch on the grass before them—arriving in the Place of Osu, and standing among the people gathered by Ụzọdị's home. And they announced themselves as coming from the village of Ichulu, then announced that perhaps they had no village at all, asking for forgiveness, kneeling before the persons among them, pleading for compassion and mercy—crying that no one is cast out before the Most Supreme, crying that no one is a slave when they are mercifully loved—as hundreds from Amalike had been hurrying from the west, entering the Place of Osu through the leadership of John, crying in many languages, "Take pity on us prisoners! Take pity on us slaves!"

And they were recognized. And when they had seen the face of Ijeọma, plainly, they each greeted her with tears, crying, "Ada Chukwu! Ada Chukwu!"

And when they told Ijeọma that Ọfọdile was dead, Ijeọma began to weep, not knowing that Ọfọdile had been given refuge in the towns of Ụmụka and Etuọdị: towns where all was as it was as in the Place of Osu. And as they told Ijeọma that this was Nnenna—Ijeọma began to weep; and as they told Ijeọma—"Here is Nnamdị," "and Chelụchi," "and Chinwe," "and the one called Chinwe's child," Ijeọma began to weep, and to kneel; and to mourn among those kneeling; weeping to a new people as she humbly sang:

> Let the man who calls the woman 'fool'
> Forget the name of his Mother.
> Let the woman who calls the man 'fool'
> Forget the name of her Father.
> And let the one who forgets the name of their chi
> Never see the coming Home;
> For if one forgets that they are as the Other
> They have begun to perish.

ACKNOWLEDGMENTS

I thank God. For giving me the grace and strength to write this novel. I thank Them for allowing Their Heaven to grant me divine inspiration, and for using me as a vessel. I thank Chukwu who is God and is the god of my ancestors for staying close to me and for not disappearing in the midst of colonialism, white hegemony, and modern-day imperialism. Eze ndi eze, ị zọputa m.

Even still, there are not enough ways to say thank you to the ones who have made this novel possible. In fact, I do not even know the names of many, since the random occurrences of everyday life—laughter on a train, dancing on the street, weeping in a church or in a movie, etc.—often happen anonymously. But it is those random occurrences that have lain in my subconscious mind—and in my spirit too: the ingredients necessary to make writing work. To the world, then, I say thank you.

And then, too, there's my world: the little community of Igbo families who raised me in Washington, D.C., who taught me Igbo on Saturday mornings and sang Igbo hymns on Sunday afternoons—to Uncle Joe and Aunty Dorothy Emeche, thank you for always challenging me to be my very best. To Uncle Alex Obodo, thank you for encouraging me to always strive for excellence. To Uncle Babie Orusakwe, thank you for continually being a model of humility and meekness. Uncle Boniface and "Aunty C" Chimah, thank you for always being so kind to me and all of us children. Aunty Julie and Uncle Chief Onunaku, I hope this novel makes me "your number one," but I know there is always space for everyone to don that title. To Uncle Geoffrey Okekeocha, thank you for always showing me the meaning of hard work and dedication to one's family. To all the families of the Igbo Catholic Community of Washington, D.C., thank you truly for raising me up to love and to love language.

And then there's my family who supported me in the daring feat of being a writer. To my mom and dad, Theresa and Joseph Nwọka, to whom this novel is dedicated, thank you for supporting me in my dream to pursue the literary arts. I hope you see yourselves in this story as much as I do. To my twin sister Adaobi

Nwọka, thank you for always being my rock. I have not known this world without you; thank you for being a supportive ejima. Thank you to Nnedimma Nwọka, my younger sister, for continually challenging me and pushing me outside of my comfort zone. I appreciate you. To Aunty Uche and Uncle Joel Uzodinma, as well as Joel, Ify, Chichi, and Ugo, thank you for being a most beautiful family to me. I love you all from the depths of my heart. To Aunty Linda and Uncle Chris Anyikude, thank you for your continued love and support; thank you for your constant joy and for the amazing gift that is Stephanie, Jennifer, Kenny, and Kerry. To Uncle Okey and Aunty Ogonna Ilochonwu, thank you for the amazing sleepovers and playtime and love I shared with Chibuzor, Obinna, Adora, and Chika. You all hold a deep, deep place in my spirit and I look forward to celebrating more of life with you. To Uncle Mike and Aunty Louisa Ewii, thank you for being the cool kids on the block. You both are the hippest Aunty and Uncle anyone could ask for and you know it! Thank you for the gift of my cousins: Chineye, Ogechi, Nnamdi, and Ginika. You guys already know that you mean the world to me. To Uncle Fred and Aunty Ngozi Udoye, thank you for always showing me the greatest benevolence and hospitality. Thank you for the amazing cousin that is Chinedu "Fred" Udoye, who beamed when I told him I would be a writer. Thank you cuzz. I am so happy for you, your wife Stephanie, and the newest addition to our growing family: Faith Sochima Udoye. Thank you also to my many cousins, aunties, and uncles in Ani Igbo (Igboland) who have supported me through this journey. I love you all.

The family with whom I spent the earliest days of my life mean the world to me, and then there is my chosen family: the ones who through a special kind of love stuck with me as I stuck with them through the craziness of life. To Reginald B. Cole, thank you for being my brother and best friend. I love you with the love of God and hope the best for our bond. To Jovan Julien, you have been at my side since day one of this writing thing; thank you for being a most loving sibling and a true friend. I love you truly and truly love you. To Chijioge "Chi" Nwogu, you are a rock. Thank you for the support, love, dedication, arguments, fights, forgiveness, and friendship. In many ways you are my hero since you often say the things I cannot say and fight the battles I shy away from. Thank you Chi for all that you have done for me. To Ian Allen, thank you for your constant wisdom and showing me that life can be fine #langstonhughes. I appreciate your humility and hard work so much and love you for all the things that you are. To Gabriel Doss, thank you for being an artist. Thank you for inspiring me to pursue art in your own way. Thank you for always challenging me to think beyond myself. To Josh Rames, thank you for teaching me that there is no need to be anxious: everything comes in time. I love you with all my heart, brother man. To Liz Morgan (or should I say Liz

Temou), you will always be my mon amie: the friend that knows that part of my heart which yearns for artful healing. To Nikkisha Smith and Fedna Jacquet, thank you both for showing me what true beauty is. Thank you both for being outstanding women who are succeeding in law and cinema. You are my sisters and I love you. To Khara Gresham: words cannot even begin to describe the amount of love and respect I have for you. Thank you for being an amazing sister to me. Thank you for being my friend. Thank you too to Shauna Higgins for always showing the world your kindness and laughter. You are a light and are so beloved by me. To Sophia Blake Roy: I love and respect you so much. Thank you for being a quiet leader; thank you for your activism (let us never forget COPAIT). I love you homie. Meaghan Robinson: you are a source of so much joy to me. Thank you for always showing up with the most radiant positivity. I love you truly. And of course, to our deceased sister Danielle Dunlap, the girl who stole my heart, the one who never kicked me out of her dorm room when I went through all her snacks, the one with the most infectious laughter. We love you Danni. Keep praying for us from wherever you are. This is my family. We call ourselves Boom Boom because of our formerly ratchet ways. The truth of the matter is that we have a most amazing love that will stay with us forever.

The Boom Boom family forged itself through Brown University: another home away from home. Many blessings to Lauren Leigh Smith, Maura Pavlow, Darnell Fine, Antonia Angress, Amanda Machado, Phil Kaye, Alia Lahlou, Tatianna Gellein, Almaz Dessie, Herma Gebru, Rebecca Burney, Alanna Tisdale, Ama Misa, Ijeoma Njaka, Tosin Fadarey, Jamal Shipman, Sharina Gordon, Michele Baer, Courtney Smith, Malcolm Shanks, Sarah Magaziner, Robert Smith III, Jennifer Anderson, Deepa Galaiya, Adam Kiki-Charles, Teng Yang, Alain Laforest, Jonathon Acosta, Pierre Arreola, Aiyah Josiah-Faeduwor, Chris Cooper, Bryant Estrada, Ross Hegtvedt, Keturah Webster, Michelle Onibukon, Kelly Murgia Sandoval, Daniel Woolridge, Daniel Bernard, Meagan Morse, Isissa Komada-John, Vyvy Trinh, Fatimah Asghar, Crystal Vance, Bradley Toney, Krys Méndez Ramirez, Deidrya Jackson, Jacquelyn Silva, Zeeshan Hussein, Kristin Jordan, Thomas Beauford, Tomás Quiñonez-Riegos, Amie Darboe, Yashua Bhatti, and Sanjay Trehan. Thank you all for your friendship, encouragement, and love. Thank you so much Owen Hill and Justin D. Williams for reading my writing early on and giving me amazing feedback and supportive words. Many thanks to my friend Rocio Bravo, who edited an early draft of this manuscript and who supported me during many trials. I am so grateful for my most beloved friend Natasha Somji, who nurtured me as a writer with amazing writer workshops and words of encouragement. Thank you, Natasha, for being a source of perseverance for me.

Thank you to my brother and friend Prab Kumar for being the first person to call me a writer and gifting me the works of Rabindranath Tagore. You mean the world to me Prab. Thank you to Yeshimabeit Milner for lifting me up on those hard days and sharing with me her dreams about what our world can be. I love you Yeshi. To Samira Thomas, who is another writer friend of mine from Brown. Thank you for the positivity and light. You are an absolute star. To my sister and friend Justine Stewart, thank you for always having space to deconstruct capitalism with me and also to celebrate our friendship that has been filled with laughter, prayer, and love. You mean the world to me. And to you my beloved sister Naïka Akpeakorang, thank you for holding my hand through the trials of life. Thank you for being a beautiful and benevolent sister who has consistently had my back. I love you with my heart. Many, many thanks to my beloved sibling Rahil Rojiani, who has been a most incredible sibling that a person could ever ask for. Thank you for always being one call away. Thank you for all the love and support, especially when I was at my most vulnerable. I love you with my heart, Rah. Thank you to Jamila Woods and Franny Choi for convincing me to take Advanced Fiction instead of the Intro. to Fiction course. Your words and friendship have influenced the course of my career. I appreciate and love you both. Many, many thanks to Dean Maria Suarez, Peggy Chang, Phil O'hara, Dean Karen E. Mclaurin, and Ann Marie Ponte. Thank you for your continued love and support of me and my life. I love and appreciate you all. Thank you especially to my home department of Africana Studies. Thank you to the African American Studies Department at Howard University, where I spent a semester; thank you so much Dr. Greg Carr and Dr. Okomfo Ama Boaky-ewa for introducing me to the work of Yvonne Chireau and the trials of children imprisoned by churches, respectively. This work is indebted to the wondrous minds and the zealous labor of my Brown Africana Studies professors: the late Anani Dzidzienyo, Corey D.B. Walker, Paget Henry, Elmo Terry-Morgan, François Hamlin, Olakunle George, Okey Ndibe, Brenda Marie Osbey, Ruth J. Simmons, and of course the late Professor Chinua Achebe. Thank you also to Professor John Edgar Wideman for taking the time to read a draft of this novel when it was in its infancy.

After Brown I spent time at the Iowa Writers' Workshop and came to meet an incredible group of storytellers. I thank Connie Brothers for being a constant ray of light and for being willing to dance with me every first of the month #payday. I also thank Lan Samantha Chang for taking a chance on me and defending me when I needed it most. Thank you Professor Marilynne Robinson for always making time to speak with me and for being a such a sage to many of us in the workshop. Thank you also to Kate Christensen for being an amazing workshop leader and helping me move forward in my literary career. I appreciate you deeply Kate. Many, many thanks to Alexia Arthurs, Novuyo Tshuma, Avro Chakraborty, and Tom Quach for being amazing friends during my time at Iowa. Thank you Jamie Watkins, Nana Nkewti, Casey Walker, and Ashley Clarke for helping me during a most dire time and for being solid support systems. I appreciate you all so much. Thank you to my amazing friend and colleague Rebekah Frumkin for reading and re-reading drafts of this novel. You are an extraordinary friend and this novel would not be in readers' hands without you.

Thank you also to my brother and friend Abraham Onche of Christ the King College, Abuja. Who would have thought that writing stories in middle school would lead to writing fiction and poetry as adults. I love you Abe. Thank you to my childhood best friend and brother Jonathan Gebretatios for continuing to support me. I love you Yoni. Thank you also to the many students whom I have had the privilege of teaching in Washington, D.C. Thank you to my students at Stanton Elementary School, Miner Elementary School, Jefferson Academy, and Inspired Teaching Demonstration School. Your enthusiasm for life and learning has made me a better person. Many thanks to my brother and friend Andrew Edghill for always being up for writing and for being encouraging of this novel. I appreciate you so much Drew. And many thanks too to the team at People Animals Love. Much love to Michael Greer, Amit Kapur, Serena Bethala, and Katrina Branch for being amazing co-workers. Thank you especially to Lillian Knudsen for reading this novel when it was a draft and providing me with great feedback. Thank you Lilly. Thank you also to my amazing English teachers Rosemary Latney of Nativity Catholic Academy and Dr. Peggy Dillon of the Hospitality High School of Washington, D.C. Thank you for introducing me to robust literature and for developing in me a love of language. Thank you also to Naomi Szekeres, who gave me a list of the classics to read in high school, which I devoured in months. Thank you Naomi for believing in me. Thank you also to Susie, my local librarian at the Hyattsville branch of the Prince George's Community Library System, for staying late one evening so that I could print out an early draft of this manuscript. I also want to thank my family at Operation Understanding DC, who taught me the importance of fighting for the most vulnerable in society. Many thanks to Rachel Feldman, Scott Dinsmore, and Raël Nelson James for being our leaders and showing us how to have difficult conversations about race and the -isms. Many thanks also to Bintu Musa, Ngozi Egbuonu, Liane Alves, Emma Hutchinson, Zachary Carroll, Ayaboe Edoh, Maurice Wilkins, Lamika Robinson, Natalie Branche, Daniel Henderson, Elizabeth Mass, Jessica Paley, Sophia Sainteus, Christina Smith, Ryan Wright, Sara Schaffer, as well as to Janell

Delaney, Natalie Friedman, James Hall, IV, Zachary Linsky, Gabriel Marwell, Jonathan Nussbaum, Robert Rome, Greg Rosenbaum, Josh Walker, Hamani Wilson, and Alison Wollack. Thank you all for having been great friends to me.

Many thanks to my Express Igbo family for teaching me enough Igbo to write this novel dutifully. Thank you to Nkem Offor, Chukwuma Okeke, Udochi Okeke, Nkiruka Christian, Adaobi Amaechi, Ijeoma Ezeonyebuchi, Oge Ezeokoli, Onyachi Chuku, Stephanie Nwogu, Tobechi Mlemchukwu, Sam Emeka Uwahemo, Oly Ebiringa, Uchenna Akalonu, Ndidiamaka Nwakalor, Uchechi Ukaoma, Uchenna Ofodile, Franklin Amaobi Eneh, Uchenna Emeche, Celeste Iroha, Tochi Ngwagwa, and Aunty Chidi Azikiwe. Also, I came to know more of myself as a writer when I was a member of The Sanctuaries: a non-profit dedicated to the arts, spirituality, and social justice. So much love to my fellow Sanctuarians: Rev. Erik Martinez Resley, Ahmane' Glover, Priya Natarajan, Adiel Suarez-Murias, Jess Lusty, Jojo Donovan, Ayari Marie Aguayo-Ceribo, Osa Obaseki, Valentina Raman, Jeremy Levine, Chimdi Ihezie, Naika Gabriel, Mahdi Asim, Thalib Razi, Hasan Bhatti, Raymond Barquero, Raven Best, Brittany Koteles, Arvind Venugopal, and Ah-reum Han. Thank you all for the love you have shown me continually. You all are the best of community for me. Thank you also to Pastor George Anazia, Cordelia Nwagbo, and Victor Amadi for your counsel and guidance as I wrote this book. I love you all with all of my heart. Many thanks to Leslie Traub for reading my work very early in my writing career and supporting me as a budding artist. And many thanks too to my friend Vijay Parameshwaran for all your encouragement and support. Thank you also to my St. Augustine's family. Thank you to my beloved sister Adaeze Okongwu for always showing me love and cooking the best meals I have encountered. I love you 'deze. Thank you also to my awesome sister Heather Nimley, who always has the best things to say about life and living. Thank you also to my beautiful friend Imani McKenzie, who is an amazing person inside and out and is a great mom to Amayah. I love you Imani. Huge appreciation and gratitude to my brother Christian Mallet, who has been such a huge support to me these past years. I love you Christian! Many thanks also to Lea Harrison, Leslie Yun, Chidiogo "Diogo" Anyigbo, Amaka Nnorom, Emmanuel Bello-Ogunu, Chanda Ikachana, Clara Jimenez, Ann Anosike, Adejoké Babington-Ashaye, Richard Osuagu, Shirley Jean, Fritz Mumbe, Rhett Engleking, Andrew and Rita Marie Larsen, Susannah Luthi, and Stella Chukwu. Thank you for being my amazing brothers and sisters in Christ. Thank you for showing the world so much love. Thank you also to John Smith, Angela Wilson-Turnbull, Lydia Curtis, and Brigid McDermott. Thank you all for being amazing lights in our parish; and thank you of course to Fr. Patrick Smith for being an amazing shepherd and guiding our community day in and day out. We love you so much Fr. Pat.

Finally, thank you to Ross Harris, the best literary agent I could have asked for; thank you for understanding the work early on and believing in it. And a world of thanks to my editor Danny Vazquez, who saw exactly what I was doing on the page and encouraged it. Thank you so much Danny for your clarity of vision and for believing in me as an artist. You truly are a dream. Thank you to Janine Barlow, the fantastic copyeditor to this work. Your editorial eye is powerful and I deeply appreciate the love you showed this text. Many thanks to Olivia Dontsov for your editorial contributions to this work. I appreciate you Olivia. Finally, I thank my publishers at Astra House for giving this novel its shelf life. Thank you to Ben Schrank and Alessandra Bastagli for putting this novel out into the world. I am forever grateful for you both.

ABOUT THE AUTHOR

Okezie Nwoka (he/they) was born and raised in Washington, DC. They are a graduate of Brown University and attended the Iowa Writers' Workshop as a Dean Graduate Research Fellow. They are presently teaching and living in their hometown. *God of Mercy* is their first novel.